The critics on Robert Ludlum

'Robert Ludlum is an ingenious storyteller with a wonderful and convincing imagination. His place as a bestselling novelist is assured'   Mario Puzo, author of *The Godfather*

'Robert Ludlum has the storytelling gift'   *TLS*

'Robert Ludlum is, of course, the bestselling thriller writer of all time, having sold more than two hundred million copies of his twenty-two novels, and he has become known for the sweep and intricacy of his plots ... Now he brings us *The Prometheus Deception* ... his most ingenious novel yet ... Ludlum transcends the genre'   *The New Yorker*

'The pace is fast, the action plentiful ... a must read'
    Booklist

'Don't ever begin a Ludlum novel if you have to go to work the next day'   *Chicago Sun-Times*

'Ludlum stuffs more surprises into his novels than any other six pack of thriller writers combined'   *New York Times*

'Ludlum is light years beyond his literary competition in piling plot twist upon plot twist, until the mesmerized reader is held captive'   *Chicago Tribune*

'Robert Ludlum is an acknowledged superstar of the political thriller'   Amazon.co.uk

'A typically baroque concoction boasting more twists than a packet of pretzels ... a hugely enjoyable caper'
    Sunday Times

'Olympic style, all-out espionage ... Good news for Ludlum's countless fans'   *Daily Express*

'Huge in scope ... Ludlum spins it all together with lots of suspense'   *Sunday Telegraph*

THE
GEMINI
CONTENDERS

ROBERT LUDLUM

ORION

An Orion paperback

First published in Great Britain in 1976
by Hart-Davis, MacGibbon Ltd
First published in paperback in 1997
by Grafton
This paperback edition published in 2004
by Orion Books Ltd,
Orion House, 5 Upper St Martin's Lane,
London WC2H 9EA

A CIP catalogue record for this book
is available from the British Library.

ISBN 0 75285 856 4

Typeset by Deltatype Ltd, Birkenhead, Merseyside

Printed and bound in Great Britain by
Clays Ltd, St Ives plc

For Richard Marek, Editor.
Brilliance cloaked in great good humour.
Perception beyond any writer's imagination.
Simply, the best there is.
And for lovely Margot, who makes it all perfect.

BOOK ONE

PROLOGUE

9 Dec 1939
SALONIKA

One by one the trucks struggled up the steep road in the pre-dawn light of Salonika. Each went a bit faster at the top; the drivers were anxious to return to the darkness of the descending country road cut out of the surrounding forests.

Yet each of the five drivers in the five trucks had to control his anxiety. None could allow his foot to slip from a brake or press an accelerator beyond a certain point; eyes had to be squinted, sharpening the focus, alert for a sudden stop or an unexpected curve in the darkness.

For it was darkness. No headlights were turned on; the column travelled with only the grey light of the Grecian night, low-flying clouds filtering the spill of the Grecian moon.

The journey was an exercise in discipline. And discipline was not foreign to these drivers, or to the riders beside the drivers.

Each was a priest. A monk. From the Order of Xenope, the harshest monastic brotherhood under the control of the Patriarchate of Constantine. Blind obedience co-existed with self-reliance; they were disciplined to the instant of death.

In the lead truck, the young bearded priest removed

his cassock, under which were the clothes of a labourer, a heavy shirt and trousers of thick fabric. He rolled up the cassock and placed it in the well behind the high-backed seat, shoving it down between odd items of canvas and cloth. He spoke to the robed driver beside him.

'It's no more than half a mile now. The stretch of track parallels the road for about three hundred feet. In the open; it will be sufficient.'

'The train will be there?' asked the middle-aged, powerfully built monk, narrowing his eyes in the darkness.

'Yes. Four goods wagons, a single driver. No stokers. No other men.'

'You'll be using a shovel, then,' said the older priest, smiling but with no humour in his eyes.

'I'll be using the shovel,' replied the younger man simply. 'Where's the weapon?'

'In the glove compartment.'

The priest in the labourer's clothes reached forward and released the catch on the compartment panel. It fell open. He put his hand inside the recess and withdrew a heavy, large-calibred pistol. Deftly, the priest sprung the magazine out of the handle, checked the ammunition, and cracked the thick steel back into the chamber. The metallic sound had a finality to it.

'A powerful instrument. Italian, isn't it?'

'Yes,' answered the older priest without comment, only the sadness in his voice.

'That's appropriate. And, I suppose, a blessing.' The younger man shoved the weapon into his belt. 'You'll call his family?'

'I've been so ordered—' It was obvious that the driver wanted to say something more, but he controlled himself. Silently he gripped the wheel more firmly than necessary.

For a moment the moonlight broke through the night clouds, illuminating the road cut out of the forest.

'I used to play here as a child,' said the younger man. 'I would run through the woods and get wet in the streams . . . then I would dry off in the mountain caves and pretend I had visions. I was happy in these hills. The Lord God wanted me to see them again. He is merciful. And kind.'

The moon disappeared. There was darkness once more.

The trucks entered a sweeping curve to the west; the woods thinned out and in the distance, barely visible, were the outlines of telegraph poles, black shafts silhouetted against grey night. The road straightened and widened and became one with a clearing that stretched perhaps a hundred yards from forest to forest. A flat, barren area imposed on the myriad hills and woodlands. In the centre of the clearing, its hulk obscured by the darkness beyond, was a train.

Immobile but not without movement. From the engine came curls of smoke spiralling up into the night.

'In the old days,' said the young priest, 'the farmers would herd their sheep and cart their produce here. There was always a great deal of confusion, my father told me. Fights broke out constantly over what belonged to whom. They were amusing stories . . . There he is!'

The beam of a flashlight shot out from the black. It circled twice and then remained stationary, the white shaft directed now at the last goods wagon. The priest in labourer's clothes unclipped a pencil light from his shirt pocket, held it forward, and pressed the button for precisely two seconds. The reflection off the truck's windshield briefly illuminated the small enclosure. The younger man's eyes were drawn swiftly to the face of his brother monk. He saw that his companion had bitten his

5

lip; a rivulet of blood trickled down his chin, matting itself in the close-cropped grey beard.

There was no reason to comment on it.

'Pull up to the third car. The others will turn around and start unloading.'

'I know,' said the driver simply. He swung the wheel gently to the right and headed towards the third goods wagon.

The driver, in overalls and goatskin cap, approached the truck as the young priest opened the door and jumped to the ground. The two men looked at each other and then embraced.

'You look different without your cassock, Petride. I'd forgotten how you looked—'

'Oh, come now. Four years out of twenty-seven is hardly the better part.'

'We don't see you often enough. Everyone in the family remarks about it.' The driver removed his large, calloused hands from the priest's shoulders. The moon broke through the clouds again; the spill lighted the trainman's face. It was a strong face, nearer fifty than forty, filled with the lines of a man constantly exposing his skin to the wind and the sun.

'How's mother, Annaxas?'

'Well. A little weaker with each month of age, but alert.'

'And your wife?'

'Pregnant again and not laughing this time. She scolds me.'

'She should. You're a lustful old dog, my brother. But better to serve the church, I rejoice to say.' The priest laughed.

'I'll tell her you said that,' said the driver, smiling.

There was a moment of silence before the young man replied. 'Yes. You tell her.' He turned to the activity taking place at the goods wagons. The loading doors had been opened and lanterns hung inside, shedding their muted light sufficiently for packing, but not bright enough to be obvious outside. The figures of robed priests began walking swiftly back and forth between the trucks and the doors, carrying crates, boxes of heavy cardboard framed with wood. Prominently displayed on each crate was the crucifix and thorns of the Order of Xenope.

'The food?' inquired the driver.

'Yes,' answered his brother. 'Fruits, vegetables, dried meats, grain. The border patrols will be satisfied.'

'Then where?' It was not necessary to be clearer.

'This vehicle. In the middle section of the carriage, beneath tobacco nets. You have the lookouts posted?'

'On the tracks and the road; both directions for over a mile. Don't worry. Before daybreak on a Sunday morning, only you priests and novices have work to do and places to go.'

The young priest glanced over at the fourth goods wagon. The work was progressing rapidly; the crates were being stacked inside. All those hours of practice were showing their value. The monk who was his driver stopped briefly by the muted light of the loading door, a carton in his hands. He exchanged looks with the younger man, then forced his attention away, back to the carton which he swung up into the well of the goods wagon.

Father Petride turned to his brother. 'When you picked up the train, did you speak with anyone?'

'Only the dispatcher. Naturally. We had black tea together.'

'What did he say?'

'Words I wouldn't offend you with, for the most part. His papers said the cars were to be loaded by the fathers of Xenope in the outlying yards. He didn't ask any questions.'

Father Petride looked over at the second goods wagon, on his right. In minutes all would be completed; they would be ready for the third wagon. 'Who prepared the engine?'

'Fuel crews and mechanics. Yesterday afternoon. The orders said it was a standby; that's normal. Equipment breaks down all the time. We are laughed at in Italy ... Naturally, I checked everything myself several hours ago.'

'Would the dispatcher have any reason to telephone the goods yards? Where supposedly we are loading the cars?'

'He was asleep, or practically so, before I left his tower. The morning schedule won't start' – the driver looked up at the grey black sky – 'for at least another hour. He'd have no reason to call anyone, unless the wireless reported an accident.'

'The wires were shorted out; water in a terminal box,' said the priest quickly, as if talking to himself.

'Why?'

'In case you did have problems. You spoke to *no one* else?'

'Not even a drifter. I checked the wagons to make sure none were inside.'

'You've studied our schedule by now. What do you think?'

The trainman whistled softly, shaking his head. 'I think I'm astounded, my brother. Can so much be ... so arranged?'

'The arrangements are taken care of. What about the time? That's the important factor.'

'If there are no track failures the speed can be maintained. The Slav border police at Bitola are hungry for bribes; and a Greek freight at Banja Luka is fair game. We'll have no trouble at Sarajevo or Zagreb; they look for larger fish than food for the religious.'

'The time, not the bribes.'

'They *are* time. One haggles.'

'Only if *not* haggling would seem suspicious. Can we reach Monfalcone in three nights?'

'If your arrangements are successful, yes. If we lose time we could make it up during the daylight hours.'

'Only as a last resort. We travel at night.'

'You're obstinate.'

'We're cautious.' Again the priest looked away. Goods wagons one and two were secure, the fourth would be loaded and packed before the minute was up. He turned back to his brother. 'Does the family think you're taking a freight to Corinth?'

'Yes. To Navpaktos. To the shipyards on the straits of Patrai. They don't expect me back for the better part of a week.'

'There are strikes at Patrai. The unions are angry. If you were a few days longer, they'd understand.'

Annaxas looked closely at his brother. He seemed startled at the young priest's worldly knowledge. There was a hesitancy in his reply. 'They'd understand. Your sister-in-law would understand.'

'Good.' The monks had gathered by Petride's truck, watching him, waiting for instructions. 'I'll join you at the engine shortly.'

'All right,' said the trainman as he walked away, glancing at the priests.

Father Petride removed the pencil light from his shirt pocket and in the darkness approached the other monks at the truck. He searched out the powerfully built man who was the driver. The monk understood and stepped away from the others, joining Petride at the side of the vehicle.

'This is the last time we speak,' said the young priest.

'May the blessings of God—'

'Please,' interrupted Petride. 'There's no time. Just

commit to memory each move we make here tonight. *Everything*. It must be duplicated exactly.'

'It will be. The same roads, the same order of trucks, the same drivers, identical papers across the borders to Monfalcone. Nothing will change, except one of us will be missing.'

'That's the will of God. For the glory of God. It's a privilege beyond my worth.'

There were two master padlocks on the truck's panel. Petride had one key; his driver held the other. Together they approached the locks and inserted the keys. The irons sprung; the locks were lifted out of the steel hasps, the hasps slapped up, and the doors opened. A lantern was hung high on the edge of the panel.

Inside were the crates with the symbols of the crucifix and thorns stencilled on the sides between the strips of wood. The monks began to remove them, manoeuvring like dancers – robes flowing in the eerie light. They carried the cartons to the loading door of the third goods wagon. Two men leaped up into the heavy-beamed deck of the wagon and started stacking the boxes at the south end.

Several minutes later half the truck was empty. In the centre of the van, separated from the surrounding cartons, was a single crate draped in black cloth. It was somewhat larger than the cases of produce and not rectangular in shape. Instead, it was a perfect cube: five feet in height, five in width, and five in depth.

The priests gathered in a semi-circle in front of the open panels of the truck. Shafts of filtered white moonlight mingled with the yellow spill of the lantern. The combined effect of the strange admixture of light, the cavernous truck, and the robed figures made Father Petride think of a catacomb, deep in the earth, housing the true relics of the cross.

The reality was not much different. Except that what

lay sealed inside the iron vault – for that was what it was – was infinitely more meaningful than the petrified wood of the crucifixion.

Several of the monks had closed their eyes in prayer; others were staring, transfixed by the presence of the holy thing, their thoughts suspended, their faith drawing sustenance from what they believed was within the tomblike chest – itself a catafalque.

Petride watched them, feeling apart from them, and that was how it should be. His mind wandered back to what seemed only hours ago, but was in reality six weeks. He had been ordered out of the fields and taken to the white concrete rooms of the Elder of Xenope. He was ushered into the presence of that most holy father; there was one other priest with the old prelate, no one else.

'Petride Dakakos,' the holy man had begun, sitting behind his thick wooden table, 'you have been chosen above all others here at Xenope for the most demanding task of your existence. For the glory of God and the preservation of Christian sanity.'

The second priest had been introduced. He was an ascetic looking man with wide penetrating eyes. He spoke slowly, precisely. 'We are the custodians of a vault, a sarcophagus, if you will, that has remained sealed in a tomb deep in the earth for over fifteen hundred years. Within that vault are documents that would rend the Christian world apart, so devastating are their writings. They are the ultimate proof of our most sacred beliefs, yet their exposure would set religion against religion, sect against sect, entire peoples against one another. In a holy war ... The German conflict is spreading. The vault must be taken out of Greece, for its existence has been rumoured for decades. The search for it would be as thorough as a hunt for microbes. Arrangements have been made to remove it where none will find it. I should

11

say, most of the arrangements. You are the final component.'

The journey had been explained. The *arrangements*. In all their glory. And fear.

'You will be in contact with only one man. Savarone Fontini-Cristi, a great *padrone* of northern Italy, who lives in the vast estates of Campo di Fiori. I, myself, have travelled there and spoken with him. He's an extraordinary man, of unparalleled integrity and utter commitment to free men.'

'He is of the Roman church?' Petride had asked incredulously.

'He is of no church, yet *all* churches. He is a powerful force for men who care to think for themselves. He is the friend of the Order of Xenope. It is he who will conceal the vault . . . You and he alone. And then you . . . but we will get to that; you are the most privileged of men.'

'I thank my God.'

'As well you should, my son,' said the holy father of Xenope, staring at him.

'We understand you have a brother. A driver for the railroads.'

'I do.'

'Do you trust him?'

'With my life. He's the finest man I know.'

'You shall look into the eyes of the Lord,' said the holy father, 'and you will not waver. In His eyes you will find perfect grace.'

'I thank God,' said Petride once again.

He shook his head and blinked his eyes, forcing the reflections out of his mind. The priests by the truck were still standing immobile; the hum of whispered chants came from rapidly moving lips in the darkness.

There was no time for meditation or prayer. There was no time for anything but swift movement – to carry out the commands of the Order of Xenope. Petride gently parted the priests in front of him and jumped up into the truck. He knew why he had been chosen. He was capable of such harshness; the holy father of Xenope had made that clear to him.

There was a time for such men as himself.

God forgive him.

'Come,' he said quietly to those on the ground. 'I'll need help.'

The monks nearest the truck looked uncertainly at one another. Then, one by one, five men climbed into the van.

Petride removed the black drape that covered the vault. Underneath, the holy receptacle was encased in the heavy cardboard, wood framing, and the stencilled symbols of Xenope; identical except for size and shape to all the other crates. But the casing was the only similarity. It required six strong backs, pushing and pulling, to nudge it to the edge of the van and on to the goods wagon.

The moment it was in place, the dancelike activity resumed. Petride remained in the goods wagon, arranging the crates so that they concealed the holy thing, obscuring it as one among so many. Nothing unusual, nothing to catch the eye.

The goods wagon was filled. Petride pulled the doors shut and inserted the iron padlock. He looked at the radium dial of his wrist-watch; it had all taken eight minutes and thirty seconds.

It had to be, he supposed, yet still it annoyed him. His fellow priests knelt on the ground. A young man – younger than he, a powerful Serbo-Croat barely out of his novitiate – could not help himself. As the tears rolled down his cheek, the young priest began the chant of Nicaea. The others picked it up and Petride knelt also, in his labourer's clothes, and listened to the holy words.

13

But not speaking them. There was no *time*! *Couldn't they understand?*

What was happening to him? In order to take his mind off the holy whispers, he put his hand inside his shirt and checked the leather pouch that was strapped to his chest. Inside that flat, uncomfortable dispatch case were the orders that would lead him across hundreds of miles of uncertainty. Twenty-seven separate pages of paper. The pouch was secure; the straps cut into his skin.

The prayer over, the priests of Xenope rose silently. Petride stood in front of them and each in turn approached him and embraced him and held him in love. The last was his driver, his dearest friend in the order. The tears that filled the rims of his eyes and rolled down his strong face said everything there was to say.

The monks raced back to the trucks; Petride ran to the front of the train and climbed up into the driver's cabin. He nodded to his brother who began to pull levers and turn wheels. Grinding shrieks of metal against metal filled the night.

In minutes the freight was travelling at high speed. The journey had begun. The journey for the glory of one Almighty God.

Petride held on to an iron bar that protruded from the iron wall. He closed his eyes and let the hammering vibrations and rushing wind numb his thoughts. His fears.

And then he opened his eyes – briefly – and saw his brother leaning out the window, his massive right hand on the throttle, his stare directed to the tracks ahead.

Annaxas the Strong, everyone called him. But Annaxas was more than strong; he was good. When their father had died, it was Annaxas who had gone out to the yards – a huge boy of thirteen – and worked the long, hard hours that exhausted grown men. The money Annaxas brought home kept them all together, made it possible for his brothers and sisters to get what schooling they could. And one brother got more. Not for the family, but for the glory of God.

The Lord God tested men. As He was testing now.

Petride bowed his head and the words seared through his brain and out of his mouth in a whisper that could not be heard.

I believe in one God, the Father Almighty, maker of all things both visible and invisible, and in one Lord, Jesus Christ, Teacher, Son of God, Only begotten of the Father. God of God, Light of Light, Very God of Very God, begotten not made . . .

They reached the sidings at Edhessa; a switch was thrown by unseen, unauthorized hands, and the wagon from Salonika plunged into the northern darkness. The Yugoslav border police at Bitola were as anxious for Greek news as they were for Greek bribes. The northern conflict was spreading rapidly, the armies of Hitler were maniacs; the Balkans were next to fall, everyone said so. And the unstable Italians were filling the piazzas, listening to the screams of war mouthed by the insane Mussolini and his strutting *fascisti*. The talk everywhere was of invasion.

The Slavs accepted several crates of fruit – Xenope fruit was the best in Greece – and wished Annaxas better fortune than they believed he would have, especially since he travelled north.

They sped through the second night north into Mitrovica. The Order of Xenope had done its work; a track was cleared on which no train was scheduled and the freight from Salonika proceeded east to Sarajevo, where a man came out of the shadows and spoke to Petride.

'In twelve minutes the track will be shifted. You will head north to Banja Luka. During the day you'll stay in the yards. They're very crowded. You'll be contacted at nightfall.'

In the crowded goods yards at Banja Luka, at precisely quarter past six in the evening, a man came to them dressed in overalls. 'You've done well,' he said to Petride. 'According to the dispatcher's flagging schedules, you don't exist.'

At six thirty-five a signal was given; another switch was thrown, and the train from Salonika entered the tracks for Zagreb.

At midnight, in the quiet yards of Zagreb, another man, emerging from other shadows, gave Petride a long manila envelope. 'These are papers signed by Il Duce's *Ministro di Viaggio*. They say your freight is part of the Venice *Ferrovia*. It is Mussolini's pride; no one stops it for anything. You will hold at the Sezana depot and pick up the *Ferrovia* out of Trieste. You'll have no trouble with the Monfalcone border patrols.'

Three hours later they waited on the Sezana track, the huge locomotive idling. Sitting on the steps, Petride watched Annaxas manipulate the valves and levers.

'You're remarkable,' he said, meaning the compliment sincerely.

'It's a small talent,' replied Annaxas. 'It takes no schooling, just doing it over and over.'

'I think it's a remarkable talent. I could never do it.'

His brother looked down at him; the glow of the coals washed over his large face, with the wide-set eyes, so firm and strong and gentle. He was a bull of a man, this brother. A decent man. 'You could do anything,' said Annaxas awkwardly. 'You have the head for thoughts and words far beyond mine.'

'That's nonsense,' laughed Petride. 'There was a time when you'd slap my backside and tell me to tend to my chores with more brains.'

'You were young; that was many years ago. You

tended to your books, you did that. You were better than the goods yards; you got out of them.'

'Only because of you, my brother.'

'Rest, Petride. We must both rest.'

They had nothing in common any longer, and the reason they had nothing was because of Annaxas's goodness and generosity. The older brother had provided the means for the younger to escape, to grow beyond him who provided . . . until there was nothing in common. What made the reality unbearable was that Annaxas the Strong understood the chasm between them now. In Bitola and Banja Luka he had also insisted they rest, not talk. They would get little sleep once they crossed the borders at Monfalcone. In Italy there would be no sleep at all.

The Lord God tested.

In the silence between them, in the open cabin, the black sky above, the dark ground below, the incessant straining of the engine's fires filling the night outside, Petride felt an odd suspension of thought and feeling. Thinking and feeling once-removed, as though he were examining another's experiences from some isolated perch, looking down through a glass. And he began to consider the man he would meet in the Italian Alps. The man who had provided the Order of Xenope with the complicated schedules of transportation through northern Italy. The expanding circles within circles that led inexorably across the Swiss borders in a way that was untraceable.

Savarone Fontini-Cristi was his name. His estate was called Campo di Fiori. The Elders of Xenope said the Fontini-Cristis were the most powerful family in Italy north of Venice. Quite possibly the richest north of Rome. The power and the wealth certainly were borne out by the twenty-seven separate papers in the leather pouch strapped so securely around his chest. Who but an extraordinarily influential man could provide them? And how did the Elders reach him? Through what means? And why would a man named Fontini-Cristi, *whose origins had to be of the Roman church*, deliver such assistance to the Order of Xenope?

The answers to these questions were not within his province, but nevertheless the questions burned. He knew what lay sealed in the vault of iron in the third goods wagon. It was more than what his brother priests believed.

Far more.

The Elders had told him so he would understand. *It* was the holiest of compelling motives that would allow him to look into the eyes of God without doubt or hesitation. And he needed that assurance.

Unconsciously, he put his hand under the coarse shirt and felt the pouch. A rash had formed around the straps; he could feel the swelling and the rough, abrasive surface of his skin. It would be infected soon. But not before the twenty-seven papers did their work. Then it did not matter.

Suddenly, a half mile away on the northern track, the Venice *Ferrovia* could be seen speeding out of Trieste. The Sezana contact raced out of the control tower and ordered them to proceed without delay.

Annaxas fired up and throttled the idling locomotive as rapidly as possible and they plunged north behind the *Ferrovia* towards Monfalcone.

The guards at the border accepted the manila envelope and gave it to their superior officer. The officer shouted at the top of his lungs for the silent Annaxas to fire up quickly. *Proceed!* The goods were part of the *Ferrovia*! The driver was not to delay!

The madness began at Legnago, when Petride gave the dispatcher the first of Fontini-Cristi's papers. The man blanched and became the most obsequious of public servants. The young priest could see the dispatcher searching his eyes, trying to unearth the level of authority Petride represented.

For the strategy devised by Fontini-Cristi was brilliant. Its strength was in its simplicity, its power over men based in fear – the threat of instant retaliation from the state.

The Greek freight was not a Greek freight at all. It was one of the highly secretive investigating trains sent out by Rome's Ministry of Transportation, the inspectors general of the Italian rail system. Such trains roamed the tracks throughout the country, manned by officials ordered to examine and evaluate all rail operations and submit reports that some said were read by Mussolini himself.

The world made jokes about *Il Duce's* railroads, but behind the humour was respect. The Italian rail system was the finest in Europe. It maintained its excellence by the time-honoured method of the fascist state: secret efficiency ratings compiled by unknown investigators. A man's livelihood – or absence of it – depended on the judgements of the *esaminatori*. Retentions, advancements, and dismissals were often the results of a few brief moments of observation. It stood to reason that when an *esaminatore* revealed himself, absolute co-operation and confidentiality were given.

The freight from Salonika was now an Italian train with the covert imprimatur of Rome as its shield. Its movements were subject only to the authorizations contained in the papers supplied by the dispatchers. And the orders within those authorizations were bizarre enough to have come from the convoluted machinations of *Il Duce* himself.

The circuitous route began. The towns and villages fled by – San Giorgio, Latisana, Motta di Levenza – as the freight from Salonika entered tracks behind Italian boxcars and passenger trains. Treviso, Montebelluna, and Valdagno, west to Malcesine on the Lago di Garda; across the large expanse of water on the sluggish freight boat and immediately north to Breno and Passo della Presolana.

There was only frightened co-operation. Everywhere.

When they reached Como the circling stopped and the dash began. They sped north on the land route and swung south to Lugano, following the tracks on the Swiss borders south and west again to Santa Maria Maggiore, crossing into Switzerland at Saas Fee, where the freight from Salonika resumed its identity, with one minor alteration.

This was determined by the twenty-second authorization in Petride's pouch. Fontini-Cristi had once again provided the simple explanation: The Swiss International Aid Commission at Geneva had granted permission for the Eastern church to cross borders and supply its retreat on the outskirts of Valde Gressoney. What was implied was that the borders would soon be closed to such supply trains. The war was gaining a terrible momentum; soon there would be no trains whatever from the Balkans or Greece.

From Saas Fee the freight rolled south into the yards at Zermatt. It was night; they would wait for the yards to close operations and a man who would come to them and confirm that another switch had been thrown. They would make the incursion south into the Italian Alps of Champoluc.

At ten minutes to nine a trainman appeared in the distance, coming out of the shadows across the Zermatt goods yard. He ran the last two hundred yards and raised his voice.

'Hurry! The rails are clear for Champoluc. There's no time to waste! The switch is tied to a master line; it could be spotted. Get *out* of here!'

Once more Annaxas went about the business of releasing the enormous pressures built up in the fires of the iron fuselage, and once again the train plunged into the darkness.

The signal would come in the mountains, high near an Alpine pass. No one knew just where.

Only Savarone Fontini-Cristi.

A light snow was falling, adding its thin layer to the alabaster cover on the moonlit ground. They passed through tunnels carved out of rock, swinging westward around the ledges of the mountains, the steep gorges menacingly beneath them on their right. It was so much colder. Petride had not expected that; he had not thought about temperatures. The snow and the ice; there was ice on the tracks.

Every mile they travelled seemed like ten, every minute that passed could have been an hour. The young priest peered through the windshield, seeing the beam of the train's searchlight reflecting off the falling snow. He leaned out; he could see only the giant trees in the darkness.

Where *was* he? Where was the Italian *padrone*, Fontini-Cristi? Perhaps he had changed his mind. O merciful God, that could not be! He could not allow himself to think such thoughts. What they carried in that holy vault would plunge the world into chaos. The Italian knew that; the Patriarchate had total confidence in the *padrone* . . .

Petride's head was aching, his temples pounded. He sat on the steps of the tender; he had to control himself. He looked at the radium dial of his watch. *Merciful God!* They'd travelled too far! In a half hour they'd be out of the mountains!

'There is your signal!' shouted Annaxas.

Petride leaped to his feet and leaned over the side, his pulse wild, his hands trembling as he gripped the roof ladder. Down the track no more than a quarter of a mile, a lantern was being raised and lowered, its light flickering through the thin sheets of snow.

Annaxas braked the locomotive. The belching engine drew out its roars like the subsiding giant furnace it was. In the snow-lit, moon-lit distance, aided by the beam of the locomotive's single headlight, Petride saw a man standing next to an odd-shaped vehicle in a small clearing at the side of the rails. The man was dressed in heavy clothing, collar and cap of fur. The vehicle was both a truck and not a truck. Its rear wheels were much larger than those in front, as though belonging to a tractor. Yet the hood beyond the windshield was not a truck's hood, or a tractor's, thought the priest. It resembled something else.

What was it?

Then he knew and he could not help but smile. He had seen hundreds of such pieces of equipment during the past four days. In front of the strange vehicle's hood was a vertically controlled cargo platform.

Fontini-Cristi was as resourceful as the monks in the Order of Xenope. But then the pouch strapped to his chest had told him that.

'You are the priest of Xenope!' Savarone Fontini-Cristi's voice was deep, aristocratic, and very used to authority. He was a tall man and slender beneath the Alpine clothing, with large, penetrating eyes recessed in the aquiline features of his face. And he was a much older man than Petride thought he would be.

'I am, *signore*,' said Petride, climbing down into the snow.

'You're very young. The holy men have given you an awesome responsibility.'

'I speak the language. I know that what I do is right.'

The *padrone* stared at him. 'I'm sure you do. What else is left for you?'

'Don't you believe it?'

The *padrone* replied simply. 'I believe in only one thing, my young father. There is but a single war that must be fought. There can be no divisions among those who battle the fascist. *That* is the extent of what I believe.' Fontini-Cristi looked up abruptly at the train. 'Come. There's no time to waste. We must return before daybreak. There are clothes for you in the tractor. Get them. I'll instruct the driver.'

'He doesn't speak Italian.'

'I speak Greek. Hurry!'

The goods wagon was lined up with the tractor. Laterally operated chains were placed around the holy vault, and the heavy iron receptacle encased in strips of wood was pulled, groaning under the tension, out on to the platform. It was secured by the chains in front; taut straps buckled over the top.

Savarone Fontini-Cristi tested the harnessing on all sides. He was satisfied; he stood back, the beam of his flashlight illuminating the monastic symbols stencilled on the encasement.

'So after fifteen hundred years it comes out of the earth. Only to be returned to the earth,' said Fontini-Cristi quietly. 'Earth and fire and sea. I should have chosen the last two, my young priest. Fire or the sea.'

'That is not the will of God.'

'I'm glad your communication is so direct. You holy men never cease to amaze me with your sense of the absolute.' Fontini-Cristi turned to Annaxas and spoke fluently in Greek. 'Pull up so that I may clear the tracks. There's a narrow trail on the other side of the woods. We'll be back before dawn.'

Annaxas nodded. He was uncomfortable in the presence of such a man as Fontini-Cristi. 'Yes, Your Excellency.'

'I'm no such thing. And you're a fine driver.'

'Thank you.' Annaxas, embarrassed, walked towards the engine.

'That man is your brother?' asked Fontini-Cristi softly of Petride.

'Yes.'

'He doesn't know?'

The young priest shook his head.

'You'll need your God then.' The Italian turned swiftly and started for the driver's side of the enclosed tractor. 'Come, Father. We have work to do. This machine was built for the avalanche. It will take our cargo where no human being could carry it.'

Petride climbed into the seat. Fontini-Cristi started the powerful engine and expertly shifted gears. The platform in front of the hood was lowered, permitting visibility, and the vehicle lunged forward, vibrating across the tracks into the Alpine forest.

The priest of Xenope sat back and closed his eyes in prayer. Fontini-Cristi manoeuvred the powerful machine through the rising woods towards the upper trails of the Champoluc mountains.

'I have two sons older than you,' said Fontini-Cristi after a while. And then he added, 'I'm taking you to the grave of a Jew. I think it's appropriate.'

They returned to the Alpine clearing as the black sky was turning grey. Fontini-Cristi stared at Petride as the young priest climbed out of the strange machine. 'You know where I live. My house is your house.'

'We all reside in the house of the Lord, *signore.*'

'So be it. Good-bye, my young friend.'

'Good-bye. May God go with you.'

'If He chooses.'

The Italian pushed the gear-lever into place and drove quickly down the barely visible road below the tracks. Petride understood. Fontini-Cristi could not lose a minute now. Every hour he was away from his estate

24

would add to the questions that might be asked. There were many in Italy who considered the Fontini-Cristis to be enemies of the state.

They were watched. All of them.

The young priest ran through the snow towards the engine. And his brother.

Dawn came over the waters of Lago Maggiore. They were on the Stresa freight bridge; the twenty-sixth authorization in the pouch was their passport. Petride wondered what would greet them in Milan, although he realized that it did not really matter.

Nothing mattered now. The journey was coming to an end.

The holy thing was in its resting place. Not to be unearthed for years; perhaps to be buried for a millennium. There was no way to tell.

They sped south-east on the main track through Varese into Castiglione. They did not wait for nightfall ... nothing mattered now. On the outskirts of Varese, Petride saw a roadsign in the bright Italian sunlight.

CAMPO DI FIORI. 20 KIL.

God had chosen a man from Campo di Fiori. The holy secret now belonged to Fontini-Cristi.

The countryside rushed by; the air was clear and cold and exhilarating. The skyline of Milan came into view. The haze of factory smoke intruded on God's sky and lay suspended like a flat, grey tarpaulin above the horizon. The freight slowed and entered the tracks of the depot sidings. They held at a stop until a disinterested *spedizioniere* in the uniform of the state railroads pointed to a curve in the rails where a green disc snapped up in front of a red one. It was the signal to enter the Milan yards.

'We're here!' shouted Annaxas. 'A day's rest, then home! I must say you people are remarkable!'

'Yes,' said Petride simply. 'We're remarkable.'

The priest looked at his brother. The sounds of the goods yard were music to Annaxas; he sang a Greek song, his whole upper body swaying rhythmically to the sharp, fast beats of the melody.

It was strange, the song Annaxas sang. It was not a song of the railroads; it belonged to the sea. A shanty that was a favourite of the fishermen of Thermaikós. There was something appropriate, thought Petride, about such a song at such a moment.

The sea was God's source of life. It was from the sea that He created the earth.

I believe in one God ... maker of all things ...

The priest of Xenope removed the Beretta from under his shirt. He took two steps forward, towards his beloved brother, and raised the barrel of the weapon. It was inches from the base of Annaxas's skull.

... both visible and invisible ... and in one Lord, Jesus Christ ... only begotten of the Father ...

He pulled the trigger.

The explosion filled the cabin. Blood and flesh and things most terrible flew through the air and matted on to glass and metal.

... substance of the Father ... God of God ... light of light ... very God of very God ...

The priest of Xenope closed his eyes and shouted in exaltation as he held the weapon against his own temple.

'*... begotten, not made! I will look into the eyes of the Lord and I shall not waver!*'

He fired.

PART ONE

CHAPTER ONE

29 Dec 1939
MILAN

Savarone walked past his son's secretary into his son's office and across the heavily carpeted floor to the window overlooking the vast factory complex that was the Fontini-Cristi Industries. His son, of course, was nowhere to be seen. His son, his *eldest* son, was rarely in his office; he was rarely in Milan, for that matter. The first son, the heir-apparent to all of Fontini-Cristi, was incorrigible. And arrogant, and far too concerned with his own comforts.

Vittorio was also brilliant. A far more brilliant man than the father who had trained him. And that fact only served to further infuriate Savarone; a man possessing such gifts had greater responsibilities than other men. *He* did not settle for the daily accomplishments that came naturally. He did not carouse and whore and gamble at roulette and baccarat. Or waste sleepless nights with the naked children of the Mediterranean. Neither did he turn his back on the events that were crippling his country, veering it into chaos.

Savarone heard a slight cough behind him and turned. Vittorio's secretary had come into the office.

'I've left word for your son at the Borsa Valori. I believe he was to see his broker this afternoon.'

'You may believe it, but I doubt you'll find it on his

29

calendar.' Savarone saw the girl flush. 'I apologize. You're not accountable for my son. Although you've probably done so, I suggest you try whatever private numbers he's given you. This is a familiar office to me. I'll wait.' He removed his overcoat of light camel's hair and his hat, a Tyrolean of green felt. He threw them on the armchair at the side of the desk.

'Yes, sir.' The girl left quickly, closing the door behind her.

It *was* a familiar office, thought Fontini-Cristi, although it had been necessary to call it to the girl's attention. Until two years ago, it had been his. Very little remained of his presence, now; only the dark wood panelling. All the furniture had been changed. Vittorio had accepted the four walls. Nothing else.

Savarone sat in the large swivel chair behind the desk. He did not like such chairs; he was too old to let his body be suddenly turned and sprung back by unseen springs and hidden ball bearings. He reached into his pocket and took out the telegram that had brought him to Milan from Campo di Fiori, the telegram from Rome that said the Fontini-Cristis were marked.

But marked for what? By whom? On whose orders?

Questions that could not be asked on the telephone, for the telephone was an instrument of the state. The state. Always the state. Seen and unseen. Observing, following, listening, prying. No telephone could be used and no answer given by the informer in Rome who employed the simple codes.

We have received no reply from Milan, therefore we take the liberty of wiring you personally. Five shipments of aircraft piston hammers defective. Rome insists on immediate replacement. Repeat: immediate. Please confirm by telephone before the end of the day.

The number 'five' referred to the Fontini-Cristis, because there were five men in the family – a father and

30

four sons. Anything to do with the word 'hammer' meant sudden, extreme danger. The repetition of the word 'immediate' was self-explanatory: not a moment could be lost, confirmation of receipt was to be made by telephone to Rome within minutes of the telegram's arrival in Milan. Other men would then be contacted, strategies analysed, plans made. It was too late now.

The wire had been sent to Savarone that morning. Vittorio must have received his cable by eleven. And yet his son had neither replied to Rome nor alerted him in Campo di Fiori. The end of the day was at hand. Too late.

It was unforgivable. Men daily risked their lives and the lives of their families in the fight against Mussolini.

It had not always been so, thought Savarone, as he stared at the office door, hoping that any second the secretary would reappear with news of Vittorio's whereabouts. It had been very different once. In the beginning, the Fontini-Cristi had endorsed *Il Duce*. The weak, indecisive Emmanuel was letting Italy die. Benito Mussolini had offered an alternative; he had come himself to Campo di Fiori to meet with the patriarch of the Fontini-Cristis, seeking alliance – as Machiavelli once sought the backing of the princes – and he had been alive, and committed, and filled with promise for all Italy.

That was sixteen years ago; since that time Mussolini had fed upon his own rhetoric. He had robbed the nation of its right to think, the people of their freedom to choose; he had deceived the aristocrats – used them and denied their common objectives. He had plunged the country into an utterly useless African war. All for the personal glory of this Caesar Maximus. He had plundered the soul of Italy, and Savarone had vowed to stop him. Fontini-Cristi had gathered the northern 'princes' together, and quietly the revolt was taking place.

Mussolini could not risk an open break with the Fontini-Cristis. Unless the charge of treason could be sustained with such clarity that even the family's most avid supporters would have to conclude they had been – if nothing else – stupid. Italy was gearing for its own entry into the German war. Mussolini had to be careful. That war was not popular, the Germans less so.

Campo di Fiori had become the meeting place of the disaffected. The sprawling acres of lawns and forests and hills and streams were suited to the clandestine nature of the conferences which generally took place at night. But not always; there were other gatherings that required the daylight hours, where younger men were trained by other experienced younger men in the arts of a new, strange warfare. The knife, the rope, the chain, and the hook. They had even coined a name for themselves: *partigiani*.

The partisans. A name that was spreading from nation to nation.

These were the games of Italy, thought Savarone. 'The games of Italy' was what his son called them, a term used in derision by an arrogant, self-centred *aristocratico* who took seriously only his own pleasures . . . No, that was not entirely true. Vittorio also took seriously the running of Fontini-Cristi, as long as pressures of the market-place conformed to his own schedules. And he made them conform. He used his financial power ruthlessly, his expertise – the expertise he had learned at his father's side – arrogantly.

The telephone rang; Savarone was tempted to pick it up, but he did not. It was his son's office, his son's telephone. Instead, he got out of the terrible chair and walked across the room to the door. He opened it. The secretary was repeating a name.

' . . . Signore Tesca?'

Savarone interrupted harshly. 'Is that Alfredo Tesca?'

The girl nodded.

'Tell him to stay on the telephone. I'll speak with him.'

Savarone walked rapidly back to his son's desk and the telephone. Alfredo Tesca was a foreman in one of the factories; he was also a *partigiano*.

'Fontini-Cristi,' Savarone said.

'*Padrone*? I'm glad it's you. This line is clear; we check it every day.'

'Nothing changes. It only accelerates.'

'Yes, *padrone*. There's an emergency. A man has flown up from Rome. He must meet with a member of your family.'

'Where?'

'The Olona house.'

'When?'

'As soon as possible.'

Savarone looked at the overcoat and the green felt hat he had thrown over the chair. 'Tesca? Do you remember two years ago? The meeting at the apartment on the Duomo?'

'Yes, *padrone*. It will be six o'clock soon. I'll be waiting for you.'

Fontini-Cristi hung up the telephone and reached for his overcoat and his hat. He put them on and checked his watch. It was five forty-five; he had to wait a few minutes. The walk across the concrete lot to the factory was short. He had to time it so that he entered the building at the height of the crowds; when the day shift was leaving and the night shift came to work.

His son had taken full advantage of Mussolini's war machine. The Fontini-Cristi Industries operated around the clock. When the father had reproached the son, the son replied. 'We don't make munitions. We're not geared for that. The conversion would be too expensive. We make only profits, father.'

33

His son. The most capable of them all had a hollowness in him.

Savarone's eyes fell on the photograph in the silver frame on Vittorio's desk. Its very existence was a cruel, self-inflicted joke. The face in the picture was that of a young woman, pretty in the accepted sense, with the pert, set features of a spoiled child growing into spoiled maturity. She had been Vittorio's wife. Ten years ago.

It had not been a good marriage. It had been more an industrial alliance between two immensely wealthy families. And the bride brought little to the union; she was a pouting, self-indulgent woman whose outlook was guided by possessions.

She died in an automobile crash in Monte Carlo, early in the morning after the casinos had closed. Vittorio never talked about that early morning; he had not been with his wife. Another had.

His son had spent four years in turbulent discomfort with a wife he could not stand, and yet the photograph was on his desk. Ten years later. Savarone once asked him why.

'Being a widower lends a certain respectability to my life-style.'

It was seven minutes to six. Time to begin. Savarone walked out of his son's office and spoke to the secretary. 'Please call downstairs and have my car brought around to the west gate. Tell my chauffeur I have a meeting at the Duomo.'

'Yes, sir ... Do you wish to leave a number where your son can reach you?'

'Campo di Fiori. But by the time he calls, I'll no doubt be asleep.'

Savarone took the private elevator to the ground floor and went out the executive entrance on to the concrete. Thirty yards away his chauffeur was walking towards the limousine with the crest of Fontini-Cristi on the door panels. The two men exchanged looks. The chauffeur nodded slightly; he knew what to do. He was a *partigiano*.

Savarone crossed the yard, aware that people were watching him. That was good; that was the way it had been two years ago when *Il Duce*'s secret police were tracking his every move, trying to unearth the whereabouts of an anti-fascist cell. The factory whistles blew; the day shift was released and within minutes the yard and the corridors would be crowded. The incoming workers – due at their stations at six fifteen – were flooding through the west gate.

He climbed the steps to the employees' entrance and entered the crowded, noisy corridor, removing his coat and hat in the confusion. Tesca stood by the wall, halfway towards the doors that led to the workers' lockers. He was tall and slender, very much like Savarone, and he took Savarone's coat and hat and helped Fontini-Cristi into his own worn, three-quarter-length raincoat with a newspaper in the pocket. Then he handed Savarone a large cloth visor cap. The exchange was completed without words in the jostling crowds. Tesca accepted Savarone's assistance in putting on the camel's hair coat; the employer saw that the employee had taken the trouble – as he had done two years ago – to change into pressed trousers, shined shoes and a white shirt and tie.

The *partigiano* entered the flow of human traffic to the exit doors. Savarone followed ten yards behind, then stood immobile on the crowded platform outside the constantly opening doors, pretending to read the newspaper.

He saw what he wanted to see. The camel's hair coat and the green Tyrolean hat stood out among the worn leather jackets and frayed workers' clothing. Two men beyond the throngs signalled each other and began the chase, making their way through the crowd as best they could in an effort to catch up. Savarone squeezed himself into the stream of workers and arrived at the gate in time to see the door of the Fontini-Cristi limousine close and the huge automobile roll into the traffic of the Via di Sempione. The two pursuers were at the kerb; a grey Fiat pulled up and they climbed in.

The Fiat took up the chase. Savarone turned north and walked swiftly to the corner bus stop.

The house on the river-front was a relic that once, perhaps a decade ago, had been painted white. From the outside it looked dilapidated, but inside the rooms were small, neat, and organized; they were places of work, an antifascist headquarters.

Savarone entered the room with the windows overlooking the murky waters of the Olona River, made black by the darkness of night. Three men rose from straight-backed chairs around a table and greeted him with feeling and respect. Two were known to him; the third, he presumed, was from Rome.

'The hammer code was sent this morning,' said Savarone. 'What does it mean?'

'You *received* the wire?' asked the man from Rome incredulously. 'All telegrams to Fontini-Cristi in Milan were intercepted. It's why I'm here. All communications to your factories were stopped.'

'I received mine at Campo di Fiori. Through the telegraph office in Varese, I imagine, not Milan.' Savarone felt a minor relief in knowing his son had not disobeyed. 'Have you the information?'

'Not all, *padrone*,' replied the man. 'But enough to know it's extremely serious. And imminent. The military is suddenly very concerned with the northern movement. The generals want it crippled; they intend to see your family exposed.'

'As what?'

'As enemies of the new Italy.'

'On what grounds?'

'For holding meetings of a treasonable nature at Campo di Fiori. Spreading anti-state lies; of attempting to undermine Rome's objectives and corrupt the industrial arm of the country.'

'Words.'

'Nevertheless, an example is to be made. They demand it, they say.'

'Nonsense. Rome wouldn't dare move against us on such tenuous grounds.'

'That is the problem, *signore*,' said the man hesitantly. 'It's not Rome. It's Berlin.'

'*What?*'

'The Germans are everywhere; giving orders to everyone. The word is that Berlin wants the Fontini-Cristis stripped of influence.'

'They look to the future, don't they,' stated one of the other two men, an older *partigiano* who had walked to the window.

'How do they propose to accomplish this?' asked Savarone.

'By smashing a meeting at Campo di Fiori. Forcing those there to bear witness to the treasons of the Fontini-Cristi. That would be less difficult than you think, I believe.'

'Agreed. It's the reason we've been careful ... When will this happen? Do you have any idea?'

'I left Rome at noon. I can only assume the code word "hammer" was used correctly.'

'There's a meeting tonight.'

'Then "hammer" was called for. Cancel it, *padrone*. Obviously, word got out.'

'I'll need your help. I'll give you names ... our telephones are unsafe.' Fontini-Cristi began writing in a notebook on the table with a pencil supplied by the third *partigiano*.

'When's the meeting scheduled?'

'Ten thirty. There's enough time,' replied Savarone. 'I hope so. Berlin is thorough.'

Fontini-Cristi stopped writing and looked over at the man. 'That's a strange thing to say. The Germans may bark orders in the Campidoglio; they're not in Milan.'

The three partisans exchanged glances. Savarone knew there was further news he had not received. The man from Rome finally spoke.

'As I said, our information is not complete. But we know certain things. The degree of Berlin's interest, for example. The German high command wants Italy to openly declare itself. Mussolini wavers; for many reasons, not the least of which is the opposition of such powerful men as yourself—' The man stopped; he was unsure. Not, apparently, of his information, but how to say it.

'What are you driving at?'

'They say that Berlin's interest in the Fontini-Cristis is Gestapo inspired. It's the Nazis who demand the example; who intend to crush Mussolini's opposition.'

'I gathered that. So?'

'They have little confidence in Rome, none in the provinces. The raiding party will be led by Germans.'

'A German raiding party out of *Milan*?'

The man nodded.

Savarone put down the pencil and stared at the man from Rome. But his thoughts were not on the man; they were on a Greek freight from Salonika he had met high in the mountains of Champoluc. On the cargo that train carried. A vault from the Patriarchate of Constantine, now buried in the frozen earth of the upper regions.

It seemed incredible, but the incredible was commonplace in these times of madness. Had Berlin found out about the train from Salonika? Did the Germans know

38

about the vault? *Mother of Christ*, it had to be kept from them! And all – *all* – *like* them!

'You're sure of your information?'

'We are.'

Rome could be managed, thought Savarone. Italy needed the Fontini-Cristi Industries. But if the German intrusion was linked to the vault from Constantine, Berlin would not consider Rome's needs in the slightest. The possession of the vault was *everything*.

And, therefore, the protection of it essential beyond all life. Above all things its secret could not fall into the wrong hands. Not now. Perhaps not ever, but certainly not now.

The key was Vittorio. It was always Vittorio, the most capable of them all. For whatever else he was, Vittorio was a Fontini-Cristi. He would honour the family's commitment; he was a match for Berlin. The time had come to tell him about the train from Salonika. Detail the family's arrangements with the monastic Order of Xenope. The timing was right, the strategy complete.

A date marked stone, etched for a millennium, was only a hint, a clue in case of a sudden failing of the heart, death from abrupt natural or unnatural causes. It was not enough.

Vittorio had to be told, charged with a responsibility beyond anything in his imagination. The documents from Constantine made everything else pale into insignificance.

Savarone looked up at the three men. 'The meeting will be cancelled tonight. The raiding party will find only a large family gathering. A holiday dinner party. All my children and their children. However, for it to be complete, my oldest son must be at Campo di Fiori. I've tried calling him all afternoon. Now you must find him. Use your telephones. Call everyone in Milan if you have to, but *find him*! If it gets late, tell him to use the stable road. It wouldn't do for him to enter with the raiding party.'

CHAPTER TWO

29 Dec 1939
LAKE COMO

The white, twelve-cylinder Hispano-Suiza, its off-white leather top rolled halfway back, uncovering the front, red leather seat, took the long curve at high speed. Below on the left were the winter-blue waters of Lake Como, to the right the mountains of Lombardy.

'*Vittorio!*' shrieked the girl beside the driver, holding her wind-shocked blonde hair with one hand, her collar of Russian pony with the other. 'I'll be undone, my lamb!'

The driver smiled, his squinting grey eyes steady on the onrushing road in the sunlight, his hands expertly, almost delicately, feeling the play in the ivory steering wheel. 'The Suiza is a far better car than the Alfa-Romeo. The British Rolls is no comparison.'

'You don't have to prove it to *me*, darling. My God, I refuse to look at the speedometer! And I'll be an absolute mess!'

'Good. If your husband's in Bellagio, he won't recognize you. I'll introduce you as a terribly sweet cousin from Verona.'

The girl laughed. 'If my husband's in Bellagio, he'll have a terribly sweet cousin to introduce to *us*.'

They both laughed. The curve came to an end, the road straightened, and the girl slid over next to the

41

driver. She slipped her hand under the arm of his tan suede jacket, enlarged by the heavy wool of the white turtleneck sweater beneath; briefly she placed her face against his shoulder.

'It was sweet of you to call. I really had to get away.'

'I knew that. It was in your eyes last night. You were bored to death.'

'Well, God, weren't *you*? Such a dreary dinner party! Talk, talk, talk! War this, war that. Rome yes, Rome no, Benito always. I'm positively sick of it! Gstaad closed! St Moritz filled with Jews throwing money at everyone! Monte Carlo an absolute fiasco! The casinos are closing, you know. Everybody says so. It's all such a *bore*!'

The driver let his right hand drop from the steering wheel and reached for the girl's overcoat. He separated the fur and caressed her inner thigh as expertly as he fingered the ivory steering wheel. She moaned pleasantly and craned her neck, putting her lips to his ear, her tongue darting.

'You continue that, we'll end up in the water. I suspect it's damned cold.'

'You started it, my lovely Vittorio.'

'I'll stop it,' he said smiling, returning his hand to the wheel. 'I won't be able to buy another car like this for a long time. Today everything is the tank. Far less profit in the tank.'

'Please! No war talk.'

'You'll get none from me,' said Fontini-Cristi, laughing again. 'Unless you want to negotiate a purchase for Rome. I'll sell you anything from conveyor belts to motorcycles to uniforms, if you like.'

'You don't make uniforms.'

'We own a company that does.'

'I forgot. Fontini-Cristi owns everything north of Parma and west of Padua. At least, that's what my husband says. Quite enviously, of course.'

'Your husband, the sleepy count, is a dreadful businessman.'

'He doesn't mean to be.'

Vittorio Fontini-Cristi smiled as he braked the long white automobile for a descending curve in the road towards the lakeshore. Halfway down, on the promontory that was Bellagio, stood the elegant Villa Lario, name for the ancient poet of Como. It was a resort lodge known for its extraordinary beauty, as well as its marked exclusivity.

When the elite moved north, they played at Villa Lario. Money and family were their methods of entry. The *commessi* were diffident, soft-spoken, aware of their clientele's every proclivity, and most alert as to the scheduling of reservations. It was not uncommon for a husband or a wife, a lover or a mistress, to receive a quiet, cautioning phone call suggesting another date for arrival. Or rapid departure.

The Hispano-Suiza swerved into the parking lot of blue brick; two uniformed attendants raced from the heated booth to both sides of the automobile, opening the doors and bowing.

The attendant at Vittorio's side spoke. 'Welcome to Villa Lario, *signore*.'

It was never nice-to-see-you-again-*signore*.

Never.

'Thank you. We have no luggage. We're here only for the day. See to the oil and petrol. Is the mechanic around?'

'Yes, sir.'

'Have him check the alignment. There's too much play.'

'Of course, *signore*.'

Fontini-Cristi got out of the car. He was a tall man, over six feet in height. His straight, dark-brown hair fell over his forehead; his features were sharp – as aquiline as his father's – and his eyes, still squinting in the bright sunlight, were at once passive and alert. He walked in front of the white hood, absently feeling the radiator cap, and smiled at his companion, the Contessa d'Avenzo. Together they crossed to the stone steps leading up to the entrance of Villa Lario.

'Where did you tell the servants you were off to?' asked Fontini-Cristi.

'Treviglio. You are a horse trainer who wants to sell me an Arabian.'

'Remind me to buy you one.'

'And you? What did you say at your office?'

'Nothing, really. Only my brothers might ask for me; everyone else waits patiently.'

'But not your brothers.' The Contessa d'Avenzo smiled. 'I like that. The important Vittorio is hounded in business by his brothers.'

'Hardly! My sweet younger brothers have between them three wives and eleven children. Their problems are continuously and forever domestic. I think sometimes I'm a referee. Which is fine; they keep occupied and *away* from business.'

They stood on the terrace outside the glass doors that led to the lobby of Villa Lario and looked down at the enormous lake and across to the mountains beyond.

'It's beautiful,' said the contessa. 'You've arranged for a room?'

'A suite. The penthouse. The view's magnificent.'

'I've heard of it. I've never been up there.'

'Few people have.'

'I imagine you lease it by the month.'

'That's not really necessary,' said Fontini-Cristi, turning towards the huge glass doors. 'You see, as it happens I own Villa Lario.'

The Contessa d'Avenzo laughed. She preceded Vittorio into the lobby. 'You are an *impossible*, *a*moral man.

You get richer from your own kind. My God, you could blackmail half of Italy!'

'Only *our* Italy, my dear.'

'That's enough!'

'Hardly. But I've never had to, if it relieves your mind. I'm merely a guest. Wait here, please.'

Vittorio walked over to the front desk. The tuxedoed clerk behind the marble counter greeted him. 'How good of you to come to see us, Signore Fontini-Cristi.'

'Are things going well?'

'Extremely so. Would you care to—?'

'No, I should not,' interrupted Vittorio. 'I assume my rooms are ready.'

'Of course, *signore*. As you requested, an early supper is being prepared. Caviar Iranian, cold pressed duck, Veuve Cliquot twenty-eight.'

'And?'

'There are flowers, naturally. The masseur is prepared to cancel his other appointments.'

'And . . . ?'

'There are no complications for the Contessa d'Aven-zo,' answered the clerk quickly, rapidly. 'None of her circle is here.'

'Thank you.' Fontini-Cristi turned, only to be stopped by the sound of the clerk's voice.

'*Signore?*'

'Yes?'

'I realize you do not care to be disturbed except in emergencies, but your office called.'

'Did my office say it was an emergency?'

'They said your father was trying to locate you.'

'That's not an emergency. It's a whim.'

'I think you may be that Arabian, after all, lamb,' mused the contessa out loud, lying beside Vittorio in the feather

45

bed. The eiderdown quilt was pulled down to her naked waist. 'You're marvellous. And so patient.'

'But not patient enough, I think,' replied Fontini-Cristi. He sat up against the pillow, looking down at the girl; he was smoking a cigarette.

'Not patient enough,' agreed the Contessa d'Avenzo, turning her face and smiling up at him. 'Why don't you put out the cigarette?'

'In a little while. Be assured of it. Some wine?' He gestured at the silver ice bucket within arm's reach. It stood on a tripod; an open bottle draped with a linen towel was pushed into the melting crushed ice.

The contessa stared at him, her breath coming shorter. 'You pour the wine. I'll drink my own.'

In swift, gentle movements, the girl turned and reached under the soft quilt with both hands to Vittorio's groin. She raised the cover and placed her face underneath, over Vittorio. The quilt fell back, covering her head as her throaty moans grew louder and her body writhed.

The waiters cleared away the dishes and rolled out the table, a *commesso* lighted a fire in the fireplace and poured brandy.

'It's been a lovely day,' said the Contessa d'Avenzo. 'May we do it often?'

'I think we should set up a schedule. By your calendar, of course.'

'Of course.' The girl laughed throatily. 'You're a very practical man.'

'Why not? It's easier.'

The telephone rang. Vittorio looked over at it, annoyed. He rose from the chair in front of the fireplace and crossed angrily to the bedside table. He picked up the instrument and spoke harshly. 'Yes?'

The voice at the other end was vaguely familiar. 'This is Tesca. Alfredo Tesca.'

'*Who?*'

'One of the foremen in the Milan factories.'

'You're *what?* How *dare* you call here! How did you get this number?'

Tesca was silent for a moment. 'I threatened the life of your secretary, young *padrone*. And I would have killed her had she not given it to me. You may fire me tomorrow. I am your foreman, but I am a *partigiano* first.'

'You *are* fired. *Now*. As of this moment!'

'So be it, *signore*.'

'I want no part—'

'*Basta!*' shouted Tesca. 'There's no time! Everyone's looking for you. The *padrone's* in danger. Your whole *family's* in danger! Go to Campo di Fiori! At once! Your father says to use the stable road!'

The telephone went dead.

Savarone walked through the great hall into the enormous dining room of Campo di Fiori. Everything was as it should be. The room was filled with sons and daughters, husbands and wives, and a thoroughly boisterous crowd of grandchildren. The servants had placed silver trays of antipasto on the tops of marble tables. A tall pine that reached the high beamed ceiling was a magnificent Christmas tree, its myriad lights and glittering ornament filling the room with reflections of colour that bounced off the tapestries and the ornate furniture.

Outside in the circular drive in front of the marble steps of the entrance were four automobiles illuminated by the floodlights that beamed down from the eaves. They could easily be mistaken for anyone's automobiles, which was what Savarone intended. For when the raiding party arrived, all it would find was an innocent, festive family gathering. A holiday dinner. Nothing else.

Except an imperiously aggravated patriarch of one of Italy's most powerful clans. The *padrone* of the Fontini-Cristis, who would demand to know who was responsible for such a barbarous intrusion.

Only Vittorio was missing; and his presence was vital. Questions might be raised that could lead to other questions. The unwilling Vittorio, who scoffed at their work, could become an unjustified target of suspicion. What was a holiday family dinner without the eldest son, the primary heir? Further, if Vittorio appeared *during* the intrusion, arrogantly reluctant – as his custom – to give an account of himself to anyone, there could be trouble. His son refused to acknowledge the extent, but Rome *was* under Berlin's thumb.

Savarone beckoned his next eldest, the serious Antonio, who stood with his wife as she admonished one of their children.

'Yes, father?'

'Go to the stables. See Barzini. Tell him that if Vittorio arrives during the fascists' visit, he's to say he was detained at one of the plants.'

'I can call him on the stable phone.'

'No. Barzini's getting on. He pretends it's not so, but he's growing deaf. Make sure he understands.'

The second son nodded dutifully. 'Yes, of course, father. Anything you say.'

What in God's name had his father *done*? What *could* he do that would give Rome the confidence, the *excuse*, to move openly against the house of Fontini-Cristi?

Your whole family is in danger.

Preposterous!

Mussolini courted the northern industrialists; he needed them. He knew that most were old men, set in their ways, and knew he could achieve more with honey than with vinegar. What did it matter if a few Savarones played their silly games? Their time was past.

But then there was only one Savarone. Separate and apart from all other men. He had become, perhaps, that terrible thing, a symbol. With his silly, goddamned *partigiani*. Ragtail lunatics who raced around the fields and the woods of Campo di Fiori pretending they were some kind of primitive tribesmen hunting tigers and killer lions.

Jesus! *Children!*

Well, it would all come to a stop. *Padrone* or no *padrone*, if his father had gone too far and embarrassed them, there would be a confrontation. He had made it clear to Savarone two years ago that when he assumed the reins of Fontini-Cristi, it meant that all the leather was in his hands.

Suddenly Vittorio remembered. Two weeks ago, Savarone had gone to Zürich for a few days. At least, he *said* he was going to Zürich. It wasn't really clear; he, Vittorio, had not been listening closely. But during those few days, it was unexpectedly necessary to get his father's signature on several contracts. So necessary that he had telephoned every hotel in Zürich, trying to locate Savarone. He was nowhere to be found. No one had seen him, and his father was not easily overlooked.

And when he returned to Campo di Fiori, he would not say where he had been. He was maddeningly enigmatic, telling his son that he would explain everything in a few days. An incident would take place in Monfalcone and when it occurred, Vittorio would be told. Vittorio *had* to be told.

What in hell was his father talking about? *What* incident at Monfalcone? Why would *anything* taking place at Monfalcone concern them?

Preposterous!

But Zürich wasn't preposterous at all. Banks were in

Zürich. Had Savarone manipulated money in Zürich? Had he transferred extraordinary sums out of Italy into Switzerland? There were specific laws against that these days. Mussolini needed every *lira* he could keep. And God knew the family had sufficient reserves in Berne and Geneva; there was no lack of Fontini-Cristi capital in Switzerland.

Whatever Savarone had done, it would be his last gesture. If his father was so politically involved, let him go somewhere else and proselytize. America, perhaps.

Vittorio shook his head slowly in defeat, as he steered the Hispano-Suiza on to the road out of Varese. What was he thinking of? Savarone was – Savarone. The head of the house of Fontini-Cristi. No matter the son's talents or expertise, the son was not the *padrone*.

Use the stable road.

What was the point of that? The stable road started at the north end of the property, three miles from the east gates. Nevertheless, he would use it; his father must have had a reason for giving the order. No doubt as implausible as the foolish games he indulged in, but a surface filial obedience was called for; the son was going to be very firm with the father.

What had happened in Zürich?

He passed the main gates on the road out of Varese and proceeded to the intersecting west road three miles beyond. He turned left and drove nearly two miles to the north gate, turning left again into Campo di Fiori. The stables were three-quarters of a mile from the entrance; the road was dirt. It was easier on the horses, for this was the road used by riders heading for the fields and trails north and west of the forest at the centre of Campo di Fiori. The forest behind the great house that was bisected by the wide stream that flowed from the northern mountains.

In the headlights he saw the figure of old Guido

Barzini waving his arms, signalling him to stop. The gnarled Barzini was something: a fixture at Campo di Fiori who had spent his life in the service of the house.

'Quickly, Signore Vittorio!' said Barzini through the open window. 'Leave your car here. There's no more time.'

'Time for what?'

'The *padrone* spoke to me not five minutes ago. He said if you drove in now, you were to call him on the stable telephone before you went to the house. It's nearly half past the hour.'

Vittorio looked at the dashboard clock. It was twenty-eight minutes past ten. 'What's going on?'

'Hurry, *signore! Please!* The *fascisti!*'

'What *fascisti?*'

'The *padrone*. He'll tell you.'

Fontini-Cristi got out of the car and followed Barzini down the stone path into the entrance of the stables. It was a tack-room; bits and braces and halters and leather were hung neatly on the walls surrounding countless plaques and ribbons, proof of the superiority of the Fontini-Cristi colours. Also on the wall was the telephone that connected the stables to the great house.

'What's going on, father? Have you any idea who called me in Bellagio?'

'*Basta!*' roared Savarone over the telephone. 'They'll be here any moment. A German raiding party.'

'*Germans?*'

'Yes. Rome expects to find a *partigiano* meeting taking place. They won't, of course. They'll intrude on a family dinner. *Remember!* A family dinner party was on your calendar. You were detained in Milan.'

'What have Germans got to do with Rome?'

'I'll explain later. Just remember—'

Suddenly, over the telephone, Vittorio heard the sounds of screeching tyres and powerful motors. A column of automobiles was speeding towards the great house from the east gates.

'*Father!*' yelled Vittorio. 'Has this anything to do with your trip to Zürich?'

There was silence over the phone. Finally Savarone spoke. 'It may have. You must stay where you are—'

'What happened? What happened in Zürich?'

'Not Zürich. Champoluc.'

'What?'

'Later! I have to get back to the others. Stay where you are! Out of sight! We'll talk when they leave.'

Vittorio heard the click. He turned to Barzini. The old stable master was riffling through a low chest of drawers filled with odd bits and braces; he found what he was looking for: a pistol and a pair of binoculars. He pulled them out and handed both to Vittorio.

'Come!' he said, his grey eyes angry. 'We'll watch. The *padrone* will teach them a lesson.'

They ran down the dirt road towards the house and the gardens above and behind it. When the dirt became pavement they cut to their left and climbed the embankment overlooking the circular drive. They were in darkness; the whole area below bathed in floodlights.

Three automobiles sped up the east-gate road; long, black, powerful vehicles, their headlights emerging out of the darkness, swallowed by the floodlamps that washed the area in white light. The cars entered the circular drive, careering to the left of the other automobiles, stopping suddenly, equidistant from each other in front of the stone steps that led to the thick oak doors of the entrance.

Men leaped out of the cars. Men dressed alike in black suits and black overcoats; men carrying weapons.

Carrying *weapons*!

Vittorio stared as the men – seven, eight, nine – raced up the steps to the door. A tall man in front assumed command; he held his hand up to those behind, ordering them to flank the doors, four on each side. He pulled the bell chain with his left hand, his right holding a pistol at his side.

Vittorio put the binoculars to his eyes. The man's face was turned away towards the door, but the weapon in his hand came into focus. It was a German Luger. Vittorio swung the binoculars to those on both sides of the doors.

The weapons were all German. Four Lugers, four Bergmann MP38 submachine guns.

Vittorio's stomach suddenly convulsed; his mind caught fire as he watched in disbelief. What had Rome *permitted*? It was incredible!

He focused the binoculars on the three automobiles. In each was a man; all were in shadows, only the backs of their heads seen through the rear windows. Vittorio concentrated on the nearest car, on the man inside that car.

The man shifted his position in the seat and looked back to his right; the light from the floodlamps caught his hair. It was close-cropped, greyish hair, but with a white streak shooting up from his forehead. There was something familiar about the man – the shape of the head, the streak of white in the hair – but Vittorio could not place him.

The door of the house opened; a maid stood in the frame, startled by the sight of the tall man with a gun. Vittorio stared in fury at the scene below. Rome would pay for the insult. The tall man pushed the maid aside and burst through the door, followed by the squad of eight men, their weapons held in front of them. The maid disappeared in the phalanx of bodies.

Rome would pay dearly!

There were shouts from inside. Vittorio could hear his father's roar and the subsequent shouted objections of his brothers.

There was a loud crash, a combination of glass and wood. Vittorio reached for the pistol in his pocket. He felt a powerful hand grip his wrist.

It was Barzini. The old stable master held Vittorio's hand, but he was looking over his shoulder, staring below.

'There are too many guns. You'll solve nothing,' he said simply.

A third crash came from below, the sound nearer now. The left panel of the huge oak double door had been thrown open and figures emerged. The children, first, bewildered, some crying in fear. Then the women, his sisters and his brothers' wives. Then his mother, her head defiant, the youngest child in her arms. His father and his brothers followed, prodded violently by the weapons in the hands of the black-suited men.

They were herded on to the pavement of the circular drive. His father's voice roared above the others, demanding to know who was responsible for the outrage.

But the outrage had not begun.

When it did, the mind of Vittorio Fontini-Cristi snapped. Cracks of thunder deafened him, streaks of lightning blinded him. He lunged forward, every ounce of his strength trying to wrench his hand free of Barzini's grip, twisting, trying desperately to free his neck and his jaw from Barzini's stranglehold.

For the black-suited men below had opened fire. Women threw themselves over the children, his brothers lurched at the weapons that shattered the night with fire and death. The screams of terror and pain and outrage swelled in the blinding light of the execution grounds. Smoke billowed; bodies froze in midair – suspended in blood-soaked garments. Children were cut in half, the bullets ripping out mouths and eyes. Pieces of flesh and skull and intestine shot through the swirling mists. A child's body exploded in its mother's arms. And still

Vittorio Fontini-Cristi could not free himself, could not go to his own.

He felt dead weight pressing him downward, then a clawing, choking, pulling at his lower jaw that blocked all sound from his lips.

And then the words pierced through the cacophony of gunshot and human screams below. The voice was tremendous, its thunder chopped by the firepower of submachine guns, but not stopped.

It was his father. Calling to him over the chasms of death.

'*Champoluc . . . Zürich is Champoluc . . . Zürich is the river . . . Champoluuuc . . .*'

Vittorio gnashed his teeth down on the fingers inside his mouth, pulling his jaw out of its socket. He wrenched his hand free for an instant – the hand with the weapon – and tried to raise the pistol and fire below.

But suddenly he could not. The sea of heaviness was over him again, his wrist twisted beyond endurance; the pistol was shaken loose. The enormous hand that had gripped his jaw was pushing his face into the cold earth. He could feel the blood in his mouth, over his lips, mingled with dirt.

And the horrible scream from the abyss of death came once more.

'*Champoluc!*'

And then was stilled.

CHAPTER THREE

30 Dec 1939
'*Champoluc ... Zürich is Champoluc ... Zürich is the river ...*'

The words were screams and they were blurred in agony. His mind's eye was filled with white light and explosions of smoke and deep red streaks of blood; his ears heard the screams of jolting shock, and terror, and the outrage of infinite pain and terrible murder.

It had happened. He had borne witness to the tableau of execution: strong men, trembling children, wives and mothers. His own.

Oh, my God!

Vittorio twisted his head and buried his face into the coarse cloth of the primitive bed, the tears flowing down his cheeks. It was cloth, not cold rough dirt; he had been moved. The last thing he remembered was his face being pressed with enormous strength into the hard ground of the embankment. Pressed down and held furiously immobile, his eyes blinded, his lips filled with warm blood and cold earth.

Only his ears bearing witness to the agony.

'*Champoluc!*'

Mother of God, it had happened!

The Fontini-Cristis were massacred in the white lights of Campo di Fiori. All the Fontini-Cristis but one. And that one would make Rome pay. The last Fontini-Cristi would cut the flesh, layer by layer, from Mussolini's face; the eyes would be last, the blade would enter slowly.

'Vittorio. Vittorio.'

He heard his name and yet he did not hear it. It was a whisper, an urgent whisper, and whispers were dreams of agony.

'Vittorio.' The weight was on his arms again; the whisper came from above, in the darkness. The face of Guido Barzini was inches from his, the sad strong eyes of the stable master were reflected in a shaft of dim light.

'Barzini?' It was all he could manage to say.

'Forgive me. There was no choice, no other way. You would have been killed with the rest.'

'Yes, I know. Executed. But *why*! In the name of God, why?'

'The Germans. That's all we know at the moment. The Germans wanted the Fontini-Cristis dead. They want you dead. The ports, the airfields, the roads, all of northern Italy is sealed off.'

'Rome allowed it.' Vittorio could still taste the blood in his mouth, still feel the pain in his jaw.

'Rome hides,' said Barzini softly. 'Only a few speak.'

'What do they say?'

'What the Germans want them to say. That the Fontini-Cristis were traitors, killed by their own people. That the family was aiding the French, sending arms and monies across the borders.'

'Preposterous.'

'Rome is preposterous. And filled with cowards. The informer was found. He hangs naked from his feet in the Piazza del Duomo, his body riddled, his tongue nailed to his head. A *partigiano* placed a sign below; it says, "This pig betrayed Italy, his blood flows from the stigmata of the Fontini-Cristis."'

Vittorio turned away. The images burned; the white smoke in the white light, the bodies suspended, abruptly immobile in death; a thousand sudden blots of thick red; the execution of children.

'Champoluc,' whispered Vittorio Fontini-Cristi.

'I beg your pardon?'

'My father. As he was dying, as the gunfire ravaged him, he shouted the name, Champoluc. Something happened in Champoluc.'

'What does it mean?'

'I don't know. Champoluc is in the Alps, deep in the mountains. "Zürich is Champoluc. Zürich is the river." He said that. He shouted it as he died. Yet there's no river in the Champoluc.'

'I cannot help you,' said Barzini, sitting up, the anxiety in his questioning eyes and in the awkward rubbing together of his large hands. 'There's not a great deal of time to dwell on it, or to think. Not now.'

Vittorio looked up at the huge, embarrassed farmhand sitting on the side of the primitive bed. They were in a room built of heavy wood. There was a door, only partially open, ten or fifteen feet away, on his left, but no windows. There were several other beds; he could not tell how many. It was a barracks for labourers.

'Where are we?'

'Across the Maggiore, south of Baveno. On a goat farm.'

'How did we get here?'

'A wild trip. The men at the river-front drove us out. They met us with a fast car on the road west of Campo di Fiori. The *partigiano* from Rome knows the drugs; he gave you a hypodermic needle.'

'You carried me from the embankment to the west road?'

'Yes.'

'It's more than a mile.'

'Perhaps. You're large, but not so heavy.' Barzini stood up.

'You saved my life.' Vittorio pressed his hands on the coarse blanket and raised himself to a sitting position, his back against the wall.

'Revenge is not found in one's own death.'

'I understand.'

'We must both travel. You out of Italy, me to Campo di Fiori.'

'You're going back?'

'It's where I can do the most good. The most damage.'

Fontini-Cristi stared for a moment at Barzini. How quickly the unimaginable became the practical reality. How rapidly did men react savagely to the savage; and how necessary was that reaction. But there was no time. Barzini was right; the thinking would come later.

'Is there a way for me to get out of the country? You said all of northern Italy was sealed off.'

'All the usual routes. It is a manhunt mounted by Rome, directed by the Germans. There are other ways. The British will help, I am told.'

'The British?'

'That is the word. They have been on *partigiano* radios all through the night.'

'The British? I don't understand.'

The vehicle was an old farm truck with poor brakes and a sliding clutch, but it was sturdy enough for the badly paved back roads. It was no match for motor-cycles or official automobiles, but excellent for travelling from one point to another in the farm country – one more truck carrying a few livestock that lurched unsteadily in the open, slatted van.

Vittorio was dressed, as was his driver, in the filthy, dung-encrusted, sweat-stained clothes of a farm labourer. He was provided with a dirty, mutilated identification card that gave his name as Aldo Ravena, former *soldato semplice* in the Italian army. It could be assumed his schooling was minimal; any conversation he might have with the police would be simple, blunt, and perhaps a touch hostile.

They had been driving since dawn, south-west into Torino, where they swung south-east towards Alba. With no serious interruptions they would reach Alba by nightfall.

At an *espresso* bar in Alba's main piazza, San Giorno, they would make contact with the British; two operatives sent by M16. It would be their job to get Fontini-Cristi down to the coast and through the patrols that guarded every mile of waterfront from Genoa to San Remo. Italian personnel, German efficiency, Vittorio was told.

This area of the coast in the Gulf of Genoa was considered the most conducive to infiltration. For years it had been a primary source route for Corsican smugglers. Indeed the *Unio Corso* claimed the beaches and rocky ocean cliffs as their own. They called this coast the soft belly of Europe; they knew every inch.

Which was fine as far as the British were concerned. They employed the Corsicans, whose services went to the highest bidders. The *Unio Corso* would aid London in getting Fontini-Cristi through the patrols and out on the water where, in a pre-arranged rendezvous north of Rogliano on the Corsican coast, a submarine from the Royal Navy would surface and pick him up.

This was the information Vittorio was given – by the ragtail lunatics he had scorned as children playing primitive games. The unkempt, wild-eyed fools who had formed an untenable alliance with such men as his father had saved his life. *Were* saving his life. Skinny peasant thugs who had direct communication with the far-off British ... far off and not so distant. No further than Alba.

How? Why? What in the name of God were the English doing? Why were they doing it? What were men he had barely acknowledged, hardly spoken to in his life before – except to order and ignore – what were *they* doing? And *why*? He was no friend; no enemy, perhaps, but certainly no friend.

These were the questions that frightened Vittorio Fontini-Cristi. A nightmare had exploded in white light and death, and he was not capable of fathoming – even wanting – his own survival.

They were eight miles from Alba on a curving dirt road that paralleled the main highway from Torino. The *partigiano* driver was weary, his eyes bloodshot from the long day of bright sunlight. The shadows of early evening were now playing tricks on his eyes; his back obviously ached from the constant strain. Except for infrequent fuel stops he had not left his seat. Time was vital.

'Let me drive for a while.'

'We're nearly there, signore. You don't know this road; I do. We'll enter Alba from the east, on the Canelli highway. There may be soldiers at the municipal limits. Remember what you're to say.'

'As little as possible, I think.'

The truck entered the light traffic on the Via Canelli and maintained a steady speed with the other vehicles. As the driver had predicted, there were two soldiers at the municipal line.

For any of a dozen reasons, the truck was signalled to stop. They pulled off the road on to the shoulder of sand and waited. A sergeant approached the driver's window, a private stood laconically outside Fontini-Cristi's.

'Where are you from?' asked the sergeant.

'A farm south of Baveno,' the *partigiano* said.

'You've come a long way for such a small delivery. I count five goats.'

'Breeding stock. They're better animals than they

look. Ten thousand *lire* for the males; eight for the females.'

The sergeant raised his eyebrows. He did not smile as he spoke. 'You don't look like *you're* worth that, *paisan*. Your identification.'

The partisan reached into his rear pocket and pulled out a worn wallet. He withdrew the state card and handed it to the soldier.

'This says you're from Varallo.'

'I come from Varallo. I work in Baveno.'

'*South* of Baveno,' corrected the soldier coldly. '*You*,' said the sergeant, addressing Vittorio. 'Your identification.'

Fontini-Cristi put his hand into his jacket, bypassing the handle of his pistol, and removed the card. He handed it to the driver, who gave it to the soldier.

'You were in Africa?'

'Yes, sergeant,' replied Vittorio bluntly.

'What corps?'

Fontini-Cristi was silent. He had no answer. His mind raced, trying to recall from the news a number, or a name. 'The Seventh,' he said.

'I see.' The sergeant returned the card; Vittorio exhaled. But the relief was short-lived. The soldier reached for the handle of the door, yanked it downward and pulled the door open swiftly. 'Get out! Both of you!'

'What? Why?' objected the partisan in a loud whine. 'We have to make our delivery by nightfall! There's barely time!'

'Get *out*.' The sergeant had removed his army revolver from the black leather holster and was pointing it at both men. He barked his order across the hood to the private. 'Pull him out! Cover him!'

Vittorio looked at the driver. The partisan's eyes told him to do as he was told. But to stay alert, be ready to move; the man's eyes told him that also.

Out of the truck on the shoulder of sand, the sergeant commanded both men to walk towards the guardhouse that stood next to a telephone pole. A telephone wire sagged down from a junction box and was attached to the roof of the small enclosure; the door was narrow, and open.

On the Via Canelli the twilight traffic was heavier now; or it seemed heavier to Fontini-Cristi. There were mostly cars, with a scattering of trucks, not unlike the farm truck they were driving. A number of drivers slowed perceptibly at the sight of the two soldiers, their weapons drawn, marching the two civilians to the guardhouse. Then the drivers speeded up, anxious to be away.

'You have no right to stop us!' cried the partisan. 'We've done nothing illegal. It's no crime to earn a living!'

'It's a crime to give false information, *paisan*.'

'We gave no false information! We are workers from Baveno, and by the Mother of God, that's the truth!'

'Be careful,' said the solder sarcastically. 'We'll add sacrilege to the charges. Get inside!'

The roadside guardhouse seemed even smaller than it appeared from the Via Canelli, the depth was no more than five feet, the length perhaps six. There was barely enough room for the four of them. And the look in the partisan's eyes told Vittorio that the close quarters was an advantage.

'Search them,' ordered the sergeant.

The private placed his rifle on the floor, barrel up. The partisan driver then did a strange thing. He pulled his arms across his chest, protectively over his coat, as though it were a conscious act of defiance. Yet the man was not armed; he had made that clear to Fontini-Cristi.

'You'll steal!' he said, louder than was necessary, his words vibrating in the wooden shack. 'Soldiers steal!'

'We're not concerned with your *lire, paisan*. There are more impressive vehicles on the highway. Take your hands from your coat.'

'Even in Rome reasons are given! *Il Duce* himself says the workers are not to be treated so! I march with the fascist guards; my rider served in Africa!'

What was the man doing? thought Vittorio. *Why was he behaving so? It would only anger the soldiers.* 'You try my patience, pig! We look for a man from Maggiore. Every road post looks for this man. You were stopped because the licence on your truck is from the Maggiore district . . . Hold out your arms!'

'*Baveno!* Not Maggiore! We are from *Baveno!* Where are the lies?'

The sergeant looked at Vittorio. 'No soldier in Africa says he was with the Seventh Corps. It was disgraced.'

The army guard had barely finished when the partisan screamed his command.

'*Now, signore!* Take the other!' The driver's hand swept down, lashing at the revolver in the sergeants's grip, only inches from his stomach. The suddenness of the action and the shattering roar of the partisan's voice in the small enclosure had the effect of an unexpected collision. Vittorio had no time to watch; he could only hope his companion knew what he was doing. The private had lurched for his rifle, his left hand on the barrel, his right surging down to the stock. Fontini-Cristi threw his weight against the man, slamming him into the wall, both hands on the side of the soldier's head, crashing the head into the hard, wooden surface. The private's barracks cap fell off; blood matted instantly throughout the hairline and streaked down over the man's head. He slumped to the floor.

Vittorio turned. The sergeant was wedged into the corner of the tiny guardhouse, the partisan over him, pistol-whipping him with his own weapon. The soldier's face was a mass of torn flesh, the blood and ripped skin sickening.

'*Quickly!*' cried the partisan as the sergeant fell. 'Bring the truck to the front! Directly to the front; squeeze it between the road and the guardhouse. Keep the motor running.'

'Very well,' said Fontini-Cristi, confused by the brutality as well as the swift decisiveness of the last thirty seconds.

'And, *signore!*' shouted the partisan, as Vittorio had one foot out of the door.

'Yes?'

'Your gun, please. Let me use it. These army issues are like thunder.'

Fontini-Cristi hesitated, then withdrew the weapon and handed it to the man. The partisan reached over to the crank-telephone on the wall and ripped it out.

Vittorio steered the truck to the front of the guardhouse, the left wheels by necessity on the hard surface of the highway; there was not sufficient room on the shoulder to pull completely off the road. He hoped the rear lights were sufficiently bright for the on-rushing traffic – far heavier now – to see the obstruction and skirt it.

The partisan came out of the guardhouse and spoke through the window. 'Race the motor, *signore*. As loud and fast as you can.'

Fontini-Cristi did so. The partisan ran back to the guardhouse. Gripped in his right hand was Vittorio's pistol.

The two shots were deep and sharp; muffled combustions that were sudden, terrible outbursts within the sounds of the rushing traffic and racing motor. Vittorio stared, his emotions a mixture of awe and fear and, inexplicably, sorrow. He had entered a world of violence he did not understand.

The partisan emerged from the guardhouse, pulling the narrow door shut behind him. He jumped into the truck, slammed the door panel and nodded to Vittorio. Fontini-Cristi waited several moments for a break in the traffic, then let out the clutch. The old truck lurched forward.

'There is a garage on the Via Monte that will hide the truck, paint it, and alter the licence plates. It's less than a mile from the Piazza San Giorno. We'll walk there from the garage. I'll tell you where to turn.'

The partisan held out the pistol for Vittorio. 'Thank you,' said Fontini-Cristi awkwardly, as he shoved the weapon into his jacket pocket. 'You killed them?'

'Of course,' was the simple reply.

'I suppose you had to.'

'Naturally. You'll be in England, *signore*. I, in Italy. I could be identified.'

'I see,' answered Vittorio, the hesitancy in his voice.

'I don't mean disrespect, Signore Fontini-Cristi, but I don't think you *do* see. You people at Campo di Fiori, it's all new to you. It's not new to us. We've been at war for twenty years; I, myself, for ten.'

'War?'

'Yes. Who do you think trains your *partigiani?*'

'What do you mean?'

'I am a Communist, *signore*. The powerful, capitalist Fontini-Cristi are shown how to fight by Communists.'

The truck was rushing forward; Vittorio held the wheel firmly, astonished but strangely unmoved by his companion's words.

'I didn't know that,' he replied.

'It's peculiar, isn't it?' said the partisan. 'No one ever asked.'

CHAPTER FOUR

30 Dec 1939
ALBA

The *espresso* bar was crowded, the tables full, the voices loud. Vittorio followed the partisan through the mass of gesturing hands and reluctantly parted bodies to the counter; they ordered coffee with Strega.

'Over there,' said the partisan, indicating a table in the corner with three labourers seated around it, their soiled clothes and stubbled faces testifying to their status. There was one empty chair.

'How do you know? I thought we were to meet two men, not three. And British. Besides, there's not enough room; there's only one chair.'

'Look at the heavyset man on the right. The identification is in the shoes. There are splotches of orange paint, not much but visible. *He's* the Corsican. The other two are English. Go over and say. 'Our trip was uneventful'; that's all. The man with the shoes will get up; take his seat.'

'What about you?'

'I'll join you in a minute, I must talk with the *Corso*.'

Vittorio did as he was told. The heavyset man with the drippings of paint on his shoes got up, heaving a sigh of discomfort; Fontini-Cristi sat down. The Britisher across from him spoke. His Italian was grammatically proper but hesitant; he had learned the language but not the idiom.

'Our sincerest regrets. Absolutely dreadful. We'll get you out.'

'Thank you. Would you prefer speaking English? I'm fluent.'

'Good,' said the second man. 'We weren't sure. We've had precious little time to read up on you. We were flown out of Lakenheath this morning. The *Corsos* picked us up in Pietra Ligure.'

'Everything's happened so fast,' said Vittorio. 'The shock hasn't worn off.'

'Don't see how it could,' said the first man. 'But we're not clear yet. You'll have to keep your wits about you. Our orders are to make bloody sure we get you to London: not to come back without you, and that's a fact.'

Vittorio looked alternately at both men. 'May I ask you why? Please understand, I'm grateful, but your concern seems to me extraordinary. I'm not humble, but neither am I a fool. Why am I so important to the British?'

'Damned if we know,' replied the second agent. 'But I can tell you, all hell broke loose last night. *All* night. We spent from midnight till four in the morning at the Air Ministry. All the radio dials in every operations room were beaming like mad. We're working with the Corsicans, you know.'

'Yes, I was told.'

The partisan walked through the crowds to the table. He pulled out the empty chair and sat down, a glass of Strega in his hand. The conversation was continued in Italian.

'We had trouble on the Canelli road. A checkpoint. Two guards had to be taken out.'

'What's the A-span?' asked the agent on Fontini-Cristi's right. He was a slender man, somewhat more intense than his partner. He saw the puzzled expression on Vittorio's face and clarified. 'How long does he think we have before the alarm goes out?'

'Midnight. When the twelve o'clock shift arrives. No one bothers with unanswered telephones. The equipment breaks down all the time.'

'Well done,' said the agent across the table. He was rounder in the face than his fellow Englishman; he spoke more slowly, as if constantly choosing his words. 'You're a Bolshevik, I imagine.'

'I am,' replied the partisan, his hostility near the surface.

'No, no, please,' added the agent. 'I like working with you chaps. You're very thorough.'

'M.I.-*Sei* is polite.'

'By the way,' said the Britisher on Vittorio's right, 'I'm Apple; he's Pear.'

'We know who you are,' said Pear to Fontini-Cristi.

'And my name's not important,' said the partisan with a slight laugh. 'I'll not be going with you.'

'Let's run through that, shall we?' Apple was anxious, but controlled to the point of being reserved. 'The going. Also, London wants to set up firmer communications.'

'We knew London would.'

The three men fell into a professional conversation that Vittorio found extraordinary. They spoke of routes and codes and radio frequencies as though they were discussing prices on the stock exchange. They touched on the necessity of *taking-out*, *eliminating* various people in specific positions – not men, not human beings, but *factors* that had to be killed.

What kind of men were these three? 'Apple', 'Pear', a Bolshevik with no name, only a false identification card. Men who killed without anger, without remorse.

He thought of Campo di Fiori. Of blinding white

floodlights, and gunfire and death. *He* could kill now. Viciously, savagely – but he could not speak of death as these men spoke of it.

'. . . get us to a trawler known to the coastal patrols. Do you understand?' Apple was speaking to him, but he had not been listening.

'I'm sorry,' said Vittorio. 'My mind was elsewhere.'

'We've a long way to go,' said Pear. 'Over fifty miles to the coast, then a minimum of three hours on the water. A lot can happen.'

'I'll try to be more attentive.'

'Do better than try,' replied Apple, his tone one of controlled irritation. 'I don't know what you've done to the Foreign Office, but you happen to be a high-priority subject. We're for the chop if we don't bring you out. So *listen*! The Corsicans will take us to the coast. There will be four changes of vehicles—'

'Wait!' The partisan reached over the table and gripped Apple's arm. 'The man who was seated with you, the paint-spattered shoes. Where did you pick him up? *Quickly.*'

'Here in Alba. About twenty minutes ago.'

'Who made contact first?'

Both Englishmen looked at each other. Briefly, with instant concern. 'He did,' said Apple.

'Get out of here! Now! Use the kitchen!'

'*What?*' Pear was looking over at the *espresso* counter.

'He's leaving,' said the partisan. 'He was to wait for me.'

The heavyset man was making his way through the crowds towards the door. He was doing so as unobtrusively as possible; a drinker going to the men's room, perhaps.

'What do you think?' asked Apple.

'I think that there are a great many men throughout Alba with paint on their shoes. They wait for strangers whose eyes stray to the floor.' The Communist rose from the table. 'The contact code was broken. It happens. The Corsicans will have to change it. Now, *go*!'

The two Englishmen got out of their chairs, but not with any overt sense of urgency. Vittorio took his cue and stood up. He reached out and touched the partisan's sleeve. The Communist was startled; his eyes were on the heavyset man; he was about to plunge into the crowds.

'I want to thank you.'

The partisan stared for an instant. 'You're wasting time,' he said.

The two Britishers knew exactly where the kitchen was, and therefore the exit *from* that kitchen. The alley outside was filthy; garbage cans were lined against the dirty stucco walls, refuse overflowing. The alley was a link between the Piazza San Giorno and the street behind, but so dimly lit and strewn with trash it was not a popular shortcut.

'This way,' said Apple, turning left, away from the piazza. 'Quickly now.'

The three men ran out of the alley. The street was sufficiently filled with pedestrians and shopkeepers to provide them with cover. Apple and Pear fell into a casual walk; Vittorio followed suit. He realized that the two agents had manoeuvred him between them.

'I'm not sure the Bolshie was right,' said Pear. 'Our *Corso* might simply have spotted a friend. He was damned convincing.'

'The Corsicans have their own language,' interjected Vittorio, excusing himself as he nearly collided with an oncoming stroller. 'Couldn't he tell by talking to him?'

'Don't do that,' said Apple incisively.

'What?'

'Don't be so damned polite. It hardly goes with the clothes. To answer your question, the Corsicans employ regional contacts everywhere. We all do. They're minor level, just messengers.'

'I see.' Fontini-Cristi looked at the man who called himself Apple. He was walking casually, but his eyes kept shifting about in the night-cloaked street. Vittorio turned his head and looked at Pear. He was doing precisely what his countryman was doing: observing the faces in the crowds, the vehicles, the recesses in the buildings on both sides of the street.

'Where are we going?' asked Fontini-Cristi.

'To within a block of where our Corsican told us to be,' replied Apple.

'But I thought you suspected him.'

Pear spoke. 'They won't see us because they don't know what to look for. The Bolshevik will catch the *Corso* in the piazza. If everything's on the up-and-up, they'll arrive together. If not, and if your friend is competent, he'll be the only one.'

The shopping area curved to the left, into the south entrance of the Piazza San Giorno. The entrance was marked by a fountain, the circular pool at its base littered with discarded papers and bottles. Men and women sat on the ledge dipping their hands in the dirty water; children shouted and ran on the cobblestones under their parents' watchful eyes.

'The road beyond,' said Apple, lighting a cigarette, gesturing towards the wide pavement seen through the spray of the fountain, 'is the Via Ligata. It leads to the coastal highway. Two hundred yards down is a side street where the *Corso* said a taxi would be waiting.'

'Would the side street, by any chance, be a dead end?' Pear asked the question with a degree of disdain. He did not really expect an answer.

'Isn't that a coincidence? I was wondering the same thing. Do let's find out. You,' said Apple to Vittorio, 'stay with my partner and do *exactly* as he says.' The

72

agent threw the match to the ground, inhaled deeply on his cigarette, and walked rapidly over the cobblestones towards the fountain. When he was within several feet of the pool, he slowed down, and then, to Vittorio's astonishment, he disappeared, lost entirely in the crowds.

'He does that rather in top form, doesn't he?' said Pear.

'I can't make him out. I don't see him.'

'Not supposed to. A good race-and-melt, done in the proper light, can be very effective.' He shrugged. 'Come along. Keep abreast and chatter a bit. And gesture. You people wave your hands like mad.'

Vittorio smiled at the Englishman's bromide. But as they walked into the crowds, he was conscious of moving hands and flailing arms and sudden exclamations. The Britisher knew his Italians. He kept pace with the agent, fascinated by the man's decisiveness. Suddenly, Pear grabbed Vittorio's sleeve and yanked him to the left, propelling them both towards a newly vacated space on the fountain's ledge. Fontini-Cristi was startled; he thought their objective was to reach the Via Ligata as rapidly and as unobtrusively as possible.

Then he understood. The Britisher's experienced, professional eyes had seen what the amateur's had not seen: the signal.

Vittorio sat on the agent's right, his head down. The first objects that came into focus were a pair of worn shoes with the splotches of orange paint on the scuffed leather. A single pair of immobile shoes in the moving shadows of moving bodies. Then Vittorio raised his head and froze. The partisan driver was cradling the heavyset body of the Corsican contact, as though succouring a friend who had drunk too much. But the contact was not drunk. His head was slumped, his eyes open, staring downward into the moving darkness. He was dead.

Vittorio leaned back on the ledge, mesmerized by the

sight below. A steady, narrow stream of blood was soaking the back of the Corsican's shirt, rolling down the stone of the fountain's inner wall, mingling with the filthy water, forming circles and swirling half circles in the intermittent light of the piazza's street lamps.

The partisan's hand gripped the cloth, bunching the shirt around the blood-soaked area, knuckles and wrist drenched. And in his grip was the handle of a knife.

Fontini-Cristi tried to control his shock.

'I was hoping you'd stop,' said the Communist to the Englishman.

'Nearly didn't,' replied Pear in his overly grammatical Italian. 'Until I noticed the couple leap up here.' The agent indicated the ledge on which he and Vittorio sat. 'They're yours, I presume.'

'No. When you were closest, I told them my friend was about to vomit. It's a trap, of course. Fishnet variety; they don't know what they'll catch. They broke the code – last night. There are a dozen or so *provocatori* in the area, flushing out what targets they can. A round-up.'

'We'll tell the Corsicans.'

'It won't do much good. The code changes tomorrow.'

'The taxi's the snare, then?'

'No. The second bait. They're not taking chances. The taxi drives the targets into the net. Only the driver knows where; he's upper level.'

'There must be others nearby.' Pear brought his hand to his mouth; it was a gesture of thought.

'Certainly.'

'But which ones?'

'There's a way to find out. Where's Apple?'

'In the Via Ligata by now. We wanted to separate in case you had trouble.'

'Join him; the trouble wasn't mine.'

'Yes. I can see that—'

'*Mother of God!*' exclaimed Vittorio under his breath,

74

incapable of silence. 'You're holding a dead man in the middle of the piazza and you chatter like women!'

'We have things to say, *signore*. Be quiet and listen.' The partisan returned his eyes to the Englishman, who had barely taken notice of Fontini-Cristi's outburst. 'I'll give you two minutes to reach Apple. Then I'll let our *Corso* friend here slide into the pool, back up, knife visible. There'll be chaos. I'll start the shouting myself. It will carry. It'll be enough.'

'And we keep our eyes on the taxi,' interrupted Pear.

'Yes. As the shouting grows, see who speaks together. See who leaves to investigate.'

'Then take the bloody taxi and be off,' added the agent with finality. 'Good show! I look forward to working with you again.' The Englishman rose; Vittorio did the same, feeling Pear's hand on his arm.

'You,' said the partisan, looking up at Vittorio while cradling the limp, heavyset body in the noisy, jostling, shadow-filled darkness. 'Something to remember. A conversation in the midst of many people is often the safest. And a blade in a crowd is the hardest to trace. Remember these things.'

Vittorio looked down at the man, not sure whether the Communist meant his words to be insulting or not.

'I'll remember,' said Vittorio.

They walked swiftly into the Via Ligata. Apple was on the other side slowly making his way towards the side street where the Corsican contact said the taxi would be waiting. The street lamps were dimmer than in the piazza.

'Hurry, now. There he is,' said Pear in English. 'Take longer steps, but don't run.'

'Shouldn't we go over and meet him?' asked Vittorio.

'No. One person crossing the street is less obvious than two ... All right. Stop now.'

Pear removed a box of matches from his pocket; he

struck one. The instant it flared, he waved it out, throwing it to the pavement – as if the flame had seared his finger – and immediately struck a second, holding it to the cigarette he had placed in his lips.

Less than a minute passed before Apple joined them by the wall of a building. Pear told him the partisan's strategy. The three walked in silence, between the strollers, down the pavement to the end of the block opposite the side street. Across, in the dim white wash of the streetlights, was the taxi, thirty feet from the corner.

'Isn't that a coincidence,' said Apple, lifting his foot to a low ledge on the building, pulling up his sock. 'It's a dead end.'

'The troops can't be far away. Is your pillow attached? Mine isn't.'

'Yes. Fix yours.'

Pear turned into the building and removed an automatic from inside his jacket. With his other hand he reached into his pocket and withdrew a cylinder about four inches long, with perforations on the iron surface, and twisted it into the barrel of his weapon. He replaced the gun inside his jacket just as the cries from the piazza began.

There were only a few at first, almost indistinguishable. And then a crescendo of sound erupted.

'*Polizia!*' '*A quale punto polizia!*' '*Assassinio!*' '*Omicidio!*' Women and children ran out of the square; men followed, shouting orders and information at no one and everyone. Among the screams came the words: '*Uomo con arancia scarpe,*' a man with orange shoes. The partisan had done his job well.

And then the partisan himself was among the crowds running down the pavement. He stopped ten feet from Fontini-Cristi and the two Englishmen and roared in a loud voice to any who would listen.

'I *saw* him! I saw *them*! I was right *next* to him! This

man – his shoes were *painted* – they put a knife into his back!'

From the dark recess of a building a figure came dashing across the street, heading for the partisan. 'You! Come here!'

'What?'

'I'm with the police. What did you see?'

'The police. Thank God! Come with me! There were two men! In sweaters—'

Before the official could adjust, the partisan started to race back towards the entrance of the piazza through the crowds. The policeman hesitated, then looked across the dimly lit street. Three men were talking together several yards in front of the taxi. The policeman gestured; two of the men broke away and started after the officer, who was now racing towards San Giorno and the disappearing partisan.

'The man left at the car. He's the driver,' said Apple. 'Here we go.'

The next moments were a blur. Vittorio followed the two agents across the Via Ligata into the side street. The man at the taxi had climbed into the driver's seat. Apple approached the car, opened the door, and without saying a word raised his gun. A muted explosion burst from the mouth of his revolver. The man slumped forward; Apple rolled him over the seat towards the opposite door. Pear spoke to Fontini-Cristi.

'Into the back. Quickly, now!'

Apple turned the ignition; the taxi was old, the engine new and powerful. The car was the usual Fiat, Vittorio thought, but the motor was a Lamborghini.

The car lurched forward, turned right at the corner and gathered speed on the Via Ligata. Apple spoke over his shoulder, addressing Pear. 'Check the glove compartment, will you? This bloody wreck belongs to some very *important people*. I daresay it would do well at Le Mans.'

Pear lunged from the seat in the speeding car, over the felt back, and across the corpse of the Italian. He pulled open the glove compartment panel, grabbed the papers, bunching them together in his hand. As he pushed himself off the dashboard, the car swerved; Apple had swung the wheel to pass two cars. The body of the dead Italian fell across Pear's arm. He gripped the lifeless neck and threw the corpse violently back into the corner.

Vittorio stared at the scene, sick and uncomprehending. Behind them a heavyset man floated in death in a piazza fountain, the handle of a knife protruding from his blood-soaked shirt. Here, in an unmarked, speeding police car disguised as a taxi, a man slumped in the front seat, a bullet in his lifeless body. Miles away, in a small guard-house on the Via Canelli, two other men lay dead, killed by the Communist who had saved his life. The continuing nightmare was destroying his mind. He held his breath, desperately trying to find an instant of sanity.

'Here we are!' shouted Pear, holding up a rectangular sheet of heavy paper he had been studying in the inadequate light. 'By God, it's a clean wicket!'

'An inland passport, I expect,' said Apple, slowing down for a curve in the road.

'Indeed it is! The bloody *veicolo* is assigned to the *ufficiale segreto*! That bunch has access to Mussolini himself.'

'It had to be something like that,' agreed Apple, nodding his head. 'The motor in this tacky box is a bloody marvel.'

'It is a Lamborghini,' said Vittorio quietly.

'What?' Apple raised his voice to be heard over the roar of the engine on the now straightaway road. They were approaching the outskirts of Alba.

'I said it's a Lamborghini.'

'Yes,' replied Apple, obviously unfamiliar with the engine. 'Well, you keep coming up with things like that.

Things Italian, that is. We're going to need your words before we reach the coast.'

Pear turned to Fontini-Cristi. The Englishman's pleasant face was barely discernible in the darkness. He spoke gently, but there was no mistaking the quiet urgency in his voice.

'I'm sure this is all very strange to you, and damned uncomfortable, I should think. But that Bolshevik had a point. Remember what you can. The most difficult part of this work isn't the *doing*; it's getting *used* to the doing, if you see what I mean. Just accepting the fact that it's real, that's the leg up a fellow needs. We've all been through it, go through it constantly, as a matter of fact. It's all so bloody outrageous, in a way. But someone's got to do it; that's what they tell us. And I'll say this: You're getting some very practical on-the-job training. Wouldn't you agree?'

'Yes,' said Vittorio softly, turning front, his eyes mesmerized by the onrushing road outlined by the beams of the headlights, and his mind frozen by the sudden question he could not avoid.

Training for what?

CHAPTER FIVE

31 Dec 1939
CELLE LIGURE

It was two hours of madness. They turned off the coastal highway and carried the body of the dead driver into a field, stripping it naked, removing all identification.

They returned to the highway and sped south towards Savona. The road checks were similar to those on the Via Canelli: single guardhouses next to telephone booths, two soldiers in attendance at each. There were four check-points; three were passed easily. The thick, official document that proclaimed the vehicle assigned to the *ufficiale segreto* was read with respect and not a little fear. Fontini-Cristi did the talking at all three posts.

'You're damned quick,' said Apple from the front, shaking his head in agreeable surprise. 'And you were right about staying back there. You roll down that window like a Punjab prince.'

The road sign was caught in the headlights.

ENTRARE MONTENOTTE SUD

Vittorio recognized the name; it was one of those medium-sized towns surrounding the Gulf of Genoa. He recognized it from a decade ago, when he and his wife had driven down the coast road on their last trip to

Monte Carlo. A journey that had ended a week later in death. In a speeding car at night.

'The coast's about fifteen miles from here, I think,' said Apple hesitantly, interrupting Fontini-Cristi's thoughts.

'Nearer eight,' corrected Vittorio.

'You know this area?' asked Pear.

'I've driven to Cap Ferrat and Villefranche a number of times.' *Why didn't he say Monte Carlo; was the name too much of a symbol?* 'Usually on the Torino road, but several times on the shore route from Genoa. Montenotte Sud is known for its inns.'

'Then would you know a dirt road that cuts north of Savona – through some hills, I gather – into Celle Ligure?'

'No. There are hills everywhere . . . But I know Celle Ligure. It's on the waterfront just beyond Albisolla. Is that where we're going?'

'Yes,' said Apple. 'It's our backup rendezvous with the Corsicans. In case anything happened, we were to make our way to Celle Ligure, to a fishing pier south of the marina. It'll be marked with a green wind-sock.'

'Well, *something* happened, as they say,' interjected Pear. 'I'm sure there's a *Corso* wandering around Alba wondering where we are.'

Several hundred yards ahead in the glare of the headlights, two soldiers stood in the centre of the road. One held a rifle at port arms; the other had his hand raised, signalling them to stop. Apple slowed the Fiat, the transposed motor emitting the low sounds of its decelerating power. 'Do your bitchy act,' he said to Vittorió. 'Be arrogant as hell.' The Britisher kept the car in the centre of the road, a sign that the inhabitants expected no interruption; pulling off to the side was unnecessary.

One of the soldiers was a lieutenant, his companion a

corporal. The officer approached Apple's open window and saluted the unkempt civilian smartly.

Too smartly, thought Vittorio.

'Your identification, *signore*,' said the soldier courteously.

Too courteously.

Apple held up the thick official paper and gestured toward the back seat. It was Vittorio's cue.

'We are the *ufficiale segreto*, Genoa garrison, and in a great hurry. We have business in Savona. You've done your job; pass us through immediately.'

'My apologies, *signore*.' The officer took the heavy paper in Apple's hand and scrutinized it. He creased the folds as his eyes scanned downward in the very dim light. He continued politely. 'I must see your identifications. There is so little traffic on the road at this hour. All vehicles must be checked.'

Fontini-Cristi slammed his hand down on the top of the front seat in sudden irritation. 'You're out of order! Don't let our appearances fool you. We're on official business and we're late for Savona!'

'Yes. Well, I must read this—'

But he was *not* reading it, thought Vittorio. A man in inadequate light did not fold a page of paper *towards* him; if he folded it at all, it would be *away* – to catch more light. The soldier was stalling. And the corporal had moved to the right of the Fiat, his rifle still held across his chest; but the left hand was now lower on the barrel grip. Any hunter knew the stance; it was ready-at-fire.

Fontini-Cristi sat back in the seat, swearing furiously as he did so. 'I demand your name and the name of your commanding officer!'

In the front, Apple had edged his shoulders to the right, trying to see into the rearview mirror, unable to do so without being obvious. But in his pretended anger, Fontini-Cristi had no such difficulty. He whipped his hand up behind Pear's shoulders, as if his irritation had reached the breaking point.

'Perhaps you did not hear me, soldier! Your name and that of your commanding officer!'

Through the rearview mirror he saw it. Quite far in the distance, beyond the clear range of the mirror, not easily seen through the window itself. A car had pulled off the road ... so far off, it was half into the field bordering the highway. Two men were getting out of the front seat, the figures barely visible, moving slowly.

' ... Marchetti, *signore*. My commanding officer is Colonel Balbo. Genoa garrison, *signore*.'

Vittorio caught Apple's eye in the rearview mirror, nodded slightly, and moved his head in a slow arc towards the back window. At the same time, he tapped his fingers rapidly on Pear's neck in the darkness. The agent understood.

Without warning, Vittorio opened his door. The rifle-bearing corporal jerked his weapon forward. 'Put that *down*, *caporale*. Since your superior sees fit to take up my time, I will put it to use. I am Major Aldo Ravena, *ufficiale segreto*, from Rome. I will inspect your quarters. I will also relieve myself.'

'*Signore!*' shouted the officer from across the Fiat's hood.

'Are you addressing me?' asked Fontini-Cristi arrogantly.

'My apologies, Major.' The officer could not help himself; he stole a quick glance to his right, to the road behind. 'There are no facilities inside the guardhouse.'

'Surely you are not immaculate in your bowels, man. The fields must be inconvenient. Perhaps Rome will install such facilities. I'll see.'

Vittorio walked swiftly toward the door of the small structure; it was open. As he expected, the corporal went with him. He walked rapidly through the door. The instant the corporal entered behind him, Fontini-Cristi turned and jammed the pistol up under the man's chin. He pushed the weapon into the flesh of the corporal's throat and with his left hand grabbed the barrel of the rifle.

'If you so much as cough, I'll have to kill you!' whispered Vittorio. 'I don't wish to do that.'

The corporal's eyes widened in shock; he had no stomach for heroics. Fontini-Cristi held the rifle and gave his order quietly, precisely.

'Call the officer. Say I'm using your telephone and you don't know what to do. Tell him I'm calling the Genoa garrison. For that Colonel Balbo. *Now!*'

The corporal shouted the words, conveying both his confusion and his fear. Vittorio pressed his back against the wall by the door. The reply from the lieutenant betrayed the officer's own fear; perhaps he had made a dreadful mistake.

'I am only following orders! I received orders from Alba!'

'Tell him Colonel Balbo is coming to the telephone,' whispered Fontini-Cristi. '*Now!*'

The corporal did so. Vittorio heard the footsteps of the officer running from the Fiat to the guardhouse.

'If you wish to live, Lieutenant, remove your pistol belt – just unbuckle both straps – and join the corporal at the wall.'

The lieutenant was stunned. His jaw dropped, his lips parted in fright. Fontini-Cristi prodded him with the rifle, lancing the barrel into his stomach. The bewildered officer winced and gasped and did as he was told. Vittorio called outside, in English.

'I've disarmed them. Now I'm not sure what to do.'

Pear's half-whispered shout came back. 'What to *do*? My God, you're a bloody marvel! Send the officer back, outside. Make sure he knows we have our weapons on him. Tell him to return to Apple's window right off. We'll take it from there.'

Fontini-Cristi translated the instructions. The officer, prodded by the barrel of Vittorio's pistol, lurched out the doors and crossed swiftly in front of the car's headlights to the driver's window.

Ten seconds later the officer's shouts were heard on the road outside.

'You men from Alba! This is not the vehicle! A mistake has been made!'

A moment passed before other voices replied. Two voices, loud and angry.

'What happened? Who are they?'

Vittorio could see the figures of two men come out of the darkness of the field. They were soldiers and held guns at their sides. The officer answered.

'These are *segreti* from Genoa. They, too, look for the vehicle from Alba.'

'Mother of Christ! How many are there?'

Suddenly, the officer pushed himself away from the window, screaming as he dived for the front of the car.

'*Shoot! Open fire!* They are—'

The muffled explosions of the British pistols erupted. Pear leaped out of the right rear door, covered by the car, and fired at the approaching soldiers. A rifle answered; it was a wild shot that thumped into the tarred surface of the road, triggered by a dying man. The checkpoint lieutenant sprang to his feet and started to race towards the opposite field into the darkness. Apple fired; three muted reports accompanied the sharp, abrupt flashes of his weapon. The officer screamed and arched his back. He fell into the dirt off the road.

'*Fontini*,' yelled Apple. 'Kill your man and get out here!'

The corporal's lips trembled, his eyes watered. He had

heard the muted explosions, the screams, and he understood the command.

'No,' said Fontini-Cristi.

'Goddamn you!' roared Apple. 'You do as I *say*! You're under *my* orders! We've no time to waste *or* chances to take!'

'You're wrong. We would waste more time and take greater risks if we could not find the road into Celle Ligure. This soldier will surely know it.'

He did. Vittorio drove, the soldier beside him in the front seat. Fontini-Cristi knew the area; if they ran into trouble, he could handle it. He had proved that.

'Relax,' said Vittorio in Italian to the frightened corporal. 'Continue to be helpful; you'll be all right.'

'What will happen to me? They'll say I deserted my post.'

'Nonsense. You were ambushed, forced at the point of a gun to accompany us, to act as a shield. You had no choice.'

They drove into Celle Ligure at ten forty; the streets of the fishing village were nearly deserted. The majority of its inhabitants began their days at four in the morning; ten at night was late. Fontini-Cristi drove into the sandy parking area behind an open fish market that fronted the wide ocean street. Across from it was the main section of the marina.

'Where are the sentries?' asked Apple. 'Where do they meet?'

At first the corporal seemed confused. Vittorio explained. 'When you are on duty here, where do you turn around?'

'I see.' The corporal was relieved; he was obviously trying to help. 'Not here, not at this section. Up farther; I mean, down farther.'

'*Damn* you!' Apple was leaning forward in the back seat. He grabbed the Italian by the hair.

86

'You'll get nowhere like that,' said Vittorio in English. 'The man's frightened.'

'So am I!' countered the agent. 'There's a dock across there with a green wind-sock on it, and a boat in that dock we have to find! We don't know what's happened behind us; there are soldiers on the piers with weapons – one shot would alert the whole area. And we have no idea what orders have been radioed the water patrols. *I'm damned* frightened!'

'I remember!' cried the corporal. 'On the left. Up the street on the left! The trucks stopped and we would walk through to the piers and wait for the man on duty. He would give us the patrol sheet and be relieved.'

'Where? *Exactly* where, Corporal?' Pear spoke urgently.

'The next street. I'm sure of it.'

'That's roughly three hundred feet, wouldn't you say?' asked Pear, looking at Fontini-Cristi. 'And the street below this another three hundred, give or take some.'

'What's your idea?' Apple had released the corporal, but kept his hands menacingly on the top of the seat.

'Same as yours,' replied Pear. 'Take the sentry at midpoint; less chance of his being seen there. Once he's out we walk south to the wind-sock, where, I trust, a Corsican or two will show themselves.'

They crossed the ocean road into an alley that led to the dock complex. The smell of fish and the sounds of half a hundred boats creaking in rhythmic rest in their slips filled the darkness. Nets were hung everywhere; the wash of the sea could be heard beyond the planked walkway that fronted the piers. A few lanterns were swaying on ropes over decks; a concertina played a simple tune in the distance.

Vittorio and Pear walked casually out of the alley, their footsteps muted by moist planks. Apple and the corporal remained in the shadows. The walkway was bordered by a railing of metal tubing above the lapping water.

'Do you see the sentry?' asked Fontini-Cristi softly.

'No. But I hear him,' answered the agent. 'He's rapping the pipe as he walks. Listen.'

It took Vittorio several seconds before he could distinguish the faint metal sounds among the rhythmic creakings of wood on water. But they were there. The unconscious, irregular tattoo of a bored man performing a dull task.

Several hundred feet south on the walkway, the figure of the soldier came under the spill of a pier light, his rifle angled down to the deck through his left arm. He was beside the railing, his right hand aimlessly tapping out his steps.

'When he gets here, ask him for a cigarette,' said Pear calmly. 'Pretend you're drunk. I will, too.'

The sentry approached. The instant he saw them he snapped up his rifle and cracked the bolt, holding his position fifteen feet away.

'*Halt! Who's there?*'

'Two fishermen without cigarettes,' replied Fontini-Cristi, slurring his words. 'Be a nice fellow and give us a couple. Even one; we'll share it.'

'You're drunk,' said the soldier. 'There's a curfew tonight on the piers. How come you're here? It was on the loudspeakers all day.'

'We've been with two whores in Albisolla,' answered Vittorio, lurching, steadying himself on the railing. 'Only things we heard were music on a phonograph and creaking beds.'

'Very nice,' mumbled Pear.

The sentry shook his head in disapproval. He lowered his rifle and approached, reaching into the pocket of his tunic for cigarettes. 'You *Ligurini* are worse than the *Napoletani*. I've done duty there.'

Behind the soldier, Vittorio could see Apple coming out of the shadows. He had forced the corporal to lie down on his back in the corner of the alley; the corporal would not move. In Apple's hands were two spools.

Before Vittorio could realize what was happening, Apple sprang out of the passageway, his arms stretched, angled upward. In two swift moves, the agent's hands whipped over the sentry's head, and with his knee jammed into the small of the soldier's back, he yanked violently, causing the guard to arch spastically and then collapse.

The only noise was an abrupt, horrible expunging of air, and the quiet fall of the man's body onto the soft, moist wood.

Pear rushed to the corporal; he held his pistol against the soldier's temple. 'Not a sound. Understood?' It was a command that left no room for debate. The corporal rose silently.

Fontini-Cristi looked down in the dim light at the guard on the walkway. What he could see he wished he had not seen. The man's neck was severed half off his body, the blood was pouring out in a dark-red stream from what had been the man's throat. Apple rolled the body through a wide space in the railing. It hit the water with a muffled splash. Pear picked up his rifle and spoke in English.

'Off we go. Down this way.'

'Come on,' said Fontini-Cristi, his hand on the trembling corporal's arm. 'You have no choice.'

The green wind-sock was limp, no breeze billowing its cloth. The pier was only half filled with boats; it seemed to extend farther out into the water than the others. The four of them walked down the steps, Apple and Pear in front, their hands in their pockets. The two Englishmen were obviously hesitant. It was apparent to Vittorio that they were concerned.

Without warning or sound, men suddenly appeared on both sides of them, their weapons drawn. They were on the decks of the boats; five, no, six men dressed as fishermen.

'Be you George the Fifth?' said the gruff voice of the man nearest the agents, standing on the deck of a small trawler.

'Thank *God*!' said Pear in relief. 'We've had a nasty time of it.'

At the spoken English, weapons were replaced in belts and pockets. The men converged, a number talking at once.

The language was Corsican.

One man, obviously the leader, turned to Apple. 'Go to the end of the pier. We've got one of the fastest trawlers in Bastia. We'll take care of the Italian. They won't find him for a month!'

'No!' Fontini-Cristi stepped between the two men. He looked at Pear. 'We gave our word. If he co-operated, he lived.'

Apple replied, instead, his whispered voice drawn out in irritation. 'Now, you see here. You've been a help, I'll not deny it, but you're not running this show. Get out to the bloody boat.'

'Not until this man is back on the walkway. We gave our word!' He spoke to the corporal. 'Go back. You won't be harmed. Strike a match when you reach a passageway to the ocean road.'

'And if I say *no*?' Apple continued to grip the soldier's tunic.

'Then I'll remain here.'

'*Damn!*' Apple released the soldier.

'Walk with him part way,' said Fontini-Cristi to the Corsican. 'Make sure your men let him pass.'

The Corsican spat on the pier.

The corporal ran as fast as he could towards the base

of the dock. Fontini-Cristi looked at the two Englishmen.

'I am sorry,' he said simply. 'There's been enough killing.'

'You're a damn fool,' replied Apple.

'Hurry,' said the Corsican leader. 'I want to get started. The water's rough beyond the rocks. And you people are crazy!'

They walked out to the end of the long pier, one by one jumping over the gunwale onto the deck of the huge trawler. Two Corsicans remained on the dock by the pilings; they unwound the thick greasy ropes while the gruff captain started the engines.

It happened without warning.

A fusillade of gunfire from the walkway. Then the blinding shaft of a searchlight shot out of the darkness, accompanied by the shouts of soldiers at the base of the pier. The voice of the corporal could be heard.

'Out *there*! At the end of the dock! The *fishing trawler*! Send out the alarms!'

One of the Corsicans was hit; he plunged to the ground, at the last second freeing the rope from the piling.

'The *light*! Shoot out the light!' screamed the Corsican from the open wheelhouse, revving the engines, heading for open water.

Apple and Pear unscrewed their silencers for greater accuracy. Apple was the first to raise himself over the protection of the gunwale; he squeezed his trigger repeatedly, steadying his hand on the wooden rail.

In the distance the searchlight exploded. Simultaneously, fragments of wood burst around Apple; the agent reeled back, screaming in pain.

His hand was shattered.

But the Corsican had steered the fast-moving trawler

out into the protective darkness of the sea. They were free of Celle Ligure.

'Our price goes up, English!' shouted the man at the wheel. 'You whoreson bastards! You'll pay for this craziness!' He looked at Fontini-Cristi crouched beneath the starboard gunwale. Their eyes met; the Corsican spat furiously.

Apple sat back sweating against a pile of ropes. In the night light reflecting the ocean's spray, Vittorio saw that the Englishman was staring at the bloody mass of flesh that was his hand, holding it by the wrist.

Fontini-Cristi got up and crossed to the agent, tearing off part of his shirt as he did so. 'Let me wrap that for you. Stop the bleeding—'

Apple jerked his hand up and spoke in quiet anger. 'Stay the hell away from me. Your goddamned principles cost too much.'

The seas were heavy, the winds strong, the rolls violent and abrupt. They had ploughed through the drenching waves of the open water for thirty-eight minutes. Arrangements had been made, the blockade run; the trawler's engines were now idling.

Beyond the swells, Vittorio could see a small flashing blue disc: on for a beat, off for a beat. The signal from a submarine. The Corsican on the bow with the lantern began his own signal. He lowered and raised the lamp, using the gunwale as a shutter, imitating the timing of the blue disc half a mile away over the waters.

'Can't you radio him?' Pear shouted his question.

'Frequencies are monitored,' replied the Corsican. 'The patrol boats would circle in; we can't bribe them all.'

The two vessels began their cautious pavane over the rough seas, the trawler making most of the moves until the huge undersea marauder was directly off the starboard rail. Fontini-Cristi was hypnotized by its size and black majesty.

The two ships drifted within fifty feet of each other, the submarine considerably higher on the mountainous waves. Four men could be seen on the deck; they were hanging on to a metal railing, the two in the centre trying to manipulate some kind of machine.

A heavy rope shot through the air and crashed against the midships of the trawler. Two Corsicans leaped at it, holding on desperately, as if the line had a hostile will of its own. They lashed the rope to an iron winch in the centre of the deck and signalled the men on the submarine.

The action was repeated. But the second rope was not the only item that had been shot from the submarine. There was a canvas pouch with metal rings on the edges, and from one of these rings was a thick coil of wire that extended back to the crew on the sub's deck.

The Corsicans ripped open the canvas pack and pulled out a shoulder harness. Fontini-Cristi recognized it immediately; it was a rig used to cross crevasses in the mountains.

Pear, bracing himself as he lurched forward on the rolling deck, approached Vittorio.

'It's a bit skin-crawling, but it's safe!' he yelled.

Vittorio shouted back, 'Send your man Apple first. His hand should be looked after.'

'You're the priority. And frankly, if the damn thing doesn't hold, I'd rather we find out with you!'

Fontini-Cristi sat on the iron bunk inside the small metal room and drank from the thick china mug of coffee. He pulled the Royal Navy blanket around his shoulders, feeling the wet clothes beneath. The discomfort did not bother him; he was grateful to be alone.

The door of the small metal room opened. It was Pear. He carried an armful of clothing which he dropped on the bunk.

'Here's a dry change for you. It wouldn't do for you to croak off with pneumonia now. That'd be a clanker in the balls, wouldn't it?'

'Thank you,' said Vittorio, getting up. 'How's your friend?'

'The ship's doctor is afraid he'll lose the use of his hand. The doctor hasn't told him, but he knows.'

'I'm sorry. I was naïve.'

'Yes,' agreed the Britisher simply. 'You were naïve.' He left, leaving the door open.

From the narrow metal corridors outside the tiny metal room, there was a sudden eruption of noise. Men raced by the door, all running in the same direction, fore or aft, Fontini-Cristi could not tell. Over the ship's intercom a piercing, deafening whistle shrieked without let-up; metal doors slammed, the shouting increased.

Vittorio lunged at the open door; his breathing stopped. The panic of helplessness under the sea gripped him.

He collided with a British sailor. But the sailor's face was not contorted in panic. Or fear. Or anything but carefree laughter.

'*Happy New Year*, mate!' cried the sailor. 'Midnight, chum! We're in 1940. A bloody new decade!'

The sailor raced on to the next hatchway, which he opened with a crash. Beyond, Fontini-Cristi could see the mess quarters. Men were gathered around holding out mugs into which two officers were pouring whisky. The shouts merged into laughter. 'Auld Lang Syne' began to fill the metal chambers.

A new decade.

The old one had ended in death. Death everywhere, most horribly in the blinding white light of Campo di

Fiori. Father, mother, brothers, sisters ... the children. *Gone*. Gone in a minute of shattering violence that was burned into his mind. A memory he would live with for the rest of his life.

Why? Why? Nothing made sense!

And then he remembered. Savarone had said he had gone to Zürich. But he had not gone to Zürich; he had gone somewhere else.

In that somewhere else lay the answer. But what?

Vittorio walked into the small metal room of the submarine and sat down on the iron ridge of the bed.

The new decade had begun.

PART TWO

CHAPTER SIX

2 Jan 1940
LONDON

Sandbags.

London was a city of sandbags. Everywhere. In doorways, windows, shop-fronts; piled in mounds on street corners. The sandbag was the symbol. Across the Channel, Adolf Hitler vowed the destruction of all England; quietly the English believed his threat, and quietly, firmly, they steeled themselves in anticipation.

Vittorio had reached the RAF airfield at Lakenheath late on the previous night, the first day of the new decade. He had been taken off an unmarked plane flown out of Majorca and whisked into operations, the purpose of which was to confirm his identity for the Admiralty. And now that he was safely in the country, the voices suddenly became calm and solicitous: Would he care to rest up after his gruelling journey? Perhaps the Savoy? It was understood that the Fontini-Cristis stayed at the Savoy when in London. Would a conference tomorrow afternoon at fourteen hundred hours be convenient? At the Admiralty. Intelligence Sector Five. Alien operations.

Of course. For God's sake, *yes*! Why have you English done what you've done? I must know, but I will be silent until you tell me.

The Savoy desk provided him with toilet articles and nightclothes, including a Savoy robe. He had drawn a very hot bath in the enormous hotel tub and immersed himself for such a length of time the skin on his fingertips wrinkled. He then proceeded to drink too many glasses of brandy and fell into bed.

He had left a wake-up call for ten but, of course, it was unnecessary. He was fully alert by eight thirty; showered and shaved by nine. He ordered an English breakfast from the floor steward and while waiting telephoned Norcross, Limited, on Savile Row. He needed clothes immediately. He could not walk around London in a borrowed raincoat, a sweater, and the ill-fitting trousers provided by an agent named Pear on a submarine in the Mediterranean.

As he hung up the phone, it struck Vittorio that he had no money other than ten pounds courtesy of Lakenheath dispersals. He assumed his credit was good; he would have funds transferred from Switzerland. He had not had time to concentrate on the logistics of living; he had been too preoccupied with staying alive.

It occurred to Fontini-Cristi that he had many things to do. And if only to control the terrible memory – the infinite pain – of Campo di Fiori, he had to keep active. Force his mind to concentrate first on the simple things, everyday things. For when the great things came into focus he could go mad pondering them.

Please, dear God, the *little* things! Spare me the time to find my sanity.

He saw her first across the Savoy lobby while waiting for the day manager to arrange for immediate monies. She was sitting in an armchair, reading *The Times*, dressed in the stern uniform of a branch of the women's service, what branch he had no idea. Beneath the officer's visor cap her dark brunette hair fell in waves to her shoulders, outlining her face. It was a face he had seen before; it was a face one remembered. But it was a younger version of that face that stuck in his mind. The woman was, perhaps, in her middle thirties; the face he recalled had been no more than twenty-two or twenty-three. The cheekbones were high, the nose more Celtic than English – sharp, slightly upturned, and delicate above the full lips. He could not see the eyes clearly, but he knew what they looked like: a very intense blue, as blue as he had ever seen a woman's eyes.

That's what he remembered. Angry blue eyes staring up at him. Angry and filled with disdain. He had not encountered that reaction often in his life; it had irritated him.

Why did he remember? When was it?

'Signore Fontini-Cristi.' The Savoy manager walked briskly out of the cashier's arch, an envelope in his hand. 'As you requested, a thousand pounds.'

Vittorio took the envelope and shoved it in the raincoat pocket. 'Thank you.'

'We've arranged for your limousine, sir. It should be here shortly. If you'd care to return to your suite, we'll ring you the moment it arrives.'

'I'll wait here. If you can put up with these clothes, I can.'

'Please, *signore*. It is always a great pleasure to welcome a member of the Fontini-Cristis. Will your father be joining you this trip? We trust he's well.'

England marched to the sudden drums of war and the Savoy inquired about families.

'He'll not be joining me.' Vittorio saw no point in further explanations. The news had not reached England, or if it had, the war dispatches made it insignificant. 'By the way, do you know that lady over there? The one seated. In the uniform.'

The manager unobtrusively glanced across the sparsely populated lobby. 'Yes, sir. She's Mrs Spane. I should say *was* Mrs Spane; they're divorced. I believe she's remarried now. Mr Spane is. We don't see her often.'

'Spane?'

'Yes, sir. I see she's with Air Defence. They're a no-nonsense group, they are.'

'Thank you,' said Vittorio, dismissing the manager courteously. 'I shall wait for my car.'

'Yes, of course. If there's anything we can do to make your stay more pleasant, don't hesitate to call upon us.'

The manager nodded and walked away. Fontini-Cristi looked again at the woman. She glanced at her watch, and then returned to her reading.

He remembered the name Spane because of its spelling, and because of the spelling, he remembered the man. It had been eleven, no, twelve years ago; he had accompanied Savarone to London to observe his father in negotiations with De Havilland – the observation part of his training. Spane had been introduced to him one night at Les Ambassadeurs, a youngish man two or three years older than he was. He'd found the English-man mildly amusing but basically tiring. Spane was a Mayfair product quite content to enjoy the fruits of ancestral labours without contributing much of anything himself, other than his expertise at the races. His father had disapproved of Spane and said as much to his eldest son, which, quite naturally, goaded the son into a brief acquaintanceship.

But it had been brief, and Vittorio suddenly remembered why. That it had not first come to mind was merely further proof that he had blocked her existence from much of his memory: not the woman across the lobby, but his wife.

His wife had come to England with them twelve years ago, the *padrone* feeling that her presence would have a restraining influence on a headstrong, wandering son.

But Savarone did not know his daughter-in-law that well; he did later, but not at the time. The heady atmosphere of Mayfair at the height of the season was a tonic to her.

His wife was attracted to Spane; one or the other seduced one or the other. He had not paid much attention; he had been occupied himself.

And somewhere along the way there'd been a disagreeable confrontation. Recriminations had been hurled, and the angry blue eyes had stared up at him.

Vittorio walked across the lobby towards the armchair. The Spane woman glanced up as he approached. There was a moment of hesitancy in her eyes, as if she were unsure. And then she *was* sure and there was no hesitance at all; the disdain he recalled so vividly replaced the hesitation. Their eyes locked a second – no more – and she returned to the newspaper.

'Mrs Spane?'

She looked up. 'The name is Holcroft.'

'We've met.'

'We have. It's Fontini—' She paused.

'Fontini-Cristi. Vittorio Fontini-Cristi.'

'Yes. A long time ago. You'll forgive me, but I've a full day. I'm waiting for someone and I shan't have the chance to get through the paper again.' She went back to her reading.

Vittorio smiled. 'You dismiss me efficiently.'

'I find it quite easy to do so,' she replied without looking at him.

'Mrs Holcroft, it *was* a long time ago. The English poet says that nothing so becomes change as the years.'

'The English poet also maintains that leopards do not change their spots. I'm really quite occupied. Good day.'

Vittorio started to nod his departure when he saw that her hands trembled ever so slightly. Mrs Holcroft was somewhat less confident than her demeanour implied.

He was not sure why he stayed; it was a time to be alone. The terrible memories of white light and death burned; he did not care to share them. On the other hand, he wanted to talk. To someone. About anything.

'Is an apology offered for childish behaviour twelve years ago a decade too late?'

The lieutenant glanced up. 'How *is* your wife?'

'She died in an automobile crash ten years ago.'

The look in her eyes was steady; the hostility lessened. She blinked in discomfort, mildly embarrassed. 'I'm sorry.'

'It is my place to apologize. Twelve years ago you were seeking an explanation. Or comfort. And I had neither to give.'

The lieutenant allowed herself the trace of a smile. Her eyes had an element – if only an element – of warmth in them. 'You were a very arrogant young man. And I'm afraid I had very little grace under pressure. I came to have more, of course.'

'You were better than the games we played. I should have understood.'

'That's a very disarming thing to say ... And I think we've said enough about the subject.'

'Will you and your husband have dinner with me tonight, Mrs Holcroft?' He heard the words he had spoken, not sure he had said them. It was the impulse of the moment.

She stared at him briefly before answering. 'You mean that, don't you?'

'Certainly. I left Italy in somewhat of a rush, courtesy of your government, as these clothes are the courtesy of your countrymen. I haven't been to London in several years. I have very few acquaintances here.'

'Now that's a provocative thing to say.'

'I beg your pardon?'

'That you left Italy in a rush and you're wearing someone else's clothes. It raises questions.'

Vittorio hesitated, then spoke quietly. 'I would appreciate your having the understanding I lacked ten years ago. I would prefer those questions not be raised. But I'd like to have dinner with you. And your husband, of course.'

She held his gaze, looking up at him curiously. Her lips curved into a gentle smile; she had made her decision. 'My husband's name was Spane. Holcroft's my own. Jane Holcroft. And I'll have dinner with you.'

The Savoy doorman interrupted. 'Signore Fontini-Cristi, your car has arrived, sir.'

'Thank you,' he replied, his eyes on Jane Holcroft. 'I'll be right there.'

'Yes, sir.' The doorman nodded and walked away.

'May I pick you up this evening? Or send my car for you?'

'Petrol's getting scarce. I'll meet you here. Eight o'clock?'

'Eight o'clock. *Arrivederci.*'

'Until then.'

He walked down the corridor at the Admiralty, escorted by a Commander Neyland who had met him at the entrance desk. Neyland was middle-aged, properly naval, and quite impressed with himself. Or perhaps he was not at all impressed with Italians. In spite of Vittorio's fluency in English, Neyland insisted on using the simplest terms, and raising his voice as though addressing a retarded child. Fontini-Cristi was convinced that Neyland had not listened to his replies; a man did not hear of pursuit, death, and escape, and respond with such banalities as 'You don't say' . . . 'Odd, isn't it?' . . . 'The Genoa gulf can be choppy in December, can't it?'

As they walked, Vittorio balanced his negative reaction

to the commander with his gratitude for old Norcross in Savile Row.

Where the commander floundered, Norcross performed. The old tailor had clothed him in a matter of hours.

The little things; concentrate on the every*day* things.

Above all, maintain a control that bordered on ice during the conference with whatever, or whoever, comprised Intelligence Sector Five. There was so much to learn, to understand. So much that was beyond his comprehension. In the cold recital of the events that were the horror of Campo di Fiori, he could not let the agony cloud his perceptions; the recital, therefore, *would* be cold and understated.

'Through here, old man,' said Neyland, indicating a cathedral-arched doorway that was more reminiscent of some venerable men's club than a military building. The commander opened the heavy door, gleaming with brass hardware, and Vittorio walked in.

There was nothing about the large room that belied the concept of a subdued but richly appointed club. Two huge windows overlooked a courtyard; everything was heavy and ornate: the drapes, the furniture, the lamps, and to some degree the three men who sat at the thick mahogany table in the centre. Two were in uniform – the insignia and breast decorations duly proclaiming rank and experience unknown to Fontini-Cristi. The man in civilian clothes had an archly diplomatic look about him, complete with a waxed moustache. Such men had come and gone in Campo di Fiori. They spoke in soft voices, their words ambiguous. The civilian was at the head of the table, the officers seated at the sides. There was one empty chair, obviously for him.

'Gentlemen,' said Commander Neyland, as if he were announcing a petitioner at the Court of St James, 'Signore Savarone Fontini-Cristi of Milan.'

Vittorio stared at the fatuous Englishman; the man had not heard a word he said.

The three men at the table rose as one. The civilian spoke. 'May I introduce myself, sir. I am Anthony Brevourt. For a number of years I was the crown's ambassador to the Greek court of George the Second in Athens. On my left, Vice-Admiral Hackett, Royal Navy; on my right, Brigadier Teague, Military Intelligence.'

At first, there were formal nods of acknowledgement, then Teague broke the formality by coming around his chair, his hand held out to Vittorio.

'I'm glad you're here, Fontini-Cristi. I received the preliminary reports. You've had a hell of a time of it.'

'Thank you,' said Vittorio, shaking the general's hand.

'Do sit down,' said Brevourt, indicating the expected chair to Vittorio and returning to his own. The two officers took their seats, Hackett rather formally, even pompously; Teague quite casually. The general withdrew a cigarette case from his pocket and offered it to Fontini-Cristi.

'No, thank you,' said Vittorio. To smoke with these men would imply a casualness he neither felt nor wanted them to think he felt. A lesson from Savarone.

Brevourt quickly continued. 'I think we'd better get on with it. I'm sure you know the subject of our anxieties. The Greek consignment.'

Vittorio looked at the ambassador. And then at the two officers. They were staring at him, apparently in anticipation. 'The Greek? I know nothing of a "Greek consignment". However, I know the gratitude I feel. There are no words to express it in either language. You saved my life; men were killed doing so. What more can I say?'

'I think,' said Brevourt slowly, 'that we should like to hear you say something about an extraordinary delivery made to the family Fontini-Cristi by the Eastern Brotherhood of Xenope.'

'I beg your pardon?' Vittorio was stunned. The words had no meaning for him. Some extraordinary error had been made.

'I told you. I was the crown's ambassador to Athens. During the tenure of my office, diplomatic liaisons were formed throughout the country, including, of course, the religious. For, in spite of the turmoil Greece is experiencing, the church hierarchy remains a powerful force.'

'I'm sure it does,' agreed Vittorio. 'But I have no idea why it concerns me.'

Teague leaned forward, the smoke curling in front of his face, his eyes riveted on Fontini-Cristi. 'Please. We've done our share, you know. As you've said – I think quite properly – we saved your life. We sent in our best men, paid thousands to the *Corsos*, took considerable gambles in dangerous waters with a submarine – of which we have precious few – and activated a barely developed aircraft escape route. All these just to get you out.' Teague paused, put down his cigarette and smiled ever so slightly. 'All human life is sacred, perhaps, but there are limits to the expenditure one makes to prolong it.'

'Speaking for the navy,' said Hackett with controlled irritation, 'we followed blindly, given only the barest facts, urged by the most commanding figures in the government. We jeopardized a vital area of operations; a decision that could cost a great many lives in the near future. Our expense was considerable. And the full tally's not in yet.'

'These gentlemen – the government itself – acted on my most urgent entreaties,' said Ambassador Anthony Brevourt with measured precision. 'I was convinced beyond any doubt that *whatever* the cost, it was imperative to get you out of Italy. Quite simply put, Signore

Fontini-Cristi, it was not your life. It was the information you possess relative to the Patriarchate of Constantine. That is my conduit. Now, if you please, the location of the delivery. Where is the vault?'

Vittorio returned Brevourt's stare until he could feel the sting in his eyes. No one spoke; the silence was strained. Things were being alluded to that moved the highest echelons of government and Fontini-Cristi knew he was the focus. But that was all he knew.

'I cannot tell you what I know nothing about.'

'*The freight from Salonika.*' Brevourt's voice was cutting. The flat of his hand descended delicately on the table, the soft slap of flesh against wood as startling as it was abrupt. 'Two dead men in the railroad yards of Milan. One a priest. Somewhere beyond Banja Luka, north of Trieste, past Monfalcone, somewhere in Italy, or Switzerland, you met that train. Now *where?*'

'I met no train, *signore*. I know nothing of Banja Luka, or Trieste. Manfalcone, yes, but it was only a phrase, and meaningless to me. An "incident" would "take place at Monfalcone". That was all. My father did not elaborate. His position was that I would be given the information *after* the incident at Monfalcone. Not before.'

'What of the two dead men in Milan? In the railroad yards.' Brevourt would not let up; his intensity was electric.

'I read of the two men you speak of – shot in the Milan goods yards. It was a newspaper story. It did not seem terribly important to me.'

'They were *Greeks.*'

'I understand that.'

'You *saw* them. They made the *delivery* to you.'

'I saw no Greeks. No delivery was made to me.'

'Oh, my God!' Brevourt drew out the words in a pained whisper. It was obvious to all at the table that the diplomat was suddenly gripped in his own particular fear; he was not feigning for negotiable effect.

'Easy,' said Vice-Admiral Hackett vacuously. The diplomat started to speak again, slowly, carefully, as though marshalling his thoughts.

'An agreement was made between the Elders of Xenope and the Italian Fontini-Cristis. It was a matter of incalculable priority. Sometime between December ninth and sixteenth – the dates the train left Salonika and arrived in Milan – it was met and a crate removed from the third goods wagon. Of such value was this cargo that the train's itinerary was prepared in isolated stages. There was only a single master plan, itself a sequence of documents, held by one man, a priest of Xenope. These, too, were destroyed before the priest took his own life and that of the driver. Only he knew where the transfer was to be made, where the crate was to be removed. He and those responsible for removing it. The Fontini-Cristis.' Brevourt paused, his deep-set eyes riveted on Vittorio. 'These are facts, sir; given to me by a courier from the Patriarchate. Coupled with the measures my government has taken, I presume they are sufficient to convince you to give us the information.'

Fontini-Cristi shifted his position in the chair and looked away from the quietly intense face of the ambassador. He was sure the three men thought he was dissembling; he would have to dissuade them of that. But first he had to think. So this was the reason. An unknown train from Salonika had caused the British government to take extraordinary measures to – what had Teague said? – prolong his life. Yet it was not his life that was important, as Brevourt had made clear. It was the information they assumed he possessed.

Which, of course, he did not.

9–16 December. His father had left for Zürich on the twelfth. But Savarone had not been in Zürich. And he would not tell his son where he had been ... Brevourt might well have cause for his anxieties. Still, there were other questions; the pattern was unclear. Vittorio turned back to the diplomat.

'Bear with me. You say Fontini-Cristis. You use the plural. A father and four sons. The father's name was Savarone. Your Commander Neyland inaccurately introduced me by that name.'

'Yes.' Brevourt was barely audible, as if he were being forced to confront a conclusion he refused to accept. 'I was aware of that.'

'So Savarone is the name you received from the Greeks. Is that correct?'

'He could not have done it alone.' Again Brevourt spoke hardly above a whisper. 'You're the eldest son; you run the companies. He would have advised you. He needed your help. There were over twenty separate documents to be prepared, we know that. He *needed* you!'

'It is what you apparently – perhaps desperately – wish to believe. And because you believed it, you took extraordinary measures to save my life, to get me out of Italy. You obviously know what happened at Campo di Fiori.'

Brigadier Teague spoke. 'We picked it up first through the partisans. The Greeks weren't far behind. The Greek embassy in Rome was keeping close tabs on the Fontini-Cristis; it wasn't told why, apparently. The Athens conduit reached the ambassador and he, in turn, got in touch with us.'

'And now you are implying,' said Brevourt icily, 'that it was all for nothing.'

'I'm not implying it. I'm stating it. During the period you spoke of, my father said he was travelling to Zürich. I'm afraid I wasn't paying much attention at the time, but several days later I had an urgent reason to ask him to return to Milan. I tried contacting him; I called every hotel in Zürich; he was nowhere to be found. He never told me where he was, where he had been. That's the truth, gentlemen.'

The two officers looked at the diplomat. Brevourt leaned slowly back in his chair – it was a gesture of futility and exhaustion; he stared at the table top. Finally, he spoke.

'You have your life, Signore Fontini-Cristi. For all our sakes, I hope the cost was not too great.'

'I can't answer that, of course. Why was this agreement made with my father?'

'*I* can't answer *that*,' replied Brevourt, his eyes still on the table. 'Apparently someone, somewhere, believed he was resourceful enough, or powerful enough, to carry it off. Either or both of which have been borne out. Perhaps we'll never know . . .'

'What was on the train from Salonika? What was in the vault that caused you to do what you did?'

Anthony Brevourt raised his eyes and looked at Vittorio and lied. 'I don't know.'

'That's preposterous.'

'I'm sure it must appear that way. I know only the . . . implications of its significance. There is no price on such things. It's an abstract value.'

'And on that judgement you made these decisions, convinced your highest authorities to make them? Moved your government?'

'I did, sir. I would do it again. And that's all I'll say on the subject.' Brevourt rose from the table. 'It's pointless to go on. Others may be in touch with you. Good day, Signore Fontini-Cristi.'

The ambassador's action startled the two officers, but they said nothing. Vittorio got out of his chair, nodded, and walked silently to the door. He turned and looked at Brevourt; the man's eyes were non-committal.

Outside, Fontini-Cristi was surprised to see

Commander Neyland standing at attention between two enlisted men. Intelligence Sector Five, Alien Operations, was taking no chances. The door of the conference room was being guarded.

Neyland turned, astonishment in his face. He obviously expected the meeting to last far longer. 'You've been released, I see.'

'I didn't think I was being held,' answered Vittorio.

'Figure of speech.'

'I never realized how unattractive it was. Are you to escort me past the desk?'

'Yes, I'll sign you out.'

They approached the Admiralty's entrance desk. Neyland checked his watch, gave Vittorio's last name to the guard. Fontini-Cristi was asked to initial the departure time; he did so, and as he stood up from the desk he was greeted by the commander's very formal salute. He nodded – formally – turned and walked across the marble floor to the huge double doors to the street.

He was on the fourth step when the words came to him. They shot through the swirling mists of white light and the shattering staccato of gunfire.

'*Champoluc . . . Zürich is Champoluc . . . Zürich is the river!*'

And then no more. Only the screams, and the white light, and the bodies suspended in death.

He stopped on the marble step, seeing nothing but the terrible visions of his mind.

'*Zürich is the river! Champoluc . . .*'

Vittorio controlled himself. He stood motionless and breathed deeply, vaguely aware that people on the pavement and the steps were staring at him. He wondered if he should walk back through the doors of the Admiralty and down a long corridor to the cathedral arch that was the conference room of Intelligence Sector Five.

Calmly he made his decision. *Others may contact you.* Let the others come. He would not share with Brevourt, the seeker of elastic who lied to him.

'If I may, Sir Anthony,' said Vice-Admiral Hackett, 'I believe there was a great deal more ground we might have covered—'

'I agree,' interrupted Brigadier Teague, his irritation showing. 'The admiral and I have our differences, but not in *this*, sir. We barely scratched the surface. We made an extraordinary investment and got nothing for it; there was more to be had.'

'It was useless,' said Brevourt wearily, walking slowly to the draped window overlooking the courtyard. 'It was in his eyes. Fontini-Cristi told the truth. He was stunned by the information. He knows nothing.'

Hackett cleared his throat, a prelude to judgement. 'He didn't strike me as foaming at the mouth. He seemed to take it rather in his stride, I'd say.'

The diplomat stared absently out of the window as he replied quietly. 'If he had foamed at the mouth, I would have kept him in that chair for a week. He behaved precisely the way such a man reacts to deeply disturbing news. The shock was too profound for theatricals.'

'Granting your premise,' said Teague coldly, 'it does not eliminate mine. He may not *realize* what he knows. Secondary information often leads to a primary source. In our business it nearly always does. I must object, Sir Anthony.'

'Your objection is noted. You're perfectly free to make further contact; I made that clear. But you'll learn no more than we did this afternoon.'

'How can you be so *sure*?' asked the Intelligence man quickly, his irritation rapidly turning into anger.

Brevourt turned from the window, his expression pained, his eyes in reflection. 'Because I knew Savarone

Fontini-Cristi. Eight years ago in Athens. He was a neutral emissary, I think is the term, from Rome. The only man Athens would trust. The circumstances are not relevant here; the methods of Fontini-Cristi are. He was a man possessed with a sense of discretion. He could move economic mountains, negotiate the most difficult international agreements, because all parties knew his word was better than any written contract. In a strange way, it was why he was feared; beware the man of total integrity. Our only hope was if he had called in his son. If he had needed him.'

Teague absorbed the diplomat's words, then leaned forward, his arms on the table. 'What was on the train from Salonika? In that damned vault?'

Brevourt paused before answering. The two officers understood that whatever the ambassador was about to say, it was *all* he would say.

'Documents hidden from the world for fourteen centuries. They could tear the Christian world apart, setting church against church . . . nation against nation, perhaps; forcing millions to choose sides in a war as profound as Hitler's.'

'And by so doing,' interrupted Teague in the form of a question, 'dividing those who fight Germany?'

'Yes. Inevitably.'

'Then we'd better pray they're not found,' concluded Teague.

'Pray strenuously, General. It's strange. Over the centuries men have willingly given their lives to protect the sanctity of those documents. Now they've disappeared. And all who knew where to are dead.'

PART THREE

CHAPTER SEVEN

Jan 1940 to Sept 1940
EUROPE

The telephone rang on the antique desk in the Savoy suite. Vittorio was at the casement window overlooking the Thames, watching the barges make their way slowly up and down the river in the afternoon rain. He checked his watch; it was exactly four thirty. The caller had to be MI6's Alec Teague.

Fontini-Cristi had learned many things about Teague over the past three weeks; one was that the man was punctual to a fault. If he said he would telephone *around* four thirty, then he would do so *at* four thirty. Alec Teague ran his life by a clock; it made for abrupt conversations.

Vittorio picked up the telephone. 'Yes?'

'Fontini?' The Intelligence man was also given to brevity when it came to names. Apparently he saw no reason to add the Cristi when the Fontini was sufficient.

'Hello, Alec, I've been expecting you.'

'I've got the papers,' said Teague rapidly. 'And your orders. The Foreign Office was reluctant. It's an equal wager whether they were concerned for your well-being, or whether they thought you'd present the crown with a bill.'

'The latter, I can assure you. My father drove "hard

bargains", I think is the term. Frankly, I've never understood the phrase; can bargains be soft?'

'Damned if I know.' Teague was not really listening. 'I think we should meet right off. How's your evening?'

'I'm having dinner with Miss Holcroft. Under the circumstances I can cancel, of course.'

'Holcroft? Oh, the Spane woman.'

'I think she prefers Holcroft.'

'Yes, can't blame her. He's a bloody fool. Still, you can't deny the ceremony.'

'She's doing her best to, I believe.'

Teague laughed. 'Damned gutsy girl. I think I'd like her.'

'Which means you don't know her, and you want *me* to know you've had me followed. I never mentioned her married name to you.'

Teague laughed again. 'For you own benefit, not ours.'

'Shall I cancel?'

'Don't bother. When will you be finished?'

'Finished?'

'Dinner. Damn, I forgot; you're Italian.'

Vittorio smiled. Alec's recollection was made in complete sincerity. 'I can see the lady home by ten thirty . . . ten o'clock. I gather you wish to meet tonight.'

'I'm afraid we have to. Your orders call for you to leave tomorrow. For Scotland. In the morning.'

The restaurant in Holborn was named Fawn's. Black curtains were drawn tautly across the windows, stretched and tacked, inhibiting any light from spilling a single shaft into the street. He was in the bar, seated at a corner stool with a clear view of the lounge and the shrouded entrance. She would arrive any minute now and he smiled at himself, realizing that he wanted to see her very much.

He knew when it had begun with Jane – their swiftly developing relationship that would shortly lead to the splendid comfort of the bed. It was not their meeting in the Savoy lobby; nor was it their first evening together. Those were pleasant distractions; he had sought no more, wanted no more.

The beginning was five days later when he had been sitting alone in his rooms. There'd been a knock on the foyer door. He had opened it; Jane was standing in the hallway. In her hand was a slightly worn copy of *The Times*. He had not seen it.

'For God's sake, what happened?' she asked.

He had shown her in without answering, unsure of her meaning. She'd handed him the newspaper. In the lower left corner of the front page was a brief article circled in red pencil.

MILAN, Jan. 2 (Reuters) – A news blackout has been lowered on the Fontini-Cristi Industries here as government officials moved in assuming managerial control. No member of the Fontini-Cristi family has been seen, and the police have sealed off the family estate at Campo di Fiori. Rumours abound as to the fate of this powerful dynasty headed by the financier Savarone Fontini-Cristi and his eldest son, Vittorio. Reliable sources indicate that they may have been killed by patriots, infuriated by recent company decisions many felt were inimicable to Italy's interests. It was reported that the mutilated body of an 'informer' was found hanging in the Piazza del Duomo, with a sign that would seem to confirm the rumours of execution. Rome has issued only the statement that the Fontini-Cristis were enemies of the state.

Vittorio had put down the paper and walked across the room, away from the girl. He knew she meant well; he did not fault her concern. Yet he was profoundly annoyed. The anguish was his alone and he did not care to share it. She had intruded.

'I'm sorry,' she'd said quietly. 'I presumed. I had no right to do that.'

'When did you first read this?'

'Less than a half hour ago. It was left on my desk. I've mentioned you to friends. I saw no reason not to.'

'And you came right over?'

'Yes.'

'Why?'

'I cared,' had been her simple answer. The honesty of it had touched him. 'I'll go now.'

'Please—'

'Do you want me to stay?'

'Yes. I think I do.'

And so he had told her. In measured tones at first, his sentences gathering momentum as he approached the hideous night of white light and death that was Campo di Fiori. His throat was dry. He did not wish to go on.

And Jane did a strange thing. Separated by the short distance between their opposing chairs, making no move to diminish that separation, she forced him to continue.

'For God's sake, *say* it. *All* of it.'

She had whispered, but the whisper was a command and in his confusion and anguish he accepted it.

When he was done, relief swept over him. For the first time in days an unbearable weight had been lifted. Not permanently, it would return; but for the moment he had found his sanity; really found it, not an imposed pretence that left his breath always a little short.

Jane had known what he had not understood. She had said it.

'Did you think you could just go on keeping it inside? Not saying the words; not hearing them. What kind of man do you think you *are*?'

What kind of man? He did not really know. He had

had not actually thought about the kind of man he was; it was not a question that had concerned him beyond certain limits. He was Vittorio Fontini-Cristi, first son of Savarone. Now he would find out what else he was. He wondered whether Jane could be a part of his new world. Or whether the hate and the war would be all-consuming. He knew only that the war – and the hate – were his springboards back to life.

Which was why he had encouraged Alec Teague when the MI6 man contacted him after the disastrous conference with Brevourt at Intelligence Sector Five. Teague wanted background material – seemingly unimportant conversations, offhand remarks, oddly repeated words – anything that might have a bearing on the train from Salonika. But Vittorio wanted something, too. From Teague. So he spaced out the isolated scraps of information: a river that might or might not have anything to do with Zürich, a district in the Italian Alps that bore the name Champoluc, but possessed no river. Whatever the puzzle was, its pieces remained separate. Still Teague probed.

And while he probed, Vittorio drew out the conceivable options MI6 might have for him. He was fluent in English and Italian, more than proficient in French and German; he had an intimate working knowledge of a score of major European industries, had negotiated with the leading financial figures throughout Europe. Certainly there was *something*.

Teague said he would look. Yesterday Teague said he would call him today at four thirty; there might be something. This afternoon at precisely four thirty Teague had called; he had Vittorio's 'orders'. There *had* been something. Fontini-Cristi wondered what it was, and even more, why the abruptness of his departure to Scotland.

'Have you been waiting long?' asked Jane Holcroft, suddenly standing beside him in the dimly lit bar.

'I'm *sorry*.' Vittorio was; he had not seen her in the lounge. Yet he had been staring at the door. 'No, not at all.'

'You were miles away. You looked right at me and when I smiled, you scowled. I trust it's not indicative.'

'Good heavens, no. You were right; I was miles away. In Scotland.'

'I beg your pardon?'

'I'll tell you about it at the table. What I know, which is very little.'

They were led to their table and ordered drinks. 'I've told you about Teague,' he said, lighting her cigarette, holding the flame of the match for his own.

'Yes. The man from Intelligence. You didn't say a great deal about him. Only that he seemed to be a good chap who asked a lot of questions.'

'He had to. My family required it.' Fontini-Cristi had not told Jane about the freight from Salonika; there was no point. 'I've been pestering him for several weeks to find me a job.'

'In the service?'

'In any service. He was a logical man to approach; he knows people everywhere. We both agreed I have qualifications that might be useful to someone.'

'What will you be doing?'

'I don't know, but whatever it is, it begins in Scotland.'

The waiter arrived with their drinks. Vittorio nodded his thanks, aware that Jane kept her eyes on his face.

'There are training camps in Scotland,' she said quietly. 'Several are listed as highly classified. They're quite secret and heavily guarded.'

Vittorio smiled. 'They can't be *too* secret.'

The girl returned his smile, the full explanation in her eyes, only half of it in her words. 'There's an elaborate system of air defence warning-relays throughout the areas. Overlapping sectors; extremely difficult for aircraft to penetrate. Especially single-engine light aircraft.'

'I forgot. The Savoy manager said you were no-nonsense people.'

'We're also given extensive training in all existing systems. As well as those in development stages. Systems vary considerably from sector to sector. When are you leaving?'

'Tomorrow.'

'I see. For how long?'

'I don't know.'

'Of course. You said that.'

'I'm to meet with Teague tonight. After dinner, but there's no need to rush. I'm not seeing him until ten thirty. I presume I'll know more then.'

Jane was silent for several moments. She locked her eyes with his and then spoke simply. 'When your meeting with Teague is over, will you come to me? To my flat? Tell me what you can.'

'Yes. I will.'

'I don't care what time it is.' She placed her hand over his. 'I want us to be together.'

'So do I.'

Brigadier Alec Teague removed his officer's cap and army overcoat and threw them on the Savoy chair. He unbuttoned his tunic and his collar and loosened his tie. He lowered his large, powerful frame into the soft couch and exhaled a sigh of relaxation. He grinned at Fontini-Cristi, who stood in front of an opposing armchair with his palms up in supplication.

'Since I've been at it since seven this morning, I do think you should offer me a drink. Whisky neat would be splendid.'

'Of course.' Vittorio crossed to the small bar against

the wall, poured two short glasses, and returned with the drinks.

'Mrs Spane's a most attractive woman,' Teague said. 'And you're quite right, you know, she does prefer her maiden name. At the Air Ministry the "Spane" is in brackets. She's called Lieutenant Holcroft.'

'Lieutenant?' Vittorio did not know why but the title seemed faintly amusing to him. 'I hadn't thought of her in such military terms.'

'Yes, I see what you mean.' Teague finished his drink quickly and placed his glass on the coffee table. Vittorio gestured for a refill. 'No more, thank you. It's time for serious talk.' The Intelligence man looked at his wrist-watch; Fontini-Cristi wondered if Teague really scheduled himself to the precise half-minute for social conversation.

'What's in Scotland?'

'Your place of residence for the next month or so. Should you accept the terms of employment. The pay's not exactly what you're accustomed to, I'm afraid.' Teague grinned again. 'As a matter of fact, we rather arbitrarily placed it at a captain's rate. I don't have the figures in my head.'

'The figures aren't my concern. You say I have a choice, but before you said that my orders had arrived. I don't understand.'

'We have no hold over you. You can reject the employment and I'll cancel the orders. It's as simple as that. However, in the interests of time, I made the purchase first. Frankly, to be sure it *could* be made.'

'All right. What is it?'

'That's rather difficult to answer quickly. If at all, really. You see, it's pretty much up to you.'

'To *me*?'

'Yes. The circumstances surrounding your getting out of Italy were unique, we all understand that. But you're not the only continental who's fled Europe. We've got dozens and dozens. And I'm not talking about the Jews and the Bolsheviks; they're in the thousands. I'm referring to scores of men like yourself. Businessmen, professionals, scientists, engineers, university people who, for one reason or another – we'd like to think it was moral repugnance – couldn't function where they lived. That's about where we are.'

'I don't understand. Where are you?'

'In Scotland. With forty of fifty ragtail continentals – all quite successful in their previous livelihoods – in search of a leader.'

'And you think I am *he*?'

'The more I think about it, the more convinced I become. Rather natural qualifications, I'd say. You've moved in the monied circles, you speak the languages. Above all, you're a businessman, you've developed markets all over Europe. Good heavens, man, the Fontini-Cristi Industries are *enormous*; you were its chief executive. Adapt to the conditions. Do what you've done splendidly for the past half-dozen years or so. Only do it from the *opposite point of view*. *Mis*management.'

'What *are* you talking about?'

The brigadier continued, speaking rapidly. 'We have men in Scotland who've worked in scores of occupations and professions in all the major cities in Europe. One step always leads to another, doesn't it?'

'That's what you're counting on, isn't it? We both ask questions.'

Teague leaned forward, suddenly reflective. 'These are hectic and complicated times. There are more questions than there are answers. But one answer was right in front of our eyes only we didn't see it. We were training these men for the wrong things! That is, we weren't sure *what* we were training them for; vaguely for the underground, contacts, routine information runs, it was amorphous.

There's something better; damned ingenious, if I say so myself. The strategy, the concept is to send them back to *disrupt* the marketplace, create havoc – not so much physical sabotage, we've enough people doing that, but bureaucratic chaos. Let them operate in their former bailiwicks. Accounting offices consistently out of balance, bills of lading constantly inaccurate, delivery schedules at sixes and sevens, mass confusion in the factories: exemplary *mis*management at all *costs*!'

Teague was excited, his enthusiasm infectious. It was difficult for Vittorio to keep his concentration on the essence of his original question. 'But why do I have to leave in the morning?'

'To put it bluntly, I said I might lose you if there were any further delays.'

'Further? How can you say that? I've been here less than—'

'Because,' broke in Teague, 'no more than five people in England know why we *really* got you out of Italy. Your complete lack of information about the train from Salonika has them stunned. They took an extraordinary gamble and lost. What you've told me leads nowhere; our agents in Zürich, Berne, Trieste, Monfalcone ... they can trace nothing. So I stepped in with a different version of why we got you out and saved a few heads in the bargain. I said this new operation was *your* idea. They leaped at it! After all, you are a Fontini-Cristi. Will you accept?'

Vittorio smiled. '"Mismanagement at all costs." That is a credo I doubt has a precedent. Yes, I do see the possibilities. Whether they are enormous – or theatrical – remains to be seen. I accept.'

Teague smiled slyly. 'There's one thing more. About your name—'

'Victor Fontine?' Jane laughed beside him on the couch in

the Kensington flat, warmed by the glow of the burning logs in the fireplace. 'That's British cheek if I ever heard it. They've *colonized* you.'

'And made me an officer in the process,' chuckled Captain Victor Fontine, holding up the envelope and dropping it on the coffee table. 'Teague was amusing. He approached the subject rather the way one expects from the cinema. "We must find you a *name*. Something immediately recognizable, easy to use in cables." I was intrigued. I was to be given a code name, something quite dramatic, I imagined. A precious stone, perhaps, with a number. Or an animal's name. Instead, he merely Anglicized my own and lopped it off.' Victor laughed. 'I'll get used to it. It's not for a lifetime.'

'I don't know if I can, but I'll try. It's rather a letdown, frankly.'

'We must all sacrifice. Am I correct in assuming a *capitano* is a higher rank than a lieutenant?'

'The lieutenant has no intention of taking orders. I don't think either of us is very military. Nor is Kensington. What about Scotland?'

He told her sketchily, keeping what facts he knew unspecific. As he spoke, he saw and could feel her unusually deep-blue eyes probing his, looking beyond the offhand phrases, knowing surely there was more, or would be. She was dressed in a comfortable lounging robe of pale yellow that accentuated her very dark brown hair and emphasized the blue of her eyes. Underneath the robe, between the wide lapels, he could see the soft white of her nightgown and he knew she meant him to see it, and to want to touch her.

It was so comfortable, thought Fontine. There was no sense of urgency or manoeuvre. At one point during his monologue he touched her shoulder; she slowly, gently reached up and held his hand, her fingers caressing his.

She led his hand down to her lap and cupped it with her other hand as he finished.

'So there we have it. "Mismanagement at all costs" wherever it can be inflicted.'

She was quiet for a moment, her eyes still probing, and then she smiled. 'It's a marvellous idea. Teague's right, the possibilities are enormous. How long will you be in Scotland? Did he say?'

'Not specifically. A "number of weeks".' He withdrew his hand from hers and casually, naturally reached around her shoulders and drew her to him. Her head rested on his upper chest; he kissed her soft hair. She pulled back and looked up at him – her eyes still searching. She parted her lips as she moved towards him, taking his hand and casually, perfectly naturally, leading it between the lapels of her robe, inside over her breast. When their lips met, Jane moaned and widened her mouth, accepting the full moisture of his own.

'It's been a long time,' she whispered finally.

'You're lovely,' he replied, stroking her soft hair with his hand, kissing her eyes.

'I wish you didn't have to go away. I don't want you to go.'

They stood up in front of the small couch. She helped him take off his jacket, pausing to press her face against his chest. They kissed again, holding each other at first gently, and then with gathering strength. For the briefest time, Victor placed his hands on her shoulders and moved her back; her lovely face was below him and he spoke into her blue eyes. 'I'll miss you terribly. You've given me so much.'

'And you've given me what I was afraid to find,' she answered, her lips forming a gentle, quiet smile. 'Afraid to look for, actually. Good heavens, I was petrified!'

She took his hand and they walked across the room to a doorway. Inside was the bedroom; a single ivory lamp shone on a night table, its yellowish white glow throwing light up on the walls of soft blue and across the ivory-coloured, simple furniture. The silk spread over the bed was, again, blue and white and filled with the intricate circles of a floral design. It was all so peaceful, so away, so lovely, as Jane was lovely.

'This is a room of great privacy. And warmth,' said Fontine, struck by the simple beauty. 'It's an extraordinary room, because it's your room and you care for it. Do I sound foolish?'

'You sound Italian,' she answered softly, smiling, her blue eyes filled with love and urgency. 'The privacy and warmth are for you to share. I want you to share them.'

She walked to one side of the bed, he to the other. Together they folded back the silk spread; their hands touched and they looked at each other. Jane walked around the bed to him. As she did so, she reached up and unbuttoned the top of her negligee, and then untied the ribbon of her gown. The fabric fell away, her round, full breasts emerged from the folds of silk, the nipples pink, taut.

He took her into his arms, his lips seeking hers in moist, soft excitement. She pressed her body against his. He could never remember being so completely, so totally aroused. Her long legs trembled and once again she pressed against him. She opened her mouth, her lips covered his, low moans of sweet pleasure coming from her throat.

'Oh, God, *take* me, Vittorio. Quickly, *quickly*, my love!'

The telephone rang on Alec Teague's desk. He looked at the office clock on the wall, then at his wristwatch. It was ten minutes to one in the morning. He picked up the receiver.

'Teague here.'

'Reynolds in surveillance. We have the report. He's

still in Kensington at the Holcroft flat. We think he'll stay the night.'

'Good! We're on schedule. Everything according to plan.'

'I wish we knew what was said. We could have set it up, sir.'

'Quite unnecessary, Reynolds. Deposit a file-insertion for the morning: Parkhurst at the Air Ministry is to be contacted. Lieutenant Holcroft is to be given flexible consideration, including a tour of the Loch Torridon warning relays in Scotland, if it can be arranged quietly. Now, I'm off for some sleep. Good night.'

CHAPTER EIGHT

Loch Torridon was west of the north-west highlands on the edge of the water, the source of the loch in the sea leading to the Hebrides. Inland there were scores of deep ravines, with streams rolling down from the upper regions, water that was icy and clear and formed pockets of marsh. The compound was between the coast and the hills. It was rough country. Isolated, invulnerable, patrolled by guards armed with weapons and dogs. Six miles north-east was a small village with a single main street that wound between a few shops and became a dirt road on the outskirts.

The hills themselves were steep, the abrupt inclines profuse with tall trees and thick foliage. It was in the hills that the continentals were put through the rigours of physical training. But the training was slow and laborious. The recruits were not soldiers but businessmen, teachers, and professionals, incapable of sustaining harsh physical exertion.

The common denominator was a hatred of the Germans. Twenty-two had their roots in Germany and Austria; in addition, there were eight Poles, nine Dutch, seven Belgians, four Italians, and three Greeks. Fifty-three once-respectable citizens who had made their own calculations months earlier.

They understood that one day they would be sent back to their homelands. But as Teague had noted, it was a formless sort of objective. And this undefined, seemingly low-level, participation was unacceptable to the continentals; undercurrents of discontent were heard in the four barracks in the middle of the camp. As the news of German victories came with alarming rapidity over the radio, the frustrations grew.

For God's sake! When? Where? How? *We are wasted!*

The camp commander greeted Victor Fontine with not a little wariness. He was a blunt officer in the Regulars and a graduate of MI6's various schools of covert operations.

'I won't pretend to understand much,' he said at their first meeting. 'My instructions are muddy, which is what they're supposed to be, I imagine. You'll spend three weeks, more or less – until Brigadier Teague gives us the order – training with our group as one of the men. You'll do everything they do, nothing out of the ordinary.'

'Yes, of course.'

With these words Victor entered the world of Loch Torridon. A strange, convoluted world that had little in common with anything he had experienced in his life before. And he understood, although he was not sure why, that the lessons of Loch Torridon would merge with the teachings of Savarone and shape the remaining years of his life.

He was issued regulation combat fatigues and equipment, including a rifle and a pistol (without ammunition), a carbine bayonet that doubled as a knife, a field pack with mess utensils, and a blanket roll. He moved into the barracks, where he was greeted casually, with as few words as possible and no curiosity. He learned quickly that there was not much camaraderie in Loch Torridon. These men lived in and with their immediate pasts; they did not seek friendship.

The daylight hours were long and exhausting; the nights spent memorizing codes and maps and in the deep sleep necessary to ease aching bodies. In some ways

Victor began to think of Loch Torridon as an extension of other, remembered games. He might have been back at the university, in competition with his classmates on the field, on the courts, on the mats, or up on the slopes racing downhill against a stopwatch. Except that the classmates at Loch Torridon were different; most were older than he was and none had known even vaguely what it was like to have been a Fontini-Cristi. He gathered that much from brief conversations; it was easy to keep to himself, and therefore to compete against himself. It was the cruellest competition.

'Hello? My name is Mikhailovic.' The man grinning and speaking to Victor sank to the ground, breathing heavily. He released the straps of his field pack and let the bulky canvas slip from his shoulders. It was midpoint in a ten-minute break between a forced march and a tactical manoeuvre exercise.

'Mine's Fontine,' replied Victor. The man was one of the two new recruits who had arrived in Loch Torridon less than a week ago. He was in his mid-twenties, the youngest trainee in the compound.

'You're Italian, aren't you? In Barracks Three?'

'Yes.'

'I'm Serbo-Croat, Barracks One.'

'Your English is very good.'

'My father is an exporter – was, I should say. The money's in the English-speaking countries.' Mikhailovic pulled out a pack of cigarettes from his fatigues pocket and offered it to Fontine.

'No, thanks. I just finished one.'

'I ache all over,' said the Slav, grinning, lighting a cigarette. 'I don't know how the old men do it.'

'We've been here longer.'

'I don't mean you. I mean the others.'

'Thank you.' Victor wondered why Mikhailovic complained. He was a stocky, powerfully built man, with a

135

bull neck and large shoulders. Too, something about him was odd: there was no perspiration whatsoever on Mikhailovic's forehead, while Fontine's own was matted with sweat.

'You got out of Italy before Mussolini made you a lackey to the German, eh?'

'Something like that.'

'Machek's taking the same road. He'll run all of Yugoslavia soon, mark my word.'

'I didn't know that.'

'Not many people do. My father did.' Mikhailovic drew on his cigarette, his eyes across the field. He added quietly. 'They executed him.'

Fontine looked compassionately at the younger man. 'I'm sorry. It's painful, I know.'

'Do you?' The Slav turned; there was bewilderment in his eyes.

'Yes. We'll talk later. We must concentrate on the manoeuvre. The object is to reach the top of the next hill through the woods without being tagged.' Victor stood and held out his hand. 'My first name's Vittor – Victor. What's yours?'

The Serbo-Croat accepted the handshake firmly. 'Petride. It's Greek. My grandmother was Greek.'

'Welcome to Loch Torridon, Petride Mikhailovic.'

As the days went by, Victor and Petride worked well together. So well, in fact, the compound sergeants paired them off against superior numbers in the infiltration exercises. Petride was allowed to move into Victor's barracks.

For Victor, it was like having one of his younger brothers suddenly return to life; curious, often bewildered, but strong and obedient. In some ways Petride filled a void, lessened the pain of his memories. If there was a liability in the relationship, it was merely one of excess on the Serbo-Croat's part. Petride was an excessive talker, forever questioning, always volunteering information about his personal life, expecting Victor to reciprocate.

Beyond a point, Fontine could not. He simply was not so inclined. He had shared the anguish of Campo di Fiori with Jane; there would be no one else. Occasionally he found it necessary to reprimand Petride Mikhailovic.

'You're my friend. Not my priest.'

'Did you have a priest?'

'Actually, no. It was a figure of speech.'

'Your family was religious. It must have been.'

'Why?'

'Your real name. "Fontini-Cristi." It means fountains of Christ, doesn't it?'

'In a language several centuries old. We're not religious in the accepted sense; not for a long time.'

'I'm very, *very* religious.'

'It's your right.'

The fifth week came and went and still there was no word from Teague. Fontine wondered if he'd been forgotten; whether MI6 had developed second thoughts over the concept of 'mismanagement at all costs'. Regardless, life at Loch Torridon had taken his mind off his self-destructive memories; he actually felt quite strong and capable again.

The compound's lieutenants had devised what they called a 'long-pursuit' exercise for the day. The four barracks operated separately, each taking forty-five degrees of the compass within a ten-mile radius of Loch Torridon. Two men from each barracks were given a fifteen-minute head start before the remaining recruits took chase; the object being for the hunted to elude the hunters for as long as possible.

It was natural for the sergeants to choose the best two

from each barracks to begin the exercise. Victor and Petride were the first eluders in Barracks Three.

They raced down the rocky slope towards the Loch Torridon woods.

'Quickly now!' ordered Fontine as they entered the thick foliage of the forest. 'We'll go left. The *mud*; step into the mud! Break as many branches as you can.'

They ran no more than fifty yards, snapping limbs, stamping their feet into the moist corridor of soft earth that angled through the woods. Victor issued his second command.

'Stop! This is far enough. Now, carefully. We'll make footprints up on to the dry ground ... That's enough. All right, step backward, directly on the prints. *Across* the mud ... Good. Now, we'll head back.'

'Head back?' asked the bewildered Petride. 'Head back where?'

'To the edge of the woods. Where we entered. We've still got eight minutes. That's enough time.'

'For what?' The Serbo-Croat looked at his older friend as if Fontine was amusingly mad.

'To climb a tree. Out of sight.'

Victor selected a tall scotch pine in the centre of a cluster of lower trees and started up, shinning to the first level of branches. Petride followed, his boyish face elated. Both men reached the three-quarter height of the pine, bracing themselves on opposite sides of the trunk. They were obscured by the surrounding branches; the ground beneath, however, was visible to them.

'We've nearly two minutes to spare,' whispered Victor, looking at his watch. 'Kick any loose branches away. Rest your weight solidly.'

Two minutes and thirty seconds later, their pursuers passed far below them. Fontine leaned forward towards the young Serbo-Croat.

'We'll give them thirty seconds and then climb down.

We'll head for the other side of the hill. A section of it fronts a ravine. It's a good hiding place.'

'A stone's throw from the starting line!' Petride grinned. 'How did you think of it?'

'You never had brothers to play games with? Race-and-hide was a favourite.'

Mikhailovic's smile disappeared. 'I have many brothers,' he said enigmatically, and looked away.

There was no time to pursue Petride's statement. Nor did Victor care to. During the past eight days or so, the young Serbo-Croat had behaved quite strangely. Morose one minute, antic the next; and incessantly asking questions that were beyond the bounds of a six-week friendship. Fontine looked at his watch. 'I'll start down first. If there's no one in sight, I'll yank the branches. That's your signal to follow.'

On the ground, Victor and Petride crouched and ran east at the edge of the woods, the base of the starting hill. Three hundred yards away, around the circle of the hill, was a slope of jagged rock that overlooked a deep ravine. It was carved out of the hill by a crack of a glacier aeons ago, a natural sanctuary. They made their way literally across the gorge. Breathing hard, Fontine lowered himself into a sitting position, his back against the stone cliff. He opened the pocket of his field jacket and took out a pack of cigarettes. Petride sat in front of him, his legs over the side of the ledge. Their isolated perch was no more than seven feet across, perhaps five in depth. Again, Victor looked at his watch. There was no need to whisper now.

'In half an hour, we'll climb over the crest and surprise the lieutenants. Cigarette?'

'No, thank you,' replied Mikhailovic harshly, his back to Fontine.

The note of anger could not be overlooked. 'What's the matter? Did you hurt yourself?'

139

Petride turned. His eyes bore into Victor. 'In a manner of speaking, yes.'

'I won't try to follow that. You either hurt yourself or you didn't. I'm not interested in manners of speech.' Fontine decided that if this was to be one of Mikhailovic's periods of depression, they could do without conversation. He was beginning to think that beneath his wide-eyed innocence, Petride Mikhailovic was a disturbed young man.

'You *choose* what interests you, don't you, Victor? You turn the world off at will. With a switch in your head, all is void. Nothing.' The Serbo-Croat stared at Fontine as he spoke.

'Be quiet. Look at the scenery, smoke a cigarette, leave me alone. You're becoming a bore.'

Mikhailovic slowly pulled his legs over the ledge, his eyes still riveted on Victor. 'You must not dismiss me. You cannot. I've shared my secrets with you. Openly, willingly. Now you must do the same.'

Fontine watched the Serbo-Croat, suddenly apprehensive. 'I think you mistake our relationship. Or, perhaps, I've mistaken your preferences.'

'Don't insult me.'

'Merely clarification—'

'My time has *run out!*' Petride raised his voice; his words formed a cry as his eyes remained wide, unblinking. 'You're not blind! You're not deaf! Yet you pretend these things!'

'Get out of here,' ordered Victor quietly. 'Go back to the starting line. To the sergeants. The exercise is over.'

'My name,' Mikhailovic whispered, one leg pulled up beneath his powerful, crouching body. 'From the beginning you refused to acknowledge it! *Petride!*'

'It is your name. I acknowledge it.'

'You've never heard it before. Is that what you're saying?'

'If I have, it made no impression.'

'That's a lie! It's the name of a priest. And you *knew that priest*!' Again the words floated upward, a cry shouted in desperation.

'I've known a number of priests. None with that name—'

'A priest on a *train*! A man devoted to the glory of God! Who walked in the grace of His holy work! You cannot, *must* not deny him!'

'*Mother of Christ!*' Fontine spoke inaudibly; the shock was overpowering. 'Salonika. The freight from Salonika.'

'Yes! That most holy train; documents that are the blood, the *soul* of the *one incorruptible, immaculate* church! You've taken them from us!'

'You're a priest of Xenope,' said Victor, incredulous at the realization. 'My God, you're a monk from Xenope!'

'With all my heart! With all my *mind* and *soul* and *body*?'

'How did you get here? How did you penetrate Loch Torridon?'

Mikhailovic pulled his other leg up; he was fully crouched now, a mad animal prepared to spring. 'It's irrelevant. I must know where that vault was taken, where it was hidden. You'll tell me, *Vittorio Fontini-Cristi*! You've no choice!'

'I'll tell you what I told the British. I know *nothing*! The English saved my life; why would I lie?'

'Because you gave your word. To another.'

'Who?'

'Your father.'

'No! He was killed before he could say the words! If you know anything, you know that!'

The priest of Xenope's eyes became suddenly fixed. His stare was clouded, his lids wide, almost thyroid. He reached under his field jacket and withdrew a small, snub-nosed automatic. With his thumb he snapped up the safety. 'You're insignificant. We're both insignificant,' he whispered. 'We're nothing.'

Victor held his breath. He pulled his knees up; the split second approached when he would have the one opportunity to save his life, when he would lash his feet out at the maniacal priest. One boot at the weapon, the other at Mikhailovic's weighted leg, sending him over the precipice. It was all there was left – if he could do it.

Abruptly, the vocal intrusion startling, the priest spoke, his tone chantlike, transfixed. 'You're telling me the truth,' he said, closing his eyes. 'You have told me the truth,' he repeated hypnotically.

'Yes.' Fontine took a deep, deep breath. As he exhaled, he knew he would plunge both legs out; the moment had come.

Petride stood up, his powerful chest expanding beneath the soldier's clothes. But the weapon was no longer aimed at Victor. Instead, both Mikhailovic's arms were extended in an attitude of crucifixion. The priest raised his head to the skies and shouted.

'*I believe in one God, the Father Almighty! I will look into the eyes of the Lord and I shall not waver!*'

The priest of Xenope bent his right arm and put the barrel of the automatic to his temple.

He fired.

'You got your first kill,' said Teague casually, sitting in a chair in front of Fontine's desk in the small, enclosed cubicle.

'I did not kill him!'

'It doesn't matter how it happens, or who pulls the bloody trigger. The result's the same.'

'For the wrong reasons! That *train*, that damned, *unholy train*! When will it stop? When will it *go away*?'

'He was your enemy. That's all I'm saying.'

'If he was, you should have known it, spotted it! You're a fool, Alec.'

Teague shifted his legs in irritation. 'That's rather harsh language for a captain to employ with a general.'

'Then I'd be delighted to purchase your command and set it right,' said Victor, returning to the papers in manila folders on his desk.

'One doesn't do that in the military.'

'It's the only reason for your continuity. You wouldn't last a week as one of my executives.'

'I don't believe this.' Teague spoke in astonishment. 'I'm sitting here being cashiered by a ragtail guinea.'

Fontine laughed. 'Don't exaggerate. I'm only doing what you asked me to do.' He gestured at the manila folders on the desk. 'Refine Loch Torridon. In that process, I've tried to learn how this priest of Xenope, this Mikhailovic, got in.'

'Have you?'

'I think so. It's a basic weakness with every one of these dossiers. There are no clear financial appraisals; there are endless words, histories, judgements – but very few figures. It should be corrected wherever possible before we make our final personnel decisions.'

'What on earth are you talking about?'

'Money. Men are proud of it; it's the symbol of their productivity. It can be traced, confirmed in a dozen different ways. Records abound. Where possible, I want financial statements on every recruit in Loch Torridon. There was none on Petride Mikhailovic.'

'*Financial—*'

'A financial statement,' completed Fontine, 'is a most penetrating look into a man's character. These are businessmen and professionals, by and large. They'll be anxious to oblige. Those that are not we'll question at length.'

Teague uncrossed his legs, his voice respectful. 'We'll get at it, there are forms for that sort of thing.'

'If not,' said Victor, glancing up, 'any bank or brokerage house can supply them. The more complex, the better.'

'Yes, of course. And beyond this, how are things going?'

Fontine shrugged, waving his hand again over the pile of folders on the desk. 'Slowly. I've read all the dossiers several times, making notes, cataloguing by professions and related professions. I've detailed geographical patterns, linguistic compatibilities. But where it's all led me, I'm not sure. It'll take time.'

'And a lot of work,' interrupted Teague. 'Remember, I told you that.'

'Yes. You also said it would be worthwhile. I hope you're right.'

Teague leaned forward. 'I have one of the finest men in the service to work with you. He'll be your communications man for the whole show. He's a crackerjack; knows more codes and ciphers than any ten of our best cryptographers. He's damned decisive, a shark at quick decisions. Which is what you'll want, of course.'

'Not for a long time.'

'Before you know it.'

'When do I meet him? What's his name?'

'Geoffrey Stone. I brought him up with me.'

'He's in Loch Torridon?'

'Yes. No doubt checking the cryps' quarters. I want him in at the beginning.'

Victor was not sure why but Teague's information disturbed him. He wanted to work alone, without distraction. 'All right. I imagine we'll see him in the mess.'

Teague smiled again and looked at his watch.

'Well, I'm not sure you'll want to dine in the Torridon mess.'

'One never *dines* in the mess, Alec. One eats.'

'Yes, well, the cuisine notwithstanding, I've a bit of news for you. A friend of yours is in the sector.'

'Sector? Is Loch Torridon a sector?'

'For air warning-relays.'

'Good Lord! *Jane* is here?'

'I found out the night before last. She's on tour for the Air Ministry. Of course, she had no idea you were in this area, until I reached her yesterday. She was in Moray Firth, on the coast.'

'You're a terrible manipulator!' Fontine laughed. 'And so obvious. Where the devil *is* she?'

'I swear to you,' said Teague with convincing innocence. 'I knew nothing. Ask her yourself. There's an inn on the outskirts of town. She'll be there at five thirty.'

My God, I've missed her! I've really missed her. It was rather extraordinary; he had not realized how deeply he felt. Her face with its sharp yet delicate features, her dark, soft hair that fell so beautifully around her shoulders; her eyes, so intensely blue; all were etched in his mind. 'I assume you'll give me a pass to leave the compound.'

Teague nodded. 'And arrange a vehicle for you. But you've a while before you should drive off. Let's spend it on specifics. I realize you've only begun, but you must have reached a conclusion or two.'

'I have. There are fifty-three men here. I doubt twenty-five will survive Loch Torridon, as I believe it should be run—'

They talked for nearly an hour. The more Fontine expanded his views, the more completely, he realized, did Teague accept them. Good, thought Victor. He was going to make many requests, including a continuing hunt for Loch Torridon talent. But now his thoughts turned to Jane.

'I'll walk you to your barracks,' Teague said, sensing his impatience. 'We might drop in at the officers' club for a minute – I promise no longer. Captain Stone will be there by now; you should meet him.'

But it was not necessary to stop off at the officers' bar to find Captain Geoffrey Stone. As they walked down the steps of the field complex, Victor saw the figure of a tall man in an army overcoat. He stood about thirty feet away in the compound, his back to them, talking to a sergeant major. There was something familiar about the officer's build, a kind of unmilitary slouch in the shoulders. Most striking was the man's right hand. It was encased in a black glove obviously several sizes too large to be normal. It was a medical glove; the hand was bandaged beneath the black leather.

The man turned; Fontine halted in his tracks, his breath suspended.

Captain Geoffrey Stone was the agent named Apple, who was shot on the pier in Celle Ligure.

They held each other. Neither spoke, for words were extraneous. It had been ten weeks since they'd been together. Ten weeks since the splendid, exciting moments of lovemaking.

At the inn, the old woman who sat in a rocking chair behind the front desk had greeted him.

'Lieutenant Holcroft arrived a half hour ago. A trust you're the captain, though the clothes dinna' say it. She said you're t' go up, if you're a mind to. She's a direct lass. Dinna' care for sly words, that one. Top of the stairs, turn left, room four.'

He had knocked softly at the door, the pounding in his chest ridiculously adolescent. He wondered if she was possessed by the same tension.

She stood inside, her hand on the doorknob, her inquisitive blue eyes bluer and more searching than he could remember ever having seen them. The tension was there, yet there was confidence, too.

He stepped in and took her hand. He shut the door; they closed the distance between them and slowly reached for each other. When their lips touched, all the questions were put to rest, the answers obvious in silence.

'I was frightened, do you know that?' whispered Jane, holding his face in her hands, kissing his lips tenderly, repeatedly.

'Yes. Because I was frightened, too.'

'I wasn't sure what I was going to say.'

'Neither was I. So here we are talking about our uncertainties. It's healthy, I suppose.'

'It's probably childish,' she said, tracing his forehead and his cheek with her fingers.

'I think not. To want . . . to *need* . . . with such feeling is a thing apart. One is afraid it may not be returned.' He took her hand from his face and kissed it, then kissed her lips and then her soft dark hair that fell framing the soft smooth skin of her lovely face. He reached around her and pulled her to him, holding her close, and whispered, 'I *do* need you. I've missed you.'

'You're a love to say it, my darling, but you don't have to. I don't require it, I won't ask for it.'

Victor pulled away gently and cupped her face, staring into her eyes, so close to his. 'Isn't it the same with you?'

'Very much the same.' She leaned into him, her lips against his cheek. 'I think of you far too often. And I'm a very busy girl.'

He knew she wanted him as fully and completely as he wanted her. The tension each had felt was transferred to their bodies, release to be found only in the act of love. Yet the swelling, aching urgency in them did not demand swiftness. Instead, they held each other in the warm excitement of the bed, explored each other in tenderness and growing insistence. And they talked softly in whispers as their excitement grew.

Oh, God, he loved her so.

They lay naked under the covers, spent. She rose on her elbow and reached across him, touching his shoulder, tracing the skin with her fingers down his thighs. Her dark hair fell over his chest; behind it, below her delicate face and penetrating blue eyes, her breasts were suspended over his flesh. He moved his right hand and reached for her, a signal that the act of love would begin again. And it suddenly occurred to Vittorio Fontini-Cristi, as they lay naked together, that he never wanted to lose this woman.

'How long can you stay in Loch Torridon?' he asked, pulling her face down to his.

'You're a horrid manipulating spoiler of not-so-young girls,' she whispered, laughing softly in his ear. 'I am currently in a state of erotic anxiety, with the memory of thunderbolts and erogenous pleasure still rippling in my most private – and you ask me how long I can stay! Forever and ever, of course. Until I return to London in three days.'

'Three days! It's better than two days. Or twenty-four hours.'

'For what? To reduce us both to babbling idiots?'

'We'll be married.'

Jane raised her head and looked at him. She looked at him for a long time before she spoke, her eyes locked with his. 'You've been through a great deal of sorrow. And terrible confusion.'

'You don't want to marry me?'

'More than my *life*, my darling. God, more than all the world . . . '

'But you don't say yes.'

'I'm yours. You don't have to marry me.'

'I *want* to marry you. It is wrong?'

'It's the rightest thing I can imagine. But you have to be sure.'

'Are *you* sure?'

She lowered her cheek on his. 'Yes. It's you. *You* must be sure.'

With his hands he swept her soft dark hair away from her face and answered her with his eyes.

Ambassador Anthony Brevourt sat behind the enormous desk in his Victorian study. It was nearly midnight, the household retired, the city of London dark. Everywhere men and women were on rooftops and on the river and in the parks talking quietly into wireless sets, watching the skies. Waiting for the siege they knew would come, but had not yet begun.

It was a matter of weeks; Brevourt knew it, the records projected it. But he could not keep his attention on the horrors that would reshape history as inevitably as the events moved forward. He was consumed by another catastrophe. Less immediately dramatic, but in many ways no less profound. It was contained in the file folder in front of him. He stared at the handwritten code name he had created for himself. And a few – very few – others.

SALONIKA

So simple in the reading, yet so complex in meaning.

How in God's name could it have happened? What were they thinking of? How could the movements of a single freight crossing half a dozen national borders be untraceable? The key had to be with the subject.

From below, in a locked drawer of his desk, a

telephone rang. Brevourt unlocked the drawer and pulled it open. He lifted the receiver.

'Yes?'

'Loch Torridon,' was the flat reply.

'Yes, Loch Torridon? I'm alone.'

'The subject was married yesterday. To the candidate.'

Brevourt momentarily stopped breathing. Then inhaled deeply. The voice on the other end of the line spoke again. 'Are you there, London? Do you hear me?'

'Yes, Torridon. I heard you. It's more than we might have hoped for, isn't it? Is Teague pleased?'

'Not actually. I think he would have preferred a convenient relationship. Not the marriage. I don't think he was prepared for that.'

'Probably not. The candidate might be considered an obstruction. Teague will have to adjust. Salonika has far greater priority.'

'Don't you ever tell MI6 that, London.'

'At this juncture,' said Brevourt coldly, 'I trust all files relative to Salonika have been *removed* from MI6. That was our understanding, Loch Torridon.'

'It is correct. Nothing remains.'

'Good. I'll be travelling with Churchill to Paris. You may reach me through the official Foreign Office channel, Code Maginot. Stay in contact; Churchill wants to be kept informed.'

CHAPTER NINE

LONDON

Fontine entered the stream of pedestrians moving towards Paddington Station. There was a numbness in the streets, a sense of disbelief that resulted in pockets of silence. Eyes searched other eyes, strangers took notice of the other strangers.

France had fallen.

Victor turned into Marylebone; he saw people buying newspapers in silence. It had happened; it had *really happened*. Across the Channel was the enemy – victorious, invincible.

The Dover boats from Calais held no crowds of laughing tourists on holiday any longer. Now there were different journeys; everyone had heard of them. The Calais boats sailed under cover of night, as men and women, some bloodied, some whole, all desperate, crouched below decks, hidden by nets and canvas, bringing out the stories of agony and defeat that were Normandy, Rouen, Strasbourg, and Paris.

Fontine remembered Alec Teague's words: *The concept, the strategy is to send them back to disrupt the marketplace ... create havoc! Mismanagement at all costs!*

The marketplace was now all of Western Europe. And Captain Victor Fontine was ready to send out his Loch Torridon mismanagers of that marketplace.

Of the original fifty-three continentals, twenty-four

remained; others would be added – slowly, selectively – as losses demanded. These twenty-four were as diverse as they were accomplished, as inventive as they were devious. They were German, Austrian, Belgian, Polish, Dutch, and Greek, but their nationalities were secondary. Labour forces were shipped across borders daily. For in Berlin, the *Reichsministerium* of Industry was pressing into service people for all occupied territories – it was a sweeping policy that would accelerate as new lands were brought under control. It was not unusual for a Hollander to be working in a Stuttgart factory. Already – only days after Paris fell – Belgians were being shipped to captured plants in Lyon.

Acting on this knowledge, the underground leaders were scouring the labour-transfer lists. Objectives: Find specialized temporary 'employment' for twenty-four skilled professionals.

In the confusion that resulted from the German obsession with maximum productivity, positions were unearthed everywhere. Krupp and I. G. Farben were exporting so many experts to get factories and laboratories rolling in conquered countries that German industrialists complained bitterly to Berlin. It led to haphazard organization, slipshod management; it reduced the effectiveness of German plants and offices.

It was into this morass that the French, Dutch, Belgian, Polish, and German undergrounds infiltrated. Job recruitment directives were sent by espionage couriers to London, for the scrutiny of Captain Victor Fontine.

Item: Frankfurt, Germany, Messerschmitt subsupplier. Three plant foremen sought.

Item: Kraków, Poland. Axle division, automobile plant. Draftsmen needed.

Item: Antwerp, Belgium. Railroad yards. Freight and scheduling divisions. Management scarce.

Item: Mannheim, Germany. Government printing offices. Bilingual technical translators needed imperatively.

Item: Turin, Italy. Turin Aircraft. Source partigiano. Mechanical engineers in short supply.

Item: Linz, Austria. Berlin claims consistent overpayment fabrics company. Cost accountants needed.

Item: Dijon, France. Wehrmacht legal department. Lawyers demanded by occupation forces . . . (So like the French, Victor had thought. In the midst of defeat, the Gallic mind sought debate in practical legalities.)

And so they went. Scores of 'requirements', dozens of possibilities that would grow in number as the German demands for productivity grew.

There was work to be had, to be done, by the small brigade of Loch Torridon continentals. It was now merely a question of proper allocations and Fontine would personally oversee the specifics. He carried in his briefcase a very small strip of reusable tape that could be attached to any part of the body. The adhesive had the tensile strength of steel, but could be removed by a simple solution of water, sugar, and citrus juice.

Within that tape were twenty-four dots, each containing a microfilm. On each microfilm was a microscopically reduced photograph and a brief résumé of talents. They would be used in concert with the underground leaders. Twenty-four positions of employment would be found . . . temporary, to be sure, for such skilled personnel would be desirable in many locations during the coming months.

But first things first, and the first item on Fontine's agenda was a business trip of undetermined length. He would be parachuted into France, in the province of Lorraine near the Franco-Swiss border. His first conference would take place in the small town of Montbéliard, where he would stay for several days. It was a strategic geographical point, affording maximum accessibility for the underground from northern and central France and southern Germany.

From Montbéliard he would head north on the Rhine as far as Wiesbaden, where contingents of anti-Reichists from Bremen, Hamburg, Berlin, and points north and west would gather for meetings. From Wiesbaden he would take the underground's routes east to Prague, then north-west into Poland and Warsaw. Schedules would be created, codes refined, official work papers provided for eventual duplication in London.

From Warsaw he would return to Lorraine. The decision would then be made whether to head south into his beloved Italy. Captain Geoffrey Stone was against it on principle. The agent Fontine had known as Apple made that clear. All things Italian filled Stone with loathing, his revulsion traced to a pier in Celle Ligure and a hand shattered because of Italian naïveté and betrayal. Stone saw no reason to waste their resources on Italy; there were too many other pressure points. The nation of incompetents was its own worst enemy.

Fontine reached Paddington and waited for the Kensington bus. He had discovered buses in London; he had never taken public conveyances in his life before. The discovery was partly defensive. Whenever official cars were used, they were shared, calling for conversation between the passengers. None was called for on a bus.

There were times, of course, when he carried highly sensitive material home to read, when Alec Teague simply refused to allow him his newfound indulgence. It was too dangerous. Tonight had been a case in point, but Victor had fought his superior; the official car had two other riders and he wanted to think. It was his last night in England. Jane had to be told.

'For heaven's sake, Alec! I'll be travelling several thousand miles in hostile territory. If I lose a briefcase that's chained to my wrist with a combination lock on a London bus, I think we're all in for immense trouble!'

Teague had capitulated, checking the chain and the lock himself.

The bus pulled up and he climbed in, threading his way down the crowded corridor to a seat in the front. It was by a window; he looked out and let his thoughts dwell first on Loch Torridon.

They *were* ready. The concept *was* valid. They *could* place their personnel in crucial managerial positions. All that remained was the implementation of the strategy. He would accomplish a great deal of that on his trip. He would find the right positions for the right personnel . . . the chaos and the havoc would shortly follow.

He was primed for the moment of departure. Yet he was not really prepared for the one thing that faced him now: telling Jane the moment had finally come.

He had moved into her Kensington flat when he returned from Scotland. She'd rejected his offer of considerably grander quarters. And these past weeks had been the happiest in his life.

And now the moment had come and fear would replace the comfort of daily existence together. It made no difference that thousands upon thousands were going through the same experience; there was no comfort in mathematics.

His stop was next. The June twilight washed the trees and scrubbed the houses. Kensington was peaceful, the war remote. He got off the bus and started down the quiet street when suddenly his attention was drawn away from the entrance gate. He had learned over the past months not to betray his concern, so he pretended to wave to an unseen neighbour in a window across the way. By doing so, while squinting his eyes against the setting sun, he was able to see more clearly the small Austin sedan parked on the opposite side of the street fifty yards diagonally in front of him. It was grey. He had seen that grey Austin before. Exactly five days ago. He remembered vividly. He and Stone had been driving up to Chelmsford to interview a Jewess who had worked for the Kraków civil service until just before the invasion. They had stopped at a service station outside of Brentwood.

The grey Austin sedan had driven in behind them to the pump beside theirs. Victor had noticed it only because an attendant who sold the driver petrol was caustic when the pump registered less than two gallons . . . and the Austin's tank was full.

'That's bein' a mite greedy,' the attendant had said.

The driver had looked embarrassed, turned the ignition, and sped out on to the highway.

Fontine had noticed because the driver was a priest. The driver of the grey Austin across from him now was a priest. The white collar could be seen clearly.

And the man, he knew, was staring at him.

Fontine walked casually to the gate of the house. He lifted the latch, entered, turned, and closed the gate; the priest in the grey Austin sat motionless, his eyes – behind what appeared to be thick glasses – still directed at him. Victor approached the door and let himself inside. The moment he was in the hallway he shut the door and moved quickly to the narrow column of windows that flanked the doorframe. A blackout curtain was draped over the glass; he parted the edge and looked out.

The priest had inched his way over to the right window of his car and was looking out and up at the front of the building. The man was grotesque, thought Fontine. He was extremely pale and thin, and the lenses of his glasses were thick.

Victor let the curtain fall back and walked rapidly to the staircase, climbing the steps two at a time to the third floor, their floor. He could hear music within; the radio was on; Jane was home. As he closed the door behind him, he heard her humming in the bedroom. There was no time to shout greetings; he wanted to get to the window. And he did not wish to alarm her if he could avoid it.

His binoculars were in the bookshelf on the fireplace wall. He pulled the case from its recess between two sections of books and took out the binoculars, went to the window and focused the glass below.

The priest was talking to someone in the back seat of the small automobile. Fontine had not seen anyone else in the car. The rear seat was in shadow and he had been concentrating on the driver. He edged the binoculars behind the priest and refined the focus.

Victor froze. The blood rushed to his head.

It was a nightmare! A nightmare that repeated itself! *Fed* upon itself!

The streak of white in the close-cropped hair! He had seen that shock of white from an embankment . . . inside an automobile . . . under the glaring lights . . . soon to erupt in smoke and death!

Campo di Fiori!

The man in the back seat of the grey Austin below had been in another back seat! Fontine had looked down at him from the darkness as he was now looking down at him thousands of miles away in a Kensington street! One of the German commanders! One of the German executioners!

'Good heavens! You startled me,' said Jane, walking into the room. 'What are you—?'

'*Get Teague on the telephone! Now!*' shouted Victor, dropping the binoculars, struggling with the combination lock on his briefcase.

'What *is* it, darling?'

'*Do as I say!*' He fought to keep control. The numbers came; the lock sprang open.

Jane stared at her husband; she dialled rapidly, asking no further questions.

Fontine raced into the bedroom. He pulled his service revolver from beneath a pile of shirts and tore it from its holster, running back into the living room towards the door.

'*Victor! Stop!* For God's sake!'

'Tell Teague to get over here! Tell him a German from Campo di Fiori is below!'

He ran out into the corridor and raced down the narrow staircase, manipulating his thumb beneath the barrel of the weapon, unlatching the safety. As he reached the top of the first flight, he heard the gunning of an engine. He yelled and plunged down to the hallway, to the front door, yanking furiously at the knob, pulling the door open with such force that it crashed against the wall. He ran outside to the gate.

The grey Austin was speeding down the street; pedestrians were on the pavements. Fontine chased it, dodging two oncoming cars, their tyres screeching as they braked. Men and women shouted at him; Victor understood. A man racing in the middle of the street at seven in the evening with a gun in his hand was a cause for violent alarms. But he could not dwell on such thoughts; there was only the grey Austin and a man in the back seat with a shock of white hair.

The *executioner*.

The Austin turned right at the corner! Oh, God! The traffic on the thoroughfare was light, only a few taxis and private cars! The Austin accelerated, speeding, weaving between the vehicles. It jumped a traffic light, narrowly missing a delivery van which jolted to a stop, blocking all vision beyond.

He had lost it. He stopped, his heart pounding, sweat pouring down his face, his weapon at his side. But he had not lost everything. There were six numbers on the grey

Austin's licence plate. He'd managed to distinguish four of them.

'The car in question is registered to the Greek embassy. The attaché assigned to it claims it must have been removed from the embassy grounds late this afternoon.' Teague spoke rapidly, annoyed not only with his conceivably false information but with the entire incident itself. It was an obstruction, a serious obstruction. The Loch Torridon operation could not tolerate barriers at this moment.

'Why the German? Who is he? I know *what* he is.' Victor spoke quietly, with enormous feeling.

'We're putting on every trace we can come up with. A dozen experienced field men are pulling the files. They're going back years, getting everything we have. The description you gave the artist was good; his sketch quite accurate, you said. If he's there, we'll find him.'

Fontine got out of the chair, started for the window and saw that the heavy black drapes had been drawn, shutting in all light. He turned and looked absently at a large map of Europe on Teague's wall. There were dozens of red mark-pins protruding from the thick paper.

'It's the train from Salonika, isn't it?' He asked the question softly, not needing an answer.

'That wouldn't explain the German. If he is German.'

'I *told* you,' interrupted Victor, turning to face the brigadier. 'He was there. In Campo di Fiori. I remembered then that I'd thought I'd seen him before.'

'And you've never been able to recall where?'

'No. There are times when it drives me mad. I don't *know*!'

'Can you associate? Go back. Think in terms of cities, or hotels; start with business dealings, contracts. Fontini-Cristi had investments in Germany.'

'I've tried all that. There's nothing. Only the face, and that not terribly clear. But the white streak in the hair, that's what stays in my mind.' Wearily, Victor returned to the chair and sat down again. He leaned back, both hands over his closed eyes. 'Oh, God, Alec, I'm frightened to death.'

'You've no reason to be.'

'You weren't in Campo di Fiori that night.'

'There'll be no repetition in London. Or anywhere else, for that matter. Tomorrow morning your wife will be escorted to the Air Ministry, where she will turn over her workload – files, letters, maps, everything – to another officer. The ministry has assured me the transition can be concluded by early afternoon. Thereupon, she'll be driven to very comfortable quarters in the countryside. Isolated and totally secure. She'll stay there until you return, or until we find your man. And break him.'

Fontine lowered his hands from his eyes. He looked questioningly at Teague. 'When did you do this? There's been no time.'

Teague smiled, but it was not the unsettling smile Victor was used to. It was, if anything, gentle. 'It's been a contingency plan since the day you were married. Within hours, as a matter of fact.'

'She'll be safe?'

'No one in England more so. Frankly, I've a twofold motive. Your wife's safety is directly related to your state of mind. You've a job to do, so I'll do mine.'

Teague looked at the wall clock, then at his wristwatch. The clock had lost nearly a minute since he'd last adjusted it. When *was* that? It must have been eight, ten days ago; he would have to take it back to the watchsmith's in Leicester Square.

It was a foolish preoccupation, he supposed, this

obsession with time. He'd heard the names: 'Stopwatch Alec', 'Timer Teague'. His colleagues often chided him; he wouldn't be so damned concerned with time if he had a wife and small ones clattering about. But he had made that decision years ago; in his profession he was better off without such attachments. He was no monk. There had, of course, been women. But no marriage. It was out of the question; it was a hindrance, an obstacle.

These passive thoughts gave rise to an active consideration: Fontine and *his* marriage. The Italian was the perfect coordinator for the Loch Torridon operation, yet now there was an obstacle – his wife.

Goddamn it! He had co-operated with Brevourt because he really *did* want to use Fontini-Cristi. If a convenient relationship with an English girl served both objectives, he was willing to go along. But not *this* far!

And now, where the hell was Brevourt? He had given up. He had faded away after having made extraordinary demands of Whitehall in the name of an unknown freight from Salonika.

Or had he merely pretended to fade away?

It seemed that Brevourt knew when to cut his losses, when to back away from an embarrassing failure. There'd been no further instructions regarding Fontine; he was now the property of MI6. Just like that. It was as though Brevourt wanted to put as much distance as possible between himself and the Italian *and* the goddamned train. When the report of the infiltrating priest of Xenope was given to Brevourt, he feigned only a mild interest, ascribing the episode to a lone fanatic.

For a man who had moved his government to do what it did, that wasn't natural. Because the priest of Xenope had not acted alone. Teague knew it; Brevourt knew it, too. The ambassador was reacting too simply, his sudden disinterest too obvious.

And the girl, Fontine's wife. When she appeared,

Brevourt had snapped up her existence like a true MI-Sixer himself. She was a short-range anchor. She could be appealed to, used. If Fontine's behaviour became suddenly strange, if he entered into or sought abnormal contacts that could be traced to the train from Salonika, she was to be called in and given her instructions: *report everything*. She was an English patriot; she would comply.

But no one had even considered a marriage. That *was* mismanagement-at-all-costs! Instructions could be given to a convenient mistress; they were not given to a wife.

Brevourt had taken the news with an equanimity that was again unnatural.

Something was happening that Teague did not understand. He had the uncomfortable feeling that Whitehall was using MI6 and that meant using him, tolerating Loch Torridon because it might lead Brevourt to a greater objective than the scattered disruption of enemy industry.

Back to the train from Salonika.

So two parallel strategies were being played out: Loch Torridon, and the search for the documents of Constantine. They allowed him the former; he was dismissed from the latter.

Dismissed and left with a married Intelligence officer – the most vulnerable kind.

It was ten minutes to three in the morning. In six hours he would be driving down to Lakenheath with Fontine to see him off.

A man with a streak of white in his hair. A sketch that eluded thousands of photographs and file descriptions, a hunt that led nowhere. A dozen MI6 staffers were down in the archives continuing the search. The field agent who broke the identity would not be overlooked when choice assignments were passed around.

His telephone rang, startling him.

'Yes?'

'It's Stone, sir. I think I have something.'

'I'll be right down.'

'If it's all the same to you, I'd prefer coming up. It's a bit mad. I'd rather see you alone.'

'Very well.'

What had Stone found? What could be so odd that it required in-house security?

'Here is the sketch Fontine approved, General,' said Captain Geoffrey Stone, standing in front of Teague's desk, placing the charcoal portrait on the blotter. An envelope was clamped awkwardly between his arm and his chest, above the immobile, gloved right hand. 'It matched nothing in the Himmler files, or any other German – or German-related – sources, including collaborationist circles in Poland, Czechoslovakia, France, the Balkans and Greece.'

'And Italy? What of the Italians?'

'That was our first consideration. Regardless of what Fontine claims to have seen that night in Campo di Fiori, he *is* Italian. The Fontini-Cristis made enemies among the fascists. But we found nothing, no one faintly resembling the subject in question. Then quite frankly, sir, I began thinking about the man. His marriage. We didn't expect that, did we, sir?'

'No, Captain. We did not expect that.'

'A small chapel in Scotland. A Church of England ceremony. Not exactly what one would have thought.'

'Why not?'

'I've worked the Italian sectors, General; the Catholic influence is most pervasive.'

'Fontine's not a religious man. What in hell are you driving at?'

'Just that. Everything's a question of degree, isn't it? One never is just this or just that. Especially a man who has wielded such power. I went back to *his* file; we've

163

photostats of every damned thing we could lay our hands on. Including his marriage application and certificate. Under the heading of "denomination" he inserted the word: "Christian".'

'Get to the point.'

'I'm doing so. One thing always leads to another. An immensely wealthy, powerful family in a Catholic country, and the surviving son purposely denies any association with its church.'

Teague narrowed his eyes. 'Go on, Captain.'

'He was *denying*. Perhaps unconsciously, we don't know. "Christian" is not a denomination. We were looking for the wrong Italian, pulling out the wrong files.' Stone raised the envelope with his left hand, unwound the small string and opened the flap. He took out a newspaper clipping, a cropped photograph of a bareheaded man with a shock of white in his dark hair. The bareheaded man wore the black robes of the church; the picture was taken at the altar of St Peter's. The man was kneeling, facing the cross. Above him was a pair of outstretched hands. They were holding the three-cornered hat of a cardinal.

'My God!' Teague looked up at Stone.

'The Vatican files. We keep records of all ecclesiastical elevations.'

'But *this*—'

'Yes, sir. The subject's name is Guillamo Donatti. He's one of the most powerful cardinals in the Curia.'

CHAPTER TEN

The aircraft began its ninety-degree turn. They were at 3,000 feet, the night clear, the windstream rushing past the open hatch with such force Fontine thought he would be sucked out before the red light above him was extinguished, replaced by the sudden glare of the white bulb that was his signal to leap. He gripped the handles at the sides of the hatch, bracing himself; his thick boots were pressed against the steel deck of the De Havilland bomber; he waited to jump.

He thought of Jane. At first, she'd objected strenuously to her confinement. She had earned her position at the Air Ministry, weeks and months of 'just plain damned hard work' were now taken away in a matter of hours. And then she abruptly stopped, seeing, he was sure, the pain in his eyes. She wanted him back. If isolation in the countryside would help his return, she would go.

He thought, too, of Teague; partially of what he said, mostly of what he did not say. MI6 had a line on the German executioner, the man-monster with the streak of white in his hair who had coldly observed the horror of Campo di Fiori. The service assumed him to be a ranking member of the *Geheimdienst Korps*, Himmler's secret police, a man who stayed far in the background, never expecting to be identified. Someone who had been stationed at the German consulate in Athens, perhaps.

'Assumed'. 'Perhaps'. Words of equivocation. Teague was concealing information. For all his experience, the Intelligence man could not hide his omissions. Nor was he entirely convincing when he subtly introduced a subject that had little to do with anything:

'—it's standard procedure, Fontine. When a man goes on assignment we list his religious affiliation. Just like a birth certificate or a passport—'

No, he had no formal affiliation. No, he was not Catholic, nor was that extraordinary; there *were* non-Catholics in Italy. Yes, Fontini-Cristi was a derivative combination that was translated as the 'fountains of Christ'; yes, the family for centuries had been allied with the church, but a number of decades ago had broken with the Vatican. But, no, he did not place undue emphasis on the break; he rarely thought about it.

What was Teague after?

The red light went off. Victor bent his knees as he had learned to do, and held his breath.

The white bulb flashed. The tap came – sharp, assured, solid. Fontine whipped his hands into reverse grips on the latch handles, leaned back, and propelled himself through the open hatch into the furious slip-stream of the aircraft. He was buffeted away from the huge fuselage, the force of the wind crashing into his body with the sudden velocity and weight of a giant wave.

He was in free fall. He forced his legs into a V, feeling the harness of his chute cutting into his thighs. He thrust his arms forward and diagonally out at his side. The spread-eagle configuration did what it was supposed to do: it stabilized his fall through the sky, just enough for Victor to concentrate on the dark earth below.

He saw them! Two tiny flares to his left.

He pulled his right hand in against the rushing air and tugged at a small ring beside the parachute release. There was a momentary flash above him, like an instantly fading spit of a Roman candle. It would be enough for those on the ground to get a sighting. The moment fell back into darkness; he yanked the rubber handle of the parachute release. The billowing folds of cloth shot out of the pack; the massive jolt came, causing him to expunge his breath, his every muscle taut in counterthrust.

He floated, swinging in quarter circles in the night sky, towards the earth.

The conferences in Montbéliard went well. It was strange, thought Victor, but in spite of the crude, even primitive surroundings – an abandoned warehouse, a barn, a rock-strewn pasture – the conferences were not unlike smoothly run management meetings, with himself acting as a visiting consultant from the home office. The objective of each conference with the teams of underground leaders who made their covert treks into Lorraine was the same: projected recruitment for the pool of skilled personnel now in exile in England.

Management personnel were in demand everywhere, for everywhere within the Third Reich's expanding sphere production facilities were instantly appropriated and geared for maximum output. But there was a major flaw in the German obsession with immediate efficiency: control remained in Berlin. Requests were processed by the *Reichsministerien* of Industry and Armaments; orders were cleared and issued hundreds of miles away from the places of origin.

Orders could be intercepted en route; requests could be altered at the source, within the ministries; infiltrated at the clerical level.

Positions could be created; personnel could be replaced. In the chaos that was the Berlin fever for instant, total efficiency, fear was inherent. Orders were rarely questioned.

Everywhere the bureaucratic environment was ripe for Loch Torridon.

'You will be taken to the Rhine and put aboard a river barge at Neuf-Brisach,' said the Frenchman, going to the small window in the rooming house overlooking Montbéliard's rue du Bac. 'Your escort will bring the papers. I understand they describe you as river garbage, strong back and small head. A loading stevedore who spends most of his waking hours drunk with very cheap wine.'

'That should be interesting.'

THE RHINE

It wasn't. It was gruelling, physically exhausting, and made almost intolerable by the stench below decks. German patrols prowled the river, stopping vessels continuously, subjecting crews to brutal interrogations. The Rhine was an underground courier route; it took no great perception to know that. And because the river 'garbage' deserved no better, the patrols took delight in wielding clubs and rifle stocks when bones and flesh were the objects of impact. Fontine's cover was successful, if revolting. He drank enough rancid wine and induced sufficient vomit to give his breath the putrid foulness of a confirmed, unkempt alcoholic.

What kept him from losing his sensibilities altogether was his escort. The man's name was Lübok, and Victor knew that whatever risks he was taking, Lübok's were far greater.

Lübok was a Jew and a homosexual. He was a blond-haired, blue-eyed, middle-aged ballet master whose Czechoslovakian parents had emigrated to Berlin thirty years ago. Fluent in the Slovak languages, as well as German, he held papers identifying him as a translator for the Wehrmacht. Along with the papers were several letters on High Command stationery that proclaimed Lübok's loyalty to the Reich.

The papers and the letterheads were genuine, the loyalty false. Lübok operated as an underground courier across the Czechoslovakian and Polish borders. At such times he wore his homosexual inclinations outrageously on his sleeve; it was common knowledge that such circles existed in the Officer *Korps*. Checkpoints never knew who was favoured by powerful men who preferred to bed with other men. And the middle-aged ballet master was an encyclopaedia of truths, half-truths and gossip as they pertained to the sexual practices and aberrations practised by the German High Command in any given sector or zone he entered. It was his inventory; it was his weapon.

Lübok had volunteered for the Loch Torridon assignment, to be the MI6 escort out of Montbéliard, through Wiesbaden, east to Prague and north to Warsaw. And as the journey progressed, and the days and the miles went by, Fontine was grateful. Lübok was the best. Beneath the well-tailored suits was a powerful man whose acid tongue and withering stare guaranteed a hot but intelligent temper.

WARSAW, POLAND

Lübok drove the motor-cycle with Victor in the sidecar, dressed in the uniform of a Wehrmacht *Oberst* attached to Occupation Transport. They sped out of Lódz on the road to Warsaw, reaching the final checkpoint a little before midnight.

Lübok performed outrageously before the patrols, dropping the names of *Kommandanten* and *Oberführerinnen* in acid rapidity, implying all manner of recriminations if their vehicle was detained. The embarrassed guards were not anxious to test him. The bike was waved through; they entered the city.

It was chaos. Although it was dark, rubble could be discerned everywhere. Street after street was deserted. Candles shone in windows – most electricity was out. Wires sagged, automobiles and trucks were immobilized – scores overturned, lying like giant steel insects waiting to be impaled on a laboratory table.

Warsaw was dead. Its armed killers walked in groups, themselves afraid of the corpse.

'We head for the Casimir,' said Lübok softly. 'The underground's waiting for you. It's no more than ten streets from here.'

'What's the Casimir?'

'An old place on the Kraków Boulevard. In the middle of the city. For years it was the university; now the Germans use it for barracks and offices.'

'We go in *there*?'

Lübok smiled in the darkness. 'You can put Nazis in universities, but it guarantees no instruction. The maintenance crews for all the buildings and the grounds are *podziemna*. Underground, to you. At least the beginnings of one.'

Lübok squeezed the motor-cycle between two staff cars on the Kraków Boulevard, halfway down the block, across from the main gate to the Casimir. Except for the guards at the gatehouse, the street was deserted. Only two streetlamps were working, but within the Casimir's grounds floodlights shot up from the grass, lighting the ornate façades of the buildings.

Out of the shadows walked a German soldier, an enlisted man. He approached Lübok and spoke quietly in Polish. Lübok nodded; the German continued diagonally across the wide boulevard up towards the Casimir gate.

'He's with the *podziemna*,' said Lübok. 'He used the

correct codes. He said you should go in first. Ask for Captain Hans Neumann, Block Seven.'

'Captain Hans Neumann,' repeated Victor. 'Block Seven. What then?'

'He's tonight's contact in the Casimir. He'll take you to the others.'

'What about you?'

'I'm to wait ten minutes and follow. I'm to ask for an Oberst Schneider, Block Five.'

Lübok seemed concerned. Victor understood. Never before had they been separated at their points of contact with the underground leaders. 'This is an unusual procedure, isn't it? You look troubled.'

'They must have their reasons.'

'But you don't know what they are. And that fellow didn't tell you.'

'He wouldn't know. He's a messenger.'

'Do you sense a trap?'

Lübok levelled his gaze at Fontine. He was thinking as he spoke. 'No, that's not really possible. The commander of this sector has been compromised. On film. I won't bore you with details, but his proclivity for children has been duly recorded. He's been shown the results and told negatives exist. He lives in fear, and we live with *him* . . . He's a Berlin favourite, a close friend of Goering's. No, it's not a trap.'

'But you're worried.'

'Needlessly. He *had* the codes; they're complicated and very precise. I'll see you later.'

Victor got out of the cramped sidecar and started across the boulevard towards the gates of the Casimir. He stood erect, the picture of arrogance, prepared to proudly display false papers that would gain him admittance.

As he walked across the Casimir's floodlit grounds, he could see German soldiers strolling in pairs and threes down the paths. A year ago these men might have been students and professors, recapping the events of the academic day. Now they were conquerors, peacefully removed from the devastation that was everywhere outside the walls of the Casimir. Death, hunger, and mutilation were within the sound of their commands, yet they talked quietly on clean paths, oblivious to the consequences of their acts.

Campo di Fiori. There were floodlights at Campo di Fiori. And death with mutilation.

He forced the images out of his mind; he could not allow his concentration to be weakened. The entranceway with the filigreed arch framing the thick double doors below the number seven was directly ahead. A Wehrmacht guard stood at attention on the single marble step.

Fontine recognized him: the soldier who had whispered in Polish to Lübok on the Kraków Boulevard.

'You're efficient,' said Victor softly in German.

The guard nodded, reached for the door and opened it. 'Be quickly now. Do use the staircase to the left. You will be met on the first landing.'

Fontine walked rapidly through the door into the huge marble hall, crossed to the stairs, and started up. Halfway to the landing he slowed his pace. A silent alarm went off in his brain.

The guard's voice, his use of German. The words were odd, strangely awkward. *Be quickly ... Do use the staircase ...*

Watch for the lack of idiom, the excessively grammatical, or conversely, unmatching end syllables. Loch Torridon.

The guard was not German. Yet why should he be? He was from the *podziemo*. Yet, again, the *podziemna* would not take chances ...

Two German officers appeared on the landing, their

pistols drawn and levelled down at him. The man on the right spoke.

'Welcome to the Casimir, Signore Fontini-Cristi.'

'Please don't stop, *padrone*. We must hurry,' said the second man.

The language they spoke was Italian, but their speech was not native. Victor recognized the source. The officers above him were no more German than the guard was German. They were *Greek*. The train from Salonika had reappeared!

There was the crack of a pistol bolt behind him, followed by rapid footsteps. Within seconds, the barrel was jammed into the small of his back, propelling him farther up the staircase.

There was no way he could move, no diversion he could employ, to distract his confronters. Weapons covered him, eyes watched his hands, bullets were locked in chambers.

Above, somewhere, in an unfamiliar corridor, he heard laughter. Perhaps if he shouted, raising alarms of an enemy within the enemy camp; the concentric circle of thought was numbing.

'Who are you?' *Words*. Begin with words. If he could raise his voice in sequence, natural sequence, that would minimize the chance of triggers pulled. 'You're not German?'

Louder. *Now* louder.

'What are you *doing* here?'

The barrel of the pistol slid up his back and was jabbed into the base of his skull. The jolt caused him to stop. A closed fist punched him in the left kidney; he lurched forward, caught by the silent, staring Greeks in front of him.

He started to shout; there was no other way. The laughter above was growing louder, nearer. Other men were descending the staircase.

'I warn you—'

Suddenly, both his hands were yanked back, his arms bent and locked, the wrists turned inward. A large, coarse cloth was shoved into his face saturated with acrid, foul-smelling liquid.

He was blinded; a breathless vacuum was being imposed on him, without light, without air. His tunic was ripped away, the cross strap pulled up from his chest. He tried to lash out his arms.

As he did so, he could feel the long needle entering his flesh; he was not sure where. Instinctively, he raised his hands in protest. They were *free*; and they were useless as his resistance was useless.

He heard the laughter again; it was deafening. He was aware of being propelled forward, and downward.

But that was all.

'You betray those who saved your life.'

He opened his eyes; images came into focus slowly. There was a burning sensation in his left arm, or shoulder. He reached for it; the touch was painful.

'You feel the antidote,' said the voice of the blurred figure somewhere in front of him. 'It raises a welt, but it isn't harmful.'

Fontine's eyes began to clear. He was sitting on a cement floor, his back against a wall of stone. Across from him, perhaps twenty feet away, a man stood in front of an opposite wall. They were on some kind of raised platform in a large tunnel. The tunnel appeared to be deep underground, carved out of rock, both ends disappearing into darkness. On the floor of the tunnel were old, narrow tracks; they were cracked, rusted. Light came from several thick candles inserted in ancient brackets on the walls.

His focus refined, Fontine concentrated on the man

across from him. He wore a black suit; around his neck was a white collar. The man was a priest.

He was bald, but not from age. The head was shaved; the man was no more than forty-five or fifty, the face ascetic, the body slender.

Beside the priest was the guard in the Wehrmacht uniform. The two Greeks impersonating German officers stood by an iron door in the left wall facing the tunnel. The priest spoke.

'We've followed you since Montbéliard. You're a thousand miles from London. The English can't protect you. We have routes south they know nothing about.'

'The English?' Fontine stared at the priest trying to understand. 'You're from the Order of Xenope.'

'We are.'

'Why do you fight the English?'

'Because Brevourt's a liar. He breaks his word.'

'Brevourt?' Victor was stunned; nothing made sense. 'You're out of your mind! Everything, *everything* he's done in *your name*! For *you*.'

'Not for us! For England. He wants the vault of Constantine for *England*! Churchill demands it! It's a more powerful weapon than a hundred armies, and they all know it! We would never see it again!' The priest's eyes were wide, furious.

'You believe that?'

'Don't be an ass!' spat the monk from Xenope. 'As Brevourt breaks his word, we broke Code Maginot. Messages were intercepted; communications between ... shall we say, interested parties.'

'You're *crazy*!' Fontine tried to think. Anthony Brevourt had faded away; there'd been no word from him – or about him – in months. 'You say you've followed me since Montbéliard. *Why?* I don't have what you want! I never did have it! I know nothing about the goddamned train!'

'Mikhailovic believed you,' said the priest softly. 'I don't.'

'Petride—' The sight of the child monk taking his own life on the rocky ledge in Loch Torridon came back to Victor.

'Petride was not his name—'

'You killed him!' said Fontine. 'You killed him as surely as if you'd pulled the trigger yourself. You're insane! All of you.'

'He failed. He knew what was expected. It was understood.'

'You're *sick*! You infect everyone you touch! You can believe me or not, but I'm telling you for the last time! I don't have the information you want!'

'Liar!'

'You're mad!'

'Then why do you travel with Lübok? Tell me that, Signore Fontini-Cristi! Why Lübok?'

Victor recoiled; the shock of Lübok's name caused him to arch his back against the stone. 'Lübok?' he whispered incredulously. 'If you know his work, you know the answer to that.'

'Loch Torridon?' asked the priest sarcastically.

'I never heard of Lübok before in my life. I only know he does his job. He's a Jew, a . . . he takes great risks.'

'He works *for Rome*!' roared the priest of Xenope. 'He conveys offers to Rome! *Your* offers!'

Victor was silent; his astonishment was so complete he had no words. The monk of Xenope continued, his voice low, penetrating. 'Strange, isn't it? Of all the escorts in the occupied territories, Lübok is chosen. He just shows up in Montbéliard. Do you expect us to believe that?'

'Believe what you will. This is madness.'

'It is *betrayal*!' the priest shouted again, taking several steps away from the wall. 'A degenerate who can pick up a telephone and blackmail half of Berlin! And most outrageous – for you – a dog who works for the monster of—'

'*Fontine! Dive!*' The piercing command came from the black hole of the tunnel. It was screamed in Lübok's high-pitched voice, the sound bouncing off the receding walls of rock, overriding the shouts of the priest.

Victor reeled and sprang forward, rolling down the stone wall, crashing from the platform to the hard ground by the old rusted track. Above him he heard the spits of bullets shattering the air, followed by two thunderous explosions of unsilenced Lugers.

In the flickering light he could see the figures of Lübok and several others lurch out of the darkness, angling their weapons, taking rapid, accurate aim; firing and spinning back into the protection of the rock.

It was over in seconds. The priest of Xenope had fallen; he was hit in the neck, his left ear blown off his head. He had crawled to the ledge of the platform, dying, staring down at Fontine. In imminent death his whispered voice was a rasp.

'We . . . are not your enemies. For the mercy of God, bring the documents to us—'

A final, muted spit was heard; the priest's forehead exploded above his staring eyes.

Victor felt a grip on his left arm; it caused shooting pains throughout his shoulder and chest. He was being yanked to his feet.

'*Get up!*' was Lübok's command. 'The shots may have been heard. Run!'

They raced into the tunnel. The beam of a flashlight pierced the black, held by one of Lübok's men up ahead. The man whispered his instructions in Polish. Lübok translated for Fontine, who ran beside him.

'About two hundred yards down there's a monk's cave. We'll be safe.'

'A *what*?'

'Monk's cave,' answered Lübok, breathing heavily. 'The history of the Casimir goes back centuries. Escapes were needed.'

They crawled on their hands and knees through a narrow, dark passageway cut out of rock. It led to the depths of a cave. The air was instantly different; there was an opening somewhere beyond in the darkness.

'I have to talk to you,' said Victor quickly.

'To answer your questions, Captain Hans Neumann is a devoted officer of the Reich with a cousin in the Gestapo. Oberst Schneider wasn't on the roster; that was sticky. We knew it was a trap . . . In all honesty we didn't expect to find you in the tunnel. That was a stroke of luck. We were on our way to Block Seven.' Lübok turned to his comrades. He spoke first in Polish, then translated for Fontine. 'We'll stay here for a quarter of an hour. That should be time enough. Then we'll proceed to the rendezvous in Seven. You'll conduct your business on schedule.'

Fontine grabbed Lübok's arm and led him away from the *podziemna* men. Two of the men had turned on their flashlights. There was enough light to see the middle-aged courier's face, and Victor was grateful for that.

'It wasn't a German trap! Those men back there were Greek! One was a priest!' Fontine whispered, but there was no mistaking his intensity.

'You're mad,' said Lübok casually, his eyes a perfect blank.

'They were from *Xenope*.'

'From what?'

'You heard me.'

'I heard you, but I haven't the faintest idea what you're talking about.'

'Goddamn you, Lübok! Who are you?'

'Many things to many people, thank heavens.'

Victor grabbed the blond-haired Czech by the lapels

178

of his jacket. Lübok's eyes became suddenly distant, filled with cold anger. 'They said you worked for Rome. That you would convey offers to Rome! *What* offers? What does it mean?'

'I don't know,' replied the Czech slowly.

'Who do you work for?'

'I work for many people. *Against* the Nazis. That's all you have to know. I keep you alive and see that you complete your negotiations. How I do it is none of your business.'

'You know *nothing* about Salonika?'

'It is a city in Greece, on the Aegean Sea . . . Now, take your hands off me.'

Fontine relaxed his grip but still held on. 'Just in case – in *case* – the many people you speak of include men interested in that train from Salonika, I know *nothing*. I never did.'

'If the subject ever comes up, and I can't imagine why, I'll convey the information. Now may we concentrate on your negotiations in Warsaw? We must complete them tonight. In the morning arrangements have been made for two couriers to fly out on the Berlin military shuttle. I'll check the airfield myself before daybreak. We'll get off at Müllheim. It's near the Franco-Swiss border, a night's trip to Montbéliard. Your business in Europe is finished.'

'*Fly* out?' Victor removed his hands. 'On a German plane?'

'Courtesy of a very distraught Warsaw commandant. He's seen too many motion pictures in which he was a prominent player. Sheer pornography.'

CHAPTER ELEVEN

The tri-motored Fokker was stationary as maintenance crews checked the engines and a fuel truck filled the tanks. They were in Munich; they had left Warsaw early in the morning with a stop at Prague. Most of the passengers had got off at Munich.

Müllheim was next, the last leg of their journey. Victor sat uncomfortably beside a seemingly relaxed Lübok in the quiet cabin of the aircraft. There was one other passenger: an ageing corporal on leave to Stuttgart.

'I'd like it better if there were a few more hitchhikers,' whispered Lübok. 'With so small a number, the pilot may insist everyone stay on board at Müllheim. He could fuel up quickly and be on his way. He takes on most of his passengers in Stuttgart.'

He was interrupted by the sound of clattering footsteps on the metal stairs outside the aircraft. Raucous, uninhibited laughter accompanied the unsteady clattering and grew louder as the new passengers approached the cabin door. Lübok looked at Fontine and smiled in relief. He returned to the newspaper provided by the attendant and sank back in the seat. Victor turned; the Munich contingent came into view.

There were three Wehrmacht officers and a woman. They were drunk. The girl was in a light-coloured cloth coat; she was pushed through the narrow door by two of the Wehrmacht and shoved into a seat by the third. She did not object; instead she laughed and made funny faces. A willing, participating toy.

She was in her late twenties, pleasant looking but not attractive. There was a frantic quality in her face, an intensity that made her appear somehow frayed. Her light-brown, windswept hair was a little too thick; it had not fallen free in the wind. The mascara about her eyes was too pronounced, the lipstick too red, the rouge too obvious.

'What are *you* looking at?' The question was shouted above the roar of the revving motors. The speaker was the third Wehrmacht officer, a broad-chested, muscular man in his thirties. He had walked past his two comrades and addressed Victor.

'I'm sorry,' said Fontine, smiling weakly. 'I didn't mean to be rude.'

The officer squinted his eyes; he was a brawler, it was unmistakable. 'We've got a *fancy* one. Listen to the lace-pants!'

'I meant no offence.'

The officer turned to his comrades; one had pulled the not-unwilling girl over onto his lap, the other was in the aisle. 'The lace-pants meant no offence! Isn't that nice?'

The two fellow officers groaned derisively. The girl laughed; a little too hysterically, thought Victor. He turned front, hoping the Wehrmacht boor would go away.

No. A huge hand reached over the seat and grabbed him by the shoulder blade. 'That's not good enough.' The officer looked at Lübok. 'You two move up front.'

Lübok's eyes sought Victor's. The message was clear: do as the man ordered.

'Certainly.' Fontine and Lübok rose and walked swiftly up the aisle. Neither spoke. Fontine could hear the uncorking of bottles. The Wehrmacht party had begun.

The Fokker sped down the runway and left the ground. Lübok had taken the aisle seat, leaving him the window. He riveted his eyes on the sky, withdrawing into the cocoon of himself, hoping to produce a blankness that would make the journey to Müllheim pass more swiftly. It could not pass swiftly enough.

The blankness would not come. Instead, involuntarily, he thought of the Xenope priest in the underground tunnel of the Casimir.

You travel with Lübok. Lübok works for Rome.

Lübok.

We are not your enemies. For the mercy of God, bring the documents to us.

Salonika. It was never far away. The vault from Constantine was capable of violently dividing men who fought a common enemy.

He heard laughter from the rear of the cabin, then a whispered voice behind him.

'*No*! Don't turn round. *Please*!' It was the flight attendant, barely audible through the narrow space between the seats. 'Don't get up. They're *Kommandos*. They just let off steam, so don't concern yourselves. Pretend there is nothing!'

'*Kommandos?*' whispered Lübok. 'In Munich? They're stationed north, in the Baltic zones.'

'Not these. These operate across the mountains in the Italian sectors. Execution teams. There are many—'

The words struck with the impact of silent thunderbolts. Victor inhaled; the muscles of his stomach hardened into a wall of stone .... *execution teams* ...

He gripped the armrests of his seat and arched his back. Then, pressing his back into the seat, he stretched his neck and turned his eyes towards the rear of the cabin, over the metal rim of the headrest. He could not believe what he saw.

The wild-eyed girl was on the floor, her coat open; she was naked except for torn undergarments, her legs spread, her buttocks moving. A Wehrmacht officer, his trousers and shorts pulled down to his knees, lowered himself on her, his penis stabbing. Kneeling above the girl's head was a second Wehrmacht, his trousers removed, an erection protruding from the opening in his shorts. He held the girl by the hair and lanced his erection around the flesh of her face; she opened her mouth and accepted it, moaning and coughing. The third Wehrmacht was sitting, bent over on the armrest above the rape. He was breathing in gasps through parted lips, his left hand extended, rubbing the girl's naked breasts in a rhythm that matched the masturbating motions of his right hand.

'*Animali!*' Fontine lunged from the seat, ripping Lübok's fingers from his wrist, hurling himself forward. The Wehrmacht were stunned beyond movement, their shock total. The officer on the armrest gaped. Victor's open hand gripped his hair and crashed the man's head into the steel rim of the seat. The skull cracked; an eruption of blood sprayed the face of the Wehrmacht lying between the spread legs of the girl. The officer caught his knees in his trousers; he fell forward on top of the girl, his hands lashing out to grab support. He rolled on his back, crushing the girl in the narrow aisle. Fontine raised the heel of his right boot and propelled it into the soft throat of the Wehrmacht. The blow was pulverizing; the veins in the German's neck swelled into huge tubes of bluish-black under the skin. His eyes rolled up into his sockets, the eyeballs white gelatine, blank and horrible.

The screams of the girl beneath were now mingled with the cries of agony from the third officer, who had sprung forward, propelling himself off the Fokker's deck towards the rear bulkhead. The man's underwear was matted with blood.

Fontine lunged; the German rolled hysterically away. His bloody, trembling hand reached under his tunic; Victor knew what he was after: the four-inch Kommando knife, strapped next to his flesh beneath his armpit. The Wehrmacht whipped out the blade – short, razor sharp – and slashed it diagonally in front of him. Fontine rose from his crouch, prepared to leap.

Suddenly an arm was lashed around Victor's neck. He struck back hard with his elbows, but the grip was unbreakable.

His neck was yanked back and a long knife sped through the air and imbedded itself deep in the German's chest. The man was dead before his body slumped to the floor of the cabin.

Abruptly Fontine's neck was released. Lübok slapped him across the face, the blow powerful, stinging his flesh.

'*Enough!* Stop it! I won't die for *you!*'

Dazed, Victor looked around. The throats of the other two Wehrmacht had been cut. The girl had crawled away, vomiting and weeping between two seats. The flight attendant lay sprawled in the aisle – dead or unconscious, there was no way to tell.

And the old corporal who had stared at nothing – in fear – only minutes ago, stood by the pilot's cabin door, a pistol in his hand.

Suddenly the girl started screaming as she got to her feet. 'They'll *kill* us! Oh, God! Why did you do it?'

Stunned, Fontine stared at the girl and spoke quietly with what breath he had left. '*You?* You can ask that?'

'Yes! Oh, my God!' She pulled her filthy coat around her as best she could. 'They'll kill me. I don't want to die!'

'You don't want to live like *that.*'

She returned his stare maniacally, her head trembling.

'They took me from the camps,' she whispered. 'I understood. They gave me drugs when I needed them, wanted them.' She pulled at her loose right sleeve; there were scores of needle marks from her wrist to her upper arm. 'But I understood. And I lived!'

'*Bestia!*' roared Victor stepping towards the girl, raising his hand. 'Whether you live or die is immaterial to me. I didn't act for you!'

'Whatever you did is done,' said Lübok quickly, touching his arm. 'Snap out of it! You've had your confrontation, there can be no more. Understand?'

Fontine saw the strength in Lübok's eyes. Breathing heavily, Victor pointed in astonishment at the fortyish corporal who stood silently by the cabin door, his weapon drawn. 'He's one of you, isn't he?'

'No,' said Lübok. 'He's a German with a conscience. He doesn't know who or what we are. At Müllheim he'll be unconscious, an innocent bystander who can tell them whatever he likes. I suspect it will be nothing. Stay with the girl.'

Lübok took charge. He went back to the bodies of the Wehrmacht and removed identification papers and weapons. In the tunic of one, he found a hypodermic kit and six vials of narcotics. He gave them to the girl, who sat by the window next to Fontine. She accepted them gratefully and without so much as looking at Victor, she proceeded to break a capsule, fill the hypodermic, and insert the needle into her left arm.

She carefully repacked the kit and shoved it into the pocket of her bloodstained coat. She leaned back and breathed deeply.

'Feel better?' asked Fontine.

She turned and looked at him. Her eyes were calmer now, only contempt showing in them. 'You don't understand, Captain. I don't *feel*. There are no feelings. One just goes on living.'

'What will you do?'

She took her eyes away from him and returned to the window. She answered him quietly, dreamily – out of contact. 'Live, if I can. It's not up to me. It's up to you.'

In the aisle the flight attendant stirred. He shook his head and got to his knees. Before he could focus, Lübok was in front of him, his gun at the attendant's head.

'If you want to stay alive, you'll do exactly as I say at Müllheim.'

Obedience was in the soldier's eyes.

Fontine got up. 'What about the girl?' he whispered.

'What about her?' countered Lübok.

'I'd like to bring her out with us.'

The Czech ran an exasperated hand through his hair. 'Oh, Christ! Well, it's that or killing her. She'd identify me for a drop of morphine.' He looked down at the girl. 'Get her to clean up. There's a raincoat in the back. She can put it on.'

'Thanks,' said Victor.

'Don't,' replied Lübok. 'I'd kill her in a second if I thought it was a better solution. But she could be valuable; she's been with a *Kommando* unit where we didn't know one existed.'

The Resistance fighters met the automobile on a back road south of Lörrach, near the Franco-Swiss border. Victor was given clean but ragged clothes to replace the German uniform. They crossed the Rhine at nightfall. The girl was taken west to a Resistance camp in the hills; she was too drugged, too erratic to make the trip south to Montbéliard.

The flight attendant was simply taken away. Fontine kept his own council. There'd been another corporal from another army on a pier in Celle Ligure.

'I leave you now,' said Lübok, crossing to him on the riverbank. The Czech's hand was extended.

Fontine was surprised. The plan had been for Lübok to go with him to Montbéliard; London might have new instructions for him. He took Lübok's hand, protesting.

'Why? I thought—'

'I know. But things change. There are problems in Wiesbaden.'

Victor held the Czech's right hand with his own, covering it with his left. 'It's difficult to know what to say. I owe you my life.'

'Whatever I did, you would have done the same. I never doubted that.'

'You're generous as well as brave.'

'That Greek priest said I was a degenerate who could blackmail half of Berlin.'

'Could you?'

'Probably,' answered Lübok quickly, looking over at a Frenchman who was beckoning him to the boat. He acknowledged with a nod of his head. He turned back to Victor. 'Listen to me,' he said softly, removing his hand. 'That priest told you something else. That I worked for Rome. You said you didn't know what that meant.'

'I don't, specifically. But I'm not blind; it has to do with the train from Salonika.'

'It has *everything* to do with it.'

'You do work for Rome, then? For the church?'

'The church is not your enemy. Believe that.'

'The Order of Xenope claims *it* is not my enemy. Yet certainly I have one. But you don't answer my question. Do you work for Rome?'

'Yes. But not in the way you think.'

'Lübok!' Fontine grabbed the middle-aged Czech by the shoulders. 'I *have* no thoughts! I don't *know*! Can't you understand that?'

Lübok stared at Victor; in the dim light his eyes were searching. 'I believe you. I gave you a dozen opportunities; you seized none of them.'

'Opportunities? *What* opportunities?'

The Frenchman by the boat called again, this time harshly. 'You! Peacock! Let's get out of here.'

'Right away,' replied Lübok, his eyes still on Fontine. 'For the last time. There are men – on both sides – who think this war is insignificant compared to the information they believe you have. In some ways I agree with them. But you don't have it, you never did. And this war must be fought. And won. In fact, your father was wiser than all of them.'

'Savarone? What do you—?'

'I go now.' Lübok raised his hands, with strength but no hostility, and removed Victor's arms. 'For these reasons, I did what I did. You'll know soon enough. That priest in the Casimir was right: there are monsters. He was one of them. There are others. But don't blame churches; they are innocent. They harbour the fanatics, but they're innocent.'

'Peacock! No more delay!'

'Coming!' said Lübok in a shouted whisper. 'Goodbye, Fontine. If for one minute I thought you were not what you say you are, I would have wracked you myself for the information. Or killed you. But you are what you are, caught in the middle. They'll leave you alone now. For a while.'

The Czech touched Victor's face briefly, gently, and ran down to the boat.

The blue lights flashed above the Montbéliard field at precisely five minutes past midnight. Instantly two rows of small flares were ignited; the runway was marked, the plane circled and made its approach.

Fontine ran across the field carrying his briefcase. By the time he reached the side of the rolling plane, the hatch was open; two men were standing in the frame, gripping the sides, their arms extended. Victor heaved the briefcase inside and reached up, making contact with the arm on his right. He ran faster, jumped, and was pulled in through the opening; he lay face down on the deck. The hatch was slammed shut, a command shouted out to the pilot, and the engines roared. The plane sprang forward, the tail of the fuselage rising in seconds and seconds later they were airborne.

Fontine raised his head and crawled to the ribbed wall opposite the hatch. He pulled the briefcase to his side and breathed deeply, letting his head fall back against the metal.

'Oh, my God!' came the words spoken in shock out of the darkness. 'It's *you*!'

Victor snapped his head to the left, in the direction of the indistinguishable figure who spoke with such alarm in his voice. The first shafts of moonlight came from the windows of the open pilot area. Fontine's eyes were drawn to the right hand of the speaker. It was encased in a black glove.

'Stone? What are you doing here?'

But Geoffrey Stone was incapable of answering. The moonlight grew brighter, illuminating the hollow shell that was the aircraft's fuselage. Stone's eyes were wide, his lips parted, immobile.

'Stone? It *is* you?'

'Oh, Jesus! We've been tricked. They've done it!'

'What are you talking about?'

The Englishman continued in a monotone. 'You were reported killed. Captured and executed in the Casimir. We were told that only one man escaped. With your papers—'

'Who?'

'The courier, Lübok.'

Victor got to his feet unsteadily, holding on to a metal brace that protruded from the wall of the vibrating aircraft. The geometric pieces were coming together. 'Where did you get this information?'

'It was relayed to us this morning.'

'By who? Who picked it up? Who relayed it?'

'The Greek embassy,' replied Stone barely above a whisper.

Fontine sank back down to the deck of the plane. Lübok had said the words.

I gave you a dozen opportunities; you seized none. There are men who think this war is insignificant . . . For these reasons I did what I did. You'll know soon enough . . . They'll leave you alone now. For a while.

Lübok had made his move. He had checked an airfield in Warsaw before daybreak and sent a false message to London.

It did not take a great deal of imagination to know what that message accomplished.

'We're immobilized. We've exposed ourselves and been taken out. We all watch each other now, but no one can make a move, or admit what we're looking for. No one can afford that.' Brevourt spoke as he stood by the leaded window overlooking the courtyard in Alien Operations. 'Checkmate.'

Across the room, standing by the long conference table, was a furious Alec Teague. They were alone.

'I don't give a *damn*. What concerns me is your blatant manipulation of Military Intelligence! You've placed an entire network in jeopardy. Loch Torridon may well have been crippled!'

'Create another strategy,' said Brevourt absently, looking out of the window. 'It's your job, isn't it?'

'Damn you!'

'For God's sake, Teague, *stop* it!' Brevourt reeled from the window. 'Do you for one minute think I was the final authority?'

'I think you compromised that authority! I should have been consulted!'

Brevourt started to reply, then stopped. He nodded his head as he walked slowly across the room to the table opposite Teague. 'You may be right, general. Tell me, you're the expert. What was our mistake?'

'Lübok,' said the brigadier coldly. 'He failed you. He took your money and turned to Rome, then made up his own mind. He was the wrong man.'

'He was your man. From your files.'

'Not for that job. You interfered.'

'He can go anywhere in Europe,' continued Brevourt almost plaintively, as if Teague had not interrupted. 'He's untouchable. If Fontini-Cristi broke away, Lübok could have followed him anywhere. Even into Switzerland.'

'You expected that, didn't you?'

'Frankly, yes. You're too good a salesman, general. I believed you. I thought Loch Torridon *was* Fontini-Cristi's brainchild. How logical it all seemed. The Italian goes back under perfect cover to make his own arrangements.' Brevourt sat down wearily, clasping his hands in front of him on the table.

'Didn't it occur to you that if such was the case, he would have come to us? To you?'

'No. We couldn't return his lands or his factories.'

'You don't know him,' concluded Teague with finality. 'You never took the trouble. That was your first mistake.'

'Yes, I expect it was. I've lived most of my life with liars. The corridors of mendacity. The simple truth is elusive.' Brevourt suddenly looked up at the Intelligence man. His face was pathetic, his pallid skin taut, the hollows of his eyes proof of exhaustion. 'You didn't believe it, did you? You didn't believe he was dead.'

'No.'

'I couldn't take the chance, you see. I accepted what you said, that the Germans wouldn't execute him, that they'd put a trace on him, find out who he was, use him. But the report said otherwise. So, if he *was* dead, it meant the fanatics in Rome or Xenope had killed him. They wouldn't do that unless – *unless* – they'd learned his secret.'

'And if they had, the vault would be theirs. Not yours. Not England's. It was never yours to begin with.'

The ambassador looked away from Teague and sank back in the chair, closing his eyes. 'Nor could it be allowed to fall into the hands of maniacs. Not now. We know who the maniac is in Rome. The Vatican will watch Donatti now. The Patriarchate will suspend activities; we've been given assurance.'

'Which was Lübok's objective, of course.'

Brevourt opened his eyes. 'Was it really?'

'In my judgement, yes. Lübok's a Jew.'

Brevourt turned his head and stared at Teague. 'There'll be no more interference, general. Get on with your war. Mine is at a stand-off.'

Anton Lübok crossed Prague's Wenceslaus Square and walked up the steps of the bombed-out cathedral. Inside, the late afternoon sun streaked through the huge gaps of stone where *Luftwaffe* bombs had exploded. Whole sections of the left wall were destroyed; primitive scaffolds had been erected everywhere for support.

He stood in the far right aisle and checked his watch. It was time.

An old priest came out of the curtained apse and crossed in front of the confessional booths. He paused briefly at the fourth. It was Lübok's signal.

He walked down the aisle cautiously, his attention on the dozen or so worshippers in the church. None was watching him. He parted the curtains and walked inside the confessional. He knelt before the tiny Bohemian crucifix, the flickering light of the prayer candle throwing shadows on the draped walls.

'Forgive me, Father, for I have sinned,' Lübok began softly. 'I have sinned in excess. I have debased the body and blood of Christ.'

'One cannot debase the Son of God,' came the proper reply from behind the drapes. 'One can only debase oneself.'

'But we are in the image of God. As was Himself.'

'A poor and imperfect image,' was the correct response.

Lübok exhaled slowly, the exercise was completed. 'You are Rome?'

'I am the conduit,' said the voice in quiet arrogance.

'I didn't think you were the city, you damn fool.'

'This is the house of God. Watch your tongue.'

'And you revile this house,' whispered Lübok. 'All who work for Donatti revile it!'

'*Silence.* We are the way of Christ!'

'You're *dirt!* Your Christ would spit on you.'

The breathing beyond the drapes was filled with controlled loathing. 'I shall pray for your soul,' came the forced words. 'What of Fontini-Cristi?'

'He had no other purpose but Loch Torridon. Your projections were wrong.'

'That won't do!' The priest's whisper was strident. 'He had to have other objectives! We're positive!'

'He never left my side from the moment we met in Montbéliard. There were no additional contacts other than those we knew about.'

'*No!* We don't believe that!'

'In a matter of days it won't make any difference what you believe. You're finished. All of you. Good men will see to it.'

'What have you done, *Jew*?' The voice behind the drapes was low now, the loathing absolute.

'What had to be done, priest.' Lübok rose to his feet and put his left hand into his pocket. With his right he suddenly ripped the drapes in front of him.

The priest was revealed. He was huge, the black robes giving him the appearance of immensity. His face was the face of a man who hated deeply; the eyes were the eyes of a predator.

Lübok withdrew an envelope from his pocket and dropped it on the prayer stall in front of the stunned priest. 'Here's your money. Give it back to Donatti. I wanted to see what you looked like.'

The priest answered quietly. 'You'd better know the rest. My name is Gaetamo. Enrici Gaetamo. And I'll come back for you.'

'I doubt it,' replied Lübok.

'Don't,' said Enrici Gaetamo.

Lübok stood for a moment looking down at the priest. When their eyes were locked, the blond-haired Czech wet the fingers of his right hand and reached for the prayer candle, extinguishing its flame. All was darkness. He parted the drapes and walked out of the confessional.

PART FOUR

CHAPTER TWELVE

The cottage was in the grounds of a large estate west of Aylesbury in Bucks. Tall metal poles strung with electrified barbed wire surrounded the area. Killer dogs guarded the enormous compound.

There was only one entrance, a gate at the base of a long, straight driveway flanked by open lawns. At the main house, a quarter of a mile from the gate, the drive split off right and left, then split again with several smaller roads leading to the various cottages.

There were fourteen cottages in all, houses built in and around the woods of the estate. The residents were men and women who needed the security: defectors and their families, double agents, couriers who'd been exposed – targets who'd been marked for an assassin's bullet.

Jane's cottage became their home and Victor was grateful for its remoteness. For nightly the *Luftwaffe* streaked through the skies, the fires of London grew, the battle for Britain had begun.

And so had Loch Torridon.

For weeks at a time, Victor was away from their miniature house in Oxfordshire, away from Jane, his mind at rest because she was safe. Teague moved the Loch Torridon headquarters into the cellars of MI6. Day and night had no essential meaning. Men worked around the clock with files and shortwave radios, and with complicated equipment that reproduced perfectly the documents required in the occupied lands: work papers, travel permits, clearances from the *Reichsministerium* of Armaments and Industry. Other men were called into the cellars and given their instructions by Captains Fontine and Stone. And they were sent to Lakenheath and beyond.

As was Victor on a growing number of occasions. At such times, he knew Alec Teague was right: *Your wife's safety is directly related to your state of mind. You have a job to do; I'll do mine.*

Jane could not be touched by the maniacs of Rome or Xenope. It was all that mattered. The freight from Salonika became a strange, painful memory. And the war went on.

24 Aug 1940
ANTWERP

> (Intercepted dispatch – duplicate – Commandant: Occupation Forces, Antwerp, to Reichsminister Speer, Armaments.)

The railroad yards at Antwerp are in chaos! Supply trains crossing Schelde River are overloaded through carelessness in shipping orders, causing cracks throughout bridge structure. Schedules and signalling codes altered without proper notice. From offices managed by *German personnel*! Reprisals ludicrous. No alien responsibility. Trains meet one another from opposing directions on the same tracks! Freights pull up for loading at sidings and depots where there are no trucks! No shipments! The situation is intolerable and I must insist that the *Reichsministerium* coordinate more thoroughly . . .

19 Sept 1940
VERDUN-SUR-MEUSE

> (Excerpts from letter received by the second command legal officer of *Gesetzbuch Besitzergreifung* from a Colonel Grep-

schedit, Verdun-Meuse.)

... It was agreed that we prepare specific rules of occupation to adjudicate disputes between ourselves and the conquered who laid down their arms. These regulations were circulated. We now find additional regulations – circulated by *your* offices – that contradict whole sections of the previous codes. We are in constant debate with even those who *welcome* us! Entire days are taken up with occupation hearings. Our own officers are faced with conflicting orders from your couriers – all under proper signatures and validated by your seals. We are at a boiling point over inconsequentials. We are going out of our minds ...

20 March 1941
BERLIN

(Extracted minutes of the meeting between accounts stabilizers of the *Finanzministerium* and the officials of *Reichsordnung*. File removed – duplicate.)

... The substance of Ordnance's unending difficulties are to be found with the *Finanzministerium*'s consistent errors in funds allocations. Accounts go unsettled for months, payrolls are miscalculated, monies are transferred to wrong dispersal depots – often to wrong geographical sectors! Whole battalions have gone without pay because the funds were somewhere in Yugoslavia when they should have been in Amsterdam! ...

23 June 1941
BREST-LITOVSK

(Courier dispatch from General Guderian to his commander, General Bock, Hdqtrs: Pripet, Poland. Intercept: Bialystok. Not delivered.)

... In two days of the offensive we are within forty-eight hours of Minsk. The Dnieper will be crossed in a matter of weeks, the Don and Moscow not far beyond! The speed of our assault requires instant communications – in the main – radio communications, but there are increasing difficulties with our radio equipment. Specifically in what the engineers tell me is frequency calibration. More than half our divisional equipment is set in differing graduations. Unless extreme caution is taken, communications are sent out on unintended frequencies, often *enemy* frequencies. It is a factory problem. Our concern is that it is impossible to determine which equipment was malfunctioning calibrations. I, myself, initiated a communication to Kleist on Rundstedt's south flank and reached our forces in eastern Lithuania . . .

2 Feb 1942
BERLIN

(Removed from correspondence file of Manfried Probst, official, *Reichsindustrie*, from Hiru Kayanaka, attaché, Japanese Embassy, Berlin.)

Dear Reichsoffiziell Probst:
Since we are now comrades in battle as well as spirit we must attempt to strive further for the perfection expected of us by our leaders.

To the subject at hand, my dear *Reichsoffiziell*. As you know, our respective governments have entered into joint radar development experiments.

We flew – at great risk – our foremost electronic scientists to Berlin to enter conferences with your people. That was six weeks ago and to date there have been no conferences whatsoever. I am now informed that our foremost scientists were flown to Greifswald on the Baltic Sea by error. They are not concerned with the rocket experiments, but with radar, my dear *Reichsoffiziell*. Unfortunately, none speak your language and the interpreters you assigned are less than fluent in ours.

Word reached my desk an hour ago that our foremost scientists are now on their way to Würzburg, where there are radio transmitters. My dear *Reichsoffiziell*, we do not know where Würzburg is. And our foremost scientists are not concerned with radio transmitters, but with *radar!*

Can you please locate our foremost scientists? When are the radar conferences? Our foremost scientists are travelling all over Germany for what purpose? . . .

25 May 1942
ST VALÉRY-EN-CAUX

> (Report filed by Captain Victor Fontine, who was dropped behind lines in the Héricourt district. Returned by trawler, Isle of Wight.)

. . . The armaments shipments along the coastal regions are primarily offensive in nature, with little thought at this point given to defensive weapons. The shipments are routed from Essen, through Düsseldorf, across the border to Roubaix and then to the French coast. The key is fuel. We have placed our people in the petrol depots. They are receiving continuous 'instructions' from the *Reichsministerium* of Industry to divert shipments of fuel immediately out of Brussels to Rotterdam, where rails will begin the journey to the Russian front. At last report, there were fourteen miles of standard armaments vehicles choking the roads between Louvain and Brussels, their tanks empty. And, of course, no reprisals. We estimate that the ploy will be operable for another four days, at which point Berlin will be forced to move in and our people will move out. Coordinate air strikes at this time . . .

(Note: Loch Torridon Command. For record. Cleared, Brigadier General Teague. Captain Victor Fontine granted leave upon return from Wight. Recommendation for majority approved—)

Fontine sped out of London on the Hempstead road towards Oxfordshire. He thought the debriefing session with Teague and Stone would never end! *God!* The repetitions! His co-administrator, Stone, was always furious when he returned from one of his trips behind the German lines. It was work Stone had been trained to do, but now was impossible for him. His shattered hand ruled out such incursions and he spent his rage on Victor. He would subject Fontine to rapid, harsh, repetitive interrogation, looking for errors in every phase of a mission. What charity Victor once felt for the cryptographer had disappeared over the months. Months? Mother of Christ, it was nearly two and a half years!

But tonight Stone's delaying tactics were unforgivable. The *Luftwaffe* strikes over England had lessened, but they had not disappeared. Should the air raid sirens begin, it might be impossible to drive out of London.

And Jane was nearly due. The doctors had said it was a matter of a fortnight. That was a week ago, when he had flown out of Lakenheath to France and dropped into the grazing fields of Héricourt.

He reached the outskirts of Aylesbury and looked at his watch, holding it under the dim light of the dashboard. It was twenty minutes past two in the morning. They would both laugh at that; he was always coming back to her at ridiculous hours.

But he was coming back. He'd be at the compound in ten minutes.

Behind him, in the distance, he could hear the wail of the sirens rising and falling in plaintive fugues. There was not the jolting, breath-catching anxiety that used to accompany the terrible sound. The sound itself had taken on a weariness; repetition had dulled its terror.

He swung the wheel of the automobile to the right; he was now on the back road that led to the Oxfordshire estate. Another two or three miles and he'd be with his wife. His foot pressed down on the accelerator. There were no cars on the road; he could speed.

Instinctively, his ears listened for the distant rumbling

of the bombing. But there was no faraway thunder, only the incessant whines of the sirens. Suddenly, there were sounds intruding where no sounds should be; he caught his breath, realizing instantly the return of forgotten anxiety. He wondered for a moment whether his exhaustion was causing tricks to be played . . .

It was no trick! No trick at all! The sounds were overhead and unmistakable. He'd heard them too often, both over London and across the Channel in scores of different, covert locations.

Heinkel aircraft. Twin-engine, German, long-range bombers. They'd passed London. And if London was bypassed, it was a good bet that the Heinkels would take a northwest heading towards the Birmingham district and the munitions factories.

My God! The aircraft were *losing altitude*. They were pitching down in rapid descent.

Directly *above* him!

In *front* of him!

A bombing run! An airstrike in the countryside of *Oxfordshire*! What in God's name? . . .

Jesus! Oh, Jesus Christ!

The compound!

The one place in England without parallel in security. From the ground, but *not* from the skies!

A low-altitude air strike had been called against the compound!

Fontine held the accelerator to the floor, his body trembling, his breath coming in short, spurting expulsions, his eyes riveted to the onrushing road.

The skies exploded. The screams of diving aircraft mingled with the manmade thunder: detonation after detonation. Immense flashes of white and yellow – jagged, shapeless, horrible – filled the open spaces above and between the woods of Oxfordshire.

He reached the compound's gate, tyres screeching as he braked the car into a turn. The iron gates were open.

Evacuation.

He stabbed the pedal to the floor and sped into the long straight drive. Beyond, fires were everywhere, explosions everywhere, people running in panic – everywhere.

The main house had taken a direct hit. The entire left front wall was blown out; the roof was collapsing in weirdly shapeless splendour, bricks and stones cascading to the grounds. Smoke spread in vertical swirls of black and grey – fires beyond, spurting upwards, jagged, yellow, terrifying.

A deafening crash; the car lurched, the ground swelled, the windows shattered, hurling fragments of glass – everywhere. Fontine felt blood streaking down his face, but he could see and that was all that mattered.

The bomb had struck less than fifty yards to his right. In the light of the fires he could see the ripped-out earth of the lawn. He swung the car to the right, skirting the crater, cutting across the grass towards the dirt road that led to their cottage. Bombs did not strike twice in the same zero target, he thought.

The road was blocked; trees had fallen, fires consuming them – everywhere.

He lurched out of the car and raced between the flaming barriers. He saw their cottage. A huge oak had been blown out of the ground, its massive trunk crashed into a pipe-tiled roof.

'*Jane! Jane!*'

God of hatred, do not do this to me! Do not do this to me again!

He smashed through the door, sending it hurtling off its hinges. Inside was total wreckage; tables, lamps, chairs were scattered, overturned, broken into a thousand fragments. Fires were burning – on the couch, in the open roof where the oak had crashed.

'*Jane!*'

'Here . . .'

Her voice came from the kitchen. He raced through the narrow doorway and felt for an instant that he should fall to his knees in supplication. Jane stood gripping the edge of the counter, her back to him, her body shaking, her head nodding up and down. He rushed to her and held her shoulders, his face against her cheek, the spastic rhythm of her movements uninterrupted.

'My darling.'

'Vittorio . . .' Suddenly Jane contracted violently, gasping as she did so. 'Sheets . . . Sheets, my love. And blankets, I think. I'm not sure, really—'

'Don't talk.' He picked her up and saw the pain in her face in the darkness. 'I'll take you to the clinic. There's a clinic, a doctor, nurses—'

'We can't get there!' she screamed. 'Do as I say.' She coughed in a spasm of pain. 'I'll show you. Carry me.'

In her hand she gripped a knife. Hot water had been running over the blade; she had been prepared to give birth alone.

Through the incessant detonations, Victor could hear the aircraft ascending, scrambling to higher altitudes. The strike was coming to an end; the distant, furious whines of Spitfires converging into the sector was a signal no *Luftwaffe* pilot overlooked.

He did as his wife told him to do, holding her in his arms, awkwardly gathering up whatever she ordered.

He kicked his way through the wreckage and the spreading flames and carried his wife out of the door. Like an animal seeking sanctuary, he hurried into the woods and found a lair that was their own.

They were together. The frenzy of death that was

several hundred yards away could not deter life. He delivered his wife of two male infants.

The sons of Fontini-Cristi were born.

Smoke spiralled up lazily, vertical coils of dignified, dead vapour interrupting the shafts of early morning sunlight. Stretchers were everywhere. Blankets covered the faces of the dead; the living and partly living were staring upward, mouths open, the shock imbedded. Ambulances were everywhere. And fire engines and police vehicles.

Jane was in an ambulance, a mobile medical unit, they called it. His sons were with their mother.

The doctor came out of the lean-to canvas extension of the strange vehicle and walked across the short stretch of lawn towards Victor. The doctor's face was haggard; he had escaped death but he lived with the dying.

'She's had a hard time of it, Fontine. I told her she would under normal circumstances—'

'Will she be all right?' interrupted Victor.

'Yes, she'll be all right. However, she'll need a long, *long* rest. I told her several months ago I suspected a multiple birth. She was not – shall I say – designed for such a delivery. In some ways it's rather amazing that she made it.'

Fontine stared at the man. 'She never mentioned that to me.'

'Didn't think she would. You're in a precarious business. Can't have too much on your mind.'

'May I see her?'

'Not for a while. She's solidly corked off; the infants are quiet. Let her be.'

The doctor's hand was gently on his arm, leading him away from the ambulance towards what remained of the main house. An officer approached them and took Victor aside.

'We found what we were looking for. We knew it was

here, or something like it. The strike was far too accurate. Even German instruments couldn't do it, and night pilotage was out; we checked. There were no markings, no flares.'

'Where are we going? What are you talking about?' Victor had heard the officer speak, but the words were elliptical.

'. . . high-arc transmitter.'

The words still did not penetrate. 'I'm sorry. What did you say?'

'I said the room's still standing. It's at the rear of the right wing. The bastard was operating a simple high-arc transmitter.'

'A transmitter?'

'Yes. That's how the Huns came in on pinpoint. They were guided by a radio beam. The chaps at MI5 and MI6 had no objection to my showing you. As a matter of fact, I think they were pleased. They're afraid with all the confusion here someone'll disturb things. You can confirm that we haven't.'

They threaded their way through the rubble and the intermittent piles of smoking debris to the right side of the large house. The major opened the door and they turned right down a corridor that seemed to be newly partitioned, as if for offices.

'A radio beam could bring a squadron into the area,' said Fontine, walking beside the officer. 'But only the area, not the target. These were bombers. I was on the road; they dove to the lowest levels. They would need more sophisticated equipment than a simple high-arc—'

'When I said there were no markings, no flares,' interrupted the major, 'I meant in a pattern; points A to B to C. Once they were over the target area, the bastard simply opened his window and shot up fireworks. He *did* use flares then. A fucking box full, from what we've found on the ground.'

At the end of the corridor a door was flanked by two uniformed guards. The officer opened it and stepped inside; Victor followed.

The room was immaculate, miraculously no part of the surrounding carnage. On a table against the wall was an open briefcase, a circular aerial protruding out of it, attached to radio equipment beneath, secured in the case.

The officer gestured to his left, to the bed, not at first visible from the doorway.

Fontine froze. His eyes locked on the sight now in front of him.

On the bed was the body of a man, the back of his head blown off, a pistol beside his right hand. In his left hand was gripped a large crucifix.

The man was in the black robes of a priest.

'Damned strange,' said the major. 'His papers said he was a member of some Greek monastic brotherhood. The Order of Xenope.'

CHAPTER THIRTEEN

He vowed it! There would be no more.

Jane and their two infant sons were taken secretly to Scotland. North of Glasgow, to an isolated house in the countryside of Dunblane. Victor would not rely on compounds *without-parallel-in-security*, nor on any guarantees from MI6 or the British government. Instead, he used his own funds, employed former soldiers, exhaustively screened by himself, and turned the house and grounds into a small but impenetrable fortress. He would not tolerate Teague's suggestions *or* objections *or* excuses. He was being pursued by forces he could not understand, an enemy beyond control, removed from the war and yet part of it.

He wondered if it would be so for the rest of his life. Mother of Christ, why didn't they believe him? How could he reach the fanatics and the killers and roar his denials? He knew nothing! *Nothing!* A train had left Salonika three years ago, at dawn on the ninth of December 1939, and he knew *nothing*! Only of its existence. Nothing more!

'Do you intend to remain here for the rest of the war?' Teague had come up to Dunblane for the day; they walked in the gardens behind the house, in sight of the high brick wall and the guards. It had been five months since they'd seen each other, although Victor permitted calls over redirected scrambler-telephones. He was too much a part of Loch Torridon; his knowledge was vital.

'You have no hold over me, Alec. I'm not British. I've sworn no allegiance to you.'

'I never thought that was necessary. I did make you a major, however,' Teague smiled.

Victor laughed. 'Without ever having been formally inducted into the service? You're a disgrace to military tradition.'

'Absolutely. I get things done.' The brigadier stopped. He bent over to pick up a long blade of grass and rose, looking at Fontine. 'Stone can't do it alone.'

'Why not? You and I talk several times a week. I tell you what I can. Stone expedites the decisions. It's a sound arrangement.'

'It's not the same and you know it.'

'It will have to do. I can't fight two wars.' Fontine paused, remembering. 'Savarone was right.'

'Who?'

'My father. He must have known that whatever was on that train could make men enemies even when they fought for a common survival.'

They reached the edge of the path. A guard was thirty yards away across the lawn by the wall; he smiled and stroked the fur of a leashed Great Dane that snarled at the sight and scent of the stranger.

'One day it will have to be resolved,' said Teague. 'You, Jane, the children: You can't live with it for the rest of your lives.'

'I've said that to myself more times than I can count. But I'm not sure how it can be.'

'Perhaps I do. At least, I'm willing to try. And I have at my disposal the finest Intelligence service in existence.'

Victor glanced at him, interested. 'Where would you start?'

'The question is not where, but when.'

'Then, *when*?'

'When this war is over.'

'Please, Alec. No more words, no strategies. Or tricks.'

'No tricks. A simple, uncomplicated agreement. I need you. The war has turned; Loch Torridon enters its most important phase. I intend to see that it does its job.'

'You're obsessed.'

'So are you. Quite rightfully. But you'll learn nothing of "Salonika" – that's Brevourt's code name, incidentally – until this war is won, take my word for it. And the war *will* be won.'

Fontine held Teague's eyes with his own. 'I want facts, not rhetoric.'

'Very well. We have identities you don't have, nor, for your own safety and the safety of your family, will I reveal them to you.'

'The man in the car? In Kensington, Campo di Fiori. The streak of white? The *executioner*?'

'Yes.'

Victor held his breath, controlling a nearly overpowering urge to grab the Englishman and force the words from him: 'You've taught me to kill; I could kill you for that.'

'To what end? I'd protect you with my life, and you know it. The point is, he's immobilized. Under control. If, indeed, he *was* the executioner.'

Victor let his breath out slowly. The muscles in his jaw ached from the tension. 'What other identities?'

'Two elders of the Patriarchate. Through Brevourt. They command the Order of Xenope.'

'Then they're responsible for *Oxfordshire*. My *God*, how can you—?'

'They're *not*,' interrupted Teague quickly. 'They were, if possible, more shocked that we were. As was pointed out, the last thing they wanted was your death.'

'The man who guided those planes was a priest! From Xenope!'

'Or someone made to appear so.'

'He killed himself,' said Fontine softly, 'in the prescribed manner.'

'No one has a quota on fanatics.'

'Go on.' Victor began walking back on the path, away from the guard and the dog.

'These people are the worst kind of extremists. They're mystics; they believe they're involved in a holy war. Their war permits only confrontation by violence, not negotiation. But we know the pressure points, those whose word cannot be disobeyed. We can bring about a confrontation through Whitehall pressure, if need be, and demand a resolution. At least one that removes you from their concerns – once and for all. You can't do this by yourself. We can. Will you come back?'

'If I do, all this will be set in motion? I, myself, a part of the planning?'

'We'll mount it with the precision we mounted Loch Torridon.'

'Has my cover in London been kept absolute?'

'Not a dent. You're somewhere in Wales. All our telephone calls are placed to the Swansea area and tripped north. Mail is regularly sent to a post office box in the village of Gwynliffen, where it's quietly put in other envelopes and returned only to me. Right now, if I'm needed, Stone places a call to a Swansea number.'

'No one knows where we are? *No one?*'

'Not even Churchill.'

'I'll talk with Jane.'

'One thing,' said Teague, his hand on Fontine's arm. 'I've given my word to Brevourt. There'll be no more trips across the Channel for you.'

'She'll like that.'

Loch Torridon flourished. The principle of mismanagement-at-all-costs became a thorn in the German craw.

In the Mannheim printing plants, 130,000 *Commandant Manuals for Occupation* came off the presses with all negatives dropped in vital restrictions. Shipments to the Messerschmitt factories in Frankfurt were routed to the Stuka assembly lines in Leipzig. In Kalach on the Russian front, it was found that three quarters of the radio equipment now operated on varying frequency calibrations. In the Krupp plants at Essen, engineering miscalculations resulted in malfunctions in the firing mechanisms of all cannon with the bore number 712. In Kraków, Poland, in the uniform factories, fabric bypassed a chemical saturation process and 200,000 units were sent out, subject to instant flammability. In Turin, Italy, where the Germans ran the aircraft plants, designs were implemented that caused metal fatigue after twenty hours of flight; entire sections of squadrons structurally collapsed in midair.

In late April of 1944, Loch Torridon concentrated on the offshore patrols throughout the coastal zones of Normandy. A strategy was conceived that would alter the petrol schedules as they were issued to the German naval personnel from the base at Pointe de Barfleur. Brigadier General Teague brought the report to Supreme Headquarters, Allied Command, and handed it personally to Dwight Eisenhower.

The German coastal predawn patrols will be removed from Normandy zones during the first eleven days in June. That is the calendar target. Repeat: 1 June through 11 June.

The supreme commander responded appropriately. 'I'll be goddamned ...'

Overlord was executed and the invading parties progressed. Under Badoglio and Grandi, the outlines of the Italian surrender and the deposition of Mussolini were negotiated in Lisbon.

It was a trip Alec Teague permitted Major Fontine. He was entitled to it.

And in a small room in Lisbon, a weary Badoglio faced Victor. 'So the son of Fontini-Cristi brings us our ultimatum. There must be a certain gratification in that for you.'

'No,' replied Victor simply. 'Merely contempt.'

26 Jul 1944
WOLFSSCHANZE

(Excerpts from the Gestapo investigation of the assassination attempt on Adolf Hitler at the Wolfsschanze High Command Headquarters. File removed and destroyed.)

... The aides of the traitor, Gen. Claus von Stauffenberg, have broken. They described a widespread conspiracy implicating such generals as Olbricht, von Falkenhausen, Hoepner, and possibly Kluge and Rommel. This conspiracy could not have been coordinated without enemy assistance. All normal channels of communications were avoided. A network of unknown couriers was employed, and a code name surfaced, unheard of previously. It is of Scottish origin, the name of a district or a village: Loch Torridon ... We have captured ...

Alec Teague stood in front of the map on his office wall. Fontine sat dejectedly in the chair by Teague's desk, his eyes on the general across the room.

'It was a gamble,' said Teague. 'We lost. Can't expect to win every time. You've had too few losses, that's your trouble, you're not used to them.' He removed three pins from the map and walked back to his desk. He sat down slowly and rubbed his eyes. 'Loch Torridon has been an extremely effective operation. We have every reason to be proud.'

Fontine was startled. 'Past tense?'

'Yes. The Allied ground offensive towards the Rhine

will commence maximum effort by October first. The Supreme Command wants no complications; they anticipate widespread defections. We're a complication, possibly a detriment. Loch Torridon will be phased out over the next two months. Terminated by the end of September.'

Victor watched Teague as the brigadier made the pronouncement. A part of the old soldier died with the words. It was painful to watch Alec. Loch Torridon was his moment in the military sun; he would get no nearer, and jealousies were not out of the question regarding its termination. But decisions had been made; they were irrevocable, and to fight them *was* out of the question. Teague was a soldier.

Fontine examined his own thoughts. At first he experienced neither elation nor depression; more a suspension, as if time were abruptly arrested. Then slowly, painfully, there was the momentary feeling of what now? Where is my purpose? What do I do?

And then suddenly these vague concerns were swiftly replaced. The obsession that was never far from his mind came sharply into focus. He got out of the chair and stood in front of Alec's desk. 'Then I call in your debt,' he said quietly to Teague. 'There's another operation that must be mounted "with all the precision of Loch Torridon". That's the way you phrased it.'

'It will be. I gave you my word. The Germans can't last a year; surrender feelers already come from the generals. Six, eight months, and the war will be over. "Salonika" will be mounted then. With all the precision of Loch Torridon.'

CHAPTER FOURTEEN

It took twelve weeks to close the books and bring the men back to England. Loch Torridon was finished; twenty-two cabinets of accomplishments were all that remained. They were put under lock and seal and stored in the vaults of Military Intelligence.

Fontine returned to the isolated compound in Scotland. To Jane and the twins. Andrew and Adrian, named for the British saint and any of several acceptable Romans. But they were neither saintly nor imperial; they were two and a half years old, with all the energy that age implied.

Victor had been surrounded by the children of his brothers all his adult life, but these were *his*. In themselves they were different. They alone would carry on the Fontini-Cristis. Jane could have no more children; the doctors had agreed. The injuries sustained in Oxfordshire were too extensive.

It was strange. After four years of furious activity and strain he was suddenly, abruptly, totally passive. The five months in '42 when he'd remained in Dunblane could not be considered a period of tranquillity. Jane's recovery had been slow and dangerous; the fortifying of the compound had obsessed him. There'd been no let-up of pressure then.

There was now. And the transition was unbearable. As unbearable as the wait for 'Salonika' to begin. It was the inactivity that gnawed at him; he was not a man for idleness. In spite of Jane and the children, Dunblane became his prison. There were men outside, across the Channel, deep within Europe and the Mediterranean, who sought him as intensely as he sought them. There was nothing until that movement could begin.

Teague would not go back on his word, Victor understood that. But neither would he deviate from it. The end of the war would mark the commencement of the strategy that would lead to the men of Salonika. Not before. With each new victory, each new penetration within Germany, Fontine's mind raced. The war *was* won; it was not over, but it was won. Lives all over the world had to be picked up, the pieces put back together and decisions made, for years of living had to be faced. For him, for Jane, everything depended on the forces that sought a vault that came out of Greece five years ago – at dawn on the ninth of December.

The inactivity was his own particular hell.

During the waiting he had reached one decision: he would not return to Campo di Fiori after the war. When he thought of his house and looked at his wife, he saw other wives slain in the white mists of light. When he saw his sons, he saw other sons, helpless, terrified, riddled by gunfire. The tortures of the mind were too vivid still. He could not live at Campo di Fiori. He could not go back to the killing ground, or to anything or anyone associated with it. They would build a new life somewhere else. The Fontini-Cristi Industries would be returned to him, the Court of Reparations in Rome had sent word to London.

And he had sent word back through MI6. The factories, the plants, all lands and properties – except Campo di Fiori – would go to the highest bidder. He would make separate arrangements for Campo di Fiori.

It was the night of 10 March. The children were asleep across the hall; the last of the winter winds blew in gusts outside the windows of their bedroom. Victor and Jane lay under the covers, the coals in the fireplace throwing an orange glow on the ceiling. And they talked quietly, as they always talked in the final hours of the day.

'Barclays will handle everything,' said Victor. 'It's a simple auction, really. I've put a cellar on the total; however they want to divide the entire purchase is up to them.'

'Are there buyers?' asked Jane, lying on her elbow, looking at him.

Fontine laughed softly. 'Packs of them. Mostly in Switzerland, mostly American. There are fortunes to be made in the reconstruction. Those who have manufacturing bases will have the advantage.'

'You sound like an economist.'

'I sincerely hope so. My father would be terribly disappointed if I didn't.' He fell silent. Jane touched his forehead, brushing aside his hair.

'What's the matter?'

'Just thinking. It'll be over with soon. First the war, then "Salonika"; that will be finished too. I trust Alec. He'll bring it off if he has to blackmail all the diplomats in the Foreign Office. The fanatics will be forced to accept the fact that I don't know a damn thing about their ungodly train.'

'I thought it was supposed to be awfully godly.' She smiled.

'Inconceivable.' He shook his head. 'What kind of god would allow it?'

'Checkmate, my darling.'

Victor raised himself on the pillow. He looked over at the windows; a March snow was silently careering off the dark panes of glass, carried by the winds. He turned to his wife. 'I can't go back to Italy.'

'I know. You've told me. I understand.'

'But I don't want to stay here. In England. Here I will

218

always be Fontini-Cristi. Son of the massacred family of *padroni*. Equal parts reality, legend, and myth.'

'You *are* Fontini-Cristi.'

Victor looked down at Jane in the dim light of the fire. 'No. For five years now I've been Fontine. I've got rather used to it. What do you think?'

'It doesn't lose too much in the translation,' said Jane, smiling again. 'Except, perhaps, a flavour of landed gentry.'

'That's part of what I mean,' he replied quickly. 'Andrew and Adrian shouldn't be burdened with such nonsense. Times are not what they were; those days will never return.'

'Probably not. It's a little sad to see them go, but it's for the best, I suppose.' His wife suddenly blinked her eyes and looked questioningly up at him. 'If not Italy, *or* England, then where?'

'America. Would you live in America?'

Jane stared at him, her eyes still searching. 'Of course, I think that's very exciting . . . Yes, it's right. For all of us.'

'And the name? You don't mind really, do you?'

She laughed, reaching up to touch his face. 'It doesn't matter. I married a man, not a name.'

'You matter,' he said, pulling her to him.

Harold Latham walked out of the old, brass-grilled elevator and looked at the arrows and the numbers on the wall. He had been transferred to the Burma theatre three years ago; it had been that long since he'd been in the corridors of MI6-London.

He tugged at the jacket of his new suit. He was a civilian now; he had to keep reminding himself of that. Soon there would be thousands upon thousands of civilians – *new* civilians. Germany had collapsed. He'd wagered five pounds that the formal announcement of surrender would come before the first of May. There were three days to go, and he didn't give a damn about the five quid. It was over; that was all that mattered.

He started walking down the hallway towards Stone's office. Good old, poor old, angry Geoff Stone. The *Apple* to his *Pear*. Rotten fucking luck it was, old Apple's hand shot to bits because of a high-handed guinea; and so early on, too.

Still, it bloody well might have saved his life. An awful lot of two-handed operatives never came back. In some ways Stone was damned fortunate. As he had been fortunate. He had a few pieces of metal in his back and stomach, but if he was careful they said he'd do fine. Practically normal, they said. Discharged him early, too.

Apple and Pear had survived. They'd made it! *Goddamn*, that called for a month of whiskies!

He had tried to call Stone but hadn't been able to reach him. He telephoned for two straight hours, both the flat and the office, but there was never an answer. There was no point in leaving messages; his own plans were so ragtail he wasn't sure how long he could stay in London.

It was better this way. Just barge in and demand to know why old Apple had taken so long to win the war.

The door was locked. He knocked; there was no answer. *Damn!* The front desk had Stone checked in; that was to say he hadn't checked *out* last night, or the night before, which was not unusual these days. Office couches were beds these days. All the Intelligence services were working around the clock, going through files, destroying records that could be embarrassing, and probably saving a few thousand lives in the process. When the dust of victory and defeat settled, informers were the least popular survivors.

He knocked louder. Nothing.

Yet there was light shining through the thin, lateral

crack at the base of the door. Perhaps Stone had stepped out for a minute. To the W.C. or the cafeteria.

And then Latham's eyes strayed to the round lock cylinder. There was something odd, something wrong. A speck of dull grey seemed to cling to the brass, a tiny scratch above it, to the right of the keyhole. Latham looked closer; he drew a match and struck it, almost afraid to do what he was about to do.

He held the flame directly below the speck of grey matter. It melted instantly and fell away: solder.

It was also an obscure but time-tested device that Apple favoured. He had used it on numerous occasions when they worked together. Come to think of it, Latham couldn't remember anyone else ever using it.

Melt the end of a small solder wire and shove the soft liquid into the lock with its key. It jammed the tumblers but did not prevent the key from going in.

It merely prevented any key from opening the lock. In quiet situations that called for a little time while a man raced out of a trap, it provided that time without raising any sudden alarms. A perfectly normal looking lock malfunctioned; most locks were old. One did not break down a door; one called a locksmith.

Had Apple needed time? Was there a trap?

Something *was* wrong.

'*Good Christ!* Don't touch anything! Get a *doctor*!' shouted Teague, lunging into the office beyond the unhinged door. 'And keep this tight!'

'He's dead,' said Latham quietly at the brigadier's side.

'I know that,' answered Teague curtly. 'I want to know how *long* he's been dead.'

'Who is he?' asked Latham, looking down at the dead man. The body had been stripped; only the undershorts and shoes remained. There was a single, clean gunshot wound in the upper centre of the naked chest; the rivulet of blood had dried.

'Colonel Aubrey Birch. Officer of the vaults.' Teague turned and spoke to the two guards holding the door. A third soldier had gone for the MI6 house surgeon on the second floor. 'Put that door back. Admit no one. Say nothing. Come with me, Latham.'

They rode the lift to the cellars. Latham saw that Teague was not only in a state of shock, he was frightened.

'What do you think happened, sir?'

'I gave him his separation papers two nights ago. He hated me for it.'

Latham was silent for a moment. Then he spoke without looking at Teague, his eyes straight ahead. 'I'm a civilian, so I'll say it. That was a rotten, goddamned thing to do. Stone was once the best man you had.'

'Your objection is noted,' said the brigadier coldly. 'You were the one they called Pear, weren't you?'

'Yes.'

Teague glanced at the discharged Intelligence agent; the panel light indicated that the cellars had been reached. 'Well, the apple soured, Mr Pear. It became rancid. What concerns me now is how far the rot penetrated.'

The door opened. They walked out of the lift and turned right towards a wall of steel that closed off the corridor. In the centre of the wall was a thick steel door; its frame was barely discernible. There was a plate of bulletproof glass in the upper section, a black button to the left, a thin rubber slot below, a metal sign above.

SECURITY AREA

No Admittance Without Proper Authorization
Ring Bell – Place Authorization in Vacuum Slot

Teague approached the glass, pushed the button and spoke firmly. 'Code Hyacinth. No delays, please; make visual confirmation. This is Brigadier Teague. I'm accompanied by one Mr Harold Latham, cleared by me.'

There was a whirring sound. The steel door receded, then was slid manually to the side. An officer on the other side saluted.

'Good afternoon, general. There's been no Hyacinth report down here.'

Teague acknowledged the salute with a nod of his head. 'I'm delivering it myself, major. Nothing is to be removed until further orders. What does the duty ledger read on Colonel Birch?'

The officer turned to a metal desk that was attached to the metal wall. 'Here it is, sir,' he said, holding open a black leather notebook. 'Colonel Birch signed out the night before last at nineteen hundred hours. He's due back in the morning. O seven hundred, sir.'

'I see. Was anyone with him?'

The major looked again at the large notebook. 'Yes, sir. Captain Stone, sir. His checkout time is the same.'

'Thank you. Mr Latham and I will be in Vault Seven. May I have the keys, please? And the combination figures.'

'Of course.'

Inside the metal room were twenty-two file cabinets. Teague stopped at the fourth cabinet against the far wall opposite the door. He looked at the page of figures in his hand and began manipulating the combination lock in the upper right corner of the cabinet. As he did so, he held out the page of figures for Latham.

'Save time,' he said brusquely, his voice hoarse. 'Locate the cabinet with the Brevourt file. B-r-e-v-o-u-r-t. Extract it.'

Latham took the paper, returned to the left wall and found the cabinet.

The lock sprung. Teague reached over and pulled out the second cabinet drawer. Rapidly his fingers separated the files.

Then he separated them again. Slowly, allowing for no oversight.

It wasn't there. The file on Victor Fontine was gone.

Teague closed the cabinet drawer and stood erect. He looked over at Latham, who knelt by the bottom drawer of his cabinet, an open folder in his hand. He was staring at it, his expression one of stunned bewilderment.

'I asked you to find it, not to read it,' said the brigadier icily.

'There's nothing to read,' replied Latham quietly, removing a single page of paper from the folder. 'Except this ... What the hell have you bastards *done*?'

The paper was a photostat. It had a black border, with room at the bottom for two seals of approval. Both men knew exactly what it was.

An order for execution. An official licence to kill.

'Who's the target?' asked Teague in a monotone, remaining by the cabinet.

'Vittorio Fontini-Cristi.'

'Who approved it?'

'Foreign Office seal, Brevourt's signature.'

'Who *else*? There must be *two*!'

'The prime minister.'

'And Captain Stone is the assignee—'

Latham nodded, although Teague had not asked a question. 'Yes.'

Teague breathed deeply, closing his eyes for a moment. He opened them and spoke. 'How well did you know Stone? His methods?'

'We worked together for eighteen months. We were like brothers.'

'Brothers? Then I remind you, Mr Latham, that in

spite of your separation from the service, the Official Secrets Act still binds you.'

CHAPTER FIFTEEN

Teague spoke into the telephone, his phrases precise, his voice cutting. 'From the beginning he was your man. From the day we placed him in Loch Torridon. His interrogations, the endless questions, Lübok's name in our files, the traps. Fontine's every move was reported to you.'

'I make no apologies,' said Anthony Brevourt on the other end of the line. 'For reasons you well know. "Salonika" was, and still remains, a highest priority of the Foreign Office.'

'I want an explanation for that order of execution! It was never cleared, never reported—'

'Nor was it *meant* to be,' interrupted Brevourt. 'That order was our backup. You may subscribe to your own immortality, general, but we don't. Air raids aside, you're a strategist for covert operations; a potential mark for assassination. If you were killed, that order permitted Stone immediate access to Fontini-Cristi's whereabouts.'

'Stone convinced you of that?'

There was a pause before the ambassador replied. 'Yes. Several years ago.'

'Did Stone also tell you he hated Fontine?'

'He didn't approve of him; he wasn't alone.'

'I said *hated*! Bordering on the pathological.'

'If you knew that, why didn't you replace him?'

'Because, damn it, he controlled it! As long as he had a reason to. He has *none* now.'

'I don't see—'

'You're a goddamn fool, Brevourt! Stone left us a photostat; he kept the original. You're helpless and he wants you to know it.'

'What are you talking about?'

'He's walking around with an official document that gives him a warrant to kill Fontine. Countermanding it now is meaningless. It would have been meaningless two *years* ago! He has the paper; he's a professional. He intends to carry out the assignment and place that document where you can't get it. Can the British government – can *you*, or the foreign secretary, or Churchill, himself, justify that execution? Would any of you care to even *comment* on it?'

Brevourt replied swiftly, urgently. 'It was a contingency. That was *all* it was.'

'It was the best,' agreed Teague harshly. 'Startling enough to cut through red tape. Sufficiently dramatic to break down bureaucratic walls. I can hear Stone mounting his argument.'

'Stone must be found. He must be stopped.' Brevourt's breathing could be heard over the line.

'We've reached one area of agreement,' said the brigadier wearily.

'What are you going to do?'

'To begin with, tell Fontine everything.'

'Is that wise?'

'It's fair.'

'We expect to be kept informed. If need be, hourly.'

Teague looked absently across the office at his wall clock. It was nine forty-five; moonlight streamed through the windows, no curtains blocked it now. 'I'm not sure that's possible.'

'*What?*'

'You're concerned with a vault taken out of Greece

five years ago. I'm concerned with the lives of Victor Fontine and his family.'

'Has it occurred to you,' said Brevourt, drawing out his words, 'that the two are inseparable?'

'Your conjecture is noted.' Teague hung up and leaned back in his chair. He would have to call Fontine now. Warn him.

There was a knock on his door.

'Come in.'

Harold Latham walked in first, followed by one of the best investigating officers in MI6. A middle-aged, former Scotland Yard forensic specialist. He carried a manila file folder in his hand.

A few weeks ago, Pear would not have walked into a general's office smoking a cigarette. He did so now; it was important to him. Yet, thought Teague, Latham's hostility had lessened. Pear was first and foremost a professional. Civilian status would not change that.

'Did you find anything?' asked Teague.

'Scratchings,' said Latham. 'They may mean something, they may not. Your man here is sharp. He can lift a book off a pinhead.'

'He knew where to point me,' added the analyst. 'He was familiar with the subject's habits.'

'What have you got?'

'Nothing on the premises; his office was clean. Nothing but case work, dossiers marked for the ovens, all quite legitimate. His flat was something else. He was a thorough chap. But the arrangements of the hangers in the closet, the clothes in his bureau, the toilet supplies ... they all indicate that Stone had been planning his departure for some time.'

'I see. And these scratchings?'

Pear answered. The professional in him needed recognition. 'Stone had a disagreeable habit. He would lie in bed making notes. Words, brackets, figures, arrows, names – doodling, I call it. But before he turned in he'd tear off the pages and burn them. We found a writing pad on the shelf of the bedside table. There was nothing on it, of course, but the Yarder here knew what to do.'

'There were depressions, sir. It wasn't difficult; we lifted them under spectrograph.' The officer handed Teague the folder across the desk. 'Here are the results.'

Teague opened the folder and stared at the spectrogram. As Pear had described, there were numbers, brackets, arrows, words. It was a disjointed puzzle, a wild diagram of incoherent meanderings.

And then the name leaped up from the mass of incoherence.

Donatti.

The man with the streak of white in his hair. The executioner of Campo di Fiori. One of the most powerful cardinals in the Curia.

'Salonika' had begun.

'. . . Guillamo Donatti.'

Fontine heard the name and it triggered the memory locked in his mind. The name was the key, the lock was sprung, and the memory revealed.

He was a child, no more than nine or ten years old. It was evening and his brothers were upstairs preparing for bed. He had come down in his pyjamas to find a book, when he'd heard the shouting from his father's study.

The door was open, no more than a foot, and the curious child had approached it. What he saw inside so shocked his sensibilities that he stood there hypnotized. A priest was in front of his father's desk, roaring at Savarone, pounding the top of the desk with his fist, his face pinched in anger, his eyes wide in fury.

That anyone should behave this way in his father's presence, even – perhaps especially – a priest, so startled the child that he involuntarily, audibly gasped.

When he did the priest whipped around, the burning eyes looking at the child, and it was then that Victor had seen the streak of white in the black hair. He had run away from the living room and up the staircase.

The next morning Savarone had taken his son aside and explained; his father never left explanations suspended. What the violent argument referred to was obscured with time, but Fontine recalled that his father had identified the priest as Guillamo Donatti, a man who was a disgrace to the Vatican ... someone who issued edicts to the uninformed and enforced them by fear. They were words a child remembered.

Guillamo Donatti, firebrand of the Curia.

'Stone's after his own, now,' said Teague over the line from London, bringing Victor's focus back to the present. 'He wants you, and whatever price you'll bring. We were looking in the wrong areas; we've traced him now. He used Birch's papers and got a military flight out of Lakenheath. To Rome.'

'To the cardinal,' corrected Fontine. 'He's not taking chances with long-distance negotiations.'

'Precisely. He'll come back for you. We'll be waiting.'

'No,' said Victor into the telephone. 'That's not the way. We won't wait, we'll go after them.'

'Oh?' The doubt was in Teague's voice.

'We know Stone's in Rome. He'll stay out of sight, probably with informer cells; they're used to hiding men.'

'Or with Donatti.'

'That's doubtful. He'll insist on neutral territory. Donatti's dangerous, unpredictable. Stone realizes that.'

'I don't know what you're thinking, but I can't—'

'Can you circulate a rumour from reliable sources?' interrupted Fontine.

'What kind of rumour?'

'That I'm about to do what everyone expects me to do:

230

return to Campo di Fiori. For unknown reasons of my own.'

'Absolutely not! It's out of the question!'

'For God's *sake*,' shouted Victor. 'I can't hide out for the rest of my life! I can't live in fear that each time my wife or my children leave the house there is a Stone or a Donatti or an execution team waiting for them! You promised me a confrontation. I want it *now*.'

There was silence on the line from London. Finally Teague spoke. 'There's still the Order of Xenope.'

'One step leads to another. Hasn't that been your premise all along? Xenope will be forced to acknowledge what *is*, not what it thinks *should* be. Donatti and Stone will be proof. There can be no other conclusion.'

'We have men in Rome, not many—'

'We don't *want* many. Very few. My being in Italy must not be linked with MI6. The cover will be the Court of Reparations. The government wants to control our factories, the properties. The court bids higher every week; they don't want the Americans.'

'Court of Reparations,' said Teague, obviously writing a note.

'There is an old man named Barzini,' continued Fontine. 'Guido Barzini. He used to be at Campo di Fiori, he tended the stables. He could give us background. Put a trace on him in the Milan district. If he's alive, he'll be found through the *partigiani*.'

'Barzini, Guido,' repeated Teague. 'I'll want safety factors.'

'So do I, but very low profile, Alec. We want to force them out in the open, not further underground.'

'Assuming the bait's taken, what will you do?'

'Make them listen. It's as simple as that.'

'I don't think it is,' said Teague.

'Then I'll kill them,' said Victor.

The word went out. The *padrone* was alive; he had

returned. In a small hotel several blocks from the Duomo, he was *seen*. Fontini-Cristi was in Milan. The news was known even in Rome.

There was a knock on the hotel door. Barzini. It was a moment Victor both looked forward to and dreaded. The memories of white light and death inadvertently came into focus. He suppressed them as he walked across the room to the door.

The old farmhand stood in the hallway, his once muscular body now bent and thin, lost within the coarse fabric of his cheap black coat. His face was wrinkled; the eyes were rheumy. The hands that had held Victor's writhing, lashing body to the earth, the fingers that had clawed at his face and saved his life, were withered, gnarled. And they shook.

To Fontine's sorrow and embarrassment, Barzini fell to his knees, his thin arms outstretched, grasping Victor's legs.

'It's true. You're alive!'

Fontine pulled him to his feet and embraced him. In silence he led the old man into the room, to the couch. Beyond his age, it was obvious that Barzini was ill. Victor offered food; Barzini asked for tea and brandy. Both were brought quickly by the hotel waiters, and when both were finished, Fontine learned the salient facts of Campo di Fiori since the night of the massacre.

For months after the German killings, the fascist troops kept the estate under guard. The servants were allowed to take their possessions and leave; the maid who had witnessed the shooting was murdered that night. No one was permitted to live in Campo di Fiori except Barzini, who was obviously mentally deficient.

'It was not difficult. The *fascisti* always thought everyone else was crazy but themselves. It was the only way they could think, and face themselves in the morning.'

In his position of stablehand and groundkeeper, Guido was able to watch the activity at Campo di Fiori. Most startling were the priests. Groups of priests were permitted in; never more than three or four at a time, but there were many such groups. At first Guido believed they had been sent by the holy father to pray for the souls of the house of Fontini-Cristi. But priests on sacred missions did not behave as these priests behaved. They went through the main house, then the cottages and, finally, the stables, searching with precision. They tagged everything; furniture was pried apart; walls tapped for hollow sections and panels removed; floors ripped up – not in anger but as experienced carpenters might do; lifted and replaced. And the grounds were combed as though they were fields of gold.

'I asked several of the younger fathers what they were looking for. I don't think they really knew. They always replied, "Thick boxes, old man. Cartons of steel and iron." And then I realized that there was one priest, an older priest, who came every day. He was forever checking the work of the others.'

'A man in his sixties,' said Victor softly, 'with a streak of white in his hair.'

'Yes! That was he! How did you know?'

'He was expected. How long did the searching go on?'

'For nearly two years. It was an unbelievable thing. And then it stopped.'

All activities stopped, according to Barzini, except German activity. The Wehrmacht officer corps appropriated Campo di Fiori, turning it into an elaborate retreat for the higher echelon commanders.

'Did you do as the Englishman from Rome told you, old friend?' Fontine poured Barzini more brandy; the trembling had partially subsided.

'Yes, *padrone*. For the past two days I have gone to the markets in Laveno, in Varese, and Legnano. I say the

233

same to a few chosen loudmouths: "Tonight I see the *padrone*! He returns! I go to Milan to meet him, but no one is to know!" They will know, son of Fontini-Cristi.' Barzini smiled.

'Did anyone ask you *why* I insisted you come to Milan?'

'Most did. I say only that you wish to talk with me privately. I tell them I am honoured. And I am.'

'It should be enough.' Victor picked up the phone and gave a number to the hotel switchboard. While he waited for the call to be placed, he turned to Barzini. 'When this is over, I want you to come back with me. To England, then America. I'm married, old friend. You'll like the *signora*. I have sons, two sons. Twins.'

Barzini's eyes shone. 'You have sons? I give thanks to God—'

There was no answer on the line. Fontine was concerned. It was *imperative* that the MI6 man be at that telephone! He was stationed halfway between Varese and Campo di Fiori. He was the contact for the others, spread out on the roads leading from Stresa, Lugano, and Morcote; he was the focal point of communications. Where the hell *was* he?

Victor hung up the phone and took his wallet out of his pocket. In a concealed recess was another telephone number. In Rome.

He gave it to the operator.

'What do you mean there's no answer?' asked the precise English voice that answered.

'Is there a clearer way to say it?' responded Fontine. 'There *is* no *answer*. When did you last hear from him?'

'About four hours ago. Everything was on schedule. He was in radio contact with all vehicles. You got the message, of course.'

'What message?'

There was a momentary silence. 'I don't like this, Fontine.'

'What *message*?'

'He said he might have been zeroed, but we weren't to worry. He'd reach you at the hotel when you arrived. He spotted the car himself. It was on the road that passes the main gates at Campo di Fiori. He didn't reach you?'

Victor suppressed a desire to shout. 'He didn't reach me. There were no messages for me. What car?'

'A green Fiat. The licence was from Savona, that's on the Genoa gulf. One of the descriptions matched a Corsican in the police files. A contrabandist London believes worked for us. The others are also *Corsi*, we think. And *him*.'

'I presume you mean—'

'Yes. Stone's the fourth man.'

Stone had taken the bait. Apple had gone back to Celle Ligure, back to the Corsicans to find his recruits. And Apple, the professional, had removed the contact in Varese.

Eliminate the couriers. Immobilize communications. Loch Torridon.

'Thank you,' said Victor to the man in Rome.

'See *here*, Fontine!' came the harried voice over the telephone. 'You're to do *nothing*! Stay where you are!'

Without answering, Victor replaced the phone and walked back to Barzini. 'I need some men. Men we can trust, who are willing to take risks.'

Barzini looked away; the old man was embarrassed. 'Things are not what they were, *padrone*.'

'*Partigiani?*' said Fontine.

'Mostly Communists. They're concerned with themselves now. With their pamphlets, their meetings. They . . .' Barzini stopped. 'Wait. There are two men who don't forget. They hid in the mountains; I brought them food, news of their families. We can trust them.'

'They'll have to do,' said Victor, starting for the

bedroom door. 'I'm going to change clothes. Can you reach them?'

'There's a telephone number,' answered Barzini, getting up from the couch.

'Call them. Tell them to meet me at Campo di Fiori. I assume there are guards.'

'Only a nightwatchman now. From Laveno. And myself.'

Fontine stopped and turned to Barzini. 'Would these men know the back road north of the stables?'

'They can find it.'

'Good. Tell them to start out now and wait for me on the bridle path at the rear of the stables. It's still there, isn't it?'

'It is still there. What are you going to do, *padrone*?'

Victor realized as he spoke that he was repeating the words he had used over the phone to Teague five days ago. 'What everyone expects me to do.' He turned and continued towards the bedroom.

CHAPTER SIXTEEN

The lessons of Loch Torridon were always present, thought Victor, as he stood in front of the hotel desk, his arms on the marble counter, watching the night clerk carry out his request. He had demanded a car for hire in a voice loud enough to draw attention. It was a difficult order considering the hour; vehicles were hard enough to come by during the day, much less in the middle of the night. But they could be had if the money was sufficient. Then, too, the argument at the front desk was sufficiently disagreeable to alert any observer. Also, there were the clothes he wore; dark grey trousers, boots, and a dark hunting jacket. It was not the hunting season.

There were only a few stragglers in the lobby; several businessmen making unsteady treks to their rooms after long, liquid conferences; a couple arguing over one or the other's behaviour; a nervous, rich youth signing in with a whore who waited discreetly in a chair. And a dark, swarthy man with the hard leather face of the sea, who was across the lobby in an armchair reading a magazine, seemingly oblivious to the hotel's night scene. A Corsican, thought Victor.

It was this man who could carry the message to other Corsicans. To the Englishman named Stone.

It was simply a matter of coordinating the upcoming sequence. To make sure there was a green Fiat on the street, probably in shadows, ready to take up a discreet position when the rented car drove away. If there was no such automobile, Victor could find reasons to delay until it arrived.

No delay was necessary. The Fiat could be seen in the middle of the next block. Captain Geoffrey Stone was sure of himself. The Fiat was positioned in front of Fontine's car, facing west, towards the road to Varese. To Campo di Fiori.

Barzini sat in the front with Victor. The brandy had done its work. The old man's head kept falling to his chest.

'Sleep,' said Victor. 'It's a long drive and I'll want you rested when we get there.'

They drove through the open gates and into the long winding entrance of Campo di Fiori. Although he was braced for it, the sight of the house filled his chest with pain; hammering seared through his temples. He approached the execution grounds. The sights and sounds of that agony returned, but he knew he could not permit them to overwhelm him. The lessons of Loch Torridon: *Divided concentrations were dangerous.*

He contracted the muscles of his stomach taut and stopped the car.

Barzini was awake, staring at him. The nightwatchman emerged from the thick oak doors beyond the marble steps, the beam of his flashlight examining the car and those inside. Barzini stepped out and spoke.

'I bring the son of Fontini-Cristi. He's the *padrone* of this house.'

The watchman threw the beam over at Victor, who had got out of the car and stood by the hood. His voice was respectful. And not a little frightened.

'I am honoured, *padrone.*'

'You may go home to Laveno,' Fontine told him. 'If you don't mind, use the north road. You probably do anyway. It's the shortest way.'

'Much the shortest, *signore*. Thank you, *signore*.'

'There may be two friends waiting for me at the stables. Don't be alarmed, I asked them to drive through the north gate. If you see them, please tell them I'll be there shortly.'

'Of course, *padrone*.' The nightwatchman nodded and walked rapidly down the marble steps into the drive. There was a bicycle in the shadows by the shrubbery. He mounted and pedalled off into the darkness towards the stables.

'Quickly,' said Victor, turning to Barzini. 'Tell me. Are the telephones as they were? Is there still a line connecting the house with the stables?'

'Yes. In your father's study and in the hall.'

'Good. Go in and turn on all the lights in the hall and in the dining room. Then go back to the study, keeping those lights out. Stay by a window. When I reach your friends, I'll call you from the stables and tell you what to do. Soon the Corsicans will appear. On foot, I'm sure. Watch for small flashlights. Tell me what you see.'

'Very well. *Padrone?*'

'Yes?'

'I have no gun. Weapons are outlawed.'

'Take mine.' Victor reached into his belt and removed his Smith & Wesson. 'I don't think you'll need it. Don't fire unless your life depends on it.'

Thirty seconds later the lights in the great hall shone through the stained-glass windows above the huge entrance doors. Victor hurried along the side of the house and waited by the edge of the building. The chandeliers in the dining room were switched on. The whole north section of the house was a blaze of light, the south section in darkness.

There were still no signs of life on the road; no beams of flashlights or flares or matches. It was as it should be.

Stone was a professional. When he moved it would be with extreme caution.

So be it. *His* moves would be cautious also.

Victor ran into the north road towards the stables. He kept low to the ground and alert, listening for the unusual. Stone might have opted for the north gates as his means of entry, but it was unlikely. Stone was anxious; he would move in swiftly, close behind his quarry, and seal off the exits.

'*Partigiani*. It's Fontini-Cristi.' Victor walked down the bridle path at the rear of the stables. The few horses left inside were old and weary, the whinnies intermittent.

'*Signore*.' The whisper came from the woods to the right of the path; Fontine approached. Suddenly a flashlight beam shot out from the opposite side. From the left. And another voice spoke.

'Stay where you are! Don't turn!'

He felt the hand of the man behind him on the small of his back, holding him steady. The flashlight moved forward over his shoulder, shining in his face, blinding him.

'It's him,' said the voice in the darkness.

The flashlight was removed. Fontine blinked and rubbed his eyes, trying to erase the residual image of the blinding light. The *partigiano* came out of the darkness. He was a tall man, nearly as tall as Victor, dressed in a worn American field jacket. The second man came from behind; he was much shorter than his comrade and barrel-chested.

'Why are we here?' asked the tall man. 'Barzini's old and doesn't think clearly. We agreed to watch you, warn you . . . nothing else. We do this because we owe Barzini much. And for old time's sake; the Fontini-Cristis fought against the fascists.'

'Thank you.'

'What do the Corsicans want? And this Englishman?' The second man moved to his friend's side.

'Something they believe I have, which I don't have.' Victor stopped. From the stables there was a soft, tired snort followed by a series of hoof thumps. The partisans heard it too; the flashlight was extinguished.

A crack of a limb. A pebble dislodged under a footstep. Someone approached, following the same path Fontine had taken. The partisans separated; the stocky man moved forward and disappeared into the foliage. His brother did the same in the opposite direction. Victor stepped to his right and crouched off the path.

Silence. The footsteps scratching over the dry earth became clearer. Suddenly the figure was there, only inches in front of Fontine, outlined in the forest night.

And then it happened. A powerful beam of light burst out of the darkness, piercing the opposite woods; at the same instant there was the sudden, muted spit of a pistol, its noise contained by a silencer.

Victor sprang up, lashing his left arm around the throat of the man, his right surging beyond for the weapon, forcing it downward. As the man's back arched, Victor crashed his knee into the base of the spine. The man's breath was expunged; Fontine yanked with all his strength at the taut neck in his hammerlock. There was a snap, sickening and final. The light rolled on the path.

The tall *partigiano* raced out of the woods, crushing the light underfoot, his pistol in his hand. He and Victor plunged into the foliage, both silently acknowledging the fear that their ally was dead.

He was not. The bullet had only creased his arm. He lay wild-eyed in shock, his mouth open, his breathing loud. Fontine knelt beside him, tearing off the partisan's shirt to check the wound. The man's brother remained standing, his gun on the stable path.

'Mother of Christ! You damn fool! Why didn't you

shoot him?' The wounded *partigiano* winced in pain. 'Another second and he would have killed me!'

'I had no weapon,' replied Victor quietly, wiping the blood from the man's flesh.

'Not even a knife?'

'No.' Fontine bound the wound and knotted the cloth. The *partigiano* stared at him.

'You've got balls,' he said. 'You could have waited out of sight. My comrade has a gun.'

'Come on, stand up. There are two other *Corsi* somewhere. I want them. But without gunfire.' Victor bent down and picked up the dead man's pistol. There were four bullets in the chamber; the silencer was one of the best. He beckoned the tall partisan off the path and spoke to both. 'I'm going to ask a favour of you. You can refuse me and I'll understand.'

'What is it?' asked the larger man.

'The other two Corsicans are back there. One's probably watching the main road, the other may be behind the house, in the gardens, there's no way to tell. The Englishman will stay out of sight, near the house. I'm sure the *Corsi* won't kill me. They'll watch every move I make, but they will not open fire.'

'That one,' said the wounded partisan, pointing to the dead man, 'did not hesitate to pull his trigger.'

'These *Corsi* know me by sight. He could see you weren't me.'

The strategy was clear. Victor was the bait; he would walk openly down to the circular drive and turn into the gardens at the rear of the house. The partisans were to follow him, staying out of sight in the trees. If Fontine was right, a Corsican would be seen. And taken. Or killed silently. It did not matter; these *Corsi* murdered Italians.

The strategy would then be repeated on the main entrance road, the partisans crossing diagonally far behind the embankment, meeting him at a juncture a quarter of a mile away. Somewhere between the circular drive and the gates, the third and last Corsican would be stationed.

The positions were logical, and Stone was nothing if not a logical man. And thorough. He *would* seal off the exits.

'You don't have to do this for me,' said Victor. 'I'll pay generously, but I understand—'

'Keep your money,' interrupted the wounded man, looking first at his comrade. 'You didn't have to do what you did for me.'

'There's a telephone in the stables. I must talk with Barzini. Then start down the road.'

The surmise was confirmed. Stone had covered both roads and the gardens. And the remaining Corsicans were taken, their lives ended with partisan knives.

They met at the stables. Fontine was sure that Stone had been watching him from the embankment. The quarry was walking the killing ground; the return was painful. Loch Torridon had taught them both to anticipate reactions. It was a weapon.

'Where's your car?' Victor asked the *partigiani*.

'Outside the north gate,' replied the tall one.

'You have my thanks. Get your friend to a doctor. Barzini will know where I can send a more concrete form of gratitude.'

'You want the Englishman for yourself?'

'There'll be no trouble. He's a man with one hand, without his *Corsi*. Barzini and I know what to do. Get to a doctor.'

'Good-bye, *signore*,' said the tall man. 'Our debts are cancelled. To old Barzini. To you, perhaps. The Fontini-Cristis were good to this land once.'

'Many thanks.'

The partisans nodded a last time and made their way swiftly up the road into the darkness towards the north gate. Fontine went down the path and let himself into the stables through a side door. He walked by the stalls, past the horses and Barzini's small bedroom, into the tack room. He found a wooden box and began filling it with braces and bits and musty, framed citations from the walls. He crossed to the telephone by the door and pushed a button beneath it.

'All is well, old friend.'

'Thank God.'

'What about the Englishman?'

'He's waiting across the drive, in the high grass. On the embankment. The same—' Barzini stopped.

'I understand. I'm starting out now. You know what to do. Remember, at the door speak slowly, clearly. The Englishman hasn't spoken Italian in recent years.'

'Old men talk louder than they must,' said Barzini, humour in his voice. 'Because we hear poorly, so must everyone else.'

Fontine replaced the phone and checked the pistol the partisans had left him; it had been taken from a dead Corsican. He unscrewed the silencer and put the weapon in his pocket. He picked up the box and went out of the tack-room door.

He walked slowly down the road to the circular drive opposite the embankment. In front of the steps, in the spill of light from the windows, he paused, giving his arms a moment of rest, conveying the fact that the box was heavier than its size might indicate.

He continued up the steps to the large oak doors. He then did the most natural thing that came to him: he kicked at the right door.

In seconds the door was opened by Barzini. Their exchange was simple, without strain. The old man spoke clearly.

'You're sure I can't bring you something, *padrone*? A pot of tea, coffee?'

'No, thank you, old friend. Get some sleep. We have a lot to do in the morning.'

'Very well. The horses will eat early today.' Barzini walked past Victor to the steps and down into the circular drive. He turned left towards the stables.

Victor stood in the great hall; everything was as it had been. The Germans knew when not to mar a thing of beauty. He turned into the darkened south section, into the enormous drawing room towards the doors of his father's study. As he walked through the familiar space, he felt pains of anguish in his chest and the catching of his breath in his throat.

He went into his father's study. Savarone's *sanctum sanctorum*. Instinctively, he turned right in the darkness; the huge desk was where it had always been. He put the box down and turned on the green-shaded lamp he remembered; it was the same lamp. Nothing had changed.

He sat down in his father's chair and removed the pistol from his pocket. He placed it on the desk, behind the wooden box, concealing it from the front.

The waiting had begun. And for the second time his life was in Barzini's hands. He could not imagine a firmer grip. For Barzini would not reach the stables. He would walk up the stable road and enter the woods, doubling back into the gardens, to the rear of the house. He would let himself in through one of the patio doors, and wait for the Englishman to come.

Stone was trapped.

The minutes dragged on. Absently, Fontine opened the drawers of his father's desk. He found sheets of Wehrmacht stationery, and methodically he placed them sheet by sheet in separate piles, a game of solitaire with huge blank playing cards.

He waited.

At first, he did not hear any sound. Instead, he felt the

presence. It was unmistakable, filling the air between himself and the intruder. Then the creak of a floorboard pierced the silence, followed by two distinct footsteps, bold, unconcealed; Fontine's hand moved towards the gun.

Suddenly, out of the dark space, a light-coloured object came flying through the shadows towards him, *at* him! Victor recoiled as the object came into focus, trailing rivulets of blood in the air. There was a harsh slap – flesh against wood – and the horrible thing made contact with the top of the desk and rolled obscenely under the spill of the lamp.

Fontine expelled his breath in an instant of total revulsion.

The object was a hand. A severed right hand cut crudely above the wrist. The fingers were old and withered and clawlike in spastic contraction, the tendons iced at the instant of primitive surgery.

It was the hand of Guido Barzini. Thrown by a maniac who had lost his own on a pier in Celle Ligure.

Victor shot up from the chair, suppressing the revulsion that welled up inside him, stabbing for the gun.

'Don't touch that! You do, you're dead!' Stone's words were spat out in English. He crouched in the shadows across the room, behind a high-backed armchair.

Victor withdrew his hand. He had to force himself to think. To survive. 'You killed him.'

'They'll find him in the woods. It's odd that *I* found him there, isn't it?'

Fontine stood motionless, accepting the awful news, suspending emotion. 'Odder still,' said Victor quietly, 'that your Corsican didn't.'

Stone's eyes reacted; only a flicker of recognition, but the reaction was there. 'The walk you took, I wondered.' The Englishman nodded his head. 'Yes, you could have done that. You could have taken them out.'

'I didn't. Others did.'

'Sorry, Fontini. That doesn't wash.'

'How can you be sure?'

'Because if there were others, you wouldn't use an old man for the last job; that's stupid. You're an arrogant son of a bitch, but you're not stupid. We're alone, all right. Just you and me and that box. *Christ!* It must have been in one hell of a hole. Enough people looked for it.'

'Then you made your deal with Donatti?'

'He thinks so. Strange, isn't it? You took everything from me. I crawled out of Liverpool and made my way up, and you took it all away on a fucking guinea pier five years ago. Now I've got it all back and then some. I may hold the biggest auction anyone's ever heard of.'

'For what? Old hunt prizes? Faded citations?'

Stone snapped the hammer of his weapon into firing position. His black glove slapped the back of the chair, his eyes bored through the shadows. 'Don't make jokes!'

'No jokes. I'm not stupid, remember? And you're not in any position to pull that trigger. You've only got one chance to deliver the contents of that vault. If you don't, another order of execution can easily be issued. Those powerful men who hired you five years ago don't like embarrassing speculations.'

'Shut up! *Stop it!*' Furiously, Stone raised the clawlike glove above the chair and smashed it down. 'Those tactics won't work on me, you guinea bastard! I used them before you ever heard of Loch Torridon.'

'Loch Torridon was based on *error*. Miscalculation! *Mismanagement!* That was its *premise*. Remember?' Fontine took a step backwards, pushing the chair with his legs, extending his hands out in a gesture of helplessness. 'Come on. Look for yourself. You wouldn't kill me before you saw what the bullet cost you.'

'Move back! *Farther!*' Stone came around the chair, his immobile right hand stretched out directly in front of him like a protruding lance. His left hand held the weapon with the cocked hammer; the slightest squeeze of the trigger and the pin would spring forward, exploding the shell.

Victor did as he was commanded, his eyes riveted on the pistol. His moment would come; it had to come or there was nothing.

The Englishman approached the desk, each step the movement of a man filled with loathing and wariness, prepared to destroy at the split second of imbalance. He took his eyes from Fontine and stared at the top of the desk. At the severed, mutilated hand of Guido Barzini. At the box. At the pile of debris inside the box.

'No,' he whispered. '*No!*'

The moment came: the shock of revelation was in Stone's eyes. It would not come again.

Victor sprang forward over the desk, his long arms plunging for the weapon; it had wavered for only a heartbeat, but that was all he could hope for.

The explosion was deafening, but Fontine's grip had deflected the shot. Only inches, but it was enough. The bullet shattered the top of the desk, hurling splinters of wood everywhere. Victor held Stone's wrist, wrenching with all the power he possessed, feeling and not feeling the blows delivered to his face and neck by the hard-gloved hand. Stone brought his right knee up, pummelling Fontine's groin and stomach; the pistol would not be dislodged. The Englishman screamed and went into a paroxysm of frenzy. He would not, *could* not be bested by strength alone.

Victor did the only thing left to him. For an instant he stopped all movement, then yanked Stone's wrist forward as if jamming the pistol into his own stomach. As the gun was about to touch the cloth of his jacket, he suddenly twisted his body and Stone's wrist, inverting the weapon, and shoved it with his full weight upward.

The explosion came. For a second Fontine was blinded, his flesh ice cold with fireburn, and for that instant he believed he had been killed.

Until he felt the body of Geoffrey Stone collapse, pulling him downward to the floor.

He opened his eyes. The bullet had entered the flesh beneath Stone's jaw, its trajectory upward, through the skull, ripping open the top of Stone's head.

And next to the mass of blood and tissue was the severed hand of Guido Barzini.

He carried Barzini's body out of the woods and to the stables. He placed the mutilated corpse on the bed and covered it with a sheet. He stood over the body, for how long he would never remember, trying to understand pain and terror and love.

Campo di Fiori was still. For him its secret was buried, never to be known. The mystery of Salonika was a confidence Savarone had not shared. And the son of Savarone would no longer dwell on it. Let others do so, if they cared to. Let Teague take care of the rest. He was finished.

He walked down the north road from the stables to the drive in front of the house and climbed into the rented car. It was dawn. The orange summer sun broke over the Italian countryside. He took one last look at the home of his childhood and started the ignition.

The trees rushed by, the foliage became a blur of green and orange and yellow and white. He looked at the speedometer. Over eighty. Eighty-four kilometres an hour on the twisting entrance road cut out of the forest. He should brake the speed, he knew that. It was foolhardy, if not dangerous. Yet his foot would not obey his mind.

Oh, God! He had to get away!

There was a long hairpin curve that preceded the gate.

In the old days – years ago – it was the custom to blow one's horn when one approached the curve. There was no cause to do so now; and he was relieved to find his foot relaxing its pressure on the pedal. Instinct was intact. Still, he took the curve at fifty, the tyres screeching as he came out of the turn and headed for the gates. Automatically, on the straightaway, he accelerated. He would whip past the gate-posts and swing on to the road for Varese. Then Milan.

Then London!

He was not sure when he saw it. *Them*. His mind had wandered, his eyes on the immediate ground in front of the hood. He only knew that he slammed the brakes with such force that he was thrown against the steering wheel, his head inches from the windshield. The car swerved, the tyres screamed, dust billowed up from the wheels, and the car skidded diagonally through the gates, stopping only feet from the two black limousines that had converged out of nowhere, blocking the road beyond the stone posts.

His body was jolted back against the seat; the whole car shook in its sudden violent arrest. Stunned, Fontine took several seconds to shake off the effects of the near collision. He blinked his eyes, quickly regaining focus. His fury was suspended in astonishment at what he saw.

Standing in front of the two limousines were five men in black suits and white clerical collars. They stared impassively at him. Then the rear door of the limousine on the right opened and a sixth man got out. He was a man of about sixty, in the black robes of the church.

With a shock of white in his hair.

CHAPTER SEVENTEEN

The cardinal had the eyes of a fanatic and the strained, clipped voice of a man possessed. He moved in slow, fluid motions, never permitting his audience's attention to waver. He was at once theatrical and ominous. It was a cultivated appearance, refined over the years in the corridors of the Vatican. Donatti was an eagle who fed on sparrows. He was beyond righteousness; he *was* righteousness.

At the sight of the man Victor lost control of himself. That this killer of the church could approach Campo di Fiori was an obscenity he could not stand. He lunged at the vile, cassocked figure, all sense of reason and survival and sanity itself destroyed in the instant of memory.

The priests were ready for him. They converged, as the limousines had converged, blocking his path of assault. They held him, twisting his arms high up behind his back; a hand with powerful fingers gripped his throat, forcing his head into an agonizing arch, choking off all speech, but not sight or hearing.

'The car,' said Donatti quietly.

The two priests who were not restraining Fontine raced to the rented car and began the search. Victor could hear the doors and the trunk and the hood being opened. Then the ripping of upholstery and the crashing of metal as the car was torn apart. For nearly a quarter of an hour the ransacking continued. Throughout, Fontine's eyes were locked with the cardinal's. Only at the end of the search did the priest of the Curia look over at the automobile, when the two men approached and spoke simultaneously.

'There's nothing, Your Grace.'

Donatti gestured to the priest whose powerful hand held Victor's throat. The grip was eased; Fontine swallowed repeatedly. His arms were still stretched taut behind his back. The cardinal spoke.

'The heretics of Constantine chose well: the apostates of Campo di Fiori. The enemies of Christ.'

'Animal! Butcher!' Victor could barely whisper; the muscles of his neck and windpipe had been damaged severely. 'You *murdered* us! I *saw* you!'

'Yes. I thought you might have.' The cardinal spoke with quiet venom. 'I would have fired the weapons myself, had it been required. And thinking thus, you are quite correct. Theologically, I was the executioner.' Donatti's eyes grew wide. 'Where is the crate from Salonika?'

'I don't know.'

'You'll tell me, heretic. Believe the word of a true priest. You haven't got a choice.'

'You hold me against my will! In the name of *God* I presume!' said Fontine coldly.

'In the name of preserving the *mother church*! No laws take precedence over that. *Where is the shipment from Salonika?*'

The eyes, the high-pitched voice triggered the memory of years ago – a small child outside a study door. 'If that knowledge was so important to you, why did you execute my father? He was the only one who knew . . .'

'A *lie*! That is a *lie*!' Donatti caught himself, his lips trembling.

Fontine understood. A raw nerve had been exposed. An error of extraordinary magnitude had been made, and the cardinal could not bear to face it. 'You know it's the truth,' said Victor quietly. '*Now* you know it's the truth and you can't stand it. *Why*? Why was he *killed*?'

The priest lowered his voice. 'The enemies of Christ deceived us. The heretics of Xenope fed lies to us.' And once more Donatti roared abruptly. '*Savarone Fontini-Cristi was the communicator of those lies!*'

'What lies could *he* tell *you*? You never believed him when he told you the truth.'

Again the cardinal trembled. He could barely be heard. 'There were two freights out of Salonika. Three days apart. The first we knew nothing about; the second we picked up at Monfalcone, making sure that Fontini-Cristi would not meet it. We did not know then that he had already made contact with the first train. And now you will tell us what we wish to know. What we *must* know.'

'I can't give you what I don't have.'

Donatti looked at the priests and said one word. 'Now.'

Victor could never remember the length of time, for there was no time, only pain. Excruciating, harrowing, stinging, conclusive pain. He was dragged within the gates of Campo di Fiori and taken into the forest. There the holy apostolic priests began the torture. They started with his bare feet; every toe was broken, the ankles twisted until they cracked. The legs and knees were next: crushed, inverted, racked. And then the groin and stomach – *O God! He wished to die!* – And always, above him, blurred in the vision of tears of pain, was the priest of the Curia with the shock of white hair.

'*Tell us! Tell us! Enemy of Christ!*'

His arms were sprung from their sockets. His wrists were turned inward until the capillaries burst, spreading purple fluid throughout the skin. There were moments of blessed void, ended suddenly by hands slapping him back to consciousness.

'*Tell us! Tell us!*' The words became a hundred thousand hammers, echoes within echoes. '*Tell us! Enemy of Christ!*'

And all was void again. And through the dark tunnels of feeling, he sensed the rhythm of waves and air and suspension. A floating that deep within his brain told him he was near death.

There was a final, convulsive crash, yet he could not feel it. He was beyond feeling.

Yet he heard the words from far, far away in the distance, spoken in a chant.

'*In nomine patris et Spiriti sanctu. Dominus vobiscum . . .*'

Last rites.

He had been left to die.

There was the floating again. The waves and the air. And voices, indistinct, too far away to be really heard. And touch. He felt touching, each contact sending shafts of pain throughout his body. Yet these were not the touches of torture; the voices in the distance were not the voices of tormentors.

The blurred images at last came into focus. He was in a white room. In the distance were shining bottles with tubes cascading in the air.

And above him was a face. The face he knew he would never see again. What was left of his mind was playing horrible tricks on him.

The face was crying; tears rolled down the cheeks.

His wife Jane whispered. 'My love. My dearest love. Oh, *God*, what have they done to you?'

Her beautiful face was next to his. Touching his.

And there was no pain.

He had been found by worried men of MI6. The priests had carried him to a car, driven him to the circular drive, and left him to die in Campo di Fiori. That he did not die was not to be explained by the doctors. He *should* have died. His recovery would take months, perhaps years. And, in truth, he would never completely recover. But with care he would regain the use of his arms and legs; he would be ambulatory, and that in itself was a miracle.

By the eighth week he was able to sit up. He concluded his business with Rome's Court of Reparations. The lands, the factories, the properties were sold for seventy-five million pounds sterling. As he had promised himself, the transaction did not include Campo di Fiori.

For Campo di Fiori he made separate arrangements, through a trusted lawyer in Milan. It, too, was to be sold but he never wanted to know the name of the buyer. There were two inviolate restrictions: The purchaser was to have nowhere in his history any connection with the fascists. Nor was he to have any association whatsoever, regardless of denomination, with any religious body.

On the ninth week an Englishman was flown over from London on instructions of his government.

Sir Anthony Brevourt stood at the foot of Fontine's bed, his jaw firm, his eyes compassionate and yet not without hardness. 'Donatti's dead, you know. He threw himself off the balustrade of St Peter's. Nobody mourns him, least of all the Curia.'

'Yes, I knew that. At the end an act of insanity.'

'The five priests who were with him have been punished. Three were excommunicated, prosecuted, and will be in prison for several decades. The other two are under life penance in the Transvaal. What was done in the church's name horrifies its leaders.'

'It seems to me that too many churches permit the fanatics, then look back in astonishment, amazed at what was done in "their names". It's not restricted to Rome.

Trappings often obscure purposes, don't they? That goes for governments, too. I want *questions answered!*'

Brevourt blinked several times at Fontine's outburst and replied rapidly, mechanically. 'I'm prepared to offer answers where I can. I've been instructed to withhold nothing.'

'First, Stone. The order of execution has been explained; I have no comment. I want to know the rest. All of it.'

'Precisely what you've been told. I didn't trust you. I was convinced when you first arrived in London that you'd made up your mind to reveal nothing about the train from Salonika. I expected you to make your own arrangements, on your own terms. We couldn't let that happen.'

'Stone reported my movements then?'

'Every one. You made eleven trips across the Channel, and one to Lisbon. With Stone's help we had you covered each time. In the event of capture, we were prepared to negotiate an exchange with the enemy.'

'Suppose I'd been killed?'

'In the beginning it was a risk we calculated, over-shadowed by the fact that you might have bolted, made contact with regard to "Salonika". And in June of forty-two, after Oxfordshire, Teague agreed not to send you across any longer.'

'What happened in Oxfordshire? The priest – if he *was* a priest – who led those planes in was Greek. From the Order of Xenope. Your first constituency, I believe.'

Brevourt pursed his lips and breathed deeply. Admissions were being made that both pained and embarrassed him. 'Stone, again. The Germans had tried for two years to locate the compound in Oxfordshire. He leaked the precise bearings to Berlin, and at the same time made his own arrangements with the Greeks. He convinced them there was a way to break you. It was worth trying; a broken man talks. He didn't give a damn himself about "Salonika", but the raid served his primary aim. He put a fanatic priest in the compound and co-ordinated the strike.'

'For God's sake, *why*?'

'To kill your wife. If she'd been killed, even severely wounded, he assumed you'd turn on all things British, get out of MI6. He was right. You nearly did, you know. He hated you; blamed you for ruining a brilliant career. As I understand it, he tried to keep you in London that night.'

Victor remembered the horrible night. Stone, the methodical psychopath, had counted the minutes, projected the speed of a car. Fontine reached for his cigarettes on the bedside table. 'The last question. And don't lie to me. What was on the train from Salonika?'

Brevourt walked away from the bed. He crossed to the hospital window and was silent for a moment.

'Parchments, writings from the past which, if made public, could bring chaos to the religious world. Specifically, they would tear the Christian world apart. Accusations and denials would be hurled back and forth, governments might have to choose sides. Above everything, in enemy hands the documents would have been an ideological weapon beyond anything imaginable.'

'Can documents do this?' asked Fontine.

'These documents can,' replied Brevourt, turning away from the window. 'Have you ever heard of the Filioque Clause?'

Victor inhaled. His mind went back over the years to the impartial lessons of his childhood. 'It's part of the Creed of Nicaea.'

'More properly, the Nicene Creed of the year 381; there were many councils, subtle alterations of the creed. The Filioque was a later addition that once and for all established the Christ figure as substance with God. It's rejected by the Eastern church as misleading. For the early Eastern church, especially the sects that followed the scholar-priest Arians, Christ as the son of God was the teacher; his divinity was not equal to God's. No such equality could exist for them in those times. When the Filioque was first proposed, the Patriarchate of Constantine recognized it for what it was: a doctrinal division that favoured Rome. A theological symbol that was the excuse to divide and conquer new territories. And quite right they were. The Holy Roman Empire became a global force – as the globe was known. Its influence spread throughout the world on that single premise, this specialized divinity of Christ: *Conquer* in the name of *Christ*.' Brevourt stopped, as if searching for words. He walked slowly back towards the foot of the bed.

'Then the documents in that vault,' said Victor, 'refute the Filioque? If so, they challenge the foundation of the Roman church and all the Christian divisions that followed.'

'Yes, they do that,' replied Brevourt quietly. 'Collectively they're called the denials ... the Filioque denials. They include agreements between crowns and caesars from as far away as Spain, in the sixth century, where the Filioque originated, for what many believe were purely political reasons. Others trace what they term the "theological corruption" ... But if that was *all* they did, the world could live with them. Son of God, teacher, one substance. These are theological differences, subjects for biblical scholars to debate. They do more, I'm afraid. In the Patriarchate's fervour to deny the Filioque, it sent out priests to search the holy lands, meet with the Aramaic scholars, unearth everything that ever existed relative to Jesus. They unearthed more than they were looking for. There were rumours of scrolls written during the years just preceding and after the turn of the first century. They traced them, discovered several, and brought them back to Constantine. It is said that one Aramaic scroll raises profound and very specific doubts as to the man known as Jesus. He may never have existed at all.'

The ocean liner headed towards the open waters of the Channel. Fontine stood at the railing and watched the skyline of Southampton. Jane was at his side, one hand gently around his waist, the other crossed in front of her, over his hand on the railing. The crutches with the large metal clasps that held his forearms were to his left, the shiny half circles of stainless steel glistening in the sunlight. He had designed them himself. If it was going to be necessary, as the doctors said, for him to use crutches for a year or more he could damn well improve on the existing product.

Their two sons, Andrew and Adrian, were with their nurse from Dunblane – one of those who had elected to sail to America with the Fontines.

Italy, Campo di Fiori, the train from Salonika were in the past. The cataclysmic parchments that had been taken from the archives of Xenope were somewhere in the vast range of the Italian Alps. Buried for a millennium; perhaps never to be found.

It was better that way. The world had passed through an era of devastation and doubt. Reason demanded that a calm be restored at least for a while, if only on the surface. It was no time for the vault from Salonika.

The future began with the rays of the afternoon sun on the waters of the English Channel. Victor leaned towards his wife and put his face next to hers. Neither spoke; she held his hand in silence.

There was a commotion on the deck. Thirty yards aft the twins had got into a quarrel. Andrew was angry

with his brother Adrian. Childish blows were exchanged.
Fontine smiled.

Children.

BOOK TWO
PART ONE

CHAPTER EIGHTEEN

June 1973

Men. They were men, thought Victor Fontine as he watched his sons thread separately through the guests in the bright sunlight. And twins, second. It was an important distinction, he felt, although it wasn't necessary to dwell on it. It seemed years since anyone had referred to them as the twins. Except Jane and himself, of course. Brothers, yes; but not twins. It was strange how that word had fallen into disuse.

Perhaps the party would revive it for a while. Jane would like that. They were always the twins to Jane. Her Geminis.

The afternoon party at the North Shore house on Long Island was *for* Andrew and Adrian; it was their birthday. The lawns and gardens behind the house, above the boathouse and the water, had been turned into an enormous outdoor *fête champêtre*, as Jane called it. 'A ruddy grown-up picnic! No one has them any more. We will.'

A small orchestra played at the south edge of the terrace, its music serving as an undercurrent to a hundred conversations. Long tables heaped with food were organized on the large expanse of manicured lawn; two bars did brisk business at either end of the rectangular buffet. *Fête champêtre*. Victor had never heard the term before. In thirty-four years of marriage he had never heard it.

How the years had flown! It was as though three decades had been compressed into a time capsule and shot through the skies at incredible speed, only to land and be opened and scanned by participants who had merely grown older.

Andrew and Adrian were near each other now. Andy chatted with the Kempsons by the canapé table. Adrian was at the bar, talking to several young people whose clothes were the only vague evidence of their gender. It was right, somehow, that Andrew should be with the Kempsons. Paul Kempson was president of Centaur Electronics; he was well thought of by the Pentagon. As, of course, was Andrew. Adrian, no doubt, had been cornered by several university students who wanted to question the singularly outspoken attorney who was Victor's son.

Victor noted with a certain satisfaction that both twins were taller than those around them. It was to be expected; neither he nor Jane were short. And they looked somewhat alike, but not identical. Andrew's hair was very light, nearly blond; Adrian's was dark, auburn. Their features were sharp, a combination of his and Jane's, but each with his own identity. The only physical thing they shared in common was their eyes: they were Jane's. Deep blue and penetrating.

At times, in very bright sunlight or in dim shadows, they could be mistaken for each other. But only at such times, under such conditions. And they did not seek them. Each was very much his own man.

The light-haired Andrew was in the army, a dedicated professional. Victor's influence had secured a congressional appointment to West Point, where Andrew had excelled. He'd made two tours of duty in Vietnam, although he despised the way the war was fought. 'Win or get out' was his credo, but none listened, and he wasn't sure it made any difference. Saigon corruption was like no other corruption on the face of the earth.

Yet Andrew was not a spoiler within the ranks, either. Victor understood that. His son was a *believer*. Deep, concerned, unwavering: the military was America's strength. When all the words were said and done, there remained only the power at hand. To be used wisely, but to be *used*.

For the dark-haired Adrian, however, there was *no* limit to be placed on the use of words, and no excuse for armed confrontation. Adrian, the lawyer, was as dedicated in his fashion as his brother, although his demeanour might seem to deny it. Adrian slouched; he gave the appearance of nonchalance where none existed. Legal adversaries had learned never to be lulled by his humour or his seeming lack of concern. Adrian *was* concerned. He was a demon in the courtroom. At least he *had* been for the prosecutor's office in Boston. He was in Washington now.

Adrian had gone from prep school to Princeton to Harvard Law, with a year taken off to wander and grow a beard and play a guitar and sleep with available girls from San Francisco to Bleecker Street. It had been a year when Victor and Jane had held their collective breath, though not always their tempers.

But the life of the open road, the provincial confines of a half-dozen communes palled on Adrian. He could no more accept the aimlessness of unprovoked experience than Victor had nearly thirty years ago at the end of the European war.

Fontine's thoughts were interrupted. The Kempsons were heading over to his chair, excusing their way through the crowd. They would not expect him to get up – no one ever did – but it annoyed Victor that he could not. Without help.

'Damn fine boy,' said Paul Kempson. 'He's got his

head on straight, that Andrew does. I told him if he ever wants to chuck the uniform, Centaur has a place for him.'

'I told him he should *wear* his uniform,' added Kempson's wife brightly. 'He's such a handsome man.'

'I'm sure he thinks it would be disconcerting,' said Fontine, not at all sure. 'No one wants to be reminded of the war at a birthday party.'

'How long's he home for, Victor?' asked Kempson.

'Home? Here? Only for a few days. He's stationed in Virginia now. At the Pentagon.'

'Your other boy's in Washington, too, isn't he? Seems I read something about him in the papers.'

'Yes, I'm sure you did.' Fontine smiled.

'Oh, then they're together. That's nice,' said Alice Kempson.

The orchestra finished one number and began another. The younger couples flocked to the terrace; the party was accelerating. The Kempsons floated away with nods and smiles. Briefly, Victor thought about Alice Kempson's remark.

. . . they're together. That's nice.

But Andrew and Adrian were not together. They worked within twenty minutes of each other but lived separate lives. At times, Fontine thought, *too* separate. They did not laugh together as they once did as children. As men, something had happened between them. Fontine wondered what it was.

Jane acknowledged for roughly the hundredth time that the party *was* a success, wasn't it. A statement. Thank heavens the weather held. The caterers had sworn they could erect the tents in less than an hour, if it was necessary, but by noon the sun was bright, the promise of a beautiful day confirmed.

Not, however, a beautiful evening. Far in the distance,

over the water near Connecticut, the sky was grey. Weather reports predicted scattered-nocturnal-thunder-showers-with-increasingly-steady-precipitation, whatever all *that* meant. Why didn't they simply say it would rain later on?

Two o'clock to six o'clock. Good hours for a Sunday *fête champêtre*. She had laughed at Victor's ignorance of the term. It was so pretentiously Victorian; the fun was in using it. It looked ridiculous on the invitations. Jane smiled, then stifled a laugh. She really *should* control her foolishness, she supposed. She was much too old for that sort of thing.

Across the lawn between the crowds, Adrian was smiling at her. Had he read her thoughts? Adrian, her dark-haired Gemini, had inherited her slightly mad English humour.

He was thirty-one years old. *They* were thirty-one years old. Where had those years gone? It seemed as if only months ago they'd all arrived in New York on the ship. Followed by months of activity that had Victor flying all over the States and back to Europe, furiously building.

And Victor had done it. Fontine Ltd became one of the most sought-after consulting firms in America. Victor's expertise primarily aimed at European reconstruction. The name Fontine on a corporation's presentation was an industrial plus. Knowledge of a given marketplace was assured.

Victor had involved himself totally, not merely for the sake of pride, or instinctive productivity, but for something else. Jane knew it, and at the same time knew she could do nothing to help him. It took his mind off the pain. Her husband was rarely without pain; the operations prolonged his life, but did little to lessen the pain.

She looked at Victor across the lawn, sitting in his hard wooden chair with the straight back, the shiny metal cane at his side. He had been so proud when the two crutches were replaced by the single cane that made it possible for him to walk without being so obvious a cripple.

'Hi, Mrs Fontine,' said the young man with the very long hair. 'It's one terrific party! Thanks for letting me bring my friends. They really wanted to meet Adrian.'

The speaker was Michael Reilly. The Reillys were their nearest neighbours on the shore, about a half a mile down the beach. Michael was in law school at Columbia. 'That's very flattering!'

'Hey, he's *great*! He wrapped up that Tesco anti-trust in Boston when even the federal courts thought it was too loose. Everyone knew it was a Centaur company, but it took Adrian to nail it.'

'Don't discuss it with Mr Kempson.'

'Don't worry. I saw him at the club and he told me to get a haircut. What the hell, so did my father.'

'You won, I see.'

Michael grinned. 'He's mad as a bull but he can't say anything. I'm on the honours list. We made a deal.'

'Good for you. Make him live up to it.'

The Reilly boy laughed and leaned over, kissing her cheek. 'You're outta sight!' He grinned again and left, beckoned by a girl at the edge of the patio.

Young people liked her, thought Jane. It was a comforting realization these days when the young found so little to like, or to approve. They liked her in spite of the fact that she refused to make concessions to youth. Or to age. Her hair was streaked – God, more than streaked – with grey; her faced was lined – as it should be lined – and there were no discussions of a skin nip here, or a tuck there, as so many of her friends had done. She thanked her stars she'd kept her figure. All things considered, not bad for sixty ... *plus*, damn it.

'Excuse me, Mrs Fontine?' It was the maid; she'd come out of the turmoil that was the kitchen.

'Yes, Grace? Problems?'

'No, ma'am. There's a gentleman at the door. He asked for you or Mr Fontine.'

'Tell him to come out.'

'He said he'd rather not. He's a foreign gentleman. A priest. I thought with so many people, Mr Fontine—'

'Yes, you were right,' interrupted Jane, understanding the maid's concerns. Victor did not relish walking among his guests as he was forced to walk. 'I'll go see him.'

The priest stood in the hallway, his black suit ill-fitting and old, his face thin and tired. He appeared awed, frightened.

Jane spoke coldly. She could not help herself. 'I'm Mrs Fontine.'

'Yes, you are the *signora*,' replied the priest awkwardly, a large, stained envelope in his hand. 'I have seen the pictures. I did not mean to intrude. So many automobiles.'

'What is it?'

'I have come from Rome, *signora*. I bring a letter for the *padrone*. You will see that he gets it, please?' The priest held out the envelope.

Andrew watched his brother at the bar with the long-haired students, dressed in their uniforms of denim and suede, medallions around their necks. Adrian would never learn; his audience was useless. They were fakes. It was not simply the profusions of unkempt hair and the offbeat clothes that bothered the soldier; those were only symptoms. It was the pretence that went with these shallow expressions of nonconformity. By and large they were insufferable; antagonistic people with unkempt minds.

They spoke so intensely, so knowingly, of 'movements' and 'countermovements' as though they were participants, shifters of political thought. *This* world, *that* world ... the *third* world. And that was the biggest joke of all, because not one in ten thousand would know how to act as a revolutionary. They had neither the commitment nor the guts nor the savvy.

They were misfits who threw plastic bags of shit when no one paid attention to their ravings. They were ... freaks, and, Christ, he couldn't stand the freaks. But Adrian did not understand; his brother looked for values where there weren't any. Adrian was a fool; but then he learned that seven years ago. Seven years ago he had discovered just how big a fool his brother was. Adrian was a misfit in the worst sense; he had every reason not to be.

Adrian glanced up at him from the bar; he turned away. His brother was a bore, and the sight of him proselytizing to that particular audience was distasteful.

The soldier hadn't always felt this way. Ten years ago when he'd got out of The Point he hadn't *hated* with the vehemence he felt now. He didn't think much of Adrian and his collection of misfits, but there was no hatred. The way the Johnson crowd began handling South-east Asia, there was something to be said for the dissenters' attitude. *Get out.*

Translated: *Obliterate Hanoi. Or get out.*

He had explained his position time and again. To the freaks. To Adrian. But no one wanted to hear it from a soldier. 'Soldier-boy', that's what they called him. And 'shell-head', and 'missile-fingers', and 'blast-ass'.

But it wasn't the names. Anyone who'd gone through West Point and Saigon could handle that. Ultimately, it was their stupidity. They didn't simply turn off the people who mattered, they antagonized them, infuriated them, and finally *embarrassed* them. And *that* was the final stupidity. They drove even those who agreed with them into opposing positions.

Seven years ago in San Francisco, Andrew had tried to make his brother see that, tried to make him understand that what he was doing was wrong. And stupid – and very dangerous to the brother who was a soldier.

He'd got back from two and a half years in the Mekong Delta with one of the finest record sheets in the army. His company had the highest body count in the battalion; he'd been decorated twice, his first-lieutenancy lasting a month before he was given his captain's bars. He was that rare commodity in armed forces, a young, brilliant military strategist from an immensely wealthy, influential family. He was on his way up to the top – where he belonged. He was being flown back for reassignment, which was another way of the Pentagon's saying: *That's our man. Keep your eye on him. Rich, solid, future Joint Chiefs material. A few more combat tours – in selected areas, a few short years – and it's the War College.*

It never hurt the Pentagon to favour a man like him, especially when it was justified. The army needed men from powerful families; they had precious few.

But regardless of what the Pentagon favoured or the army needed, G2 agents had shown up when he got off that plane in California seven years ago. They'd taken him to an office and given him a two-month-old newspaper. On the second page was a story about an insurrection at the army's Presidio in San Francisco. Accompanying the article were photographs of the riot, one showing a group of civilians marching in support of mutinying enlisted men. A face had been circled in red pencil.

It was Adrian. It seemed impossible, but there he was! He wasn't supposed to be there; he was in his last year at law school. In Boston. But he was not in Boston, he was in San Francisco harbouring three convicted deserters who had escaped; that's what the G2 men said. His twin brother was working for the *enemy*! Goddamn it, that's what they *were* and that's what he was *doing*! The Pentagon wouldn't look upon *that* with a whole lot of laughs. Jesus! His brother! His *twin*!

So G2 flew him up north and, out of uniform, he had wandered the streets of Haight-Ashbury until he'd found Adrian.

'These aren't men, they're confused kids,' his brother said in a quiet bar. 'They were never even told what their legal alternatives were; they've been railroaded.'

'They took oaths like everybody else. You can't make exceptions,' Andrew had replied.

'Oh, come on. Two of them didn't know what that oath meant, and the other one genuinely changed his mind. But nobody wants to listen. The judge advocates want examples, and the defence attorneys don't want to make waves.'

'Sometimes examples *have* to be made,' the soldier had insisted.

'And the law says they're entitled to competent counsel. Not barracks drinking buddies who want to look good—'

'Get with it, Adrian!' he interrupted. 'There's a war out there! The firepower's real! Bastards like these cost *lives*.'

'Not if they're over here.'

'Yes, they do! Because others will begin to wonder why they're over *there*.'

'Maybe they should.'

'For Christ's sake, you're talking about *rights*, aren't you?' asked the soldier.

'You better believe it.'

'Well, doesn't the poor son of a bitch on patrol in a rice paddy have any? Maybe *he* didn't know what he was getting into; he just went along because the law said he had to. Maybe *he* changed his mind. But he doesn't have time to think about it; he's trying to stay alive. He gets confused, he gets sloppy, he gets *killed*!'

'We can't reach everybody; it's one of the law's oversights, an abuse built into the system. But we do what we can.'

Adrian would not give him any information seven years ago. He refused to tell him where the deserters were hidden. So the soldier said good-bye in the quiet bar and waited in a San Francisco alley until his brother came out. He followed Adrian for three hours through the acid streets. The soldier was an expert in tracking stray patrols in jungles; San Francisco was just another jungle.

His brother made contact with one of the deserters five blocks from the waterfront. The boy was a black, with a growth of beard on his face. He was tall and thin and matched the photograph in Andrew's pocket. His twin gave the deserter money; it was a simple matter to follow the black down to the waterfront, to a filthy tenement that was as good a hiding place as any in the area.

The phone call was made to the military police. Ten minutes later three convicted deserters were dragged out of the filthy tenement, to spend eight years in the stockades.

The misfit network went to work; the crowds gathered, screeching their epithets, swaying to their adolescent, useless chants. And throwing their plastic bags of faeces.

His brother came up to him in the crowds that night and for several moments just stared at him. Finally he said, 'You've driven me back. Thanks.'

Then Adrian had walked swiftly away to the barricades of would-be revolutionaries.

Andrew's reflections were interrupted by Al Winston,

né Weinstein, an engineer with an aerospace company. Winston had called out his name and was making his way over. Al Winston was heavy into air force contracts, and lived in the Hamptons. Andrew didn't like Winston-Weinstein. Whenever he ran into him he thought of another Jew – and compared them. The Jew he thought of was stationed at the Pentagon after four years under heavy fire in the worst sections of the Delta. Captain Martin Greene was a tough son of a bitch, a great soldier – not a flabby Winston-Weinstein from the Hamptons. And Greene didn't gouge profits from cost over-runs; instead he watched them, catalogued them. Marty Greene was one of *them*. One of Eye Corps.

'Many happy returns, Major,' said Winston, raising his glass.

'Thanks, Al. How are you?'

'Be a lot better if I could sell you boys something. I get no support from the ground troops.' Winston grinned.

'You do pretty well *off* the ground. I read where you're in on the Grumman contract.'

'Nickels and dimes. I've got a laser homing device that can be adapted to heavy artillery. But I can't get to first base.'

Andrew toyed with the idea of sending Winston-Weinstein to Martin Greene. By the time Greene got finished with him, Al Winston would wish he'd never heard of the Pentagon. 'I'll see what I can do. I'm not in procurement—'

'They *listen* to you, Andy.'

'You never stop working, Al.'

'Big house, big bills, rotten kids.' Winston grinned again, then stopped smiling long enough to get across his point. 'Put in a word for me. I'll make it worth your while.'

'With what?' asked Andrew, his eyes straying towards

the boathouse and the Chris-Craft and the sailboats moored in the water. 'Money?'

Winston's grin returned, now nervous, awkward. 'No offence,' said the engineer softly.

Andrew looked at the Jew, thinking again of Captain Martin Greene and the difference between the two men. 'No offence,' he said, walking away.

Christ! Next to the freaks, he despised the *corrupters*. No, that wasn't true. Next to the corrupters, he despised those who allowed themselves to *be* corrupted. They were everywhere. Sitting in boardrooms, playing the golf courses in Georgia and Palm Springs, lapping up the sauce in the country clubs of Evanston and Grosse Pointe. They'd sold their ranks!

Colonels, generals, commanders, admirals. The whole god-damned military establishment was riddled with a new brand of thieves. Men who winked and smiled and put their signatures on committee recommendations, on procurements approvals, on contracts, on over-runs. Because there were understandings made. Today's brigadier was tomorrow's 'consultant' or 'Washington representative'.

Christ, it was easy to hate! The misfits, the corrupters, the corrupted . . .

It was why Eye Corps was formed. A very small, select group of officers who were sick to death of the apathy and corruption and venality that pervaded every branch of the armed forces. Eye Corps was the answer, the medicine that would cure the sickness. For Eye Corps was compiling records from Saigon to Washington. The men of Eye Corps were putting it all together: names, dates, connections, illegal profits.

To hell with the so-called proper channels: up the chain of command. To the inspector general. To the secretary of the army. Who vouched for command?

Who for the IG? Who in his right *mind* would vouch for the civilians?

No one they trusted. So they would do it themselves. Every general – every brigadier and admiral – *anyone* who tolerated any form of deviation would be smoked out and confronted with his crimes.

Eye Corps. That's what it was all about. A handful of the best young officers in the field. And one day they'd walk into the Pentagon and take over. None would dare stand in their way. The Eye Corps indictments would hang like grenades over the heads of the high brass. The grenades would explode if the brass didn't move out, leaving their chairs for the men of the Eye Corps. The Pentagon belonged to them. They would give it meaning again. Strength. *Their* strength.

Adrian Fontine leaned on the bar and listened to the intense young students arguing, aware that his brother was staring at them. He looked up at Andrew; the soldier's cold eyes held their usual veiled contempt and then glanced away as Al Winston approached, raising his glass to the major.

Andrew was beginning to wear his contempt too openly, thought Adrian. His brother had lost some of his well-known cool; things aggravated the soldier too quickly these days.

God, how they'd veered from each other! They'd been so close once. The Geminis . . . brothers, twins, friends. The Geminis were the *best*! And somewhere along the line – in their teens, in prep school – it all started to change. Andrew began to think he was better than best, and Adrian became less than convinced he was adequate. Andrew never questioned his abilities; Adrian wasn't sure he had very many.

He was sure now. The terrible years of indecision were over; he'd passed through uncertainty and found his own way. Thanks in large measure to his very positive brother, the soldier.

And today, on their birthday, he had to confront his brother and ask some very disturbing questions. Questions that went to the core of Andrew's strength.

Core? It was appropriate; the sound was right, the spelling wrong.

Eye Corps was the name they'd uncovered. His brother was on the list. Eight self-deluded elitists who concealed evidence for their own purposes. A small band of officers who had convinced themselves they should run the Pentagon through what amounted to sheer blackmail. The situation might have been comic except that the evidence was there, and Eye Corps had it. The Pentagon was not above being manipulated by fear. Eye Corps was dangerous; it had to be ripped out.

They'd settle for that. They'd hand over a blanket subpoena to the army lawyers and let them handle it quietly. As long as the army lawyers did handle it and did not cover up. Perhaps it wasn't the time for demoralizing trials and long prison sentences. The guilt was so widespread and the motives so complex. But there was one irreducible condition. *Get the elitists out of uniform; clean your military house.*

Jesus, the irony of it! In San Francisco, Andrew had blown a crude whistle in the name of military law. Now, seven years later, he, Adrian, was blowing the whistle. Less crudely, he hoped, but the law was no less specific. The charge was obstruction of justice.

So much had changed. Nine months ago he was an assistant prosecutor in Boston, happy doing what he was doing, building a reputation that could lead to just about anywhere. Building it *himself*. Not having it *given* to him because he was Adrian Fontine, son of Victor Fontine, Limited; brother of West Point's celebrated Major Andrew Fontine, immaculate warrior.

Then a man had called him in early October, asking him to have drinks at the Copely bar late in the afternoon. The man's name was James Nevins and he was black; he was also an attorney and he worked for the Justice Department in Washington.

Nevins was the spokesman for a small contingent of harassed, disaffected government lawyers who burned under the tactics of the most politicized Justice Department in memory. The phrase 'White House calling' simply meant that another manipulation was taking place. The lawyers were worried, genuinely worried. Those manipulations were taking the country too close to the spectre of a police state.

The lawyers needed help. From the outside. Someone who could organize and evaluate, who could set up and pay for a command centre where they could meet privately and discuss their progress.

Someone, frankly, who could not be harassed. For reasons more obvious than not, one Adrian Fontine fitted the bill. Would he accept?

Adrian hadn't wanted to leave Boston. He had his work; he had his girl. A slightly mad, brilliant girl he adored. Barbara Pierson, BA, MA, PhD, Associate Professor, Anthropology Laboratories, Harvard University. She of the quick deep laugh, the light-brown hair and the dark-brown eyes. They'd been living together for a year and a half; it wasn't easy to leave. But Barbara had packed for him and sent him on his way because she knew he had to go.

Just as he had had to go seven, eight years ago. He had to leave Boston then, too. A depression had swept over him. He was the wealthy son of a powerful father; the twin brother of a man the army paraded in dispatches as one of the brightest young lights in the military.

What was left? For him? Who *was* he?

So he fled the trappings of a lifetime to see what he

could find for himself. That was *his*. It was his own personal crisis; he couldn't explain it to anyone. And he ended up in San Francisco where there was a fight, a struggle he could understand. Where he could help. Until the immaculate warrior came along and ripped the scene apart.

Adrian smiled, remembering the morning after that terrible night in San Francisco. He'd got roaring drunk and woke up in the house of a legal aid lawyer in Cape Mendocino sick and vomiting.

'If you're who you say you are, you can do more than any of us,' said the lawyer in Cape Mendocino that morning. 'Hell, my old man was a janitor at the May Company.'

In the seven intervening years Adrian had tried. But he knew he had only just begun.

'It's a constitutional ambiguity! Isn't that right, Adrian?'

'What? Sorry, I didn't hear what you said.' The students at the bar had been arguing among themselves; now all eyes were on him.

'Free press versus pre-trial bias,' said an intense young girl, stumbling over the words.

'It's a grey area, I think,' replied Adrian. 'Each case is judged by itself.'

The youngsters wanted more than he gave them, so they went back to yelling at each other.

Grey area. Saigon's Eye Corps had been a grey area only weeks ago. Rumours had filtered back to Washington that a small cadre of young senior officers were regularly harassing enlisted personnel on the docks and in the warehouses, insisting on copies of shipment manifests and destination schedules. Shortly after, in one of the numerous, halfheartedly pursued anti-trust cases at Justice, there was a plaintiff's allegation that records had been stolen from the corporation's Saigon offices, thus constituting illegally obtained evidence. The case would be dropped.

The lawyers at Justice wondered whether there was a connection between the strange group of officers who scoured the shipment manifests and corporations under contract to the Pentagon. Had the military gone that far? The conjecture was enough to send Jim Nevins to Saigon.

The black attorney found what he was looking for. In a warehouse in the Tan Son Nhut cargo area. An officer was in the process of illegally transcribing security-related information on armaments supplies. Threatened with charges, the officer broke, and Eye Corps was revealed for everything it was. There were eight officers; the man caught knew the names of seven. The eighth was in Washington, that's all he knew.

Andrew Fontine headed the list of those identified.

Eye Corps. Nice fellows, thought Adrian. Just what the country needed; storm troopers out to save the nation.

Seven years ago in San Francisco his brother had not given him any warning before the action started, and the sirens came screaming into Haight-Ashbury. Adrian would be more considerate. He was going to give Andrew five days. There'd be no sirens, no riots . . . no eight-year sentences in the stockades. But the celebrated Major Andrew Fontine would be out of the army.

And although the work in Washington was nowhere near completed, Adrian would go back to Boston for a while. Back to Barbara.

He was tired. And sick with what faced him in an hour or so. The pain was real. Whatever else, Andrew was his brother.

The final guests had left. The orchestra was packing its instruments, and the caterers were cleaning up the lawn.

The sky was growing darker, as much because of the threatening clouds over the water as by the approach of nightfall.

Adrian walked across the lawn to the flagstone steps and down to the boathouse. Andrew was waiting for him; he had told the soldier to be there.

'Happy birthday, counsellor,' said Andrew as Adrian came through the boathouse door. The soldier leaned against the wall beyond the boat slip, his arms folded, smoking a cigarette.

'Same to you,' answered Adrian, stopping at the edge of the slip. 'You staying tonight?'

'Are you?' asked Andrew.

'I thought I might. The old man looks pretty bad.'

'Then I won't,' said the soldier politely.

Adrian paused; he knew he was expected to speak. He wasn't quite sure how to begin, so instead he looked around the boathouse. 'We had some good laughs down here.'

'Did you want to reminisce? Is that why you asked me to come down here?'

'No ... I wish it were that simple.'

The soldier flipped the cigarette into the water. 'I hear you left Boston. You're in Washington.'

'Yes. For a while. I keep thinking we'll run into each other.'

'I doubt it,' said the major, smiling. 'We don't travel in the same circles. You working for a DC firm?'

'No. I guess you might say I'm a consultant.'

'That's the best job in Washington.' Andrew's voice was laced with quiet contempt. 'Who are you counselling?'

'Some people who are very upset—'

'Oh, a consumer group; isn't that nice.' It was an insulting statement. 'Good for you!'

Adrian stared at his brother; the soldier returned the

look. 'Don't dismiss me, Andy. You're in no position to do that. You're in trouble. I'm not here to help you, I can't do that. I'm here to warn you.'

'What the hell are you talking about?' asked the major softly.

'A deposition was taken from an officer in Saigon by one of our people. We have a complete statement about the activities of a group of eight men who call themselves Eye Corps.'

Andrew bolted upright against the wall, his face pinched, his fingers stretched, curved, immobile. He seemed to freeze; he spoke barely above a whisper, spacing his words out. 'Who is "we"?'

'You'll know the origin soon enough. It's on the subpoena.'

'*Subpoena?*'

'Yes. The Justice Department, a specialist division . . . I won't tell you the individual attorneys, but I will tell you that your name heads the Eye Corps list. We know there are eight of you; seven have been identified, the eighth is at the Pentagon. In procurement. We'll find him.'

Andrew held his position against the wall; everything about him remained immobile, except the muscles of his jaw, which moved slowly, steadily. Once again his voice was low, measured. 'What have you done? What have you bastards *done*?'

'Stopped you,' answered Adrian simply.

'What do you know? What have you been told?'

'The truth. We've no reason to doubt it.'

'You need proof for a subpoena!'

'We need probable cause. We have that.'

'One deposition! *Nothing!*'

'Others'll follow. What difference does it make? You're finished.'

Andrew's voice calmed. He spoke matter-of-factly.

'Officers complain. Up and down the zones, officers complain every day—'

'Not this way. There's no fine line between complaints and blackmail. It's very defined, very distinct. You crossed over it.'

'*Who have we blackmailed?*' asked Andrew swiftly. 'No one!'

'Records were kept, evidence suppressed; the intent was clear. That's in the deposition.'

'There *are* no records!'

'Oh, come on, they're *somewhere*,' said Adrian wearily. 'But I repeat, who gives a goddamn? You're finished.'

The soldier moved. He breathed deeply and stood erect against the wall. 'Listen to me,' he said quietly, his voice strained. 'You don't know what you're doing. You say you're a consultant to men who are upset. We both know what that means; we're the Fontines. Who needs resources when they have us?'

'I don't see it that way,' broke in Adrian.

'It's *true*!' shouted the soldier. And then he lowered his voice. 'You don't have to spell out what you're doing, the Boston newspapers did that. You nail the big fellows, the vested interests, you call them. You're good. Well, what the hell do you think *I'm* doing? We're nailing them, too! You stop Eye Corps, you're destroying the finest young senior officers in the field, men who want to rip out the garbage! Don't *do* that, Adree! *Join* us! I mean that.'

'Join—' Adrian repeated the word in disbelief. Then he added quietly, 'You're out of your mind. What makes you think that's remotely possible?'

Andrew took a step away from the wall; his eyes were steady on his brother. 'Because we want the same thing.'

'No, we don't.'

'*Think*, for God's sake! "Vested interests." You use this

a lot, "vested interests". I read your summation in the Tesco case; you repeated it continuously.'

'It applied. One company owning many, setting a single policy when there should have been competition. What's your point?'

'You use the term negatively because that's the way you find it. Okay, I'll buy that. But I submit there's another way to look at it. There can be *good* vested interests. Like us. Our interest isn't ourselves; we don't *need* anything. Our interest is the country and our resources are considerable. We're in positions to *do* something. I'm doing it. For Christ's sake, don't *stop* me!'

Adrian turned away from his brother and walked aimlessly along the moist planks of the boathouse towards the huge opening that led to the open water. The waves slapped against the pilings. 'You're very glib, Andy. You were always very glib and sure and truly confident. But it's not going to work.' He turned again and faced the soldier diagonally across the slip. 'You say we don't need anything. I think we do; we both need – want – something. And what you want frightens me because I've got the idea what your concept of finest is. Frankly, it scares the hell out of me. The thought of your "finest senior officers" controlling the country's hardware is enough to send me running to the library to reread the Constitution.'

'That's arrogant horseshit! You don't know them!'

'I know the way they operate, the way you operate. If it'll make you feel better, you made some sense in San Francisco. I didn't like it, but I recognized it.' Adrian walked back along the slip. 'You're not making sense now, which is why I'm warning you. Save what you can of your neck, I owe you that much. Get out as gracefully as you can.'

'You can't force me,' said Andrew scathingly. 'My record's one of the best. Who the hell are *you*? One lousy statement from a disgruntled officer in a combat zone. Bullshit!'

'I'll spell it out!' Adrian stopped by the boathouse doorway, raising his voice. 'In five days – next Friday, to be precise – a blanket subpoena will be served on the adjutant general of the Courts of Military Justice. He'll have the weekend to negotiate his arrangements. Arrangements *can* be negotiated, but there's one irrevocable condition. You're *out*. All of you!'

The soldier started forward, then stopped, his foot on the edge of the slip, as if he were about to spring across, lunging at his enemy. He held himself in check; waves of nausea and fury seemed to pass over him and through him. 'I could ... kill you,' he whispered. 'You're everything I despise.'

'I guess I am,' said Adrian, closing his eyes briefly, rubbing them in weariness. 'You'd better get to the airport,' he continued, now looking at his brother. 'You've got a lot to do. I suggest you start with this so-called evidence you've been sitting on. We understand you've been collecting it for damn near three years. Get it to the proper authorities.'

In angry silence the soldier lurched in rapid strides around the slip, past Adrian, and out to the boathouse steps. He began climbing, taking the flagstone stairs two at a time.

Adrian moved swiftly to the door and called out, halting his brother on the border of the lawn.

'Andy!'

The soldier stood motionless. But he did not turn around, or speak. So the lawyer continued.

'I admire your strength, I always have. Just as I admire father's. You're part of him, but you're not all of him. You missed something, so let's understand each other. You're everything I consider dangerous. I guess that means you're everything *I* despise.'

'We understand each other,' said Andrew, repeating the words in a monotone. He started up across the lawn towards the house.

CHAPTER NINETEEN

The orchestra and the caterers left. Andrew was driven to La Guardia Airport. There was a nine o'clock plane to Washington.

Adrian remained on the beach by himself for nearly thirty minutes after his brother left. Finally he wandered up to the house to talk to his parents. He told them he had intended to stay the night but now thought he should leave. He had to get back to Washington.

'You should have gone with your brother,' said Jane at the front door.

'Yes, I should have,' said Adrian softly. 'I didn't think.' He said his good-byes.

When he left, Jane walked out to the terrace, carrying the letter brought by the priest. She held it out for her husband, unable to conceal her fear. 'A man brought this. About three hours ago. He was a priest. He said he was from Rome.'

Victor looked up at his wife. There was no comment in his eyes, and by the lack of it, there was. 'Why did you wait?'

'Because it was your sons' birthday.'

'They're strangers to each other,' said Fontine, taking the envelope. 'They're both our children, but they're very far apart.'

'It won't last. It's the war.'

'I hope you're right,' said Victor, opening the envelope and taking out the letter. It ran several pages, the handwriting small but precise. 'Do we know a man named Aldobrini?'

'Who?'

'Guido Aldobrini. That's the signature.' Fontine held up the last page.

'I don't think so,' answered Jane, sitting down in the nearest chair, her eyes on the threatening sky. 'Can you see in this light? It's getting darker.'

'It is sufficient.' Victor put the pages in sequence and began to read.

Signor Fontini-Cristi:

You do not know me although we met many years ago. That meeting cost me the better part of my life. I have spent over a quarter of a century in the Transvaal in holy penance for an act of shame. I did not touch you myself, but I observed and did not raise my voice for mercy, which was an indecent and unholy thing.

Yes, Signore, I was one of the priests with the Cardinal Donatti that dawn at Campo di Fiori. For what we believed was the preservation of Christ's Mother Church on earth, the Cardinal convinced us that there were no laws of God or man or mercy standing between our actions and the preservation of God's church. All our scholastic training and vows of obedience – not only to our superiors, but to the highest authority of conscience – were twisted by the power of Donatti's influence. I have spent twenty-five years trying to understand, but that is another story not pertinent here. One would have had to know the Cardinal to understand.

I am retired from my cloth. The illnesses of the African forests have taken their toll, and thanks be to Christ I do not fear death. For I have given of myself as fully as I knew how. I am cleansed and await the judgement of God.

Before I face our merciful Lord, however, there is information I must impart to you, for to withhold it now would be no less a sin than that for which I have paid holy penance.

The work of Donatti continues. A man, one of the three defrocked priests who were imprisoned by the civil court for their assault on you, has been released. As you perhaps know, one took his own life, the other died of natural causes while in prison. This third man survives and for motives beyond my comprehension, has rededicated himself to the pursuit of the Salonika documents. I say beyond my comprehension, for Cardinal Donatti was discredited in the highest circles of the Vatican. The Grecian documents cannot affect the Holy Mother Church. Divine revelation cannot be contravened by the hand of mortal man.

This defrocked priest goes by the name of Enrici Gaetamo, and he has taken to wearing the collar denied him by apostolic decree. It is my understanding that his years spent in the criminal institution have done nothing to enlighten his soul or show him the ways of a merciful Christ. On the contrary, I am told he is Donatti incarnate. A man to be feared.

He currently, painstakingly, researches every detail he can unearth relative to the train from Salonika thirty-three years ago. His travels have carried him from the yards at Edhessa, through the Balkans, over the rail routes beyond Monfalcone into the northern Alpine regions. He seeks out all he can find who knew the son of Fontini-Cristi. He is a man possessed. He subscribes to the code of Donatti. There is no law of God or man that will interfere with his 'journey for Christ', as he phrases it. Nor will he reveal to anyone the objective of his journey. But I know, and now you do. And soon I shall depart this life.

Gaetamo resides in a small hunting lodge in the hills of Varese. I'm sure the proximity to Campo di Fiori does not escape you.

This is all I can tell you; it is all I know. That he will attempt to reach you, I am certain. That you be warned and remain safe in God's hands, is my prayer.

In sorrow and personal anguish for my past, I remain,

Guido Aldobrini

There was the sound of thunder over the water; Fontine wished the symbolism were not so crudely simple. The clouds were above them now; the sun was gone and the rains began. He was grateful for the diversion. He looked at Jane. She was staring at him; somehow he had communicated to her his profound uneasiness.

'Go in,' he said softly. 'I'll follow in a minute or two.'

'The letter—'

'Of course,' he answered her unspoken question as he replaced the pages in the envelope and handed it to her. 'Read it.'

'You'll be drenched. The rain will get stronger.'

'It's refreshing; you know I like the rain.' He smiled up at her. 'Then perhaps you'll help me change the brace while we talk.'

She stood above him for a moment, and he could feel her eyes on him. But as always, she would leave him alone when he wished it.

He was chilled by his thoughts, not the rain. The letter from Aldobrini was not the first time Salonika had reappeared. He had said nothing to Jane for there was nothing concrete, only a series of obscurely disturbing – seemingly minor – occurrences.

Three months ago he had gone to Harkness for yet another week of corrective surgery. Several days after the operation he'd had a visitor whose appearance startled him; a monsignor from the Archdiocese of New York. His name was Land, he said. He had returned to the United States after many years in Rome, and wanted to meet Victor because of information he had come across in the Vatican archives.

The priest was solicitous; what struck Fontine was that the cleric knew a great deal about his physical condition, far more than a casual visitor would know.

It was a very odd half hour. The priest was a student of history, he said. He had come across archive documents that raised profoundly disturbing questions between the house of Fontini-Cristi and the Vatican. Historical questions that led to the break between the *padroni* of the north and the Holy See. When Victor was well again, perhaps they could discuss the past. The *historical* past. He had ended his good-byes with a direct reference to the assault at Campo di Fiori. The pain and anguish inflicted by one maniacal prelate could not be laid at the soul of the church, he said.

About five weeks later there'd been a second incident. Victor had been in his Washington office, preparing to testify before a congressional committee looking into the tax concessions enjoyed by American shippers sailing under the Paraguayan flag, when his intercom buzzed.

'Mr Fontine, Mr Theodore Dakakos is here. He says he wants to pay his respects.'

Dakakos was one of the young Greek shipping giants, an impertinent rival of Onassis and Niarchos, and far better liked. Fontine told his secretary to send him in.

Dakakos was a large man with a blunt open expression on his face that might become an American football player more than a tycoon. He was around forty years of age; his English was precise, the language of a student.

He had flown to Washington to observe the hearings, perhaps to learn something, he said smiling. Victor laughed; the Greek's reputation for integrity was matched only by the legend of his acute business sense. Fontine told him so.

'I was most fortunate. At a very young age I was given the advantages of an education by a sympathetic but remote religious brotherhood.'

'You were, indeed, fortunate.'

'My family was not wealthy, but they served their church, I'm told. In ways that today I do not understand.'

The young Greek magnate was saying something beyond his words, but Victor could not determine what it was. 'Gratitude as well as God, then, moves in strange ways,' said Victor, smiling. 'Your reputation is a fine one. You do credit to those who aided you.'

'Theodore is my first name, Mr Fontine. My full name is Theodore Annaxas Dakakos. Throughout my schooling I was known as Annaxas the Younger. Does that mean anything to you?'

'In what way?'

'The name Annaxas.'

'I've dealt with literally hundreds of your countrymen over the years. I don't think I've ever run across the name Annaxas.'

The Greek had remained silent for several moments. Then he spoke quietly. 'I believe you.'

Dakakos left soon after.

The third occurrence was the strangest of all; it triggered a memory of violence so sharply into focus that Fontine lost his breath. It had happened only ten days ago in Los Angeles. He was at the Beverly Hills Hotel for conferences between two widely divergent companies trying to merge their interests. He had been called in to salvage what he could; the task was impossible.

Which was why he was taking the sun in the early afternoon, instead of sitting inside the hotel listening to lawyers trying to justify their retainers. He was drinking a Campari at a table in the outside pool area, astonished at the number of good-looking people who apparently did not have to work for a living.

'*Guten Tag, mein Herr.*'

The speaker was a woman in her late forties or early fifties, that age so well cosmeticized by the well-to-do. She was of medium height, quite well proportioned, with streaked blonde hair. She wore white slacks and a blue blouse. Covering her eyes were a pair of large silver-rimmed sunglasses. Her German was natural, not studied. He replied in his own – academic less natural – as he rose awkwardly.

'Good afternoon. Have we met? I'm sorry, but I don't seem to remember.'

'Please sit down. It's difficult for you. I know that.'

'You do? Then we *have* met.'

The woman sat down opposite him. She continued in English. 'Yes. But you had no such difficulties then. You were a soldier then.'

'During the war?'

'There was a flight from Munich to Müllheim. And a whore from the camps escorted on that flight by three Wehrmacht pigs. More pigs than she, I try to tell myself.'

'My God!' Fontine caught his breath. 'You were a *child*. What happened to you?'

She told him briefly. She had been taken by the French Resistance fighters to a transit camp southwest of Montbéliard. There for several months she endured agonies best left undescribed, as she experienced the process of narcotics withdrawal. She had tried to commit suicide numerous times, but the Resistance people had other ideas. They banked on the fact that once the drugs were expunged, her memories would be motive enough to turn her into an effective underground agent. She was already tough; that much they could see.

'They were right, of course,' the woman said, ten days ago at the table on the patio of the Beverly Hills Hotel. 'They kept watch over me night and day, men and women. The men had more fun; the French never waste anything, do they?'

'You survived the war,' Fontine replied, not caring to probe.

'With a bucket full of medals. *Croix de guerre, Légion d'honneur, Légion de résistance*.'

'And so you became a great motion picture star and I was too stupid to recognize you.' Victor smiled gently.

'Hardly. Although I've had occasions to be associated, as it were, with many prominent people of the motion picture industry.'

'I'm afraid I don't understand.'

'I became – and at the risk of sounding immodest, still am – the most successful madame in the south of France. The Cannes Film Festival alone provides sufficient income for a perfectly adequate subsistence.' It was the woman's turn to smile. It was a good smile, thought Fontine. Genuine, alive.

'Then I'm very happy for you. I'm Italian enough to find a certain honourableness in your profession.'

'I knew you were. And would. I'm here on a talent hunt. It would be my pleasure to grant any request you might have. There are a number of my girls out there in the pool.'

'No, thank you. You're most kind, but, as you said, I am not the man I was.'

'I think you're magnificent,' she said simply. 'I always have.' She smiled at him. 'I must go. I recognized you and wanted to speak to you, that's all.' She rose from the table and extended her hand. 'Don't get up.'

The handshake was firm. 'It's been a pleasure – and a relief – to see you again,' he said.

She held his eyes and spoke quietly. 'I was in Zürich a few months ago. They traced me through a man named Lübok. To you. He was a Czech. A queen, I'm told. He was the man on the plane with us, wasn't he?'

'Yes. A very brave man, I must add. A king, in my judgement.' Victor was so startled he replied instinctively, without comprehending. He had not thought of Lübok in years.

'Yes, I remember. He saved all of us. They broke him.' The woman released his hand.

'Broke him? About *what*? My God, the man, if he's alive, is my age or more. Seventy or better. Who would be interested in such old men? What are you talking about?'

'About a man named Vittorio Fontini-Cristi, son of Savarone.'

'You're talking nonsense. Nonsense I understand, but I don't see how it might concern you. *Or* Lübok.'

'I don't know any more. Nor do I care to. A man in Zürich came to my hotel room and asked questions about you. Naturally, I couldn't answer them. You were merely an Allied Intelligence officer who saved a whore's life. But he knew about Anton Lübok.'

'Who was this man?'

'A priest. That is all I know. Good-bye, *Kapitän*.' She turned and walked away, waving and smiling at various girls who were splashing about in the pool and laughing too obviously.

A priest. In Zürich.

... He seeks out all he can find who knew the son of Fontini-Cristi ...

Now he understood the enigmatic meeting at the pool-side in Los Angeles. A defrocked priest had been released after nearly thirty years in prison and revived the hunt for the documents of Constantine.

The work of Donatti continues, the letter said. *He currently, painstakingly, researches every detail he can unearth ... his travels have carried him from the yards at Edhessa, through the Balkans ... beyond Monfalcone into the northern Alpine regions.*

He seeks out all he can find who knew the son of Fontini-Cristi.

And thousands of miles away in New York City, another priest – very much *of* the cloth – comes into a hospital room and speaks of an act of barbarism that could not be separated from those documents. Lost three decades ago and hunted still.

And in Washington, a young industrial giant walks into an office and for no apparent reasons says his family served the church in ways he did not understand.

'... I was given ... advantages ... by a sympathetic but remote religious brotherhood ...'

The *Order of Xenope*. It was suddenly so very clear.

Nothing was coincidence.

It had come back. The train from Salonika had plunged through thirty years of sleep and reawakened. It had to be controlled before the hatreds collided, before the fanatics turned the search into a holy war, as they had done three decades ago. Victor knew he owed that much to his father, his mother, to the loved ones slain in the white lights of Campo di Fiori; to those who had died in Oxfordshire. To a misguided young monk named Petride who took his own life on a rocky slope in Loch Torridon, to a man named Teague, to an undergrounder named Lübok, to an old man named Guido Barzini who had saved him from himself.

The violence could not be allowed to return.

The rain came faster now, harder, in diagonal sheets blown by the wind. Fontine reached for the wrought iron chair beside him and struggled to his feet, his arm clamped within the steel band of his cane.

He stood on the terrace looking out over the water. The wind and the rain cleared his mind. He knew what he had to do, where he had to go.

To the hills of Varese.

To Campo di Fiori.

CHAPTER TWENTY

The heavy car approached the gates of Campo di Fiori. Victor stared out of the window, aware of the spasm in his back; the eye was recording, the mind remembering.

His life had been altered, in pain, on the stretch of ground beyond the gates. He tried to control the memory; he could not suppress it. The images he observed were forced out of his mind's eye, replaced by black suits and white collars.

The car went through the gates; Victor held his breath. He had flown into Milan from Paris as unobtrusively as possible. In Milan he had taken a single room at the Albergo Milano, registering simply as: V. Fontine, New York City.

The years had done their work. There were no raised eyebrows, no curious glances; the name triggered no surprises. Thirty years ago a Fontine or a Fontini in Milan would be reason enough for comment. Not now.

Before he left New York he had made one inquiry – any more might have raised an alarm. He had learned the identity of the owners of Campo di Fiori. The purchase had been made twenty-seven years ago; there had been no change of ownership since that time. Yet the name had no impact in Milan. None had heard of it.

Baricours, Père et Fils. A Franco-Swiss company out of Grenoble, that's what the transfer papers said. Yet there was no Baricours, Père et Fils, in Grenoble. No details could be learned from the lawyer who had negotiated the sale. He had died in 1951.

The automobile rolled past the embankment into the circular drive in front of the main house. The spasm in Victor's back was compounded by a sharp stinging sensation behind his eyes; his head throbbed as he re-entered the execution grounds.

He gripped his wrist and dug his fingers into his own flesh. The pain helped; he was able to look out of the window and see what was there now, not thirty-three years ago.

What he saw was a mausoleum. Dead but cared for. Everything was as it had been, but not for the living. Even the orange rays of the setting sun had a dead quality to them: majestically ornamental, but not alive.

'Aren't there ground keepers or men at the gates?' he asked.

The driver turned in his seat. 'Not this afternoon, *padrone*,' he replied. 'There are no guards. And no priests of the Curia.'

Fontine lurched forward in his seat; his metal cane slipped. He stared at the driver.

'I've been tricked.'

'Watched. Expected. Not tricked, really. Inside, a man is waiting for you.'

'One man?'

'Yes.'

'Would his name be Enrici Gaetamo?'

'I told you. There are no priests of the Curia here. Please, go inside. Do you need help?'

'No, I can manage.' Victor got out of the car slowly, each movement a struggle. He understood. His mind was refocusing itself. He had come to Campo di Fiori for answers. For a confrontation. But he had not expected it to be this way.

He walked up the wide marble steps to the oak door of

298

his childhood. He paused and waited for what he thought was inevitable: a sense of overwhelming sorrow. But it did not come, because there was no life here.

He heard the gunning of the engine behind him and turned. The driver had swung the car out into the curve, and driven past the embankment into the road towards the main gate. Whoever he was, he wanted to be away as rapidly as possible.

As he watched, Victor heard the metallic sound of a latch. He turned again to the huge oak door; it had opened.

The shock was impossible to conceal. Nor did he bother to hide it. The rage inside him welled; his whole body trembled in anger.

The man at the door was a *priest*! Dressed in the black cassock of the church. He was an old man and frail. Had he been otherwise, Fontine might have struck out at him.

Instead he stared at the old man and spoke quietly. 'That a priest would be in this house is most painful to me.'

'I'm sorry you feel that way,' replied the priest in a foreigner's Italian, his voice thin but firm. 'We revered the *padrone* of the Fontini-Cristis. We placed our most precious treasures in his hands.'

Their eyes were locked; neither wavered, but the anger within Victor was slowly replaced with incredulity. 'You're Greek,' he said, barely audible.

'I am, but that's not relevant. I'm a monk from Constantine. Please. Come in.' The old priest stepped back to allow Victor to pass. He added softly, 'Take your time. Let your eyes roam. Little has been changed; photographs and inventories were taken of each room. We have maintained everything as it was.'

A mausoleum.

'So did the Germans.' Fontine walked into the

enormous hall. 'It's strange that those who went to such lengths to own Campo di Fiori don't want to change it.'

'One doesn't cut a great jewel or deface a worthy painting. There's nothing strange in that.'

Victor did not reply. Instead, he gripped his cane and walked with difficulty towards the staircase. He stopped in front of the arch that led to the huge drawing room on the left. Everything *was* as it had been. The paintings, the half-tables against the massive walls, the glazed antique mirrors above the tables, the oriental rugs covering the polished floor, the wide staircase, its balustrade glistening.

He looked over through the north arch into the dining room. Twilight shadows fell across the enormous table, now bare, polished, empty, where once the family had sat. He pictured them now; he could hear the chatter and the laughter. Arguments and anecdotes, never-ending talk; dinners were important events at Campo di Fiori.

The figures froze, the voices disappeared. It was time to look away.

Victor turned. The monk gestured at the south arch. 'Shall we go into your father's study?'

He preceded the old man into the drawing room. Involuntarily – for he did not care to activate memories – his eyes fell on the furnishings, suddenly so familiar. Every chair, every lamp, every tapestry and sconce and table was precisely as he remembered it.

Fontine breathed deeply and closed his eyes for a moment. It was macabre. He was passing through a museum that had once been a living part of his existence. In some ways it was the cruellest form of anguish.

He continued on through the door into Savarone's study; it had never been his, although his life nearly ended in that room. He passed by the doorframe through which a severed, bloody hand had been thrown in the shadows.

If there was anything that startled him it was the desk lamp; and the light that spilled downward over the floor from the green shade. It was *precisely* as it was nearly three decades ago. His memory of it was vivid, for it was the light from the lamp that had washed over the shattered skull of Geoffrey Stone.

'Would you care to sit down?' asked the priest.

'In a minute.'

'May I?'

'I beg your pardon?'

'May I sit at your father's desk?' said the monk. 'I've watched your eyes.'

'It's your house, your desk. I'm a visitor.'

'But not a stranger.'

'Obviously. Am I speaking with a representative of Baricours, Père et Fils?'

The old priest nodded silently. He walked slowly around the desk, pulled out the chair, and lowered his frail body into it. 'Don't blame the lawyer in Milan; he couldn't have known. Baricours met your conditions, we made sure of it. Baricours is the Order of Xenope.'

'And my enemy,' said Victor quietly. 'In 1942 there was an MI6 compound in Oxfordshire. You tried to kill my wife. Many innocent people lost their lives.'

'Decisions were made beyond the control of the Elders. The extremists had their way; we couldn't stop them. I don't expect you to accept that.'

'I don't. How did you know I was in Italy?'

'We are not what we once were, but we still have resources. One in particular keeps his eye on you. Don't ask me who it is; I won't tell you. Why did you come back? After thirty years, why did you return to Campo di Fiori?'

'To find a man named Gaetamo,' answered Fontine. 'Enrici Gaetamo.'

'Gaetamo lives in the hills of Varese,' said the monk.

'He's still looking for the train from Salonika. He's travelled from Edhessa, through the Balkans, across Italy, into the northern mountains. Why have you stayed here all these years?'

'Because the *key* is here,' replied the monk. 'A pact was made. In October of 1939, I travelled to Campo di Fiori. It was I who negotiated Savarone Fontini-Cristi's participation. I who sent a dedicated priest on that train with his brother, an engineer. And demanded their deaths in the name of God.'

Victor stared at the monk. The spill of the lamp illuminated the pale, taut flesh and the sad, dead eyes. Fontine recalled the visitor in his Washington office. 'A Greek came to me saying his family served their church once in ways he didn't understand. Was this priest's brother the engineer, named Annaxas?'

The old cleric's head snapped up; the eyes became briefly alive. 'Where did you hear that name?'

Fontine looked away, his eyes falling on a painting beneath a Madonna on the wall. A hunting scene, birds being flushed from a thicket by men with guns. Other birds flew above. 'We'll trade information,' he said quietly. 'Why did my father agree to work with Xenope?'

'You know the answer. He had only one concern: not to divide the Christian world. The defeat of the fascists was all he cared about.'

'Why was the vault taken from Greece in the first place?'

'The Germans were scavengers and Constantine was marked. That was the information we received from Poland and Czechoslovakia. The Nazi commanders stole from museums, tore apart retreats and monasteries. We couldn't take the chance of leaving it there. Your father engineered the removal. Brilliantly. Donatti was tricked.'

'By the use of a second train,' added Victor. 'Mounted and routed identically. Sent three days later.'

302

'Yes. Word of this second train was leaked to Donatti through the Germans, who had no concept of the significance of the vault from Constantine. They looked for treasures – paintings, sculpture, art objects – not obscure writings they were told were valuable only to scholars. But Donatti, the fanatic, could not resist; the Filioque denials had been rumoured for decades. He had to possess them.' The priest of Xenope paused, the memory painful. 'The cardinal's and the German interests coincided. Berlin wanted Savarone Fontini-Cristi's influence destroyed; Donatti wanted to keep him from that train. At all costs.'

'Why was Donatti involved at all?'

'Again, your father. He knew the Nazis had a powerful friend in the Vatican. He wanted Donatti exposed for what he was. The cardinal could not know about that second train unless the Germans told him. Your father intended to make use of this fact. It was the only price Fontini-Cristi asked of us. As it turned out, that price brought about the executions of Campo di Fiori.'

Victor could hear his father's voice piercing through the decades ... *He issues edicts to the uninformed and enforces them by fear ... A disgrace to the Vatican.* Savarone knew the enemy, but not the extremes of his monstrousness.

The brace across Fontine's back was cutting into his flesh. He had been standing too long. He gripped his cane and walked towards the chair in front of the desk.

'Do you know what was on that train?' asked the old monk gently.

'Yes. Brevourt told me.'

'Brevourt never knew. He was told part of the truth. Not all of it. What did he tell you?'

Victor was suddenly alarmed. He locked eyes once again with the priest.

'He spoke of the Filioque denials, studies that refuted

the divinity of Christ. The most damaging of which was an Aramaic scroll that raised questions as to whether Jesus ever existed at all. The conclusion would appear to be that he did not.'

'It was never the denials. Never the scroll. It was – *is* – a confession written in its entirety that predates all the other documents.' The priest of Xenope looked away. He raised his hands; his bony fingers touched the pale skin of his cheek. 'The Filioque denials are artefacts for scholars to ponder. As one of them, the Aramaic scroll was ambiguous, as the scrolls of the Dead Sea were ambiguous when studied fifteen hundred years later. However, thirty years ago, at the height of a moral war – if that's not a contradiction in terms – that scroll's exposure might have been catastrophic. It was enough for Brevourt.'

Fontine was mesmerized. 'What is this confession? I've never heard it mentioned.'

The monk returned his eyes to Victor. During the brief silence before he spoke, the old priest conveyed the pain of his immediate decision. 'It is everything. It was written on a parchment brought out of a Roman prison in the year sixty-seven. We know the date because the document speaks of the death of Jesus in terms of the Hebrew calendar that places the figure at thirty-four years. It coincides with archaelogical scholarship. The parchment was written by a man who wandered blindly; he speaks of Gethsemane and Capernaum, Gennesaret and Corinth, Pontus, Galatia and Cappadocia. The writer can be no one else but Simon of Bethsaida, given the name of Peter by the man he called Christ. What is contained in the parchment is beyond anything in your imagination. It must be found.'

The priest stopped and stared across at Victor.

'And destroyed?' asked Fontine softly.

'Destroyed,' replied the monk. 'But not for any reason

you might think of. For *nothing* is changed, yet *all* is changed. My vows forbid me to tell you more. We're old men: we haven't much time. If you can help, you must. That parchment can alter history. It should have been destroyed centuries ago, but arrogance prevailed. It could plunge a great part of the world into a terrible agony. No one can justify the pain.'

'But you say nothing is changed,' replied Victor, repeating the monk's words, 'yet *all* is changed. One cancels the other; it doesn't make sense.'

'The confession on that parchment makes sense. In all its anguish. I can tell you no more.'

Fontine held the priest's eyes. 'Did my father know about the parchment? Or was he told only what Brevourt was told?'

'He knew,' said the monk of Xenope. 'The Filioque denials were like your American articles of impeachment, charges for canonical debate. Even the most damaging – as you called it – the Aramaic scroll, was subject to the linguistic interpretations of antiquity. Fontini-Cristi would have perceived these issues; Brevourt did not. But the confession on that parchment is not debatable. It was the single, awesome thing that demanded Fontini-Cristi's commitment. He understood and accepted it.'

'A confession on a parchment taken out of a Roman prison.' Fontine spoke quietly; the issue was clear. 'That's what the vault of Constantine is all about.'

'Yes.'

Victor let the moment pass. He leaned forward in the chair, his hand on his metal cane. 'You said the key is here. But why? Donatti searched – every wall, every floor, every inch of ground. You've remained here for twenty-seven years, and still there's nothing. What's left for you?'

'Your father's words, said in this room.'

'What were they?'

'That the markings would be here in Campo di Fiori. Etched for a millennium. That was the phrase he used: "etched for a millennium". And his son would understand. It was part of his childhood. But his son was told nothing. We came to know that.'

Fontine refused a bed in the great house. He would rest in the stables, in the bed on which he had placed the dead Barzini a lifetime ago.

He wanted to be alone, isolated, and above all, out of the house, away from the dead relics. He had to think, to go back over the horror again and again until he found the missing connection. For it was there now; the pattern existed. What remained missing was the line that completed the design.

Part of his childhood. No, not there, not yet. Don't start there; it would come later. Begin with what one knew, one saw, one heard for oneself.

He reached the stables and walked through the empty rooms and past the empty stalls. There was no electricity now; the old monk had given him a flashlight. Barzini's room was as he remembered it. Bare, without ornament; the narrow bed, the worn-out armchair, the simple trunk for his few possessions.

The tack room, too, was as he had seen it last. Bridles and leather straps on the walls. He sat down on a small wooden stirrup bench, exhaling in pain as he did so. He put out the flashlight. The moon shone through the windows. He inhaled deeply and forced his mind back to the horrible night.

The shattering of machine gun fire filled his ears, evoking the memory he abhorred. The swirling clouds of smoke were there, the arched bodies of loved ones in succeeding instants of death, seen in the blinding light of the floodlamps.

Champoluc is the river! Zürich is the river!

The words were screamed, then repeated, twice, three times! Roared up at him but aimed higher than where he was, above him, as the bullets pierced his father's chest and stomach.

Champoluc is the river!

The head raised? Was that it? The head, the *eyes*. It's always in *the eyes*! A split fraction of time before the words poured out, his father's eyes had *not* been on the embankment, *not on him*.

They had been levelled to his right, on a diagonal. Savarone had been staring at the automobiles, into the *third automobile*.

Savarone had seen Guillamo Donatti! He had recognized him in the shadows of the back seat of the car. At the instant of death, he knew the identity of his executioner.

And the roars of fury had poured forth, up at his son, but beyond his son. Up and beyond and ... what *was* it? What *was* it his father had done at that last instant of life? It was the missing connection, the line that completed the pattern!

Oh, Christ! Some part of his body. His head, his shoulders, his hands. What *was* it?

The *whole* body! My God, it was the gesture in *death* of the *whole body*! Head, arms, hands. Savarone's body had been stretched in one final gesture! *To his left!* But not the house, not the lighted rooms so viciously invaded, but beyond the house. *Beyond the house!*

Champoluc is the river ...

Beyond the house!

The *woods* of Campo di Fiori!

The *river!* The wide mountain stream in the forest! Their own personal '*river*'!

It was part of his childhood. The river of his childhood was a quarter of a mile beyond the gardens of Campo di Fiori!

Sweat fell from Victor's face; his breath was erratic, his hands trembled. He gripped the edge of the stirrup bench in the darkness. He was spent, but certain; it was all suddenly, totally clear.

The *river* was not in the Champoluc, nor in Zürich. It was minutes away from *here*. A brief walk down a forest path made by generations of children.

Etched for a millennium.

Part of his *childhood*.

He pictured the woods, the flowing stream, the rocks . . . the rocks . . . the *rocks*. The *boulders* that bordered the stream in the deepest section of the water! There was one *large* boulder used for diving and jumping and lying in the sun, and *scratching initials* and childish *messages*, and secret *codes* between very young brothers!

Etched for a millennium. His *childhood*!

Had Savarone chosen *this* rock on which to etch his message?

It was suddenly so clear. So *consistent*.

Of course he had.

CHAPTER TWENTY-ONE

The night sky turned gradually to grey, but no rays of the Italian sun broke through the overcast. Instead, there would be rain soon, and a cold summer wind whipping down from the northern mountains.

Victor walked down the stable road into the gardens. It was too dark to make out the colours. Then, too, there were not the rows of flowers bordering the paths as there had been; he could see that much.

He found the path with difficulty, only after examining the uncut grass, angling the beam of his flashlight into the ground, looking for signs of the past. As he penetrated the woods beyond the garden familiar things came back to him: a gnarled olive tree with thick limbs; a cluster of white birches, now concealed by beechwood vine and dying spruce.

The stream was no more than a hundred yards away, diagonally to his right, if memory served. There were birches and tall pines; giant weeds formed a wall of tentacles, soft but uncomfortable to the touch.

He stopped. There was a rustle of bird wings, the snap of a twig. He turned and peered into the black shapes of the overgrowth.

Silence.

Then the sound of a small animal intruded on the quiet. He had probably disturbed a hare. Strange he should assume so naturally that it was a hare. The surroundings jogged memories long forgotten; as a boy he had trapped hares in these woods.

He could smell the water now. He had always been able to smell the moistness when he approached the stream, smell it before he heard the sounds of the flow. The foliage nearest the water was thick, almost impenetrable. Seepage from the stream had fed a hundred thousand roots, allowing rampant, uncontrolled growth. He had to force back limbs and spread thickets to approach the stream.

His left foot was entangled in a tangle of ground vine. He stepped back on his right and, with his cane, worked it free, losing his balance as he did so. The cane whipped out of his hand, spiralling into the darkness. He grabbed for a branch to break his fall; the small limb cracked, stripping itself from its source. On one knee, he used the thick stick to push himself off the ground; his cane was gone; he could not see it. He held on to the stick and threaded his way through the mass of foliage to the water's edge.

The stream seemed narrower than he remembered. Then he realized it was the grey darkness and the overgrown forest that made it appear so. Three decades of inattention had allowed the woods to impinge upon the water.

The massive boulder was on his right, upstream, no more than twenty feet away, but the wall of overgrowth was such that it might have been half a mile. He began edging his way towards it, crouching, rising, separating, each movement a struggle. Twice he butted against hard obstacles in the earth, too high, too thin and narrow, for rocks. He swung the beam of the flashlight down; the obstacles were iron stakes, rusted and pitted as though relics from a sunken galleon.

He reached the base of the huge rock; its body

extended over the water. He looked below, the flashlight illuminating the separation of earth and flowing stream, and realized the years had made him cautious. The distance to the water was only a few feet, but it appeared a gulf to him now. He sidestepped his way down into the stream, the thick stick in his left hand prodding the depth.

The water was cold – as he remembered, it was always cold – and came up to his thighs, lapped over his waist below the brace, sending chills throughout his body. He shivered and swore at the years.

But he was *here*. It was all that mattered.

He focused the flashlight on the rock. He was several feet from the edge of the bank; he would have to organize his search. Too many minutes could be wasted going over areas twice or three times because he could not remember examining them. He was honest with himself: He was not sure how long he could take the cold.

He reached up, pressing the end of the stick into the surface of the rock. The moss that covered it peeled easily. The details of the boulder's surface, made vivid by the harsh, white beam of the flashlight, looked like thousands of tiny craters and ravines.

His pulse accelerated at the first signs of human intrusion. They were faint, barely visible, but they were there. And they were his marks, from more than half a century ago. Descending lines scratched deeply into the rock as part of a long forgotten boyhood game.

The **V** was the clearest letter; he had made sure his mark was vivid, properly recorded. Then there was **b**, followed by what might have been numbers. And a **t**, again followed by what were probably numbers. He had no idea what they meant.

He peeled the moss above and below the scratchings.

There were other faint markings, some seemed meaningful. Initials, mainly; here and there, rough drawings of trees and arrows and quarter circles drawn by children.

His eyes strained under the glare of the flashlight; his fingers peeled and rubbed and caressed a larger and larger area. He made two vertical lines with the stick to show where he had searched and moved farther into the cold water; but soon the cold grew too much and he climbed on to the bank, seeking warmth. His hands and arms and legs were trembling with cold and age. He knelt in the damp overgrowth and watched the vapour of his breath diffuse itself in the air.

He went back into the water, to the point where he had left off. The moss was thicker; underneath he found several more markings similar to the first set nearer the embankment. **V**'s and **b**'s and **t**'s and very faint numbers.

Then it came back to him through the years – faintly, as faintly as the letters and the numbers. And he *knew* he was right to be in that stream, at that boulder.

Burrone! Traccia! He had forgotten but now recalled. 'Ravine', 'trail'. He had always scratched – recorded – their journeys into the mountains!

Part of his childhood.

My God, what a part! Every summer Savarone gathered his sons together and took them north for several days of climbing. Not dangerous climbing, more hiking and camping. For them all, a high point of the summers. And he gave them maps so they knew where they had been; and Vittorio, the eldest, would indelibly, soberly record the journeys on the boulder down at the stream, their 'river'.

They had christened the rock The Argonaut. And the scratchings of The Argonaut served as a permanent record of their mountain odysseys. Into the mountains of their boyhood.

Into the mountains.

The train from Salonika had gone into the mountains! The vault of Constantine was somewhere in the mountains!

He balanced himself with the stick and continued. He was near the face of the rock; the water came up to his chest, chilling the steel brace beneath his clothes. The farther out he went the more convinced he became; he was *right* to be there! The faint scratchings – the faded scars of half lines and zigzags – were more and more numerous. *The Argonaut*'s hull was covered with graffiti related to journeys long forgotten.

The cold water sent a spasm through the base of his spine; the stick fell from his hands. He slapped at the water, grabbing the stick, shifting his feet in the effort. He fell – glided, actually – into the rock and righted himself by pressing the stick into the mud below for balance.

He stared at the sight inches from his eyes in the water. There was a short, straight, horizontal line deeply defined in the rock. It was *chiselled*.

He braced himself as best he could, transferred the stick to his right hand, manipulating it between his thumb and the flashlight, and pressed his fingers into the surface of the boulder.

He traced the line. It angled sharply downward into the water; across and down and then it abruptly stopped.

7. It was a 7.

Unlike any other faded hieroglyphics on the rock; not scratches made by awkward, youthful hands, but a work of precision. The figure was no more than two inches high – but the impression itself was a good half inch deep.

He'd *found* it! *Etched for a millennium!* A message carved in rock, *chiselled in stone*!

He brought the flashlight closer and carefully moved his trembling fingers about the area. My God, was this *it*? Was this the *moment*? In spite of the cold and the wet, the blood raced to his head, his heart accelerated. He felt like shouting; but he had to be *sure*!

At midpoint of the vertical line of the **7**, about an inch to its right, was a dash. Then another vertical line . . . a **1**, followed by yet another vertical that was shorter, angling to the right . . . and intersected by a line straight up and down . . . A **4**. It was a **4**.

Seven – dash – one – four. More below the surface of the water than above it.

Beyond the **4** was another short, horizontal line. A dash. It was followed by a . . . **Z**, but not a **Z**. The angles were not abrupt, they were rounded.

2.

Seven – dash – one – four – dash – two . . .

There was a final impression but it was not a figure. It was a series of four short, straight lines joined together. A box . . . a square. A perfect geometric square.

Of course, it *was* a figure! A *zero*.

0.

What did it *mean*? Had Savarone's age caused him to leave a message that meant nothing to anyone but *him*? Had everything been so brilliantly logical but the message itself? It meant *nothing*.

7–14–20 . . . A date? Was it a *date*?

My God! thought Victor. 7–14. 14 July! His birthday!

Bastille Day. Throughout his life that had been a minor source of amusement. A Fontini-Cristi born on the celebrated day of the French Revolution.

14 July . . . two-zero . . . 20. 1920.

That was Savarone's key. Something had happened on 14 July 1920. What was it? What incident had occurred that his father considered so meaningful to his first son? Something that had a significance beyond other times, other birthdays.

A shaft of pain – the second of what he knew would be

many – shot through his body, originating, once again, at the base of his spine. The brace was like ice; the cold of the water had chilled his skin and penetrated the tendons and muscle tissue.

With the sensitivity of a surgeon he pressed his fingers around the area of the chiselled numbers. There was only the date; all else was flat and unspoiled. He took the stick in his left hand and thrust it below the water into the mud. Painfully, he sidestepped his way back towards the embankment, until the level of the water had receded to his thighs. Then he paused for breath. The flashes of pain accelerated; he had done more damage to himself than he had realized. A full convulsion was developing; he tensed the muscles of his jaw and throat. He had to get out of the water and lie down. Lurching for the overhanging vines on the embankment, he fell to his knees in the water. The flashlight spun out of his hand and rolled over some matted fern, its beam shooting out into the dense woods. He grabbed a cluster of thick, exposed roots and pulled himself up towards the ground, pushing the stick behind him into the mud for propulsion.

All movement was arrested in a paralysing instant of shock.

Above him, in the darkness on the embankment, stood the figure of a man. A huge man dressed in black, and motionless, staring down at him. Around his throat – in jarring counterpoint to the pitch-black clothing – was a rim of white. A priest's collar. The face – what he could see of it in the dim forest light – was impassive. But the eyes that bore down at him had fire in them, and hatred.

The man spoke. His speech was deliberate, slow, born of loathing.

'The enemy of Christ returns.'

'You are Gaetamo,' said Fontine.

'A man came in a car to watch my cabin in the hills. I

315

knew that car, that man. He serves the heretic of Xenope. The monk who lives his life in Campo di Fiori. He was there to keep me away.'

'But he couldn't.'

'No.' The defrocked priest elaborated no further. 'So this is where it was. All those years and the answer was here.' His deep voice seemed to float, beginning nowhere, ending abruptly in mid-statement. 'What did he leave? A name? Of what? A bank? A building in the Milan factories? We thought of those; we took them apart.'

'Whatever it was, it has no meaning for you. Nor for me.'

'Liar,' replied Gaetamo quietly, in his chilling monotone. He turned his head right, then left; he was remembering. 'We staked out every inch of these woods. We ran yellow strings from stake to stake and marked each area as we studied it. We considered burning, cutting . . . but were afraid of what we might destroy. We dammed the stream and probed the mud. The Germans gave us instruments . . . but always nothing. The large rocks were filled with meaningless markings, including the birthdate of an arrogant seventeen-year-old who had to leave his conceit in stone. And always nothing.'

Victor tensed. *Gaetamo had said it.* In one brief phrase the defrocked priest had unlocked the door! *An arrogant seventeen-year-old*, leaving his mark in stone. But *he* had not left it! Donatti had found the key but had not recognized it! The reasoning was so simple, so uncomplicated: a seventeen-year-old carving a memorable day on a familiar rock. It was so logical, so essentially unremarkable. And so *clear*.

As the memory was now clear. Most of it.

7–14–20. His seventeenth birthday. It came back to him because there had been none like it in his life. My God, thought Victor, Savarone was incredible! *Part of his childhood.* It was on his seventeenth birthday that his father had given him the present he had wanted so badly he had dreamed of it, pleaded for it: the chance to go up into the mountains without his younger brothers. To really do some climbing . . . *above* the usual and – for him – dreary campsites in the foothills.

On his seventeenth birthday, Savarone had presented him with an authentic Alpine pack, the sort used by experienced climbers. Not that his father was about to take him up the Jungfrau; they never really scaled anything extraordinary. But that first trip – *alone with his father* – was a landmark in his early manhood. That pack and that journey were symbols of something very important to him; proof that he was growing up in his father's eyes.

He had forgotten; he was not sure of it even now, for there had been other trips, other years. Had it – that first trip – been in the Champoluc? It must have been, but *where?* That *was* beyond memory.

'. . . end your life in this water.'

Gaetamo had spoken, but Fontine had not heard him: only the threat had penetrated. Of all men – all priests – this madman could be told nothing. 'I found only meaningless scribblings. Childish markings, as you said.'

'You found what rightfully belongs to *Christ*!' Gaetamo's words sliced through the forest. He lowered himself to one knee, his immense chest and head inches from Victor, his eyes wide and burning. 'You found the *sword of the archangel of hell*! No more lies. Tell me what you've found!'

'Nothing.'

'Liar! Why are you *here*? An old man in water and mud! What was in this stream? On this *rock*!'

Victor stared at the grotesque eyes. 'Why am I here?' he repeated, stretching his neck, arching his tortured back, his features pinched. 'I'm old. With memories. I convinced myself that the answer *might* be here. When we were children we left messages for one another here. You saw for yourself. Childish markings, scribblings, stone scratched against stone. I thought perhaps – But I found nothing. If there was anything, it's gone now.'

'You examined the rock, and then you stopped! You were prepared to leave.'

'*Look* at me! How long do you think I can stay in this water?'

Gaetamo shook his head slowly. 'I watched you. You were a man who found what he had come to find.'

'You saw what you wanted to see. Not what was there.'

Victor's foot slipped; the stick that braced him in the water slid in the mud, sinking deeper. The priest thrust out a hand and grabbed Fontine's hair. He yanked viciously, pulling Victor into the embankment, forcing his head and neck to one side. The sudden contortion was unbearable; wrenching pain spread throughout Fontine's body. The wide maniacal eyes above him in the dim light were not those of an ageing man in the clothes of a priest but, instead, the eyes of a young fanatic thirty years ago.

Gaetamo saw. And understood. 'We thought you were dead then. There was no way you could have survived. The fact that you did convinced our holy men that you were from *hell*! . . . You remember. For now I'll continue what was begun thirty years ago! And with each crack of your bones you'll have the chance – as you did then – to tell me what you've found. But don't lie. The pain will only stop when you tell me the truth.'

Gaetamo bent forward. He began to twist Victor's head, pressing the face downward into the rocky embankment, cutting the flesh, forcing the air out of Fontine's throat.

Victor tried to pull back; the priest slammed his forehead into a gnarled root. Blood spurted from the gash, flowing into Victor's eyes, blinding him, infuriating him. He raised his right hand, grappling for Gaetamo's wrist; the defrocked priest clasped the hand and wrenched it inward, snapping the fingers. He pulled Fontine higher on the ground, twisting, always twisting his head and his neck, causing the brace to cut into his back.

'It won't end until you tell me the truth!'

'*Pig! Pig from Donatti!*' Victor lurched to the side. Gaetamo countered by crashing his fist into Fontine's rib cage. The impact was paralysing, the pain excruciating.

The stick. The *stick*! Fontine rolled to his left, his left hand below, still gripped around the broken limb, gripped as one holds an object in a moment of agony. Gaetamo had felt the brace; he pulled on it, wrenching it back and forth until the steel lacerated the surrounding flesh.

Victor inched the long stick up, by pressing it into the embankment. It touched his chest; he felt it. The end was jagged. If he could only find the smallest opening between himself and the monster above, space enough to thrust it upward, towards the face, the neck.

It came. Gaetamo raised one knee. It was *enough*.

Fontine shoved the stick up, driving it with every ounce of strength he could summon, impaling it into the stunned body above. He heard a cry of shock, a scream filled the forest.

And then an explosion filled the grey darkness. A powerful gun had been fired. The screeches of birds and animals swelled in the woods – and the body of Gaetamo fell forward on top of him. It rolled to the side.

The stick was lodged in his throat. Below his neck a huge gaping mass of torn flesh saturated with blood was in his upper chest; he had been blown apart by the gun that had been fired out of the darkness.

'May god forgive me,' said the monk of Xenope from the shadows.

A black void came over Victor; he felt himself slipping into the water as trembling hands grabbed him. His last thoughts – strangely peaceful – were of his sons. The Geminis. The hands might have been the hands of his sons, trying to save him. But his sons' hands did not tremble.

PART TWO

CHAPTER TWENTY-TWO

Major Andrew Fontine sat rigidly at his desk, listening to the sounds of morning. It was five minutes to eight; the offices were beginning to fill up. Voices rose and fell in the corridors as the Pentagon started the day.

He had five days to think. No, not to think, to *move*. There wasn't that much to think about; it was only necessary to move out and cut *down*. Stop whatever Adrian and his 'concerned citizens' had started.

Eye Corps was the most legitimate clandestine unit in the army. It was doing exactly what the dissenters *thought they* were doing, but without tearing down the system, without revealing weakness. Maintain strength and the illusion of strength. It was all-important. They'd tried it the other way. Eye Corps wasn't born in Georgetown, over brandy and cigars and pictures of the Pentagon on the walls. *Bullshit!* It was born in a hut in the Mekong Delta. After he had come back from Saigon and told his three subordinate officers what had happened at command headquarters.

He had gone to Saigon with legitimate field complaints, proof of corruption in the supply lines. Hundreds of thousands of dollars' worth of equipment was being drained off all over the Mekong every week, abandoned by ARVN troops at the first sign of hostilities, routed back into the black market. Payrolls were banked by ARVN commanders, drugs bought and distributed by Vietnamese networks out of Hue and

Da-nang. Millions were piped out of the South-east Asia operation, and no one seemed to know what to do about it.

So he brought his proof to Saigon, right up to the command brass. And what did the brass do? They thanked him and said they would investigate. What was there to investigate? He'd brought enough proof to institute a dozen charges.

A brigadier had taken him out for a drink.

'Listen, Fontine. Better a little corruption that blow the whole ammo dump. These people are thieves by nature, we're not going to change that.'

'We could make a few examples, sir. Openly.'

'For Christ's sake! We've got enough Stateside problems! That kind of publicity would play right into the anti-military hands. Now, you've got a fine record; don't louse it up.'

That's when it started, when Eye Corps was born. The name itself said it: a unit of men who watched and recorded. And as the months went on, the four of them expanded to five, then seven. Recently, they'd added the eighth man: Captain Martin Greene, in the Pentagon. They were born of disgust. The army was led by weak-kneed whores – *women* – afraid to *offend*. What kind of stature was that for the military leaders of the strongest nation on earth?

Something else happened, too, along the way. As the records grew and the enemies within were tagged for what they were, the obvious stared the men of Eye Corps in the face: *they* were the inheritors! They were the incorruptible; they were the elite.

Since regular channels didn't work, they would do it their way. Build up the records, get files on every misfit, every deviate, every corrupter, large and small. Strength lay with those who could confront the misfits and make them crawl. Make them do exactly what strong, incorruptible men wanted them to do.

Eye Corps was nearly there. Almost three years' worth of recorded garbage. Christ! South-east Asia was the place to find it. They'd take over soon; go right into the Pentagon and take over! It was men like themselves who had the skill and the training and the commitment to oversee the vast complexities that were the armed might of the country. It was not a delusion; they *were* the elite.

It was so logical for him, too. His father would understand that, if he could ever talk to him about it. And one day he might. Since his earliest memories, he felt the presence of influence, of pride, of consequence. And power ... yes, power, it wasn't a dirty word! It belonged to those who knew how to handle it; it was his birthright.

And Adrian wanted to tear it all down! Well, the spoiler was not going to tear it down. He was not going to rip Eye Corps apart.

... *arrangements can be made*. That's what Adrian had said in the boathouse.

How right he was! Arrangements could be made; but not any arrangements considered by Adrian and his concerned citizens. A lot would happen before then.

Five days. Adrian wasn't trained to consider the options. Practical, physical alternatives, not words and abstractions and 'positions'. The army would have a hell of a time trying to reach him in five days from now if he was 10,000 miles away in a combat zone, involved in operations covered by an umbrella of security. He had enough clout to do that; to get over there and build that umbrella.

There was a weakling in Saigon who had betrayed them. Betrayed the rest of Eye Corps. To learn who he was – and he was one of six – was the first reason to get over there. Find him ... then make a decision.

Once he was found – and the decision made – the rest was easy. He'd brief the remaining men of Eye Corps. The stories would be integrated, synchronized.

Even the army needed proof. And there was no way it could get that proof.

Here in Washington, Eye Corps' eighth member could take care of himself. Captain Martin Greene was steel and leather. And smart. He could hold his own against any flak levelled at him. His people had come from the Irgun, the toughest fighters in *Jew* history. If the DC brass gave him any static, he'd cut out for Israel in a second, and the Jew army would be better for it.

Andrew looked at his watch. It was a little past eight, time to reach Greene. He couldn't take the chance last night. Adrian and his civilians were trying to find an unknown officer who worked at the Pentagon. Outside telephones could not be trusted. He and Marty would have to talk; they couldn't wait for their next scheduled meeting. He would be on a plane for Saigon before the day was over.

They had agreed never to be seen together. If they met by chance at a conference or a cocktail party, both pretended they were meeting for the first time. It was vital that no connection between them be apparent. When they did meet, it was in out-of-the-way places and always by pre-arranged schedule. During the meetings they would combine whatever damaging information they'd culled from Pentagon files during the week, seal the pages in an envelope, and mail it to a post office box in Baltimore. The enemies of Eye Corps were being catalogued everywhere.

In times of emergencies, or when one needed the other's immediate advice, they sent word to each other by placing a 'mistaken' call through the Pentagon switchboard. It was the signal to invent some excuse, get out of the office, and head for a bar in downtown Washington. Andrew had made the 'mistaken' call two hours ago.

The bar was dark and cheap and gaudy, with booths in the back that afforded a clear view of the entrance. Andrew sat in a booth by the back wall, toying with his boredom, not interested in it. He kept looking up at the entrance fifty feet away. Whenever the door opened, the morning sun burst through briefly, a harsh intruder on the interior darkness. Greene was late; it wasn't like him to be late.

The door opened again and the silhouette of a stocky, muscular man with broad, thick shoulders was arrested in the glare. It was Marty; he was out of uniform, dressed in an open white shirt and what appeared to be plaid trousers. He nodded to the bartender and started towards the rear of the bar. Everything about Greene was powerful, thought Andrew. From his thick legs to the shock of bright-red hair, shaped in a bristling crew cut.

'Sorry it took me so long,' said Greene, sliding into the booth opposite Andrew. 'I stopped off at the apartment to change. Then I went out the back way.'

'Any particular reason?'

'Maybe, maybe not. Last night I took the car out of the garage and thought I picked up surveillance – a dark green Electra. I reversed directions; it was still there. I went home.'

'What time was it?'

'Around eight thirty, quarter to nine.'

'It figures. It's why I called you. They expected me to contact someone in your section; set up a meeting right away. They probably had half a dozen others followed.'

'Who?'

'One of them's my brother.'

'Your *brother*?'

'He's a lawyer. He's working with—'

'I know *exactly* who he is,' interrupted Greene, '*and* who he's working with. They're about as subtle as jackals.'

'You never mentioned him to me. How come?'

'There was no reason to. They're a bunch of hotheads over at Justice. They were organized by a black named Nevins. We keep close tabs on them; they mess around with hardware contracts more than we'd like. But they haven't got anything to do with *us*.'

'They do now. It's why I called you. One of the six in Nam broke. They've got a deposition. A list. Eight officers, seven identified.'

Greene's cold eyes narrowed. He spoke slowly, quietly. 'What the hell are you saying?'

Andrew told him. When he finished, Greene spoke without moving an inch of his powerful body.

'The black son of a bitch, Nevins, flew to Saigon two weeks ago. The matter wasn't related.'

'It is now,' said the major.

'Who has the deposition? Are there copies?'

'I don't know.'

'Why is the subpoena being delayed?'

'Again, I don't know,' said Andrew.

'There must be a reason! For Christ's sake, why didn't you ask?'

'Hold it, Marty. Everything came as a shock—'

'We're trained for shock,' interrupted Greene icily. 'Can you find out?'

Andrew swallowed part of his bourbon. He had not seen the captain like this before. 'I can't call my brother. He wouldn't tell me if I did.'

'Nice family. May the brothers live and be well. Maybe I can do better. We've got people at Justice; procurement covers itself. I'll do what I can. Where are our files in Saigon? They're the bottom line.'

'They're not in Saigon. They're in Phan-thiet, on the

coast. In a fenced-off area of a warehouse. I'm the only one who knows the location. A couple of cabinets among a thousand G-2 crates.'

'Very smart.' Greene nodded his head in approval.

'I'll check them the first thing. I'm flying out this afternoon. A sudden inspection trip.'

'Very nice.' Greene nodded again. 'You'll find the man?'

'Yes.'

'Check Barstow. He's a smartass. Too many decorations.'

'You don't know him.'

'I know the way he operates,' said Greene.

Andrew was stung by the similarity of words. His brother had applied them to Eye Corps. 'He's a good man in the field—'

'Bravery,' interrupted the captain, 'hasn't got a goddamn thing to do with it. Check Barstow first.'

'I will.' Andrew smarted under Greene's pronouncements. He had to get some of his own back. 'What about Baltimore? I'm worried about that.'

The envelopes in Baltimore were picked up by Greene's twenty-year-old nephew.

'He's perfect. He'd kill himself first. I was up there last weekend. I would have known.'

'Are you sure?'

'It's not worth discussing. I want to know more about that goddamned deposition. When you crack Barstow make sure you get every word he put down. They probably gave him a copy; see if he's got a military lawyer.'

The major drank again, avoiding Greene's narrow eyes. Andrew did not like the captain's tone of voice. He was actually giving orders; he was out of line. But on the bottom line Greene was a good man to have around in a crisis. 'What can you find out over at Justice?'

'More than that black bastard would ever guess. We've got funds set up for the mavericks who interfere with armaments contracts. We don't care who makes a few extra dollars, we want the hardware. You'd be surprised how the lowly paid government lawyers take to Caribbean vacations.' Greene smiled and sat back in the booth. 'I think we can handle this. The subpoena won't mean a damn thing without our records. Line officers bitch all the time, what else is new?'

'That's what I told my brother,' said Andrew.

'Him I can't figure,' said Greene. And then the captain leaned forward. 'Whatever you do in Nam, think it out. If you use prejudice, get your facts and do it by remote.'

'I think I've had more experience in those areas than you.' Andrew lighted a cigarette; his hand was steady in spite of his increased irritation. He was pleased with that.

'You probably do,' said Greene casually. 'Now, I've got something for you. I figured it could wait till our next meeting, but there's no point in holding it.'

'What is it?'

'A congressional tracer came in last Friday. From a pol named Sandor; he's on the Armed Services Committee. It concerned you, so I pulled it.'

'What did they want?'

'Limited. Your rotation schedule. How permanent you were in Washington. I inserted a routine response. You were high-echelon material, War College candidate. Very permanent.'

'I wonder what—'

'I haven't finished,' interrupted Greene. 'I called this Sandor's aide and asked why the congressman was interested in you. He checked his papers and said the request came from a friend of Sandor's, a man named Dakakos. Theodore Dakakos.'

'Who is he?'

'A Greek shipper. In your family's class. He's got millions.'

'Dakakos? Never heard of him.'

'These Greeks are pistols. Maybe he wants to give you a present. Like a small yacht or your own battalion.'

Fontine shrugged. 'Dakakos? I can buy a yacht. I'll take the battalion.'

'You can buy that, too,' said Greene, sliding across the seat out of the booth. 'Have a prosperous trip. Call me when you get back.'

'What are you going to do?'

'Find out everything there is to know about a black son of a bitch named Nevins.'

Greene walked rapidly past the booths towards the entrance. Andrew would wait five minutes before leaving. He had to get to his apartment and pack. His plane left at one thirty.

Dakakos? Theodore Dakakos.

Who was he?

Adrian got out of bed slowly, one foot after the other, as quietly as possible so he would not wake her. Barbara was asleep, but her sleep was fitful.

It was barely nine thirty in the evening. He had picked her up at the airport shortly after five. She'd cancelled her Thursday and Friday seminars, too excited to lecture detached summer students.

She had been awarded a grant to assist the anthropologist Sorkis Khertepain at the University of Chicago. Khertepain was in the process of analysing artefacts taken from the site of the Aswan Dam. Barbara was exhilarated; she had to fly down and tell Adrian about it. She was intensely alive when things went right in her world, a scholar who would never lose her sense of wonder.

It was strange. Both he and Barbara had entered their

professions in a sense of outrage. His was traced to the acid streets of San Francisco, hers to a brilliant mother denied her rightful place in a midwest college because she *was* a mother. A woman who had no place in the world of anthropology. Yet each had found values that far outweighed the anger.

It was part of the bond between them.

He walked quietly across the room and sat down in an armchair. His eyes fell on his briefcase on the bedroom desk. He never left it in the sitting room at night; Jim Nevins had cautioned him about being careless. Nevins was at times a little paranoid about such matters.

Nevins, too, had come to his profession in outrage. It was the outrage that often sustained him. Not merely the frustrations of a black man climbing over the barriers erected by a sceptical white establishment, but the anger of a lawyer who saw so much illegality in the city where laws were made.

But nothing outraged him more than the discovery of Eye Corps. The idea of military elitists suppressing evidence of massive corruption for their own ends was more dangerous than anything the black lawyer could think of.

When Major Andrew Fontine's named appeared on the list, Nevins had asked Adrian to remove himself. Adrian had become one of his closest friends, but nothing could stand in the way of prosecuting Eye Corps.

Brothers were brothers. Even white brothers.

'You look so serious. And so naked.' Barbara swept her light-brown hair away from her face, and rolled on her side, hugging the pillow.

'I'm sorry. Did I wake you?'

'Heavens, no. I was only dozing.'

'Correction. Your snoring could be heard on Capitol Hill.'

'You lie through your legal teeth . . . What time is it?'

'Twenty to ten,' he answered, looking at his watch.

She sat up and stretched. The sheet fell away to her waist; her lovely, full breasts separated, their slow expansion, the movement of the nipples holding his eyes, arousing him. She saw him watching her and smiled, pulling the sheet over her as she leaned against the headrest.

'We talk,' she said firmly. 'We have three days to wear ourselves to a frazzle. While you're out during the day slaying bears, I'll preen myself like a concubine. Satisfaction guaranteed.'

'You should do all those things non-academic ladies do. Spend hours at Elizabeth Arden's, wallow in milk baths, eat bonbons with your gin. You're a tired girl.'

'Let's put me aside,' said Barbara smiling. 'I've been talking about me all night – almost. How's everything down here? Or shouldn't you say? I'm sure Jim Nevins thinks the suite is bugged.'

Adrian laughed, crossing his legs. He reached for a pack of cigarettes next to a lighter on the armchair table. 'Jim's conspiracy complex remains undaunted. He refuses to leave case files at the office anymore. He keeps all his important papers in his briefcase, which is the biggest damn thing you ever saw.' Adrian chuckled.

'Why does he do that?'

'He doesn't want copies made. He knows the crowd upstairs would take him off the cases if they knew how much progress he was making.'

'That's astonishing.'

'It's chilling,' he said.

The telephone rang. Adrian got out of the chair quickly and crossed to the bedside table.

It was his mother. She could not hide the anxiety in her voice. 'I've heard from your father.'

'What do you mean, you've *heard* from him?'

'He flew to Paris last Monday. Then went on to Milan—'

'*Milan*? What for?'

'He'll tell you himself. He wants you and Andrew here on Sunday.'

'Wait a minute,' Adrian's mind raced. 'I don't think I can do that.'

'You *must*.'

'You don't understand, and I can't explain right now. But Andy's not going to want to see me. I'm not sure I want to see him. I'm not even sure it's advisable under the circumstances.'

'What are you talking about?' His mother's voice was suddenly cold. 'What have you done?'

Adrian paused before answering. 'We're on the opposite sides of a . . . dispute.'

'Whatever it is, it doesn't matter! Your father *needs* you.' She was losing control. 'Something happened to him. Something *happened* to him! He could barely talk!'

There were several clicks on the line, followed by the urgent voice of a hotel operator. 'Mr Fontine, I'm sorry to break in, but there's an emergency call for you.'

'Oh, God.' His mother whispered over the line from New York. 'Victor—'

'I'll call you back if it's got anything to do with him. I promise you that,' said Adrian swiftly. 'All right, operator. I'll take—'

It was as far as he got. The voice now on the line was hysterical. It was a woman, crying and screaming and barely coherent.

'*Adrian! My God, Adrian!* He's *dead*! He was *killed*! They *killed him!* Adriannnnnnn!'

The screams filled the room. And the terror of the screams filled Adrian with a shock he had never felt before . . . Death. Death that touched *him*.

The woman on the telephone was Carol Nevins. Jim's wife.

'I'll be right there!'

'Call my mother,' he told Barbara, as he dressed as fast as he could. 'The North Shore number. Tell her it's not dad.'

'Who is it?'

'Nevins.'

'Oh, my God!'

He raced into the corridor and down to the elevators. He kept his finger on the button; the elevators were slow – *too* slow! He ran to the exit doors, crashed them open and leaped down the angling staircase to the lobby. He sped to the glass doors of the entrance.

'Excuse me! Pardon me! Let me through, *please!*'

Out on the kerb he ran to his right, to the lighted sign of an empty taxi. He gave the address of Nevins's apartment.

What had happened? What in God's name *had happened?!* What did Carol mean? *They killed him! Who* killed him? Jesus! Was he *dead?!*

Jim Nevins dead? Corruption, yes. Greed, of course. Mendacity, normal. But not *murder!*

There was a traffic light at New Hampshire, and he thought he would go mad. Two more blocks!

The cab plunged forward the instant the light flickered. The driver accelerated, then halfway down the block came to a sudden stop. The street was jammed with traffic. There were circling lights up ahead; nothing was moving.

Adrian jumped out on the street and began threading his way as fast as possible between the cars. Across Florida Avenue police cars blocked the entrance. Patrolmen were blowing whistles, signalling with iridescent orange gloves, funnelling the traffic west.

He ran into the blockade; two police officers several yards away at either side yelled at him.

'No one goes past here, mister!'

'Get back, buddy! You don't want to go in there!'

But he did want to go; he had to go! He ducked between two patrol cars and raced towards the swirling lights near a mass of twisted metal and shattered glass that Adrian instantly recognized. It was Jim Nevins's car. What was left of it.

An ambulance's rear doors were opened; a stretcher on which a body lay strapped, covered completely with a white hospital blanket, was being carried from the wreckage by two attendants. A third man, holding a black medical bag, walked alongside.

Adrian approached, pushing away a policeman who held out a prohibiting arm. 'Get out of the way,' he said firmly, but with his voice trembling.

'Sorry, mister. I can't let—'

'I'm an attorney! And that man, I *think*, is my friend.'

The doctor heard the desperation in his words and waved the officer away. Adrian reached down for the blanket; the doctor's hand shot out and held his wrist.

'Is your friend black?'

'Yes.'

'With identification that says his name is Nevins?'

'Yes.'

'He's dead, take my word for it. You don't want to look.'

'You don't understand. I *have* to look.'

Adrian pulled back the blanket. Nausea swept over him; he was at once hypnotized and terrified at what he saw. Nevins's face was half ripped off, blood and bone more apparent than flesh. The area of the throat was worse; half his neck was gone.

'Oh, Jesus. My *God!*'

The doctor replaced the blanket and ordered the

attendants to continue on. He was a young man with long blond hair and the face of a boy. 'You better sit down,' he said to Adrian. 'I tried to tell you. Come on, let me take you to a car.'

'No. No, thanks.' Adrian suppressed the sickness and tried to breathe. There wasn't enough air! 'What happened?'

'We don't know all the details yet. Are you really a lawyer?'

'Yes. And he was my friend. What happened?'

'Seems he made a left turn to go into the apartment driveway and halfway across, some outsized rig rammed him at full speed.'

'Rig?'

'A trailer truck, the kind with steel gridwork. It barrelassed down like it was on a freeway.'

'Where is it?'

'We don't know. It stopped for a couple of moments, its horn blasting like hell, then pulled out. A witness said it was a rental; it had one of those rent-a-truck signs on the side. You can bet the cops have APB's out all over the place.'

Suddenly, Adrian remembered, amazed that he was able to do so. He grabbed the doctor's sleeve. 'Can you get me through the police to his car? It's important.'

'I'm a doctor, not a cop.'

'Please. Will you try?'

The young doctor sucked air through his teeth, then nodded his head. 'Okay. I'll take you over. Don't pull any shit, though.'

'I just want to see something. You said a witness saw the truck stop.'

'I *know* it stopped,' replied the blond-haired doctor enigmatically. 'Come on!'

They walked over to the wreck. Nevins's car was caved in on the left side, metal stripped everywhere, windows shattered. Foam had been sprayed around the gas tank; white globules had drifted through the smashed windows.

'Hey, Doc! What are you doing?' The policeman's voice was tired and angry.

'Come on, kid, get back. You too!' A second patrolman yelled.

The young doctor raised his black bag. 'Forensic washout, fellas. Don't argue with me, call the station!'

'What?'

'What forensic?'

'Pathology, for Christ's sake!' He propelled Adrian forward. 'Come on, lab man, take the samples and let's get out of here. I'm beat.' Adrian looked into the car. 'See anything?' asked the doctor pointedly.

Adrian did. Nevins's briefcase was missing.

They walked back through the cordon of police to the ambulance.

'Did you really find anything?' asked the young doctor.

'Yes,' answered Adrian, numbed, not sure he was thinking clearly. 'Something that should have been there, but wasn't.'

'Okay. Good. Now I'll tell you why I took you over.'

'What?'

'You saw your friend; I wouldn't let his wife see him. His face and neck were blown apart with broken glass and metal fragments.'

'Yes . . . I know. I saw.' Adrian felt the wave of nausea spreading over him again.

'But it's a pretty warm night. I think the window on the driver's side was rolled down. I couldn't swear to it – that car's totalled – but your friend could have taken a short blast from a shotgun.'

Adrian raised his eyes. Something inside his head

snapped; the words his brother said seven years ago in San Francisco seared into his brain.

'... *There's a war out there ... the firepower's real!*'

Among the papers in Nevins's briefcase was the deposition taken from an officer in Saigon. The indictment of Eye Corps.

And he had given his brother five days' warning.

Oh, God! What had he done?

He took a cab to the precinct police station. His credentials as an attorney gained him a brief conversation with a sergeant.

'If there's foul play involved, we'll find it,' said the man, looking at Adrian with the distaste the police reserved for lawyers who followed up accidents.

'He was a friend of mine and I have reason to believe there was. Did you find the truck?'

'Nope. We know it's not on any of the highways. The state troopers are watching for it.'

'It was a rental.'

'We know that, too. The rental agencies are being checked. Why don't you go home, mister?'

Adrian bent over the sergeant's desk, his hands on the edge. 'I don't think you are taking me very seriously.'

'Fatality sheets come into this station a dozen an hour. Now, what the hell do you want me to do? Suspend everything else and put a whole goddamned platoon on one hit-and-run?'

'I'll tell you what I want, sergeant. I want a pathology report on all cranial injuries sustained by the deceased. Is that clear?'

'What are you talking about?' replied the police officer disdainfully. 'Cranial—'

'I want to know what blew that man apart.'

CHAPTER TWENTY-THREE

The train from Salonika had claimed its last sacrifice, thought Victor, as he lay in his bed, the morning sun streaming through the oceanside windows of the North Shore house. There was no reason on earth why any further life should be lost in its name. Enrici Gaetamo was the last victim, and there was no sorrow in that death.

He himself had very little time remaining. He could see it in Jane's eyes, in the eyes of the doctors. It was to be expected; he had been granted too many reprieves.

He had dictated everything he could remember about that day in July a lifetime ago. He had probed forgotten recesses in his mind, refused the narcotics that would numb the pain because they would equally numb the memories.

The vault from Constantine had to be found, its contents evaluated by responsible men. What had to be prevented – however remote it might be – was a chance discovery, exposure without thought. He would charge his sons. Salonika was now theirs. The Geminis. They would do what he could not do: find the vault of Constantine.

But there was a piece of the puzzle that was missing. He had to find it before he spoke to his sons. What did Rome know? How much had the Vatican learned about Salonika? Which was why he had asked a man to visit him this morning. A priest named Land, the monsignor from New York's Archdiocese who had come to his hospital room months ago.

Fontine heard the footsteps outside the bedroom, and the quiet voices of Jane and the visitor. The priest had arrived.

The heavy door opened silently. Jane ushered in the monsignor, then went back into the hallway, closing the door behind her. The priest stood across the room, a leather book in his hand.

'Thank you for coming,' Victor said.

The priest smiled. He touched the leather cover of the book. '*Conquest with Mercy. In the Name of God.* The history of the Fontini-Cristis. I thought you might like this, Mr Fontine. I found it in a bookshop in Rome years ago.'

The monsignor placed the book on the bedside table. They shook hands; each, Victor realized, was appraising the other.

Land was no more than fifty. He was of medium height, broad in the chest and shoulders. His features were sharp, Anglican; his eyes hazel beneath generous eyebrows that were darker than his short, greying hair. It was a pleasant face with intelligent eyes.

'A vanity publication, I'm afraid. A custom of dubious value at the turn of the century. It's long been out of print. The language is Italian—'

'An obsolete northern idiom,' completed Land. 'Court Victorian would be the English equivalent, I think. Somewhere between "you" and "thee".'

'You have the advantage over me. My knowledge of languages is not nearly so erudite.'

'It was sufficient for Loch Torridon,' said the priest.

'Yes, it was. Please sit down, Monsignor Land.' Victor gestured to the chair by the bed. The priest sat. The two men looked at each other. Fontine spoke.

'Several months ago you came to my hospital room. Why?'

'I wanted to meet the man whose life I had studied so thoroughly. Shall I speak frankly?'

'You wouldn't have come here this morning if you meant to do otherwise.'

'I was told you might die. I was presumptuous enough to hope you'd allow me to administer last rites.'

'That *is* frank. And *was* presumptuous.'

'I realized that. It's why I never returned. You're a courteous man, Mr Fontine, but you couldn't conceal your feelings.'

Victor examined the priest's face. There was the same sorrow he had remembered in the hospital. 'Why did you study my life? Does the Vatican still investigate? Wasn't Donatti's cause rejected?'

'The Vatican is always engaged in study. In examination. It doesn't stop. And Donatti was more than rejected. He was excommunicated, his remains refused the sanctity of Catholic burial.'

'You answer my last two questions. Not the first. Why you?'

The monsignor crossed his legs, clasping his hands in front of him on his knees, his fingers entwined. 'I'm a political and social historian. Which is another way of saying that I look for incompatible relationships between the church and its environs at given periods of time.' Land smiled, his eyes reflective. 'The original reason for such work was to prove the virtue of the church and the error of any who opposed her. But virtue wasn't always found. And it certainly wasn't found in the countless lapses of judgement, or morality, as they were exposed.' Land's smile had gone; his admission was clear.

'The execution of the Fontini-Cristis was a lapse? Of *judgement*? *Morality*?'

'Please.' The priest spoke swiftly, his voice soft but

emphatic. 'You and I both know what it was. An act of murder. Impossible to sanction and unforgivable.'

Victor saw once again the sorrow in the man's eyes. 'I accept what you say. I don't understand it, but I accept it. So I became an object of your social and political examinations?'

'Among many other questions of the time. I'm sure you're aware of them. Although there was a great deal of good during those years, there was *much* that was unforgivable. You and your family were obviously in this category.'

'You became interested in me?'

'You became my obsession.' Land smiled again, awkwardly. 'Remember, I'm American. I was studying in Rome, and the name Victor Fontine was well known to me. I had read of your work in post-war Europe; the newspapers were filled with it. I was aware of your influence in both the public and the private sectors. You can imagine my astonishment when in studying the period, I found that Vittorio Fontini-Cristi and Victor Fontine were the same person.'

'Was there a great deal of information in your Vatican files?'

'About the Fontini-Cristis, yes.' Land gestured his head towards the leather-bound volume he had placed on the bedside table. 'Like that book, somewhat biased, I'm afraid. Hardly as flattering, naturally. But of you, there was substantively nothing. Your existence was acknowledged: the first male child of Savarone, now an American citizen known as Victor Fontine. Nothing more. The files ended abruptly with the information that the remaining Fontini-Cristis had been executed by the Germans. It was an incomplete ending. Even the date was missing.'

'The less written down, the better.'

'Yes. So I studied the records of the Court of

Reparations. They were far more complete. What began as curiosity turned into shock. You made accusations to the tribunal of judges. Accusations I found unbelievable, intolerable, for you included the church. And you named a man in the Curia, Guillamo Donatti. That was the link that was missing. It was all I needed.'

'Are you telling me Donatti's name was nowhere in the files of the Fontini-Cristis?'

'It is now. It wasn't then. It was as if the archivists couldn't bring themselves to acknowledge the connection. Donatti's papers had been sealed, as usual with excommunicants. After his death, they had been found in the possession of an aide—'

'Father Enrici Gaetamo. Defrocked,' interrupted Fontine softly.

Land paused. 'Yes. Gaetamo. I received permission to break the seals. I read the paranoid ramblings of a madman, a self-canonized fanatic.' Again the monsignor stopped briefly, his eyes wandering. 'What I found there took me to England. To a man named Teague. I met him only once, at his country house. It was raining and he repeatedly got up to stoke the fire. I never saw a man finger a watch so. Yet he was retired and had no place to go.'

Victor smiled. 'It was an annoying habit, that watch. I told him so many times.'

'Yes, you were good friends, I learned that quickly. He was in awe of you, you know.'

'In awe of me? Alec? I can't believe that. He was far too direct.'

'He said he never admitted it to you, but he was. He said he felt inadequate around you.'

'He didn't convey it.'

'He said a great deal more, too. Everything. The execution at Campo di Fiori, the escape through Celle

344

Ligure, Loch Torridon, Oxfordshire, your wife, your sons. And Donatti; how he had kept the name from you.'

'He had no choice. The knowledge would have interfered with Loch Torridon.'

Land unclasped his hands and uncrossed his legs. He seemed to have difficulty finding the words. 'It was the first time I heard of the train from Salonika.'

Victor raised his eyes abruptly; they had been focused on the priest's hands. 'That's not logical. You read Donatti's papers.'

'And suddenly they were clear. The insane ramblings, the disjointed phrases, the seemingly deranged references to out-of-the-way places and times . . . suddenly made sense. Even in his most private papers, Donatti wouldn't spell it out; his fear was too great . . . Everything was reduced to that train. And whatever was on it.'

'You don't know?'

'I came to. I would have learned more quickly, but Brevourt refused to see me. He died several months after I tried to reach him.

'I went to the prison where Gaetamo was held. He spat at me through the wire mesh, clawing his hands over it until they were bleeding. Still, I had the source. Constantine. The Patriarchate. I gained an audience with a priest of the Elders. He was a very old man and he told me. The train from Salonika carried the Filioque denials.'

'That was all?'

Monsignor Land smiled. 'Theologically speaking, it was enough. To that old man and his counterparts in Rome, the Filioque documents represented triumph and cataclysm.'

'They don't represent the same to you?' Victor watched the priest closely, concentrating on the steady hazel eyes.

'No. The church isn't the church of past centuries,

even past generations. Simply put, it couldn't survive if it were. There are the old men who cling to what they believe is incontrovertible ... in most cases it's all they have left; there's no need to strip them of their convictions. Time mandates change gracefully; nothing is as it was. With each year – as the old guard leaves us – the church moves more swiftly into the realm of social responsibility. It has the power to effect extraordinary good, the wherewithal – spiritually and pragmatically – to alleviate enormous suffering. I speak with a certain expertise, for I'm part of this movement. We're in every diocese over the globe. It's our future. We are *with* the world now.'

Fontine looked away. The priest had finished; he described a force for good in a sadly lacking world. Victor turned back to Land.

'You don't know precisely, then, what is in those documents from Salonika.'

'What does it matter? At the worst, theological debate. Doctrinal equivocation. A man *existed* and his name was Jesus of Nazareth ... or the Essenian Archangel of Light ... and he spoke from the heart. His words have come down to us, historically authenticated by the Aramaics and Biblical scholars, Christian and non-Christian alike. What difference does it really make whether he is called carpenter, or prophet, or son of God? What matters is that he spoke the truth as he saw it, as it was *revealed* to him. His sincerity, if you will, is the only issue, and on that there *is* no debate.'

Fontine caught his breath. His mind raced back to Campo di Fiori, to an old monk of Xenope who spoke of a parchment taken out of a Roman prison.

... what is contained in that parchment is beyond anything in your imagination ... it must be found ... destroyed ... for nothing has changed, yet all is changed ...

Destroyed.

. . . what matters is that he spoke the truth as he saw it, as it was revealed to him . . . His sincerity is the only issue, and on that there is no debate . . .

Or was there?

Was this scholar-priest, this good man beside him, prepared to face what had to be faced? Was it remotely fair to ask him to do so?

For nothing has changed, yet all is changed.

Whatever those contradictory words meant, it would take exceptional men to know what to do. He would prepare a list for his sons.

The priest named Land was a candidate.

The four massive overhead blades slowed to a stop, sending metallic thuds throughout the aircraft. An airman opened the hatch and sprang the lever that swung the short flight of steps out from the undercarriage. Major Andrew Fontine emerged into the morning sunlight and climbed down the metal stairs on to the helicopter pad at Air Force Base Cobra in Phan-thiet.

His papers authorized priority transportation and access to the restricted warehouses down at the water-front. He would commandeer a jeep from the officer's pool and head directly to the piers. And to a file cabinet in Warehouse Four. The Eye Corps records were there; and they would stay there, the safest place in South-east Asia, once he saw for himself that nothing was disturbed. He had two more stops to make after the warehouse: north to Da-nang, then south again, past Saigon into the Delta. To Can-tho.

Captain Jerome Barstow was in Can-tho. Marty Greene was right; it was Barstow who had betrayed Eye Corps. The others agreed; his behaviour was that of a man who had broken. He had been seen in Saigon with a legal officer named Tarkington. It wasn't difficult to understand what had happened: Barstow was preparing a defence, and if that was so, a defence meant he would testify. Barstow did not know where the Eye Corps records were, but he had seen them. Seen them, *hell*! He'd prepared twenty or thirty himself. Barstow's testimony could finish Eye Corps. They could not allow that.

The legal officer named Tarkington was in Da-nang. He didn't know it but he was going to meet another man from Eye Corps. It would be the last person he met. In an alley, with a knife in his stomach, and whisky on his shirt and in his mouth.

And then Andrew would fly to the Delta. To the betrayer named Barstow. Barstow would be shot by a whore; they were easy to buy.

He walked across the hot concrete towards the transit building. A lieutenant-colonel was waiting for him. At first Andrew was alarmed; had something gone wrong? The five days weren't up! Then he saw that the colonel was smiling, somewhat patronizingly, but nevertheless in friendship.

'Major Fontine?' The greeting was accompanied by an extension of the hand; no salute was expected.

'Yes, sir?' The handshake was brief.

'Washington cable, straight from the secretary of the army. You have to get home, major. As soon as possible. I'm sorry to be the one to tell you, but it concerns your father.'

'My *father*? Is he dead?'

'It's only a matter of time. You have priority clearance for any aircraft leaving Tan Son Nhut.' The colonel handed him a red-bordered envelope with the imprimatur of General Headquarters, Saigon, across the top. It was the sort of envelope reserved for White House liaisons and couriers from the joint chiefs.

'My father's been a sick man for many years,' said

Fontine slowly. 'This isn't unexpected. I have another day's work here. I'll be at Tan San Nhut tomorrow night.'

'Whatever you say. The main thing is we found you. You've got the message.'

'I've got the message,' said Andrew.

In the phone booth, Adrian listened to the weary voice of the police sergeant. The sergeant was lying; more credible still, someone had lied to him. The pathology report on Nevins, James, black male, victim of hit-and-run, showed no apparent evidence of cranial, neck, or upper thorax injuries unrelated to the impact of collision.

'Send the report and the X-rays to me,' said Adrian curtly. 'You've got my address.'

'There were no X-rays accompanying the pathology report,' replied the police officer mechanically.

'Get them,' said Adrian, hanging up the phone.

Lies. Everywhere lies and evasions.

His was the biggest lie of all; he had lied to himself, and accepted that lie and used it to convince others. He had stood up in front of a group of very frightened young lawyers from the Justice Department and told them that under the circumstances, the subpoena on Eye Corps should be delayed. They needed to regroup their evidence, obtain a second desposition; to go to the adjutant general with only a list of names was meaningless.

It *wasn't* meaningless! The moment was right to confront the military and demand an immediate investigation. A man was murdered; the evidence he carried with him removed from the scene of his death. That evidence was the indictment of Eye Corps! Here are the names! This is the gist of the deposition!

Now, *move* on it!

But he could not do that. His brother's name was at the top of the list. To serve the subpoena was to charge his brother with murder. There was no other conclusion. Andrew was his brother, his twin, and he was not prepared to call him killer.

Adrian walked out of the phone booth and down the block towards his hotel. Andrew was on his way back from Saigon. He had left the country last Monday; it didn't take a great deal of imagination to know why. His brother wasn't stupid; Andrew was building his defence at the source of his crimes; crimes that included conspiracy, suppression of evidence, and obstruction of justice. Motives: complex and not without fundamental substance, but still crimes.

But not murder at night in a Washington street.

Oh, Christ! Even now he lied to himself! Or to be charitable, he refused to face the possible. Come on! *Say it, think it!*

The probable.

There was an eighth member of Eye Corps in Washington. Whoever that man was, he was Nevins's killer. And Nevins's killer could not have acted without the knowledge given by brother to brother in a boathouse on Long Island's North Shore.

When Andrew's plane landed, he would learn that the subpoena had not been served. Eye Corps was intact for a while longer, free to manoeuvre and manipulate.

There was one thing that would stop it, though. Stop it instantly and recharge a group of frightened lawyers who wondered if what happened to Nevins could happen to them; they were attorneys, not commandos.

Adrian would look into his brother's eyes, and if he saw Jim Nevins's death in them, he would avenge it. If the soldier had given the order of execution, then the soldier would be destroyed.

Or was he lying to himself again? Could he call his brother killer? Could he *really*?

What the hell did his father want? What difference did it make?

CHAPTER TWENTY-FOUR

The two chairs were placed on opposite sides of the bed. It was proper this way. He could divide his attention between his sons; they were different people, their reactions would be different. Jane preferred to stand. He had asked a terrible thing of her: to tell his sons the story of Salonika. Everything, leaving out nothing. They had to be made to understand that powerful men, institutions, even governments could be moved by the vault from Constantine. As they had been moved before.

He could not tell the story himself. He was dying; his mind was clear enough to know that. He had to have the simple energy to answer their questions; he had to have the strength to give his charge to his sons. For theirs was now the responsibility of the Fontini-Cristis.

They walked into the room with their mother. So tall, so alike, yet so different. One in uniform, the other in a nondescript tweed jacket and flannel trousers. Blond-haired Andrew was angry. It was in his face, the continuous tensing of his jaw muscles, the firm set of his mouth, the neutral, clouded gaze of his eyes.

Adrian, on the other hand, seemed unsure of himself. His blue eyes were questioning, his mouth slack, the lips parted. He drew his hand through his dark hair as he stared down, his expression equal parts of compassion and astonishment.

Victor indicated the chairs. The brothers looked at each other briefly; it was impossible to define the communication. Whatever had happened to alienate them had to be erased. Their responsibility demanded it. They sat down, the Xeroxed pages of recollections of 14 July 1920 in their hands. He had instructed Jane to give them each a copy; they were to read them through before seeing him. No moments were to be lost on explanations that could be covered beforehand. He hadn't the strength.

'We won't waste words on sentiment. You've heard your mother; you've read what I've written. You'll have questions.'

Andrew spoke. 'Assuming this vault can be found – and we'll get to that – what then?'

'I'll prepare a list of names. Five or six men, no more; they are not easily arrived at. You'll bring the vault to them.'

'What'll they do?' pressed Andrew.

'That will depend on what the vault contains, *specifically*. Release it, destroy it, rebury it.'

Adrian interrupted quietly. The lawyer was suddenly disturbed. 'Is there a choice? I don't think so. It doesn't belong to us; it should be public knowledge.'

'With public chaos? The consequences have to be weighed.'

'Does anyone else have the key?' asked the soldier. 'The location of this trip on 14 July 1920?'

'No. It would be meaningless. There are only a few left who knew of the train, knew what was *really* on it. Old men from the Patriarchate; one remains in Campo di Fiori and cannot have much time.'

'And we're to say nothing to anyone,' continued the major. 'No one but ourselves is to know.'

'No one. There are those who would trade off half the arsenals in this world for the information.'

'I wouldn't go that far.'

'Then you wouldn't be thinking. I'm sure your mother

explained. Besides the Filioque denials, including the Aramaic scroll, in that vault there is a parchment on which is written a confession that could alter religious history. If you think governments, whole nations, are disinterested bystanders, you are grossly mistaken.'

Andrew fell silent. Adrian looked at him and then at Victor.

'How long do you figure it'll take? To find this . . . this vault?' he asked.

'I'd estimate a month. You'll need equipment, Alpine guides, a week of instruction – no more, I should think.'

Adrian raised the Xeroxed pages several inches. 'Can you estimate how large an area there is to cover?'

'It's difficult to say; much will depend on what you find, what has changed. But if my memory serves, no more that five to eight square miles.'

'Five to eight! That's out of the question,' said Andrew emphatically, but without raising his voice. 'I'm sorry, but it's crazy. It could take years. You're talking about the Alps. One hole in the ground, a box no larger than a coffin, anywhere in a dozen mountains.'

'The most logical recesses are limited; they are reduced to one of perhaps three or four passes, high above, I suspect, where we were never allowed to climb.'

'I've mapped terrain in half a hundred field situations,' said the soldier slowly, so courteously his words bordered on condescension. 'You're minimizing an unbelievably difficult problem.'

'I don't think so. I meant what I just said to Adrian. Much will depend on what you find. Your grandfather was nothing if not meticulous. He considered all aspects of a situation, and most eventualities.' Victor stopped and shifted his position on the pillows. 'Savarone was an old man; there was a war going on and no one knew it better than he did. He would leave nothing that was recognizable to anyone in Campo di Fiori, but I can't believe he would not leave *something* within the area itself. A sign, a message – something. He was like that.'

'Where would we look?' asked Adrian, his eyes straying for an instant to his brother in the leather chair opposite him. The major was staring at the pages in his hand.

'I've written down the possibilities,' said Victor. 'There was a family of guides in the village of Champoluc. The Goldonis. They were used by my father, his father before him. And there was an inn north of the village. Run for generations by a family named Capomonti. We never travelled to the Champoluc without staying there. These were the people *closest* to Savarone. If he spoke with anyone, it would be to them.'

'That's over fifty years ago,' protested Adrian softly.

'Families in the mountains are closely knit. Two generations isn't a particularly wide gap. If Savarone left word it would be passed on from father to eldest child. Remember that: *child*. Son *or* daughter.' He smiled weakly at them. 'What else occurs to you? Questions may trigger further memories.'

The questions began but they triggered nothing. Victor had traced and retraced all he could. Whatever else remained was beyond memory.

Until Jane caught something. And as he listened to her words, Victor smiled. His blue-eyed, English Jane was remarkable for details.

'You wrote that the tracks of the railroad wound through the mountains south of Zermatt and descended into Champoluc, past flagging stops. Clearings between stations for the convenience of climbers and skiers.'

'Yes. Before the war. Nowadays, vehicles are more flexible in the snow.'

'It seems logical that a train carrying a vault, described to you as heavy and awkward, would find it necessary to stop at one of those clearings. For it to be transferred to another vehicle.'

'Agreed. What's your point?'

'Well, there are, or *were*, only so many stops between Zermatt and Champoluc. How many would you say?'

'Quite a few. At least nine or ten.'

'That's not much help. I'm sorry.'

'North of Champoluc, the first clearing was called Eagle's Peak, I believe. Then Crow's Lookout, and Condor's—' Victor stopped. *Birds*. The *names of birds*. A memory had been triggered, but it was not a memory that reached back three decades. It was barely days ago. In Campo di Fiori. 'The painting,' he said softly.

'What painting?' asked Adrian.

'Beneath the Madonna. In my father's study. A hunting scene, with *birds*.'

'And each clearing on the tracks,' said Andrew swiftly, sitting forward in the chair, 'is – or was – described in part with the name of a bird. What were the birds in the painting?'

'I don't remember. The light was dim and I was trying to find a few moments to think. I didn't concentrate on that painting.'

'Was it your father's?' asked Adrian.

'I'm not sure.'

'Can you call?' said the major, his question less a request than an order.

'No. Campo di Fiori is a tomb without lines of communication. Only a postal box in Milan, and that under the name of Baricours, Père et Fils.'

'Mother told us an old priest lives there. How does he exist?' The soldier was not satisfied.

'I never thought to ask,' replied the father. 'There was a man, a driver who picked me up in Milan. I assumed he was the monk's contact with the outside. The old priest and I talked most of the night, but my concerns were limited. He was still my enemy. He understood that.'

Andrew looked over at his brother. 'We stop at Campo di Fiori,' said the soldier curtly.

Adrian nodded and turned back to Victor. 'There's no way I can convince you to turn this over to others? To responsible scholars?'

'No,' answered Victor simply. 'The scholars will come later. Before then, nothing. Bear in mind what you're dealing with. The contents of that vault are as staggering to the civilized world as anything in history. The confession on that parchment is a devastating weapon, make no mistake about it. No *committee* can be asked to assume the responsibility, at this stage. The dangers are too great.'

'I see,' said Adrian, sitting back in his chair, looking at the pages. 'You mention the name Annaxas, but you're not clear about it. You say the father of Annaxas was the engineer on the train, killed by the priest of Xenope? Who is Annaxas?'

'In the event those papers fell into hands other than yours, I wanted no connection made. Annaxas is Theodore Dakakos.'

There was a snap. The soldier was holding a wooden pencil in his hand. He had broken it in half. Father and brother looked at him. Andrew said one word.

'Sorry.'

'I've heard that name,' continued Adrian. 'I'm not sure where.'

'He's Greek. A very successful shipper. The priest on that train was his father's brother, his uncle. Brother killed brother. It was ordered by Xenope, the location of the vault buried with them.'

'Dakakos knows this?' asked the soldier quietly.

'Yes. Where he precisely fits in, I don't know. I know only that he's looking for answers. And for the vault.'

'Can you trust him?' asked the lawyer.

'No. I trust no one where Salonika is concerned.' Victor inhaled deeply. It was difficult to talk now; his breath was shorter, his strength going.

'Are you all right?' Jane crossed quickly in front of Adrian to her husband. She leaned over and placed her hand on his cheek.

'Yes,' he answered, smiling up at her. And then he looked at Andrew and Adrian, holding each with his eyes.

'I don't ask what I ask of you lightly. You have your own lives, your interests are your own. You have money.' Victor raised a hand quickly. 'I hasten to add that this, too, was your right. I was given no less, nor should you be. In this respect we are a privileged family. But this privilege extracts responsibilities from those who enjoy it. There must inevitably come periods when you're asked to suspend your own pursuits for an unexpected urgency. I submit to you that such an urgency now exists.

'You've separated. Opponents, I suspect, philosophically and politically. There's nothing wrong with that, but these differences are insignificant compared to what faces you now. You're brothers, the grandsons of Savarone Fontini-Cristi, and you now must do what *his* son can't do. There's no appeal from privilege. Don't look for it.'

He was finished. It was all he could say; each breath was painful.

'All these years, you never said—' Adrian's eyes were questioning once again; there was awe and sadness in them. 'My God, how you must have felt.'

'I had two choices,' replied Victor, barely audible. 'To be productive. Or die a neuter. It was not a difficult choice.'

'You should have killed them,' said the soldier quietly.

They stood outside in the drive in front of the North

Shore house. Andrew leaned against the bonnet of his rented Lincoln Continental, his arms folded across his pressed uniform, the afternoon sun bouncing off the brass buttons and the insignia.

'He's going,' he said.

'I know,' answered Adrian. 'He knows it, too.'

'And here we are.'

'Here we are,' agreed the lawyer.

'What he wants is easier for me than it is for you.' Andrew looked up at the windows of the front bedroom on the second floor.

'What does that mean?'

'I'm practical. You're not. We'll do better working together than apart.'

'I'm surprised you concede I might help. It must hurt your vanity.'

'There's no ego in field decisions. It's the objective that counts.' Andrew spoke casually. 'We can cut the time in half if we divide the possibilities. His recollections are disjointed, he wanders all over the place. His terrain-recall is confused; I've had some experience in that.' Andrew straightened up, away from the car. 'I think we'll have to go back, Adrian. Seven years ago. Before San Francisco. Can you do that?'

Adrian stared at his brother. 'You're the only one who can answer that. And please don't lie; you were never any good at lying. Not with me.'

'Nor you with me.'

Their eyes locked; neither wavered.

'A man was killed Wednesday night. In Washington.'

'I was in Saigon. You know that. Who was he?'

'A black lawyer from Justice. A man named—'

'Nevins,' completed Andrew, interrupting his brother. 'My God! You *knew*!'

'*About* him, yes. About his being *killed*, no. Why would I?'

'Eye Corps! He took a deposition on Eye Corps! It was with him! It was taken from his car!'

'Are you out of your goddamned mind?' The soldier spoke slowly, without urgency. 'You may not like us, but we're not stupid. A target like that man, even remotely linked to us, would bring on investigations by the hundreds. There are better ways. Killing's an instrument; you don't use it against yourself.'

Adrian continued to look at his brother, searching his eyes. Finally, he spoke. Softly, barely above a whisper. 'I think that's the most cold-blooded thing I've ever heard.'

'What is?'

'"Killing's an instrument." You mean it, don't you?'

'Of course I do. It's the truth. Have I answered your question?'

'Yes,' said Adrian quietly. 'We'll go back ... before San Francisco. For a while; you have to know that. Only until this is over.'

'Good ... You've got things to straighten up before we leave, and so do I. Let's say a week from tomorrow.'

'All right. A week from tomorrow.'

'I'm catching the six o'clock plane to Washington. Want to come along?'

'No, I'm meeting someone in town. I'll use one of the cars here.'

'It's funny,' said Andrew, shaking his head slowly, as if what he was about to say wasn't funny at all. 'I've never asked for your telephone number, or where you lived.'

'It's the District Towers. On Nebraska.'

'The District Towers. All right. A week from tomorrow. I'll make the plane reservations. Straight through to Milan. Is your passport current?'

'I think so. It's at the hotel. I'll check.'

'Good. I'll call you. A week from tomorrow.' Andrew reached for the door handle. 'Incidentally, what happened to that subpoena?'

'You know what happened. It wasn't served.'

The soldier smiled as he climbed into the car. 'It wouldn't have worked anyway.'

They sat at a corner table in the St Moritz pavement café on Central Park South. They were partial to such places; they would select pedestrians and invent instant biographies.

They invented none now. Instead, Adrian decided that his father's instructions to tell no one about the train from Salonika would not include Barbara. His decision was based on his belief that were their roles reversed, she would tell him. He wasn't going to leave the country for five to ten weeks without saying why. She deserved better than that.

'So there it is. Religious documents that go back fifteen hundred years, an Aramaic scroll that made the British government go half out of its collective mind in the middle of the war, and a confession written on a parchment two *thousand* years ago that contains God only knows what. That vault's caused more violence than I want to think about. If what my father says is true, those documents, that scroll – the parchment, most of all – could alter a large part of history.'

Barbara leaned back in the chair, her brown eyes levelled at him. She watched him without replying for several moments. 'That seems highly unlikely. Documents are unearthed every day. History doesn't change,' she said simply.

'Have you ever heard of something called the Filioque Clause?'

'Certainly. It was incorporated in the Nicene Creed. It was the first issue that separated the Western and Eastern church. The debate went on for hundreds of years, and led to the Photian schism in ... the ninth century, I think. Which in turn brought about the schism of 1054. The issue ultimately became papal infallibility.'

'How the hell do you know that?'

Barbara laughed. 'It's my field. Remember? At least the behavioural aspects.'

'You said the ninth century. My father said fifteen hundred years—'

'Early Christian history is confusing, date-happy. From the first to the seventh centuries there were so many councils, so much seesawing back and forth, so much debate over *this* doctrine and *that* law, it's nearly impossible to sort out. Do these documents concern the Filioque? Are they supposed to be the denials?'

Adrian's glass was suspended on the way to his lips. 'Yes. That's what my father said; he used the term. The Filioque denials.'

'They don't exist.'

'What?'

'They were destroyed – ceremonially, I believe – in Istanbul, in the Mosque of Saint Sophia, early in the Second World War. There's documentation ... witnesses, if I remember correctly. Even charred fragments confirmed by spectrochemical analyses.'

Adrian stared at her. Something was terribly wrong. It was all too simple. Too negatively simple. 'Where did you get that information?'

'Where? You mean *specifically* where?'

'Yes.'

Barbara leaned forward, moving her glass absently in thought. Her forehead was creased. 'It's not my area, but I can find out, of course. It goes back several years. I *do* remember that it was quite a shock to a lot of people.'

'Do me a favour,' he said rapidly. 'When you get back, find out everything you can about that fire. It doesn't make sense! My father would know about it.'

'I don't know why. It's awfully academic stuff.'

'It still doesn't make sense—'

'Speaking of Boston,' she interrupted. 'My answering service had two calls from someone trying to locate you. A man named Dakakos.'

'*Dakakos?*'

'Yes. A Theodore Dakakos. He said it was urgent.'

'What did you say?'

'That I'd give you the message. I wrote down the number. I didn't *want* to give it to you. You don't need hysterical phone calls from Washington. You've had a horrid few days.'

'He's not from Washington.'

'The phone calls were.'

Adrian looked up from the table, past the miniature hedges in the boxes bordering the café. He saw what he was looking for: a telephone booth.

'I'll be right back.'

He walked to the phone and called the District Towers in Washington.

'Front desk, please.'

'Yes, Mr Fontine. We've had several calls from a Mr Dakakos. There's an aide to Mr Dakakos in the lobby now waiting for you.'

Adrian thought quickly. His father's words came back to him; he had asked his father if he could trust Dakakos. *Where Salonika is concerned, I trust no one . . .*

'Listen to me. Tell the man in the lobby you just heard from me. I won't be back for several days. I don't want to see this Dakakos.'

'Of course, Mr Fontine.'

Adrian hung up. His passport was in Washington. In the room. He'd go by way of the garage. But not tonight; that was too soon. He'd wait until tomorrow. He'd stay in New York tonight . . . His father. His father should be told about Dakakos. He called the North Shore house.

Jane's voice was strained. 'The doctor's with him now.

Thank God he allowed them to give him something. I don't think he could have stood it much longer. He's had spasms—'

'I'll phone you tonight.'

Adrian walked out of the booth and threaded his way between the strollers back to the café, to the table.

'What *is* it?' Barbara was alarmed.

'Get in touch with your service in Boston. Tell them to call Dakakos and say we missed each other. I had to fly to – hell, Chicago. On business. That was the message for you at the hotel here.'

'You really don't want to see him, do you?'

'I've got to avoid him. I want to throw him off the track. He's probably tried to reach my brother.'

The path in Rock Creek Park. It was Martin Greene's idea, his selection. Greene had sounded strange on the telephone, somehow defiant. As though he didn't care about anything anymore.

Whatever was gnawing at Greene would vanish in the time it took to tell him the story. My God, would it! In one afternoon, Eye Corps had taken a giant step! Beyond anything they could have imagined. If the things his father said about the vault – the lengths powerful men, entire *governments* went to possess it – if it was all only half true, Eye Corps was in the catbird seat! Unreachable!

His father said he was going to prepare a list. Well, his father didn't have to; there *was* a list. The seven men of Eye Corps would control that vault. And he would control the seven men of Eye Corps.

Christ, it was incredible! But events did not lie; his father did not lie. Whoever possessed those documents, that parchment from a forgotten Roman prison, had the leverage to make extraordinary demands. Everywhere! An omission of recorded history, kept from the world out of unbelievable fear. Its revelation could not be tolerated. Well, fear, too, was an instrument. As great a one as death. Often greater.

Bear in mind that the contents of that vault are as staggering to the civilized world as anything in history . . .

The decisions of extraordinary men – in peace and in war – supported his father's judgement. And now other extraordinary men, led by one extraordinary man, would find that vault and help shape the last quarter of the twentieth century. One had to begin to think like that, think in large blocks, concepts beyond ordinary men. His training, his heritage. All was coming into focus, and he was ready for the weight of enormous responsibility. He was primed for it; it was his with a vault buried in the Italian Alps.

Adrian would have to be immobilized. Not seriously; his brother was weak, indecisive, no contender at all. It would be enough to slow him down. He would visit his brother's rooms and do just that.

Andrew started down the Rock Creek path. There were very few strollers; the park was not a place for walking at night. Where was Greene? He should have been there; his apartment was a lot closer than the airport. And Greene had told him to hurry.

Andrew walked out on the grass and lighted a cigarette. There was no point standing under the spill of the park lamps. He'd see Greene when he came down the path.

'Fontine!'

The soldier turned around, startled. Twenty yards away at the side of a tree trunk stood Martin Greene. He was in civilian clothes; there was a large briefcase in his left hand.

'Marty? What the hell—'

'Get over here,' ordered the captain tersely.

Andrew walked rapidly into the cluster of trees. 'What's going on?'

'It's gone, Fontine. The whole goddamned thing. I've been calling you since yesterday morning.'

'I was in New York. What are you talking about?'

'Five men are in a maximum security jail in Saigon. Want to take a guess who?'

'*What?* The subpoena wasn't served! You confirmed it, *I* confirmed it!'

'Nobody needed a subpoena. The IG crawled out of the rocks. They hit us on all points. My guess is that I've got about twelve hours before they figure I'm the one in procurement. You, you're marked.'

'Wait a minute. Just wait a minute! This is crazy! The subpoena was cancelled!'

'I'm the only one who benefits from that. You never mentioned my name in Saigon, did you?'

'Of course not. Just that we've got a man here.'

'That's all they'll need; they'll put it together.'

'How?'

'A dozen different ways. Locking in and comparing my checkout times with yours is the first that comes to mind. Something happened over there; something blew everything apart.' Greene's eyes strayed.

Andrew breathed steadily, staring down at the captain. 'No, it didn't,' he said softly. 'It happened over here. Last Wednesday night.'

Greene's head snapped up. 'What *about* Wednesday night?'

'That black lawyer. Nevins. You had him killed, you stupid son of a bitch. My brother accused me! Accused *us*! He believed me because I believed it myself! It was too stupid!' The soldier's voice was a strained whisper. It was all he could do to keep from lashing out at the man staring up at him.

Greene replied calmly, with assurance. 'You're getting

the right total but the wrong numbers. I had it done, that's true, and I've got the bastard's briefcase, including the deposition against us. But the contract was so remote the people who did it don't know I exist. To bring you up to date, they were caught this morning. In West Virginia. They've got laundered money that can be traced to a company up for fraud. And we're not it . . . No, Fontine, it wasn't me. Whatever it was, happened over there. I think you blew it.'

Andrew shook his head. 'Impossible. I handled—'

'Please. No burdens. I don't want to know, because I don't give a damn any more. I've got a suitcase at Dulles and a one-way ticket to Tel Aviv. But I'm going to do you one last favour. When everything hit, I called a few friends at IG; they owed me. That deposition from Barstow we worried so much about wasn't even in the prize money.'

'What do you mean?'

'Remember the routine congressional inquiry? The Greek you never heard of—?'

'*Dakakos?*'

'That's right. Theodore Dakakos. Over at IG they call it the Dakakos probe. It was him. Nobody knows how, but that Greek was the one who got everything there was to get on Eye Corps. He funnelled it piece by piece into the IG files.'

Theodore Dakakos, thought Andrew. Theodore Annaxas Dakakos, son of a Greek railwayman slain thirty years ago in the Milan goods yards by a priest who was his brother. Extraordinary men went to extraordinary lengths to control the vault of Constantine. A calm swept over the soldier.

'Thanks for telling me,' he said. Greene held up the briefcase. 'By the way, I made a trip to Baltimore.'

'The Baltimore records are among the best,' said Fontine.

'Where I'm going, we may need some quick firepower in the Negev. These could get it.'

'Very possibly.'

Greene hesitated, and then asked quietly, 'You want to come along? We can hide you. You could do worse.'

'I can do better.'

'Stop kidding yourself, Fontine! Use some of your well-advertised money and get out of here as fast as you can. Buy sanctuary. You're *finished*.'

'You're wrong. I've just begun.'

CHAPTER TWENTY-FIVE

Washington's noonday traffic was slowed further by the June thunderstorm. It was one of those deluges without spells of relief that allowed pedestrians to dash from doorway to awning to doorway. Windscreen wipers did little but intrude on the sheets of water that blanketed the glass, distorting all vision.

Adrian sat in the backseat of a taxi, his thoughts divided equally in three parts, on three people, Barbara, Dakakos, and his brother.

Barbara was in Boston, probably in the library archives by now, researching the information – the extraordinary information – about the destruction of the Filioque denials. If those ancient documents had been in the vault from Constantine, and proof of their destruction established beyond doubt ... had the vault been found? A equals B equals C. Therefore A equals C. Or did it?

Theodore Dakakos, the indefatigable Annaxas, would be scouring the Chicago hotels and law firms looking for him. There was no reason for the Greek not to; a business trip to Chicago was perfectly normal. The distraction was all Adrian needed. He would go up to his rooms, grab his passport, and call Andrew. They could both get out of Washington, avoiding Dakakos. The assumption had to be that Dakakos was trying to stop them. Which meant that somehow Dakakos-Annaxas knew what their father had planned. It was easy enough.

An old man returns from Italy, his life expectancy short. And he summons his two sons.

One of those sons was Adrian's third concern. Where was his brother? He had telephoned Andrew's apartment in Virginia repeatedly throughout the night. What bothered Adrian, and the admission wasn't easy for him, was that his brother was more equipped to deal with someone like Dakakos than he. Move and countermove was part of his life, not thesis and antithesis.

'Garage entrance,' said the cab driver. 'Here it is.'

Adrian dashed through the rain into the District Towers' garage. He had to orient himself before walking towards the lift. As he did so, he reached into his pocket for the key with the plastic tag; he never left it at the front desk.

'Hi, Mr Fontine. How are ya'?'

It was the garage attendant; Adrian vaguely remembered the face. A sallow, twenty-year-old hustler with the eyes of a ferret.

'Hello,' replied Adrian, pushing the lift button.

'Hey, thanks again. I appreciated it, ya' know what I mean? I mean it was real nice of you.'

'Sure,' Adrian said blankly, wishing the lift would arrive.

'Hey.' The attendant winked at him. 'You look a lot better'n you did last night. A real broiler, huh?'

'What?'

The attendant smiled. No, it wasn't a smile, it was a leer. 'I tied one on, too. Real good. Just like you said.'

'What did you say? You saw me last night?'

'Hey, come on. Ya' don't remember even? I gotta admit, you was fried, man.'

Andrew! Andrew could do it when he wanted to! Slouch, wear a hat, draw out his words. He'd pulled that caricature dozens of times.

'Tell me, I'm a little hazy. What time did I get in?'

'Jee-*sus*! You was flat out. Around eight o'clock, don't you remember? You gimme—' The attendant stopped; the hustler in him prevented full disclosure.

The lift doors opened. Adrian walked inside. So Andrew had come to see him while he was trying to call *him* in Virginia. Had Andy found out about Dakakos? Had he already left town? Maybe Andy was upstairs now. Again the realization was disquieting, but Adrian felt a certain relief at the prospect. His brother would know what to do.

Adrian walked down the corridor to the door of his suite and let himself in. As he did so, he heard the footsteps behind him. He whipped around and saw an army officer standing in the bedroom door; not Andrew, a colonel.

'Who the hell are you?'

The officer did not immediately reply. Instead, he stood immobile, his eyes angry. When he did speak there was a slight drawl in his cold voice.

'Yeah, you do look like him. Put on a uniform and straighten you up and you could *be* him. Now, all you have to do is tell me where he is.'

'How did you get in here? Who the hell let you in?'

'No question for a question. Mine comes first.'

'What comes first is that you're trespassing.' Adrian walked rapidly to the telephone, crossing in front of the officer. 'Unless you've got a warrant from a civilian court, you're going to march into a civilian police station.'

The colonel undid one button on his tunic, reached inside, and took out a pistol. He snapped the safety catch and levelled the weapon.

Adrian held the telephone in his left hand, his right poised above the dial. Stunned, he stopped all movement; the expression on the officer's face had not changed.

'You listen to me,' said the colonel softly. 'I could shoot both your kneecaps off just for looking like him. Can you understand that? I'm a civilized man, a lawyer like you; but where Eye Corps' Major Fontine is concerned, all the rules go out the window. I'll do anything to get that son of a bitch. Do you read me?'

Adrian slowly put down the telephone. 'You're a maniac.'

'Minor compared to him. Now, you tell me where he is.'

'I don't know.'

'I don't believe you.'

'Wait a minute!' In his shock, Adrian had not been sure of what he'd heard. Now he was. 'What do you know about *Eye Corps*?'

'A lot more than you paranoid bastards want me to know. Did you two really think you could pull it off?'

'You're way off base! You'd know that if you knew anything about me! About Eye Corps we're on the same side! Now, for God's sake, what have you got on him?'

The officer replied slowly. 'He killed two men. A captain named Barstow, and a legal officer named Tarkington. Both killings were made to look *kai-sai* – whore-and-booze oriented. They weren't. In Tarkington's case it was inconsistent. He didn't drink.'

'Oh, Christ!'

'And a file was taken from Tarkington's Saigon office. Which *was* consistent. What they didn't know was that we had a complete copy.'

'Who's "we"?'

'The Inspector General's Office.' The colonel did not lower his pistol; his answers were delivered in a flat Southwestern drawl. 'Now, I just gave you the benefit of a doubt. You know why I want him, so tell me where he is. My name's Tarkington, too. I drink and I'm not mild-mannered and I want the son of a bitch who killed my brother.'

Adrian felt the breath leave his lungs. 'I'm sorry—'

'Now you know why this gun is out and why I'll use it. Where did he go? How did he go?'

It took Adrian a moment to focus. 'Where? How? I didn't know he *was* gone. Why are your sure he is?'

'Because he knows we're after him. We know he got the word; we made the connection this morning. A captain named Greene in the Pentagon. In procurement. Needless to say, he's gone too. Probably halfway across the world by now.'

... *halfway across the world* ... the words penetrated, the realization began to surface. *Halfway across the world. To Italy. Campo di Fiori. A painting on the wall and the memories of a half a century ago. The vault from Constantine!*

'Did you check the airports?'

'He has a standard military passport. All military ...'

'Oh, Jesus!' Adrian started for the bedroom.

'Hold it!' The colonel grabbed his arm.

'Let me go!' Fontine shook off the officer's hand and raced into the bedroom. To the bureau.

He pulled open the right-hand top drawer. From behind the colonel's hand shot out and slammed it, trapping his wrist.

'You pull out anything I don't like, you're dead.' The colonel released the drawer.

Fontine could feel the pain and see the swelling on his wrist. He could not think about either. He opened a large leather case. His passport was gone. So, too, his international driver's licence and his Banque Genève cheque book with the coded numbers and photograph on the flap.

Adrian turned and walked across the room in silence. He dropped the leather pouch on the bed and continued to the window. The rain outside came down in torrents against the glass.

His brother had stalled him. Andrew had gone after the vault, leaving him behind, wanting no assistance at all, never having wanted it. The vault from Constantine was Andrew's final weapon. In his hands a deadly thing.

The irony was, reflected Adrian, that the army officer behind him in that room could *help*. He could break down bureaucratic barriers, provide instant transportation – but the army officer could be told nothing about the train from Salonika.

There are those who would trade off half the arsenals in the world for the information. His father's words.

He spoke quietly. 'There's your proof, colonel.'

'I guess so.'

Adrian turned and faced the officer. 'Tell me, as one brother to another – how did you lock in on Eye Corps?'

The colonel put away the gun. 'A man named Dakakos.'

'Dakakos?'

'Yes, he's Greek. You know him?'

'No, I don't.'

'The data came in slowly at first. Right into my department, marked for me by name. When Barstow broke and gave his deposition in Saigon, there was Dakakos again. He sent word to my brother to get to Barstow. Eye Corps was covered both over here and over there—'

'By two brothers who could pick up a phone and keep it all together,' said Adrian, interrupting. 'Without bureaucratic interference.'

'We figured that. We don't know why, but this Dakakos was after Eye Corps.'

'He certainly was,' agreed Adrian, marvelling at Dakakos's clarity of method.

'Yesterday, *everything* came in. Dakakos had Fontine

followed to Phan-thiet. To a warehouse. We've got Eye Corps' records now, we've got the proof—'

The telephone rang, interrupting the army man. Adrian barely heard it, so total was his concentration on the colonel's words.

It rang again.

'May I?' asked Adrian.

'You'd better.' Tarkington's eyes became cold again. 'I'll be right next to you.'

It was Barbara, calling from Boston. 'I'm in the archives. I've got the information on that church fire in 'forty-one that destroyed the Filioque.'

'Just a minute.' Adrian turned his head towards the officer, the phone between them. He wondered if he could sound natural. 'You can get on a line in the other room, if you like. It's just some research I asked for.'

The ruse worked. Tarkington shrugged and walked to the window.

'Go ahead,' he said into the phone.

Barbara spoke as an expert does, scanning a report whose form is familiar; her voice rose and fell as salient points were enumerated. 'There was a gathering of elders on 9 January 1941, at eleven o'clock in the evening at the Mosque of Saint Sophia, Istanbul, a ceremony of deliverance. According to the witnesses a consigning of holy property to the heavens . . . sloppy work here; it's all narrative. There should be direct quotes and literal translations. Anyway, it goes on to verify the act and list the laboratories in Istanbul and Athens where fragments of the ash were confirmed for age and materials. There you are, my doubting Thomas.'

'What about those witnesses? The narrative?'

'I'm being overly critical. I could be more so; the report should include authorizing credentials and graphic plate numbers, but that's all academic lacework. The main thing is, it's got the archival seal; you don't buy that. You can't play games with it. It means someone beyond reproach was at the scene and confirmed the burning. The Annaxas grant got what it paid for. The seals says it.'

'What grant?' he asked quietly.

'Annaxas. It's the company that put up the money for the research.'

'Thanks. I'll talk to you later.' He hung up. Tarkington was standing by the window, looking out at the rain. This was the man he had to get away from; he had to get to the vault!

Barbara was right in one respect. Dakakos-Annaxas got *exactly* what he paid for: a false report in the archives.

He knew where he had to go.

Campo di Fiori.

Dakakos.

Dakakos, Dakakos, *Dakakos*!

The named burned into Andrew's brain as he watched the coast of Italy go by 30,000 feet below. Theodore Annaxas Dakakos had destroyed Eye Corps for the sole purpose of destroying *him*, eliminating *him* from the search for a vault buried in the mountains. What triggered his decision? How did he do it? It was vital to learn all he could about the man himself. The better one knew his enemy, the better one could fight. As things stood, Dakakos was the only barrier, the only contender.

There was a man in Rome who could help. He was a banker who showed up with increasing frequency in Saigon, a large-scale buyer who bought whole piers, shipped the contents back to Naples and sold the stolen goods throughout Italy. Eye Corps had nailed him and used him; he had provided names that went right back to Washington.

Such a man would know about Dakakos.

The announcement came over the Air Canada loud-speaker. They would begin their descent into Rome's Leonardo da Vinci Airport in fifteen minutes.

Fontine took out his passport. He had bought it in Quebec. Adrian's passport had got him through Canadian customs, but he knew it would be worthless after that. Washington would flash the name Fontine to every airport in the hemisphere.

Ironically, he made a connection with several army deserters at two in the morning in Montreal. The exiled moralists needed money; morality could not be proselytized without hard cash. A stringy-haired intellectual in a GI field jacket took him to an apartment that reeked of hash, and for $10,000 he got a passport within an hour.

Adrian was so far behind he'd never catch up.

. . . He could dismiss Adrian. If Dakakos wanted to stop one of them, he obviously wanted to stop both. The Greek was no match for the soldier; he was more than a match for the lawyer. And if Dakakos didn't stop Adrian, the lack of a passport would slow him down more than enough. His brother was out of the picture, no contender at all.

The plane touched ground. Andrew unbuckled his seat belt; he would be among the first out of the aircraft. He was in a hurry to get to a telephone.

The evening crowds on the Via Veneto were heavy, the pavement tables under the awnings of the Café de Paris nearly filled. The banker had secured one near the service door, where the traffic was concentrated. He was a gaunt, middle-aged, impeccably dressed man, and he was cautious. No listener could overhear anything said at that table.

Their greeting was perfunctory, the banker obviously anxious to have the meeting over with as quickly as possible.

'I won't ask why you're in Rome. No address, out of your celebrated uniform.' The Italian spoke rapidly in a monotone that gave no emphasis to any word and thus emphasis to all. 'I honoured your demand to make no inquiries. It wasn't necessary. You're a hunted man.'

'How do you know that?'

The slender Italian paused, his thin lips stretched into a slight smile. 'You just told me.'

'I warn you—'

'Oh, stop it. A man flies in unannounced, says he'll meet only in crowds. It's enough to send me to Malta so I won't run into you. Besides, it's all over your face. You're uncomfortable.'

The banker was essentially right. He *was* uncomfortable. He would have to adjust better, be more relaxed. 'You're clever, but then we knew that in Saigon.'

'I never saw you before in my life,' replied the Italian, signalling a waiter. '*Due Campari, per favore.*'

'I don't drink Campari . . .'

'Then don't. Two Italians who order Campari on the Via Veneto are not conspicuous. Which is precisely what I intend to be. What did you wish to discuss?'

'A man named Dakakos. A Greek.'

The banker raised his eyebrows. 'If by Dakakos you mean Theo Dakakos, he is indeed Greek.'

'You know him?'

'Who in the world of finance doesn't? You have business with Dakakos?'

'Maybe. He's a shipper, isn't he?'

'Among many other interests. He's also quite young and very powerful. Even the colonels in Athens think twice before issuing edicts unfavourable to him. His older competitors are wary of him. What he lacks in experience he makes up for in energy. He's a bull.'

'What are his politics?'

The Italian's eyebrows once more rose. 'Himself.'

'What are his interests in South-east Asia? Whom does he work for out of Saigon?'

'He doesn't work *for* anyone.' The waiter returned with the drinks. 'He ships middle-manned supplies to the AID in Vientiane. Into northern Laos and Cambodia. As you know, it's all intelligence-operated. He pulled out, I understand.'

That was it, thought Fontine, pushing away the glass of Campari. Eye Corps had tagged the corruption in AID, and Dakakos had tagged *them*. 'He went to a lot of trouble to interfere.'

'Did he succeed in interfering? ... I see he did. Annaxas the Younger usually does succeed; he's perverse and predictable in that department.' The Italian raised his glass delicately.

'What was that name?'

'Annaxas. Annaxas the Younger, son of Annaxas the Strong. Sounds Theban, does it not? The Greek bloodlines, however insignificant, are always on the tips of their tongues. Pretentious, I think.'

'Does he use it a lot?'

'Not often for himself. His yacht is named *Annaxas*, several planes are *Annaxas – One, Two, Three*. He works the name into a few corporate titles. It's an obsession with him. Theodore Annaxas Dakakos. The first son of a poor family raised by some religious order in the north. The circumstances are cloudy; he doesn't encourage curiosity.' The Italian drained his glass.

'That's interesting.'

'Have I told you something you didn't know?'

'Maybe,' said Fontine casually. 'It's not important.'

'By which you mean it is.' The Italian smiled his thin, bloodless smile. 'Dakakos is in Italy, you know.'

Fontine concealed his surprise. 'Is he really?'

'So you *do* have business with him. Is there anything else?'

'No.'

The banker rose and walked rapidly into the crowds of the Via Veneto.

Andrew remained at the table. So Dakakos was in Italy. Andrew wondered where they would meet. He wanted that meeting very much; almost as much as he wanted to find the vault from Salonika.

He wanted to kill Theodore Annaxas Dakakos. The man who had destroyed Eye Corps did not deserve to live.

Andrew got up from the table. He could feel the bulge of papers in his jacket pocket. His father's recollections of half a century ago.

CHAPTER TWENTY-SIX

Adrian shifted the soft leather suitcase into his left hand and fell behind the surge of passengers in the wide corridor of London's Heathrow Airport. He did not wish to be among the first in the passport line. He wanted to be in the middle group, even the last section; he would have more time to look around, be less conspicuous doing so. He wondered who among the scores of people in the terminal had him in their sights.

Colonel Tarkington was no fool; he'd have known within minutes of the application that one Adrian Fontine was at the emigration offices in Rockefeller Center waiting for the issuance of a substitute passport. It was entirely possible that an IG agent had picked him up before he'd left the building. If no one had, he knew it was only a question of time. And because of that certainty, Adrian had flown to London, not Rome.

Tomorrow he would begin the chase. An amateur against professionals. His first step was to disappear, but he wasn't sure how. On the one hand it seemed simple: a single human being among millions; how difficult could it be? Then came second thoughts: one had to travel across national borders – that meant clearly one had to have identification; one had to sleep and eat – that meant shelter and purchases, places that could be watched, alerted.

It wasn't simple at all; not if the single human being in question had no experience. He had no contacts in the underworld; he wouldn't know how to behave if he met them. He doubted that he could approach someone and say the words *'I'll pay for a false passport'*, ... or *'Get me to Italy illegally'*, ... or even *'I won't tell you my name but I'll give money for certain services.'* Such boldness belonged in fiction. Normal men and women did not do such things; their awkwardness would be laughed at. But professionals – the sort he was up against – were not normal. They did such things quite easily.

He saw the passport lines. There were six in all; he chose the longest. Yet as he walked over to it, he realized that the decision was amateurish. True, he had more time to look around, but conversely, so did others.

'Occupation, sir?' asked the immigration officer.

'I'm a lawyer.'

'Here on business?'

'In a manner of speaking. Also pleasure.'

'Anticipated length of stay?'

'I'm not sure. No more than a week.'

'Do you have hotel accommodations?'

'I didn't make reservations. Probably the Savoy.'

The official glanced up; it was difficult to tell whether he was impressed or whether he resented Adrian's tone. Or whether the name Fontine, A., was on a concealed list somewhere in the drawer of his lectern, and he wanted to look at the face.

Regardless, he smiled mechanically, stamped the pages of the newly issued passport, and handed it to Adrian. 'Have a pleasant stay in Great Britain, Mr Fontine.'

'Thank you.'

The Savoy found him a room above the court, offering to switch him to a suite on the Thames side as soon as one became available. He accepted the offer, saying he expected to remain in England for the better part of the month. He would be travelling around – away from

London for much of the time – but would like a suite available during the period of his stay.

What astonished him was the ease with which he lied. It all flowed casually, with a certain businesslike assurance. It wasn't an important manoeuvre, but the fact that he was able to do it so well gave him a sense of confidence. He had seized an advantage when it was presented; that was the important thing. He had spotted an opportunity and acted on it.

He sat on the bed, airline schedules scattered over the spread. He found what he wanted. An SAS flight from Paris to Stockholm at 10:30 AM. And an Air Afrique from Paris to Rome. Time: 10:15 AM. The SAS left from the de Gaulle field, the Air Afrique from Orly.

Fifteen minutes between flights, departure before arrival, from adjacent airfields. He wondered – almost academically now – if he was capable of conceiving a deception, organizing the facts and executing the manipulation from beginning to end.

Odd things would have to be considered. Items that were part of the . . . 'dressing', that was the word. Part of the ruse that would draw the proper attention in a crowded, bustling airport. He picked up a Savoy note pad and wrote:

Three suitcases – unusual.
Overcoat – conspicuous.
Glasses.
Hat – wide-brimmed.
Small paste-on beard.

The last item – the beard – caused him to smile uncomfortably, embarrassed at his own imagination. Was he crazy? Who did he think he was? What did he think he was doing? He moved the pencil instinctively to the left of the line, prepared to cross it out. Then he stopped. He wasn't crazy. It was part of the boldness he had to absorb, the unnatural with which he had to be comfortable. He took the pencil away and without thinking wrote the name: 'Andrew'.

Where was he now? Had his brother reached Italy? Had he travelled halfway around the world without being found? Would he be waiting for him at Campo di Fiori?

And if he *was* waiting, what would they say to each other? He hadn't thought about that; he hadn't wanted to think about it. Like a difficult summing-up in front of a hostile jury, he could not rehearse the words. He could only marshal the facts in his head and trust his thought processes when the moment came. But what did one say to a twin who was the killer of Eye Corps? What was there *to* say?

... Bear in mind, the contents of that vault are as staggering to the civilized world as anything in history ...

His brother had to be stopped. It was as simple as that.

He looked at his watch. It was one in the morning. He was thankful that he had had little sleep during the past several days. It would make sleeping possible now. He had to rest; he had a great deal to do tomorrow. Paris.

He walked up to the desk clerk in the Hôtel Pont Royale and handed him the room key. He hadn't been to the Louvre in five years; it would be a cultural sin to avoid it since it was so close by. The clerk agreed politely but Adrian saw the shaded curiosity in the man's eyes. It was further confirmation of what Adrian suspected: he was being followed; questions were being asked.

He walked into the bright sunlight on the rue du Bac. He nodded, smiling, at the doorman and shook his head in response to the offer of a taxi.

'I'm going to the Louvre. I'll walk, thanks.'

At the kerb he lit a cigarette, turning slightly as if to

avoid a breeze, and let his eyes wander over the large windows of the hotel. Inside, through the glass, obscured by the sun's reflection, he could see the clerk talking to a man in a light-brown coat. Adrian was not certain, but he was fairly sure he had seen that gabardine coat at the airport two hours ago.

He started east down the rue du Bac, towards the Seine and the Pont Royale.

The Louvre was crowded. Tourists mingled with bus-loads of students. Adrian climbed the steps past Winged Victory and continued up the staircase to the right, to the second landing, and into the hall of the nineteenth-century masters. He fell in with a group of German tourists.

The Germans moved in unison down to the next painting, a Delacroix. Adrian was now in the centre of the group. Keeping his head below the level of the tallest German, he turned and looked between the sagging bodies, beyond the impassive faces. He saw what he was both afraid of and wanted to see.

The light-brown coat.

The man was fifty feet away, pretending to read from a museum pamphlet, relating it to an Ingres in front of him. But he was neither reading nor relating; his eyes kept straying up from the paper to the crowd of Germans.

The group turned the corner into the intersecting corridor. Adrian was against the wall. He parted the bodies in front of him, excusing himself until he was past the guide and free of the group. He walked swiftly down the right side of the enormous hall and turned left into a dimly lit room. Tiny spotlights shone down from the dark ceiling on a dozen marble statues.

It suddenly occurred to him that if the man in the light brown gabardine coat came into that room, there was no way out.

On the other hand, if the man entered there was no way out for him, either. Adrian wondered which of them had more to lose. He had no answer and so he stood in shadows at the farthest end of the room, beyond the shafts of light, and waited.

He could see the group of Germans go past the doorway. Seconds later there was the blur of the light brown coat; the man was running, actually running.

Adrian went to the door, paused long enough to see the Germans swing left to yet another intersecting corridor, turned right and walked rapidly towards the hall to the stairs.

The crowds on the staircase were denser than before. There was a contingent of uniformed schoolgirls reaching the steps. Behind the girls was the man in the light-brown gabardine coat, frustrated in his attempts to pass and reach the steps.

It was suddenly clear to Adrian. The man had lost him and would wait at the exit.

There remained the obvious; reach the main doors first.

Adrian hurried down the steps, doing his best to look unhurried; a man late for a lunch date.

Out by the steps in front of the entrance a taxi was disgorging four Japanese. An elderly couple, obviously British, was walking across the pavement towards the cab. He ran, overtaking the couple, and reached the taxi first.

'*Dépêchez-vous, s'il vous plaît. Très important.*'

The driver grinned and started up the car. Adrian turned in the seat and looked out the rear window. On the steps the man in the light-brown coat stood looking up and down, confused and angry.

'Orly Airport,' ordered Adrian. 'Air Afrique.'

There were more crowds and more lines but the line

he was in was short. And nowhere in sight was the light-brown coat. No one seemed interested in him at all.

The black girl in the Air Afrique uniform smiled at him.

'I'd like a ticket to Rome on your ten fifteen flight tomorrow morning. The name's Llewellyn. That's two *l*'s in front, two in back, with a *y*. First class, please, and if it's possible, I'd like seat location now. I'll be very rushed in the morning, but hold the reservation. I'll pay in cash.'

He walked out the automatic doors of the Orly terminal and hailed another taxi.

'De Gaulle field, please. SAS Airlines.'

The line was longer, the service slower; that was fine, thought Adrian. Here he wanted to see the light-brown gabardine coat, but there was no sign of it. On the other hand, there was a man staring at him beyond a row of plastic chairs. There'd been no one looking at him like that in the Orly terminal. He wondered: he hoped.

'Round trip to Stockholm,' he said arrogantly to the SAS attendant behind the counter. 'You have a flight tomorrow at ten thirty. That's the one I want.'

The attendant looked up from his papers. 'I'll see what we have, sir,' he replied in muted irritation, his accent heavily Scandinavian. 'What would be the return date?'

'I'm not sure, so leave it open. I'm not interested in bargains. The name's Fontine.'

Five minutes later the tickets were processed, the payment made.

'Please be here an hour prior to departure, sir,' said the clerk, smarting under Adrian's impatience.

'Of course. Now, there's a small problem. I have some valuable, very fragile objects in my luggage. I'd like—'

'We cannot take responsibility for such things,' interrupted the attendant.

'Don't be a damn fool. I know you can't. I just want to make sure you have "Fragile" stickers in Swedish or

Norwegian or whatever the hell it is. My bags are easily recognized—'

He left the de Gaulle terminal convinced he'd alienated a very nice fellow who would complain to his colleagues about him, and got into a taxi.

'The Hôtel Pont Royal, please. Rue du Bac.'

Adrian saw him at a table in a small sidewalk café on the rue Dumont. He was an American, drinking white wine, and looked like a student who would nurse a drink because of the price. His age was no problem; he seemed tall enough. Adrian walked up to him.

'Hello?'

'Hi,' replied the young man.

'May I sit down? Buy you a drink?'

'Hell, why not?'

Adrian sat. 'You go to the Sorbonne?'

'Nope. L'Ecole des Beaux Arts. I'm a bona-fide, real-life painter. I'll sketch you for thirty francs. How about it?'

'No thanks. But I'll give you a lot more than that if you'll do something else for me.'

The student eyed him suspiciously, distastefully. 'I don't think I want to hear about it.'

'Don't get me wrong. I'll pay you just to get on an airplane. First-class seat, come back the same day.'

'You're nuts, man. I don't smuggle anything for anybody. You'd better beat it. I'm a very legal type.'

'I'm more than that. I'm a lawyer. A prosecuting attorney, as a matter of fact. With a card to prove it.'

'You don't sound it.'

'Just hear me out. What can it cost? Five minutes and some decent wine?'

At nine fifteen in the morning Adrian emerged from the limousine in front of the glass doors of SAS Airlines at de

388

Gaulle airport. He was dressed in a long, flared Edwardian overcoat of white fabric; he looked like an ass, but he couldn't be missed. On his head he wore a matching white, wide-brimmed fedora, the cloth pulled down over his face in Barrymore style, his features in shadow. Beneath the hat were huge dark glasses that covered far more than his eyes, and below his chin was a blue scarf, billowing above and out of the white coat.

The uniformed chauffeur scrambled around to the boot of the limousine, opened it, and called for porters to serve his very important passenger. Three large white leather suitcases were stacked on a hand rack, to Adrian's complaints that they were being scuffed.

He strode through the electronically parted doors and up to the SAS counter.

'I feel like hell!' he said scathingly, conveying the effects of a hangover, 'and I would appreciate as little difficulty as possible. I want my luggage to be loaded last; please keep it behind the counter until the final baggage call. It's done for me all the time. The gentleman yesterday assured me there'd be no trouble.'

The clerk behind the counter looked bewildered. Adrian slapped his ticket envelope down.

'Gate forty-two, sir,' the clerk said, handing back the envelope. 'Boarding time is at ten o'clock.'

'I'll wait over there,' replied Adrian, indicating the line of plastic chairs inside the SAS area. 'I meant what I said about the luggage. Where's the men's room?'

At twenty minutes to ten a tall, slender man in khaki trousers, cowboy boots, and an American army field jacket came through the doors of the terminal. On his face there was a pronounced beard; on his head a wide Australian bush hat. He entered the men's room.

At eighteen minutes to ten, Adrian got out of the plastic chair and walked across the crowded terminal. He pushed the door marked 'Hommes' and entered.

Inside the toilet stall they awkwardly manipulated the exchange of clothes.

'This is weird, man. You swear there's nothing in that crazy coat?'

'It's not even old enough to have lint . . . Here are the tickets, go to gate forty-two. You can throw away the baggage stubs, I don't care. Unless you want the suitcases; they're damned expensive. And clean.'

'In Stockholm no one busts me. You guarantee.'

'As long as you use your *own* passport and don't say you're me. I gave you my tickets, that's all. You've got my note to prove it. Take my word for it, nobody'll press you. You don't know where I am and there's no warrant. There's nothing.'

'You're a nut. But you've paid my tuition for a couple of years, plus some nice living expenses. You're a good nut.'

'Let's hope I'm good enough. Hold the mirror for me.' Adrian pressed the beard on his chin; it adhered quickly. He studied the results and, satisfied, put on the bush hat, pulling it down on the side of his head. 'Okay, let's go. You look fine.'

At eleven minutes to ten, a man in a long white coat, matching white hat, blue scarf, and dark glasses strode past the SAS desk towards gate forty-two.

Thirty seconds later a bearded young man – obviously American – in a soiled field jacket, khaki trousers, cowboy boots, and bush hat slipped out of the door of the men's room, turned sharply left into the crowds, and headed for the exit door. Out on the pavement he rushed to a waiting taxi, got in and removed the beard.

'The name's Llewellyn!' he shouted to the Air Afrique attendant at the lectern by the departure gate. 'I'm sorry I'm late; did I make it?'

The pleasant-faced black woman smiled and replied in

a French accent. 'Just barely, monsieur. We've given the last call. Have you any hand luggage?'

'Not a thing.'

At twenty-three minutes past ten, the ten fifteen Air Afrique flight to Rome taxied out towards runway seven. By ten twenty-eight it was airborne. It was only thirteen minutes late.

The man who called himself Llewellyn sat by the window, the bush hat on his left in the adjacent, empty first-class seat. He felt the hardening globules of facial cement on his chin, and he rubbed them in a kind of wonder.

He had done it. Disappeared.

The man in the light-brown coat boarded the SAS flight to Stockholm at ten twenty-nine. Departure was delayed. As he walked towards the economy section, he passed the fashionably dressed passenger in the long white overcoat and matching white hat. He thought to himself that the man he was following was a fucking idiot. Who did he think he was, wearing that outfit?

By ten fifty the flight to Stockholm was airborne. It was twenty minutes late, not unusual. The man in the economy section had removed his coat and was seated in the forward area of the cabin, diagonally behind the target of his surveillance. When the curtains were parted – as they were now – he could see the subject clearly.

Twelve minutes into the flight the pilot turned off the seat-belt sign. The fashionably dressed subject in the first-class section rose from his aisle seat and removed the long white overcoat and matching white hat.

The man diagonally behind in the economy section jerked forward in his seat, stunned.

'Oh, shit,' he muttered.

CHAPTER TWENTY-SEVEN

Andrew peered through the windshield at the sign caught in the dull wash of the headlights. It was dawn but pockets of fog were everywhere.

MILANO 5 KM

He had driven through the night, renting the fastest car he could find in Rome. The journey at night minimized the risk of being followed. Headlights were giveaways on long stretches of dark roads.

But he had not expected to be followed. In Rock Creek Park, Greene said he was marked. What the Jew did not know was that if IG wanted him that quickly, they would have picked him up at the airport. The Pentagon knew exactly where he was; a cable from the secretary of the army had brought him back from Saigon.

So the word to take him had not been given. That it would within days, perhaps hours, was not the issue; of course it would. But he was the son of Victor Fontine. The Pentagon would not be hasty in issuing any formal orders for arrest. The army did not bring charges against a Rockefeller or a Kennedy or a Fontine lightly. The Pentagon would insist on flying back the Eye Corps officers for corroborating testimony. The Pentagon would not leave anything to chance or error.

Which meant he had the time to get out. For by the time the army was prepared to move, he would be in the mountains tracing a vault that would change the ground rules as they had never been changed before.

Andrew stepped on the accelerator. He needed sleep. A professional knew when the body hungered for rest in spite of the high-pitched moment, and the eyes became aware of their sockets. He would find a small boarding house or a country inn and sleep for most of the day. Late in the afternoon he would drive north to Campo di Fiori, and find a picture on the wall. The first clue in the search for a vault buried in the mountains.

He drove by the crumbling stone gates of the entrance without slowing down, and continued for several miles. He allowed two cars to pass him, observing the drivers; they were not interested in him. He turned around and went past the gates a second time. There was no way to tell what was inside; whether there were any security measures – trip alarms or dogs. All he could see was a winding paved road that disappeared into the woods.

The sound of a car on that road would be its own alarm. He could not chance that; he had no intention of announcing his arrival at Campo di Fiori. He slowed the car down, and turned into the bordering woods, driving as far off the road as possible.

Five minutes later he approached the gates. By habit he checked for wires and photoelectric cells; there were none, and he passed through the gates and walked down the road cut out of the woods.

He stayed at the edge, concealed by the trees of the overgrowth until he was in sight of the main house. It was as his father had described: more dead than alive.

The windows were dark, no lamps were on inside. There should have been. The house was in shadows. An old man living alone needed light; old men did not trust their eyes. Had the priest died?

Suddenly, out of nowhere, there came the sound of a

voice, high-pitched and plaintive. Then footsteps. They came from the road beyond the north bend of the drive; the road he remembered his father describing as leading to the stables. Fontine dropped to the ground, below the level of the grass, and remained motionless. He raised his head by inches; he waited and watched.

The old priest came into view. He was wearing a long black cassock and carried a basket. He spoke out loud, but Andrew could not see who he was talking to. Nor could he understand the words. The monk stopped and turned and spoke again.

There was a reply. It was rapid, authoritative, in a language Fontine did not immediately recognize. Then he saw the monk's companion and instantly appraised him as one might an adversary. The man was large, the shoulders wide and heavy, encased in a camel-hair jacket above well-tailored slacks. The last rays of the sun illuminated both men; not well – the light was at their backs – but enough to distinguish the faces.

Andrew concentrated on the younger, powerfully built man walking behind the priest. His face was large, the eyes wide apart, beneath light brows and a tanned forehead that set off short, sun-bleached hair. He was in his middle forties, certainly no more. And the walk: it was of a deliberate man, capable of moving swiftly, but not anxious for observers to know it. Fontine had commanded such men.

The old monk proceeded towards the marble steps, shifting the small basket to his left arm, his right hand lifting the folds of his habit. He stopped at the top step and turned again to the younger man. His voice was calmer, resigned to the layman's presence or instructions or both. He spoke slowly and Fontine had no trouble now in recognizing the language. It was Greek.

As he listened to the priest he reached another, equally

obvious conclusion. The powerfully built man was
Theodore Annaxas Dakakos. *He is a bull.*

The priest continued across the wide marble porch to
the doors; Dakakos climbed the steps and followed. Both
men went inside.

Fontine lay in the grass on the border of the drive for
several minutes. He had to think. What brought Dakakos to Campo di Fiori? What was here for him?

And as the questions formed, the single answer was
apparent. Dakakos, the loner, was the unseen power
here. The conversation that had just taken place in the
circular drive was not a conversation between strangers.

What had to be established was whether Dakakos had
come alone to Campo di Fiori. Or had he brought his
own protection, his own fire-power? There was no one
in the house, no lights in the windows, no sounds from
inside. That left the stables.

Andrew scrambled backward in the wet grass until all
sightlines from the windows were blocked by the overgrowth. He rose behind a clump of bushes and removed
a small Beretta revolver from his pocket. He climbed to
the embankment above the drive and estimated the angle
of the stable road across the knoll. If Dakakos's men
were in the stables, it would be a simple matter to
eliminate them. Without gunfire; that was essential. The
weapon was merely a device; men collapsed under its
threat.

Fontine crouched and weaved his way across the knoll
towards the stable road. The early evening breezes bent
the upper grass and the branches of trees; the professional soldier fell instinctively into the rhythm of their
movement. The roofs of the stables came into view and
he stepped silently down the incline towards the road.

In front of the stable door was a long steel-grey
Maserati, its tyres caked with mud. There were no
voices, no signs of life; there was only the quiet hum of

the surrounding woods. Andrew lowered himself to his knees, picked up a handful of dirt, and threw it twenty yards in the air across the road, hitting the stable windows.

No one emerged. Fontine repeated the action, using more dirt mixed with small pieces of rock. The splattering was louder; there was no way it could go unobserved.

Nothing. No one.

Cautiously, Andrew walked out on the road towards the car. He stopped before he reached it. The surface of the road was hard, but still partially wet from the earlier rain.

The Maserati was headed north; there were no footsteps on the passenger side of the car in front of him. He walked around the car; there were distinct imprints on the driver's side: the shoe marks of a man.

Dakakos had conformed to the profile constructed at a table in the Via Veneto. He had come alone.

There was no time to waste now. There was a picture on a wall to be taken, and a journey to Champoluc that had to begin. Too, there was a fine irony in finding Dakakos at Campo di Fiori. The informer's life would end where his obsession had begun. Eye Corps was owed that much.

He could see lights inside the house now, but only in the windows to the left of the main entrance. Andrew kept to the wall, ducking under the ledges, until he was at the side of the window where the light was brightest. He inched his face to the frame and looked inside.

The room was huge. There were couches and chairs and a fireplace. Two lamps were lit; one by the far couch, the second nearer, to the right of an armchair. Dakakos was standing by the mantel, gesturing in slow, deliberate movements with his hands. The priest was in the chair, his back to Fontine, and barely visible. Their conversation was muted, indistinguishable. It was impossible to determine whether the Greek had a weapon; the assumption had to be that he did.

Andrew pried a brick loose from the border of the drive and returned to the window. He rose, the Beretta in his right hand, the brick gripped in his left. Dakakos approached the priest in the chair; the Greek was pleading, or explaining, his concentration absolute.

The moment was now.

Shielding his eyes with the gun, Fontine extended his left arm behind him, then arched it forward, hurling the brick into the centre of the window, shattering glass and wood strips everwhere. On impact he slashed the remaining, obstructing glass with the Beretta, thrusting the weapon through the space, and screamed at the top of his voice.

'*You move one inch, you're dead!*'

Dakakos froze. '*You?*' he whispered. 'You were *taken*!'

The Greek's head slumped forward, the gashes from the pistol barrel on his face deep, ugly, and bleeding profusely. There was nothing that so became this man as a painful death, thought Fontine.

'In the name of God have *mercy!*' screamed the priest from the opposite chair, where he sat bound and helpless.

'Shut up!' roared the soldier, his eyes on Dakakos. 'Why did you do it? Why are you here?'

The Greek stared, his breathing erratic, his eyes swollen. 'They said you were taken. They had everything they needed.' He could barely be heard, speaking as much to himself as to the man above him.

'They made a mistake, old man,' said Andrew. 'Their signals got crossed. You didn't expect them to wire you their apologies, did you? What did they tell you? That they were picking me up?'

Dakakos remained silent, blinking from the rivulets of

blood that rolled down his forehead into his eyes. Fontine could hear the Pentagon commanders. *Never admit. Never explain. Take the objective, the rest is no strain.*

'Forget it,' he said quietly to Dakakos. 'Just tell me why you're here.'

The Greek's eyes swam in his head: his lips moved. 'You are *filth*. And we'll *stop you*!'

'Who's we?'

Dakakos arched his neck, thrusting it forward, and spat into the soldier's face. Fontine swung the barrel of the pistol up into the Greek's jaw. The head slumped forward.

'*Stop!*' cried the monk. 'I'll tell you. There's a priest named Land. Dakakos and Land work together.'

'Who?' Fontine turned abruptly to the monk.

'It's all I know. The name! They've been in contact for years.'

'Who is he? *What* is he?'

'I don't know. Dakakos doesn't say.'

'Is he waiting for him? Is this priest coming here?'

The monk's expression suddenly changed. His eyelids quivered, his lips trembled.

Andrew understood. Dakakos was waiting for someone, but not Land. Fontine raised the barrel of the pistol and shoved it into the mouth of the semiconscious Greek. 'All right, Father, you've two seconds to tell me who it is. Who's this son of a bitch waiting for?'

'The other one . . .'

'The other *what*?'

The old monk stared at him. Fontine felt a hard emptiness in his stomach. He removed the pistol.

Adrian.

Adrian was on his way to Campo di Fiori! His brother had broken away and sold out to Dakakos!

The *picture*! He had to make sure the picture was there! He turned, looking for the door of the . . .

When the blow came it was paralysing. Dakakos had snapped the lamp cord binding his wrists and lunged forward, his fist pummelling into Andrew's kidney, his other hand wrapped around the Beretta's barrel, twisting Fontine's forearm until he thought his elbow would crack.

Andrew countered by falling sideways, rolling with the force of Dakakos's lunge. The Greek sprang on top of him, crushing him like some elephantine hammer. He smashed Fontine's knuckles against the floor until the gun exploded, the bullet embedding itself in the wooden arch of the doorway. Andrew brought his knee up, pounding the base of Dakakos's groin, crushing the Greek's testicles until he arched his back, grimacing in torment.

Fontine rolled again, freeing his left hand, clawing the bleeding face above, tearing at the hanging flesh. Still, Dakakos would not retreat, would not let up; he slammed his forearms into Andrew's throat.

It was the instant! Andrew arched forwards, sinking his teeth into the flesh of Dakakos's arm, biting deeply, as a mad dog would bite, feeling the warm blood flowing into his throat. The Greek pulled his arm up – his hand away – and it was the space Fontine needed. He crashed his knee up once again in Dakakos's groin, and slid his whole body under the giant; as he did so he shot his left hand into the well of Dakakos's armpit, and pressed the nerve with all the force he could summon.

The Greek raised his right side in agony. Andrew rolled to his left, kicking the heavy body away, pulling his arm free.

With the speed born of a hundred fire-fights, Fontine was on his haunches, the Beretta levelled, spitting five bullets into the exposed chest of the informer who had come to close to killing him. Dakakos was dead. Annaxas was no more.

Andrew rose unsteadily; he was covered with blood, his whole body wracked. He looked at the priest of Xenope in the chair. The old man's eyes were closed, his lips moving in silent prayer.

There was one shell left in the Beretta. Andrew raised the gun and fired.

CHAPTER TWENTY-EIGHT

Stunned, Adrian took the cablegram held out for him by the desk clerk. He walked towards the front entrance of the hotel, stopped, and opened it.

Mr Adrian Fontine
Excelsior Hotel
Rome, Italy
My dear Fontine:

It is urgent we confer, for you must not act alone. You must trust me. You have nothing to fear from me. I understand your anxieties, consequently there will be no intermediaries, none of my people will intercept you. I will wait for you alone and alone we can make our decisions. Check your source.

Theo Dakakos

Dakakos had traced him! The Greek expected to MEET. But where? How?

Adrian knew that once he passed through customs in Rome, there was no way he could stop those looking for him from knowing he'd come to Italy; it was the reason for the next step in his strategy. But that Dakakos would openly contact him seemed extraordinary. It was as though Dakakos assumed they were working *together*. Yet it was Dakakos who had gone after Andrew; gone after his brother relentlessly, ingeniously, wrapping up Eye Corps in a seditious ribbon that had eluded the combined efforts of the inspector general and the Justice Department.

The sons of Victor Fontine – the grandsons of Savarone Fontini-Cristi – were after the vault. Why would Dakakos stop one and not the other?

The answer had to be that he was trying to do just that. Carrots held out in front of the donkey's nose; offers of safety and trust that were translated to mean *control, confinement.*

. . . I will wait for you alone and alone we can make our decisions. Check your source . . .

Was Dakakos on his way to Campo di Fiori? How was that possible? And what was the *source*? An IG colonel named Tarkington with whom Dakakos had set up lines of communication to trap Eye Corps? What other source did he and Dakakos have in common?

'Signore Fontine?' It was the Excelsior manager; the door to his office was open behind him. He had come out quickly.

'Yes?'

'I tried your room, of course. You were not there.' The man smiled nervously.

'Right,' said Adrian. 'I'm here. What is it?'

'Our guests are always our first consideration.' The Italian smiled again. It was maddening.

'Please. I'm in a hurry.'

'A few moments ago we had a call from the American embassy. They say they are calling all the hotels in Rome. They are looking for you.'

'What did you say?'

'Our guests are always—'

'What did you *say*?'

'That you had checked out. You *have* checked out, *signore*. However, if you wish to use my telephone . . .'

'No, thank you,' said Adrian, starting towards the entrance. Then he stopped and turned to the manager.

402

'Call the embassy back. Tell them where I've gone. The front desk knows.'

It was a second part of his strategy in Rome, and when he conceived it, he realized it was merely an extension of what he had done in Paris. Before the day was over the professionals who followed him would know exactly where he was. Computers and passport entries and international co-operation made for swift relays of information. He had to make them all think he was going somewhere that he wasn't.

Rome was the best place to start. Had he flow to Milan, the IG men would dig into their files; Campo di Fiori would appear. He could not allow that.

He had asked the front desk of the Excelsior to draw up a route for a drive south. To Naples, Salerno and Policastro, along roads that would take him east through Calabria to the Adriatic. He had rented a car at the airport.

Now Theodore Dakakos had joined the hunt. Dakakos, whose relays of information were faster than those of United States Army Intelligence, and far more dangerous. Adrian knew what the United States Army wanted: the killer from Eye Corps. But Dakakos wanted the vault from Constantine. It was a greater prize.

Adrian drove through Rome's melodramatic traffic back to Leonardo da Vinci Airport. He returned the rented car and bought a ticket on Itavia Airlines for Milan. He stood in line at the departure gate, his head down, his body slouched, seeking the protective cover of the crowd. As he was jostled forward – and for reasons he didn't know – the words of an extraordinary lawyer came back to him.

You can run with the pack, in the middle of the pack, but if you want to do something, get to the edges and peel away. Darrow.

In Milan he would call his father. He'd lie about

Andrew; he'd invent *something*, he couldn't think about that now. But he had to know more about Theodore Dakakos.

Dakakos was closing in.

He sat on his bed in Milan's Hotel di Piermonte as he'd sat on the bed at the Savoy in London, staring at papers in front of him. But these were not airline schedules, they were the Xeroxed pages of his father's recollection of fifty years ago. He was re-reading them – not for any new information; he knew the contents – but because the reading postponed the moment when he would pick up the phone. He wondered how thoroughly his brother had studied these pages, with their rambling descriptions and hesitant, often obscure reflections. Andrew would probably pore over them with the scrutiny of a soldier in combat. There were names. Goldoni, Cadpomonti, Lefrac. Men who had to be reached.

Adrian knew he could not procrastinate any longer. He folded the pages, put them in his jacket pocket, and reached for the telephone.

Ten minutes later the switchboard called him back; the phone 5,000 miles away in the North Shore house was ringing. His mother answered and when she said the words, she did so simply, without the trappings of grief, for they were extraneous, the grief was private.

'Your father died last night.'

Neither spoke for several moments. The silence conveyed a sense of love. As though they were touching.

'I'll come home right away,' he said.

'No, don't do that. He wouldn't want you to. You know what you have to do.'

Again there was silence. 'Yes,' he said finally.

'Adrian?'

'Yes?'

'I have two things to tell you, but I don't want to discuss them. Can you understand that?'

Adrian paused. 'I think so.'

'An army officer came to see us. A Colonel Tarkington. He was kind enough to speak only with me. I know about Andrew.'

'I'm sorry.'

'Bring him back. He needs help. All the help we can give him.'

'I'll try.'

'It's so easy to look back and say, "Yes, I see now. I realize." He always saw the results of strength; he never understood its complications, its essential compassion, I think.'

'Let's not discuss it,' reminded the son.

'Yes. I don't want to discuss – Oh, God, I'm so *frightened*!'

'*Please*, mother.'

Jane breathed deeply, the sound carried over the wire. 'There's something else. Dakakos was here. He spoke to your father. To both of us together. You must trust him. Your father wished it; he was convinced of it. So am I.'

. . . check your source . . .

'He sent me a cable. He said he'd be waiting for me.'

'At Campo di Fiori,' completed Jane.

'What did he say about Andrew?'

'That he thought your brother might be delayed. He didn't elaborate; he talked only about you. He used your name repeatedly.'

'You're sure you don't want me to come home?'

'No. There's nothing you can do here. He wouldn't want it.' She paused for a moment. 'Adrian, tell your brother his father never knew. He died thinking both his Geminis were the men he believed them to be.'

'I'll tell him. I'll call again soon.'

They said quiet good-byes.

His father was dead. The source had gone, and the void was terrible. He sat by the telephone, aware that perspiration had formed on his forehead, though the room was cool. He got up from the bed; there were things to do and he had to move quickly. Dakakos was on his way to Campo di Fiori. So was the killer of Eye Corps, and Dakakos did not know that.

So he sat down at his desk and began writing. He might have been back in his Boston apartment, jotting down items in preparation for the next day's cross-examination.

But in this case it was not the next day. It was tonight. And very few items came to mind.

He stopped the car at the fork in the road, picked up the map, and held it under the dashboard light. The fork was detailed on the map. There were no other roads until the town of Laveno. His father had said there were large stone gateposts on the left; they were the entrance to Campo di Fiori.

He started the car up, straining his eyes in the darkness, waiting to catch a glimpse of erected stone in the wall of forest on his left. Four miles up the road he found them. He stopped the car opposite the huge, crumbling stone pillars and aimed his flashlight out of the window. There was the winding road beyond as his father had described it, angling sharply, disappearing into the woods.

He swung the car to the left and drove through the gates. His mouth was suddenly dry, his heart accelerated, its beat echoing in his throat. It was the fear of the immediate unknown that gripped him. He wanted to face it quickly, before the fear controlled him. He drove faster.

There were no lights anywhere.

The enormous white house stood in eerie stillness, a deathlike splendour in the darkness. Adrian parked the car on the left side of the circle, opposite the marble steps, shut off the motor and, reluctantly, the headlights. He got out, took the flashlight from his raincoat pocket, and started across the rutted pavement towards the stairs.

Dull moonlight briefly illuminated the macabre setting and then disappeared. The sky was overcast but no rain would come; the clouds were everywhere above, but thin and travelling too fast. The air was dry; everything was still.

Adrian reached the bottom step and switched on his flashlight to look at his watch. It was eleven thirty. Dakakos was not there. Nor his brother. Either or both would have heard the car; neither nor both would be asleep at this hour. That left the old priest. An old man in the country would have gone to bed by now. He called out.

'Hello in there! My name is Adrian Fontine and I'd like to talk to you!'

Nothing.

And not nothing! There was movement. A pattering, a series of scratches accompanied by tiny, indistinguishable screeches. He swung the flashlight to the source. In its beam were caught the blurred, rushing figures of rats – three, four, five – scampering over the ledge of an open window.

He held the flashlight steady. The window was smashed; he could see jagged edges of glass. He approached it slowly, suddenly afraid.

His feet sank into the earth; his shoes crunched broken glass. He stood in front of the window and raised the flashlight.

He lost his breath in an involuntary gasp as two pairs of animal's eyes were suddenly caught in the blinding shaft. They darted up, startled yet furious, and a terrible muted screeching was heard as the creatures fled into the darkness to another part of the house. There was a crash. A crazed, frightened animal had collided with an unstable object of china or glass.

Adrian breathed again, then shuddered. His nostrils were filled with an overpowering stench, a putrid, rotting aroma that caused his eyes to water and his throat to swell and choke. He held his breath and he climbed over the window ledge. He pressed his open left hand against his mouth and his nose, filtering the foul stench; he cast the beam of the flashlight over the enormous room.

The shock of it staggered him. The figures of two dead men, one in torn robes strapped to a chair, the other half-naked on the floor, were hideous. The clothes were torn by animal teeth, flesh ripped out by animal jaws, dried blood made moist by animal urine and saliva.

Adrian reeled. Vomit spewed out of his mouth. He lurched to his left; the light caught a doorway and he lunged into it, gasping for breath, for air that could be swallowed.

He was in the study of Savarone Fontini-Cristi, a man he never knew, but now hated with all the hatred of which he was capable. The grandfather who had triggered a chain of killing and suspicion that in itself brought more death and greater hatred.

Over *what*? For what?

'*Goddamnnn youuu!* . . .

He screamed uncontrollably; he gripped the high back of an old chair and threw it crashing to the floor.

Suddenly, in silence and in full knowledge of what he had to do, Adrian stood immobile and aimed the flashlight on the wall behind the desk. To the right, he remembered, beneath a painting of the Madonna.

The frame was there, the glass shattered.

And the painting was gone.

He sank to his knees, trembling. Tears welled in his eyes and he sobbed uncontrollably.

'Oh, *God*,' he whispered, the pain unbearable. 'Oh, my brother!'

PART THREE

CHAPTER TWENTY-NINE

Andrew pulled the Land Rover off to the side of the Alpine road and poured steaming hot coffee into the lid of the thermos. He had made good time; according to the Michelin map he was ten miles from the village of Champoluc. It was morning; the rays of the early sun shot up from behind the surrounding mountains. In a little while he would drive into Champoluc and buy the equipment he needed.

Adrian was far behind. Andrew knew he could slow down for a while, think things out. Besides, his brother was walking into a situation that would paralyse him. Adrian would find the bodies at Campo di Fiori and panic; his thoughts would be confused, indecisive. He wouldn't know what to do next. His brother wasn't trained to confront death from violence; it was too far removed from him. It was different for soldiers: it was different for him. The physical confrontation – even the bloodshed – primed his senses, infused him with an intense feeling of exhilaration. His energies were peaked, he was confident, sure of his movements.

The vault was as good as his. Now was the time to concentrate. Study each word, each clue. He took his father's Xeroxed pages and held them up, catching the morning light through the windshield.

... *In the village of Champoluc was the family Goldoni. According to current Zermatt records, they exist still and are scattered throughout the area. The present head of the family*

413

*is one Alfredo Goldoni. He resides in the house of his father –
and his father before him – on several acres of land at the base
of the mountains in the west outskirts. For generations the
Goldonis have been the most experienced guides in the Italian
Alps. Savarone employed them frequently, and beyond this,
they were 'northern friends' – a phrase my father used to
distinguish men of the land from those in the marketplace. His
trust was placed in the former far more quickly than the latter.
It is possible that he left information with Alfredo Goldoni's
father. With his death, arrangements would be made to pass
this information on to the surviving eldest child – whether
man or woman – as is the Italian-Swiss custom. Therefore,
should Alfredo not be the eldest, look for an older sister.*

*North, into the mountains – between the railroad clearings
Kraben Ausblick and Greier Gipfel, I believe – is a small inn
run by the family Capomonti. Again, according to Zermatt (I
made no inquiries in the Champoluc district to avoid raising
suspicion) the inn, too, still exists. I gather it has been
somewhat expanded. It is currently under the management of
Natan Lefrac, a descendant by marriage of the Capomontis. I
remember this man. He was not a man then, of course, for he
was one or two years younger than I, the son of a merchant
who dealt with the Capomontis. We became quite good friends.
I recall clearly that he was much beloved of the Capomontis
and the hope was that he would marry a daughter of the house.
Obviously he did so.*

*As children – and young men – we never went into the
Champoluc without staying at the Locanda Capomonti. I have
recollections of warm welcomes and laughter and roaring
fireplaces and much comfort. The family was simple – in the
uncomplicated sense – and extremely outgoing and sincere.
Savarone was particularly taken with them. If there were
secrets to leave in the Champoluc, old Capomonti would have
been a rock of silence and trust . . .*

Andrew put down the pages and picked up the
Michelin road map. Once again he traced the minute

markings of the Zermatt railroad, his concern returning. Of the many clearings his father recalled, only four remained. And none bore the name of *hawk*.

For the hunting picture in the study at Campo di Fiori was not as his father remembered; it did not show birds being flushed from bushes. Instead, there were hunters in overgrown fields, their eyes and weapons levelled forward as hawks flew lazily above in the distant sky; an artist's comment on the futility of the hunt.

His father said that the clearings were called Eagle's Peak, Condor's Lookout, and Crow's Summit. There had to be a clearing with the name hawk in it. But if there had been, it no longer existed. And a half century had gone by; obscure railroad clearings below Alpine passes scores of miles apart were not landmarks. Who recalled the precise location of a trolley stop thirty years after the tracks were covered with asphalt? He put down the map and picked up the Xeroxed pages again. The initial key was somewhere in these words.

We stopped in the centre of the village for a late lunch, or afternoon tea, I cannot remember which – and Savarone left the restaurant to check the telegraph office for messages – I do remember that. When he returned he was very upset, and I feared our trip to the mountains would be cancelled before it began. However, during the meal another message was delivered and Savarone was both placated and relieved. There was no more talk of returning to Campo di Fiori. The dreadful moment had passed for an anxious seventeen-year-old.

From the restaurant we dropped by the shop of a merchant whose name was German in sound and spelling, not Italian or French. My father was prone to order supplies and equipment from this man because he felt sorry for him. He was a Jew and for Savarone, who fought bitterly against the czarist pogroms and dealt on a hand-shake with the Rothschilds, such thinking was indefensible. There is a blurred memory of an unpleasant incident at the store that evening. What the unpleasant incident specifically entailed, I have no recall, but it was most serious and provoked my father to quiet but definite anger. A sad anger if, again, memory serves. I seem to have the vague impression that details were withheld from me, but now, so many years later, it is only an impression and could well be false.

We left the merchant's shop and proceeded by horse and cart to the Goldoni farm. I remember showing off my Alpine pack with its straps and hammer and cleats and forged double-clamps for the ropes. I was terribly proud of it, believing it signified manhood. Again there is a dim impression that while at the Goldonis' an undercurrent of distress was prevalent, but not obvious. I cannot tell you why this feeling remains after so many years, but I relate it to the fact that I had difficulty holding the attention of the male Goldonis while exhibiting my new pack. The father, an uncle or two, and certainly the older sons seemed distracted. Arrangements were made with one of the Goldoni sons to meet us the next day and take us into the mountains. We stayed at the Goldonis for several hours before leaving to resume our journey by cart to the Locando Capomonti. I do recall it was dark when we left, and, as it was summer, the hour had to be past 7.30 or 8.00.

What were the facts, thought Andrew. Man and boy arrived at the village, had something to eat, bought supplies from a disliked Jew, went to the house of the guides they were hiring, and a spoiled child was insulted because not enough attention was paid to his mountain-climbing equipment. The relevant information was reduced to the name Goldoni.

Andrew finished the coffee and screwed the lid back on the thermos. The sun was higher now; it was time to move. Exhilaration filled him. All the years of training and experience and decisions in the field had prepared him for the next few days. There was a vault in the mountains and he would find it!

Eye Corps would be paid in full.

The soldier turned the ignition and gunned the motor. He had clothing and equipment and weapons to buy. And a man named Goldoni to see. Perhaps a woman named Goldoni; he'd know shortly.

Adrian sat in the darkness behind the wheel of the stationary car and wiped his mouth with his handkerchief. He could not erase the taste of sickness in his throat any more than he could erase the sight of the ravaged bodies inside the house from his mind's eye. Or the stench of death from his nostrils.

Sweat rolled down his face, produced by a tension he had never known, a fear he had never experienced.

He felt the need to vomit returning; he suppressed it by inhaling rapidly. He had to find some semblance of sanity, he had to function. He could not remain in darkness, in an immobile car for the rest of the night. He had to pass through the shock and find his mind again. It was all he had left: the ability to think.

Instinctively, he pulled the pages of his father's memories from his pocket and switched on the flashlight. Words had come to be his refuge; he was an analyst of words – their shadings, their subtle interpretations, their simplicity and complexity. He was an expert with words, as much an expert as his brother was with death.

Adrian separated the pages, reading slowly, meticulously. Child and man had come to the village of Champoluc; there were immediate impressions of discord, perhaps more than discord. *When he returned he was very upset . . . I feared for our trip.* There was the shop of the Jew, and anger. *What the unpleasant incident specifically entailed, I have no recall . . . It was most serious and provoked my father.* A sadness. *A sad anger if, again, memory serves.* Then the anger and the sadness faded away, replaced by vague feelings of distress and embarrassment; the child was not heeded by those whose attentions he sought. *The*

father, *an uncle or two, and certainly the older sons were
distracted*. Their attentions were elsewhere – on the
anger, the discord? The sadness? And these obscure
recollections were in turn displaced by memories of
warmth, and an inn north of the village, *a warm welcome,
which was like a dozen other similar welcomes*. This peaceful
interlude was followed a short while later once again by
vague feelings of distress and concern.

*At the Capomonti inn there is little I can recall specifically
except a warm welcome, which was like a dozen other similar
welcomes. One thing I do remember was that for the first time
in the mountains I had my own room, no younger brothers
sharing it with me. It was a significant departure and I felt
quite grown up. There was another meal, and my father and
old Capomonti drank a good deal of whisky afterwards. I recall
this because I went to bed, thinking of the next day's climbing,
and later heard loud, belligerent voices below, and wondered if
the noise might wake the other guests. It was a small inn then
and there were perhaps three or four others registered. This
concern was unusual for I had never seen my father drunk. I
do not know to this day if he was, but the noise was
considerable. To a young man on his seventeenth birthday,
about to be given the present of his life – a real climb in the
Champoluc – the thoughts of a weakened, angry father in the
morning were disturbing.*

*It was not the case, however. The Goldoni guide arrived
with our supplies, shared breakfast with us, and we departed.*

*A Capomonti son – or it might have been young Lefrac –
drove the three of us several miles north in the cart. We bade
him good-bye and it was agreed he would meet us at the same
place late in the afternoon on the following day. Two days in
the mountains and an overnight camp with adults! I was
overjoyed for I knew we would make camp at a higher altitude
than was ever possible with younger brothers in tow.*

Adrian put down the pages on the seat of the car. The
remaining paragraphs described sketchily remembered

hills and trails and views that seemed to overlap. The journey into the mountains had begun.

Specific information might well lie in these rambling descriptions. Isolated landmarks might be revealed, and a pattern emerge; but which landmarks, which patterns?

Oh, God! The painting on the wall! Andrew had the painting!

Adrian suppressed his sudden alarm. The painting from Savarone's study might narrow down the location of a clearing, but what then? Fifty years had passed. A half century of ice and water and summer thaws and natural growth and erosion.

The painting on the wall might well be one clue, perhaps the most important. But Adrian had the feeling that there were others as vital as that painting. They were contained in the words of his father's testament. Memories that survived fifty years of extraordinary living.

Something had happened fifty years ago that had nothing to do with a father and son going into the mountains.

He had found part of his mind again. He was exercising his ability to think. The shock and horror were still there, but he was passing through to the beginnings of sanity.

. . . Bear in mind, the contents of that vault are as staggering to the civilized world as anything in history . . .

He had to reach it, find it. He had to stop the killer from Eye Corps.

CHAPTER THIRTY

Andrew parked the Land Rover by a fence bordering a field. The Goldoni farmhouse was two hundred yards down the road, on the left; the field was part of the Goldoni property. There was a man driving a tractor along the upturned earth, his body turned in the seat, watching the progress behind him. There were no other houses in the area, no other people in sight. Andrew decided to stop and speak to the man.

It was shortly past five in the afternoon. He had spent the day wandering about Champoluc, buying clothes, supplies, and climbing equipment, including the finest Alpine pack available, filled with those items recommended for the mountains, and one that was not. A Magnum .357-calibre pistol. He had made these purchases at the much-expanded shop referred to in his father's recollections. The name was Leinkraus; it had a mezuzah on the doorframe of the front entrance. The clerk behind the counter allowed that Leinkraus had been selling the finest equipment in the Italian Alps since 1913. There were now branches in Gstaad and Lake Lucerne.

Andrew got out of the Land Rover and walked to the fence, waving his hand back and forth to get the attention of the man on the tractor. He was a short, stocky Italian-Swiss, ruffled brown hair above dark eyebrows, and the rugged, sharp features of a northern Mediterranean. He was at least ten years older than

Fontine; his expression was cautious, as if he were not used to unfamiliar faces.

'Do you speak English?' Andrew asked.

'Passably, *signore*,' said the man.

'I'm looking for Alfredo Goldoni. I was directed out here.'

'You were directed correctly,' replied the Italian-Swiss in more than passable English. 'Goldoni is my uncle. I tend his land for him. He can't work for himself.' The man stopped, offering no further clarification.

'Where can I find him?'

'Where he always is. In the back room of his house. My aunt will show you to him. He likes visitors.'

'Thank you.' Andrew turned towards the Land Rover.

'You're American?' asked the man.

'No, Canadian,' he replied, extending his cover for any of a dozen immediate possibilities. He climbed into the vehicle and looked at the man through the open window. 'We sound the same.'

'You look the same, dress the same,' countered the farmhand quietly, eyeing the fur-lined Alpine jacket. 'The clothes are new,' he added.

'Your English isn't,' said Fontine. He turned the ignition.

Goldoni's wife was gaunt and ascetic looking. Her straight grey hair was pulled back, the taut bun a crown of self-denial. She ushered the visitor through several neat, sparsely furnished rooms to a doorway at the rear of the house. There was no door attached; where once there'd been a sill in the frame, it had been removed, the floor levelled. Fontine walked through; he entered the bedroom. Alfredo Goldoni sat in a wheelchair by a window overlooking the fields at the base of the mountains.

He had no legs. The stubs of his once-massive limbs were encased in the folds of his trousers, the cloth held together by safety pins. The rest of his body, like his face, was large and awkward. Age and mutilation had extracted their price.

Old Goldini greeted him with false energy. A tired cripple, afraid of offending a newcomer, grateful for the all-too-infrequent interruption.

The introductions over, the directions and the journey from town described, and wine brought by a sullen wife, Fontine sat down in a chair opposite the legless man. The stumps were within an arm's reach; the word *grotesque* came repeatedly to his mind. Andrew did not like ugliness; he did not care to put up with it.

'You don't recognize the name Fontine?'

'I do not, sir. It's French, I think. But you're American.'

'Do you recognize the name Fontini-Cristi?'

Goldoni's eyes changed. A long-forgotten alarm was triggered. 'Yes, of course, I recognize it,' replied the amputee, his voice also changing, his words measured. 'Fontine; Fontini-Cristi. So the Italian becomes French and the possessor American. It's been many years. You're a Fontini-Cristi?'

'Yes. Savarone was my grandfather.'

'A great *padrone* from the northern provinces. I remember him. Not well, of course. He stopped coming to Champoluc in the late twenties, I believe.'

'The Goldonis were his guides. Father and sons.'

'We were everyone's guides.'

'Were you ever a guide for my grandfather?'

'It's possible. I worked the mountains as a very young man.'

'Can't you remember?'

'In my time I have taken thousands into the Alps—'

'You just said you remembered him.'

'Not well. And more by the name than by the person. What is it you want?'

'Information. About a trip to the mountains taken by my father fifty years ago.'

'Are you joking?'

'Hardly. My father, Victor – Vittorio Fontini-Cristi – sent me from America to get that information. At great inconvenience to me. I haven't much time, so I need your help.'

'It's freely given, but I wouldn't know where to begin. A single climb fifty years ago! Who would remember?'

'The man who led them. The guide. According to my father he was a son of Goldoni. The date is July the fourteenth, 1920.'

Fontine could not be sure – perhaps the grotesque cripple merely suppressed a sharp pain from his massive stumps, or shifted his legless clump of a body in reflection – but Goldini *did react*. It was the *date*. He reacted to the date. And immediately covered that reaction by talking.

'July of 1920. It's two generations ago. It's impossible. You must have something more, how do you say, specific than that?'

'The *guide*. He was a Goldoni.'

'Not I. I was no more than fifteen years old. I went into the mountains young, but not that young. Not as a *prima guida*.'

Andrew held the cripple's eye with his own. Goldoni was uncomfortable; he did not like the exchange of stares and looked away. Fontine leaned forward. 'But you remember something, don't you?' he asked quietly, unable to keep the coldness out of his voice.

'No, Signore Fontini-Cristi. There's nothing.'

'Just a few seconds ago, I gave you the date: July the fourteenth 1920. You knew that date.'

'I knew only that it was too long ago for me to think about.'

'I should tell you, I'm a soldier. I've interrogated hundreds of men; very few ever fooled me.'

'It wouldn't be my intention, *signore*. For what purpose? I should like to be helpful to you.'

Andrew continued to stare. 'Years ago there were clearings on the railroad tracks south of Zermatt.'

'A few are left,' added Goldoni. 'Not many, of course. They're not necessary these days.'

'Tell me. Each was given the name of a bird—'

'Some,' interrupted the Alpiner. 'Not all.'

'Was there a *hawk*? A hawk's ... *something*?'

'A hawk? Why do you ask that?' The outsized amputee looked up, his gaze now steady, unwavering.

'Just tell me. Was there a clearing with "hawk" as part of its name?'

Goldoni remained silent for several moments. 'No,' he said finally.

Andrew sat back in the chair. 'Are you the eldest son of the Goldoni family?'

'No. It was obviously one of my brothers who was hired for that climb fifty years ago.'

Fontine was beginning to understand. Alfredo Goldoni was given the house because he had lost his legs. 'Where are your brothers? I'll talk with them.'

'Again, I must ask if you joke, *signore*. My brothers are dead, everyone knows that. My brothers, an uncle, two cousins. All dead. There are no Goldoni guides left in Champoluc.'

Andrew's breathing stopped. He absorbed the information and inhaled deeply. His short cut had been eliminated with a single sentence.

'I find that hard to believe,' he said coldly. '*All* those men dead? What killed them?'

'Avalanche, *signore*. A whole village was buried in 'sixty-eight. Near Valtournanche. Rescue teams were sent from as far north as Zermatt, south from Châtillon.

The Goldonis led them. Three nations awarded us their highest honours. They were of little good to the rest. For me, they provided a small pension. I lost my legs through exposure.' He tapped the stumps of his once muscular legs.

'And you have no information about that trip on July the fourteenth, 1920?'

'Without particular details, how can I?'

'I have descriptions. Written down by my father.' Fontine withdrew the Xeroxed pages from his jacket.

'Good! You should have said so before! Read them to me.'

Andrew did so. The descriptions were disjointed, the pictures evoked contradictory. Time sequences jumped back and forth, and landmarks seemed to be confused with each other.

Goldoni listened; every now and then he closed his puffed, creased eyes and turned his neck to one side, as though conjuring up his own visual recollections. When Fontine finished he shook his head slowly. 'I'm sorry, *signore*. What you have read could be any twenty, thirty different trails. Much that's there doesn't even exist in our district. Forgive me, but I think that your father has confused the trails farther west in Valais. It's easy to do.'

'There's nothing that sounds familiar?'

'On the contrary. Everything. *And* nothing. Fragments of many locations for hundreds of square miles. I'm sorry. It's impossible.'

Andrew was confused. He still had the gut feeling that the Alpiner was lying. There was another option to pursue before he forced the issue. If it, too, led nowhere, he would come back and face the cripple with different tactics.

... *Should Alfredo not be the eldest, look for a sister* ...

'Are you the eldest surviving member of the family?'

'No. Two sisters were born before me. One lives.'

'Where?'

'In Champoluc. On the Via Sestina. Her son works my land.'

'What's the name? Her married name?'

'Capomonti.'

'Capomonti? That's the name of the people who run the inn.'

'Yes, *signore*. She married into the family.'

Fontine got out of the chair, putting the Xeroxed pages into his pocket. He reached the door and turned. 'It's possible I'll be back.'

'It will be a pleasure to welcome you.'

Fontine got into the Land Rover and started the engine. Across the fence in the field, the nephew-farmhand sat motionless on the tractor and watched him, his vehicle idling. The gut feeling returned; the look on the farmhand's face seemed to be saying, *Get out of here. I must run to the house and hear what you said.*

Andrew released the brake and pressed the accelerator. The Land Rover shot forward on to the road; he made a rapid U-turn and started back towards the village.

Suddenly his eyes became riveted on the most obvious, unstartling sight in the world. He swore. It was so obvious he had not taken notice.

The road was lined with telephone poles.

There was no point in looking for an old woman on the Via Sestina; she would not be there. Another strategy came to the soldier's mind. The odds favoured it.

Woman!' shouted Goldoni.

'Quickly! Help me! The telephone!'

Goldini's wife walked swiftly into the room and gripped the handles of the chair. 'Should I make the calls?' she asked, wheeling him to the telephone.

'No. I'll do it.' He dialled. 'Lefrac? Can you hear me? ... He's come. After all these years. Fontini-Cristi. But he does not bring the words. He seeks a clearing named for *hawks*. He tells me nothing else, and that's nothing. I don't trust him. I must reach my sister. Gather the others. We'll meet in an hour . . . Not *here*! At the inn.'

Andrew lay prone in the field across from the farmhouse. He focused the binoculars alternately on the door and on the windows. The sun was going down behind the western Alps; it would be dark soon. Lights had been put on in the farmhouse; the shadows moved back and forth. There was activity.

A car was being backed out of a dirt drive to the right of the house; it stopped and the farmhand-nephew got out. He raced to the front door; it opened.

Goldoni was in his wheelchair, his wife behind him. The nephew replaced her and started wheeling his legless uncle across the lawn towards the car, whose motor was idling.

Goldoni was clutching something in his arms. Andrew focused the binoculars on the object.

It was a large book; but it was more than a book. It was some kind of heavy, wide volume. A ledger.

At the car Goldoni's wife held the door open while the nephew grabbed the grotesque amputee under the arms and swung the carcass across into the seat. Goldoni twitched and squirmed; his wife drew a strap across him and buckled it.

Through the frame of the open door's window, Andrew had a clear view of the legless, former Alpine guide. The centre of focus once again was the huge ledger in Goldoni's arms, held almost desperately, as though it were a thing of extraordinary value he dared not let go. Then Andrew realized there was something else in Goldoni's arms, something infinitely more familiar to the soldier. A shaft of glistening metal was wedged between the large volume and the Alpiner's thick chest.

It was the barrel of a small, powerful shotgun; a model particularly identified with warring Italian families in the south. In Sicily. It was called the *lupo*, the 'wolf'. It was without much accuracy beyond twenty yards, but at short range could blow a man ten feet off the ground.

Goldoni was guarding the volume in his arms with a weapon more powerful than the .357 Magnum in the soldier's Alpine pack. Briefly, Andrew focused on Goldoni's nephew; the man had a new addition to his garb. Jammed into his belt was a pistol, the large handle indicative of its heavy calibre.

Both Alpiners were guarding that ledger. No one could get near it. What was—

Christ! Suddenly, Fontine understood. *Records!* Records of *journeys into the mountains*! It couldn't be anything else! It never occurred to him – *or* to Victor – to ask if such records were kept. Especially in light of the years; it was simply not a consideration. My God, a half century had passed!

But according to his father, and *his* father, the Goldonis were the finest guides in the Alps. Such professionals with such a collective reputation to uphold *would* keep records; it was the most natural thing to do. Records of past trips into the mountains, going back decades!

Goldoni had lied. The information his visitor wanted was in that house. But Goldoni did not want the visitor to have it.

Andrew watched. The nephew collapsed the wheel-chair, opened the boot of the car, threw it in, and ran to the driver's side. He climbed behind the wheel as Goldoni's wife closed her husband's door.

The car lurched out of the drive and headed north towards Champoluc. Goldoni's wife returned to the house.

The soldier lay prone in the grass and slowly replaced

the binoculars in the case as he considered his options. He could race to the hidden Land Rover and go after Goldoni, but to what purpose, and how great a risk? The Alpiner was only half a man, but the *lupo* in his hands more than made up for his missing legs. Too, the surly nephew wouldn't hesitate to use the pistol in his belt.

If the ledger carried by Goldoni was what he suspected, it was being rushed away to be hidden. Not to be destroyed; one did not destroy a record of such incalculable value.

If. He had to be sure, certain of his judgement. Then he could move.

It was funny. He had not expected Goldoni to leave; he had expected others to come to him. That Goldoni did leave meant that panic had set in. A legless man who never went anywhere did not race away into the indignity and discomfort of the outside world unless the motive was extraordinary.

The soldier made up his mind. The circumstances were optimum; Goldoni's wife was alone. First, he would find out if that ledger was what he thought it was; then he would find out where Goldoni had gone.

Once he learned these things, the decision would be made: whether to follow or to wait.

Andrew rose from the grass; there was no point wasting time. He started for the house.

'There's no one here, *signore*,' said the stunned, gaunt woman, her eyes frightened. 'My husband has gone with his nephew. They play cards in the village.'

Andrew pushed the woman aside without replying. He walked directly through the house to Goldoni's room. There was nothing but old magazines and out-of-date Italian newspapers. He looked in the closet; it was at once ugly and pathetic. Trousers hung, the cloth folded, the folds held in place by safety pins. There were no books, no ledgers like the one the Alpiner had clutched in his arms.

He returned to the front room. The sullen, frightened wife was at the telephone, depressing the bar in short, panicked jabs with her bony fingers.

'The wire's cut,' he said simply, approaching her.

'No,' the woman whispered. 'What do you want? I have nothing! *We* have nothing!'

'I think you do,' answered Fontine, backing the woman against the wall, his face inches above hers. 'Your husband lied to me. He said he couldn't tell me anything, but he left in a hurry carrying a very large book. It was a journal, wasn't it! An old journal that described a climb in the mountains fifty years ago. The journals! Show me the journals!'

'I do not know what you talk about, *signore*! We have nothing! We live on a *pensione*!'

'Shut up! Give me those records!'

'*Per favore . . .*'

'Goddamn you!' Fontine grabbed the woman's straight grey hair and yanked it forward, then suddenly, brutally backward, crashing her head into the wall. 'I haven't got time. Your husband lied to me. Show me where those books are! *Now!*' He wrenched the hair again, and again slammed her skull into the wall. Blood appeared on her wrinkled neck, tears welled in her unfocused eyes.

The soldier realized he had gone too far. The combat option was now defined; it wouldn't be the first time. There'd been no lack of unco-operative peasants in Nam. He pulled the woman away from the wall.

'Do you understand me?' he said in a monotone. 'I'll light a match in front of your eyes. Do you know what happens then? I'm asking you for the last time. Where are those records?'

Goldoni's wife collapsed, sobbing. Fontine held her by

the cloth of her dress. With a trembling arm and frenzied, shaking fingers she pointed to a door in the right wall of the room.

Andrew dragged her across the floor. He withdrew his Beretta and smashed the door with his boot. It crashed open. There was no one inside.

'The light switch. Where is it?'

She raised her head, her mouth open, the breath coming shorter, and moved her eyes to the left. '*Lampada, lampada,*' she whispered.

He pulled her inside the small room, releasing the cloth of her dress, and found the lamp. She lay trembling, curled up on the floor. The light reflected off the glass-enclosed bookcase on the opposite wall. There were five shelves, and on each a row of books. He rushed to the case, grabbed a knob in the middle and tried to raise the pane of glass. It was locked; he tried the others. All locked.

With his Beretta he smashed the glass of two panels. The light from the lamp was dim but sufficient. The faded, handwritten letters and numbers on the brown bindings were clear enough.

Each year was divided into two six-month periods, the volumes differing in thickness. The books were hand-made. He looked at the upper left panel; he had not broken the glass and the reflection of light obscured the lettering. He smashed it, clearing the fragments of glass away with repeated thrusts of the steel barrel.

The first volume read 1907. There was no month noted underneath; that was a system which had evolved.

He raced the barrel over the volumes to the year 1920.

January to June was there.

July to December was missing. In its place, filling the space, was a hastily inserted volume dated 1967.

Alfredo Goldoni, the legless cripple, had outrun him. He had removed the key from the locked door that held the secret of a journey into the mountains fifty years ago, and raced away. Fontine turned to Goldoni's wife. She was on her knees, her gaunt arms supporting her shaking, gaunt body.

It would not be difficult to do what he had to do, learn what had to be learned.

'Get up,' he said.

He carried the lifeless body across the field and into the woods. There was still no moon; instead the air smelled of impending rain, the sky pitch black with clouds, no stars in evidence. The beam of the flashlight wavered.

Time. Time was the only thing that counted now.

And shock. He would need shock.

Alfredo Goldoni had gone to the inn of the Capomontis, according to the dead woman. They had all gone there, she said. The *consigliatori* of Fontini-Cristi had gathered together. A stranger had come among them bringing the wrong words.

CHAPTER THIRTY-ONE

Adrian drove back to Milan but he did not go to the hotel, he followed the highway signs to the airport, not entirely sure of *how* he was going to do what he had to do, but certain that he would do it.

He had to get to Champoluc. A killer was loose and that killer was his brother.

Somewhere in the vast complex of Milan airport was a pilot and a plane. Or someone who knew where both could be found, for whatever price was necessary.

He drove as fast as he could, all the windows open, the wind whipping through the car. It helped him control himself; it helped him not to think, for thought was too painful.

'There's a small, private field on the outskirts of Champoluc, used by the rich in the mountains,' said the unshaven pilot who had been awakened and summoned to the airport by a well-tipped clerk on the night shift for Alitalia. 'But it's not operational at these hours.'

'Can you fly in?'

'It's not so far away, but the terrain's bad.'

'Can you *do* it?'

'I'll have enough petrol to return if I cannot. That will be my decision, not yours. But not one *lira* will be given back, is that understood?'

'I don't care.'

The pilot turned to the Alitalia clerk, speaking authoritatively, obviously for the benefit of the man who would pay such money for such a flight. 'Get me the weather. Zermatt, stations south, heading two-eighty degrees sweep to two-ninety-five out of Milan. I want radar fronts.'

The Alitalia clerk shrugged and sighed.

'You'll be paid,' said Adrian curtly.

The clerk picked up a red telephone. '*Operazioni*,' he said officiously.

The landing at Champoluc was not as hazardous as the pilot wanted Adrian to believe. The field, it was true, was not operational – there was no radio contact, no tower to guide a plane in – but the single strip was outlined, the east and west perimeters marked by red lights.

Adrian walked across the field towards the only structure with lights on inside. It was a semi-circular metal shell, perhaps fifty feet long, twenty-five feet high at its midpoint. It was a hangar for small private aircraft. The door opened, brighter light spilled out on the ground, and a man in overalls was silhouetted in the doorway. He hunched his shoulders, peering out into the darkness; then he stretched, stifling a yawn.

'Can you speak English?' asked Fontine.

The man did – reluctantly and poorly, but clearly enough to be understood. And the information Adrian was given was pretty much what he expected. It was four in the morning and there was no place open where a car could be found for hire; there was no place open at all. What pilot was crazy enough to fly into Champoluc at such an hour? Perhaps the *polizia* should be called.

Fontine withdrew several large notes from his pocket and held them in the light of the doorway. The watchman's eyes became riveted on the money. Adrian suspected that it was over a month's pay for the angry man.

'I came a long way to find someone. I've done nothing

wrong except hire a plane to fly me here from Milan. The police are not interested in me, but I *must* find the person I'm looking for. I need a car and directions.'

'You're no criminal? Flying up at such an hour—'

'No criminal,' interrupted Adrian, suppressing his impatience, speaking as calmly as he could. 'I'm a lawyer. An ... *avvocato*,' he added.

'*Avvocato?*' The man's voice conveyed his respect.

'I must find the house of Alfredo Goldoni. That's the name I've been given.'

'The legless one?'

'I didn't know that.'

The car was an old Fiat with torn upholstery and cracked side windows. The Goldoni farmhouse was eight to ten miles out of town, according to the watchman, on the west road. The man drew a simple diagram; it was easy to follow.

A post-and-rail fence could be seen in the glare of the headlights, the outlines of a house farther in the distance. And there was a dim wash of light coming from the house, shining through windows, dimly illuminating cascading branches of pine trees that fronted the old building near the road. Adrian removed his foot from the Fiat's accelerator, wondering whether he should stop and go the rest of the way on foot. Lights on in a farmhouse at a quarter to five in the morning was not what he expected.

He saw the telephone poles. Had the night watchman at the airport called Goldoni and told him to expect a visitor? Or did farmers in Champoluc normally rise at such an early hour?

He decided against approaching on foot. If the watchman had telephoned, or the Goldonis were starting their day, a car was not the alarming intruder a man alone, walking quietly in the night, would be.

Adrian turned into a wide dirt path between the tall

pines: there was no other entrance for a car. He pulled up parallel to the house; the dirt drive extended far back into the property, ending at a barn. Farm equipment could be seen through the open barn doors in the wash of the headlights. He got out of the car, passed the lighted front windows covered by curtains, and walked to the front door. It was a farmhouse door – wide and thick, the upper section a panel itself, separated from the lower to let in the summer breezes and keep the animals out. There was a heavy, pitted brass knocker in the centre. He used it.

He waited. There was no response, no sounds of movement within.

He rapped again, louder, with longer spaces between the sharp metallic reports.

There was a sound from behind the door. Indistinct, brief. A rustle of cloth or paper; a hand scratching on fabric? What?

'Please,' he called out courteously. 'My name's Fontine. You knew my father, and his father. From Milan. From Campo di Fiori. Please let me speak to you! I mean no harm.'

Only silence now. Nothing.

He stepped back on to the grass and walked to the lighted windows. He put his face against the glass and tried to see through the white sheer curtains beyond. They were in opaque folds. The blurred images inside were further distorted by the thick glass of the Alpine window.

Then he saw it, and for a moment – as his eyes adjusted to the blurred distortion – he thought he had lost his mind for the second time that night.

At the far left side of the room was the figure of a legless man writhing in short, spastic twitches across the floor. The deformed body was large from the waist up, dressed in some kind of shirt that ended at the huge

436

stumps, what remained of the legs hidden in the cloth of white undershorts.

The legless one.

Alfredo Goldoni. Adrian watched now as Goldoni manoeuvred himself into a dark corner at the far wall. He carried something in his arms, clutching it as though it were a lifeline in a heavy sea. It was a rifle, a large-barrelled rifle. Why?

'*Goldoni! Please!*' Fontine cried out at the window. 'I just want to *talk* to you. If the watchman called you, he must have told you that.'

The report was thunderous; glass shattered in all directions, fragments penetrating Adrian's raincoat and jacket. At the last instant he had seen the black barrel raised and had lurched to the side, covering his face. Thick, jagged points of glass were like a hundred pieces of ice across his arm. But for the heavy sweater he had bought in Milan, he would have been a mass of blood. As it was, his arms and neck were bleeding slightly.

Above, through the billows of smoke and the shattered glass of the window, he could hear the metallic snap of the rifle; Goldoni had reloaded. He sat up, his back against the stone foundation of the house. He felt along his left arm and removed as much of the glass as he could. He could feel the rivulets of blood on his neck.

He sat there, breathing heavily, ministering to himself, then called out again. Goldoni could not possibly negotiate the space between the dark corner and the window. They were two prisoners, one intent on killing the other, held at bay by an invisible, unclimbable wall.

'Listen to me! I don't know what you've been told, but it's not true! I'm not your enemy!'

'*Animale!*' roared Goldoni from within. 'I'll see you dead!'

'For God's sake, why? I don't want to harm you!'

'You are Fontini-Cristi! You are a killer of women! An abductor of children! *Maligno! Animale!*'

He was too late. Oh, Jesus! He was *too late*! The killer had reached Champoluc before him.

But the killer was still loose. There was a chance.

'One last time, Goldoni,' he said, without shouting now. 'I'm a Fontini-Cristi, but I'm not the man you want dead. I'm not a killer of women and I've abducted no children. I know the man you're talking about and he's not me. That's as clear and as simple as I can put it. Now, I'm going to stand up in front of this window. I haven't got any gun – I've never owned one. If you don't believe me, I guess you'll have to shoot. I haven't got time to argue any longer. And I don't think you do, either. Any of you.'

Adrian pressed his bleeding hand on the ground and rose unsteadily. He walked slowly in front of the shattered glass of the window.

Alfredo Goldoni called out quietly, 'Walk in with your arms in front of you. There's no way you'll live if you hesitate or break your step.'

Fontine came out of the shadows of the darkened back room. The legless man had directed him to a window through which he could enter; the cripple would not risk the manipulations required of him to open the front door. As Adrian emerged from the darkness, Goldoni cocked the hammer of the rifle, prepared to fire. He spoke in a whisper.

'You're the man and, yet, you are not the man.'

'He's my brother,' said Adrian softly. 'And I have to stop him.'

Goldoni stared at him in silence. Finally, his eyes still concentrated on Fontine's face, he uncocked the rifle and lowered it beside him in the corner.

'Help me into my chair,' he said.

Adrian sat in front of the legless man, bare to the waist, his back within reach of Goldoni's hands. The Italian-Swiss had removed the fragments of glass, applying an alcohol solution that stung but did its work; the bleeding stopped.

'In the mountains blood is precious. Our countrymen in the north call this fluid *leimen*. It's better than the powder. I doubt if the medical doctors approve, but it does the trick. Put on your shirt.'

'Thank you.' Fontine rose and did as he was told. They had spoken only briefly of things that had to be said. With an Alpiner's practicality, Goldoni had ordered Adrian to remove his clothes where the glass had penetrated. A wounded man, uncared for, was of little good to anyone. His role of rural physician, however, did not lessen his anger or his agony.

'He's a man from hell,' said the cripple as Fontine buttoned his shirt.

'He's sick, though I realize that's no help for you. He's looking for something. A vault, hidden somewhere in the mountains. It was carried there years ago, before the war, by my grandfather.'

'We know. We've known someone would come someday. But that's all we know. We don't know where in the mountains.'

Adrian didn't believe the legless man and yet he could not be sure. 'You said killer of women. Who?'

'My wife. She's gone.'

'Gone? How do you know she's dead?'

'He lied. He said she ran away down the road. That he took chase and caught her and keeps her hidden in the village.'

'It's possible.'

'It is not. I can't walk, *signore*. My wife can't run. She has the swollen veins in her legs. She wears thick shoes to get around this house. Those shoes are in front of your eyes.'

Adrian looked down where Goldoni gestured. A pair of heavy, ugly shoes were placed neatly at the side of a chair.

'People do things they don't think they can do—'

'There's blood on the floor,' interrupted Goldoni, his voice trembling, pointing to an open doorway. 'There were no wounds on the man who calls himself a soldier. Go! Look for yourself.'

Fontine walked to the open door and went inside the small room. A glass bookcase was smashed, sharp fragments everywhere. He reached inside and removed a volume from behind one of the shattered panels. He opened it. In clear handscript were pages detailing successive climbs into the mountains. The dates extended back beyond 1920. And there was blood on the floor by the door.

He was too late.

He walked swiftly back into the front room.

'Tell me everything. As quickly as you can. *Everything.*'

The soldier had been thorough. He had immobilized his enemy, rendered them helpless through fear and panic. The major from Eye Corps had mounted his own invasion of the Capomonti inn. He had done so swiftly, without a wasted move, finding Lefrac and the members of the Capomonti and Goldoni families in an upstairs room where they were holding their hastily summoned conference.

The door of the room had crashed open, a terrified desk clerk propelled through it so harshly he fell to the floor. The soldier entered quickly, closing the door before any in the room knew what was happening, and held them all rigid at the point of a gun.

The soldier then issued his demands. First, the old ledger describing the journey into the mountains over fifty years ago. And maps. Minutely detailed maps used by climbers in the Champoluc district. Second, the services of either Lefrac's son or eighteen-year-old grandson to lead him into the hills. Third, the grand-daughter as a second hostage. The child's father had lost his head and lunged at the man with the gun; but the soldier was expert and the father subdued without a shot.

Old Lefrac was ordered to open the door and call for a housemaid. Proper clothing was brought to the room and the children dressed under gunpoint. It was then that the man-from-hell told Goldoni his wife was a prisoner. He was to return to his house and remain there alone, sending his driver – his nephew – away. If he stopped to reach the police, he would never see his wife again.

'Why?' asked Adrian quickly. 'Why did he do that? Why did he want you back here alone?'

'He separates us. My sister returns with my nephew to her house on the Via Sestina; Lefrac and his son remain at the inn. Together we might make each other bold. Apart we're frightened, helpless. A gun against a child's head is not easily forgotten. He knows that alone we'll do nothing but wait.'

Adrian closed his eyes. 'God,' he said.

'The soldier's an expert, that one.' Goldoni's voice was low, the hatred seething.

Fontine glanced at him. *I have run with the pack – in the middle of the pack – but now I have reached the edges and I will peel away.*

'Why did you shoot at me? If you thought it was him, how could you take the chance? Not knowing what he did.'

'I saw your face against the glass. I wanted to blind you, not to kill you. A dead man can't tell me where he's taken my wife. Or the body of my wife. Or the children. I'm a good shot; I fired inches above your head.'

Fontine crossed to the chair where he had thrown his jacket and took out the Xeroxed pages of his father's recollections of fifty years ago. 'You must have read that journal. Can you remember what was written?'

'You can't go after him. He'll kill.'

'Can you *remember*?'

'It was a two-day climb with many crossing trails! He could be anywhere. He narrows down the place he seeks. He travels blindly. If he saw you, he'd kill the children.'

'He won't see me. Not if I get there first! Not if I *wait* for *him*!' Adrian unfolded the Xeroxed pages.

'They've been read to me. There's nothing that can help you.'

'There has to be! It's *here*!'

'You're wrong,' said Goldoni, and Adrian knew he was not lying. 'I tried to tell *him* that, but he wouldn't listen. Your grandfather made his arrangements, but the *padrone* did not consider unexpected death, or human failing.'

Fontine looked up from the pages. Helplessness was in the old man's eyes. A killer was in the mountains and he was helpless. Death would surely follow death, for surely his wife was gone.

'What were these arrangements?' asked Adrian softly.

'I'll tell you. You're not your brother. We've kept the secret for thirty-five years, Lefrac, the Capomontis and ourselves. And one other – not one of us – whose death came suddenly, before he made his own arrangements.'

'Who was that?'

'A merchant named Leinkraus. We didn't know him well.'

'Tell me.'

'We've waited all these years for a Fontini-Cristi to come.' So the legless man began:

The man they – the Goldonis, Lefrac, and the Capomontis – expected would come quietly in peace, seeking the iron crate buried high in the mountains. This man would speak of the journey taken so many years ago by father and son, and he would know that journey was recorded in the Goldoni ledgers – as all who employed the Goldoni guides would know. And because that climb lasted for two days over considerable terrain, the man would specify an abandoned railroad clearing known as *Sciocchezza di Cacciatori* – Hunter's Folly. The clearing had been left to nature over forty years ago, long before the iron crate had been buried, but it had existed when father and son journeyed to Champoluc in the summer of 1920.

'I thought those clearings were given—'

'The names of birds?'

'Yes.'

'Most were, not all. The soldier asked if there was a clearing known by the name of a hawk. There are no hawks in the mountains of Champoluc.'

'The painting on the wall,' said Adrian, more to himself than for the benefit of the Alpiner.

'What?'

'My father remembered a painting on a wall in Campo di Fiori, a painting of a hunt. He thought it might be significant.'

'The soldier did not speak of it. Nor did he speak of why he sought the information; only that he had to have it. He wouldn't mention the *search* to me. *Or* the ledgers. Or the reason why the railroad clearing was important. He was *secretive*. And, clearly, he did not come in peace. A soldier who threatens a legless man is a hollow commander. I didn't trust him.'

Everything his brother had done was contrary to the memory of the Fontini-Cristis as these people remembered them. It might have been so simple had he been open with them, had he *come in peace*; but the soldier couldn't do that. He was always at war.

443

'Then the area around this abandoned clearing – Hunter's Folly – is where the vault is buried?'

'Presumably. There are several old trails to the east that lead away from the tracks, up to the higher ridges. But which trail, which ridge? We do not know.'

'The records would describe it.'

'If one knew where to look. The soldier doesn't.'

Adrian thought. His brother had travelled across the world, eluding the Intelligence network of the most powerful nation on earth. 'You may be underestimating him.'

'He's not one of us. He's not a man of the mountains.'

'No,' mused Fontine quietly. 'He's something else. What would he *look* for? That's what we have to think about.'

'An inaccessible place. Away from the trails. Ground that would not be travelled easily for any of several reasons. There are many such areas. The mountains are filled with them.'

'But you said it a few minutes ago. He'd narrow down his . . . options.'

'*Signore?*'

'Nothing. I was thinking of – never mind. You see, he knows what *not* to look for. He knows that the vault was heavy; it had to be transported – mechanically. He starts with something *besides* the record book.'

'We weren't aware of that.'

'He is.'

'It will do him little good in the darkness.'

'Look at the window,' said Adrian. Outside, the first morning light could be seen. 'Tell me about this other man. The merchant.'

'Leinkraus?'

'Yes. How was he involved?'

'That answer went with his death. Even Francesca doesn't know.'

'Francesca?'

'My sister. When my brothers died, she was the eldest. The envelope was given to her . . .'

'*Envelope?* What envelope?'

'Your grandfather's instructions.'

. . . Therefore, should Alfredo not be the eldest, look for a sister, as is the Italian-Swiss custom . . .

Adrian unfolded the pages of his father's testament. If such fragments of truth came through the distance of years with such accuracy, more attention had to be paid to his father's disjointed remembrances.

'My sister has lived in Champoluc since her marriage to Capomonti. She knew the Leinkraus family better than any of us. Old Leinkraus died in his store. There was a fire; many thought it wasn't accidental.'

'I don't understand.'

'The family Leinkraus are Jews.'

'I see. Go on.' Adrian shifted the pages.

. . . The merchant was not popular. He was a Jew and for one who fought bitterly . . . such thinking was indefensible.

Goldoni continued. The man who came to Champoluc and spoke of the iron crate and the long-forgotten journey and the old railroad clearing was to be given the envelope left with the eldest Goldoni.

'You must understand, *signore*.' The legless man interrupted himself. 'We are *all* family now. The Capomontis and the Goldonis. After so many years and no one came, we discussed it between ourselves.'

'You're ahead of me.'

'The envelope directed the man who had come to Champoluc to old Capomonti . . .'

Adrian turned back the pages. *If there were secrets to leave in the Champoluc, old Capomonti would have been a rock of silence and trust.*

'When Capomonti died, he gave *his* instructions to his son-in-law, Lefrac.'

'Then Lefrac *knows*.'

'Only one word. The name Leinkraus.'

Fontine bolted forward in his seat. He remained on the edge, bewildered. Yet something was triggered in his mind. As in long, complex cross-examination, isolated phrases and solitary words were suddenly brought into focus, given meaning where no meaning had existed previously.

The *words*. Look to the words, as Andrew looked to violence.

He scanned the pages in his hands, turning them rapidly until he found what he was looking for.

. . . There is a blurred memory of an unpleasant incident . . . what the unpleasant incident specifically entailed, I have no recall . . . serious and provoked my father . . . a sad anger . . . impression that details were withheld from me . . .

Withheld. Anger. Sadness.

. . . provoked my father . . .

'Goldoni, listen to me. You've got to think back. Way back. Something happened. Something unpleasant, sad, angry. And it concerned the Leinkraus family.'

'No.'

Adrian stopped. The legless Goldoni had not let him finish. 'What do you mean, "No"?' he asked quietly.

'I told you. I didn't know them well. We barely spoke.'

'Because they were Jews? Is that the way it came down from the north in those days?'

'I don't understand you.'

'I think you do,' Adrian stared at him; the Alpiner avoided his eyes. Fontine continued softly. 'You didn't have to know them – at all, perhaps. But for the first time, you're lying to me. Why?'

'I'm not lying. They weren't friends of the Goldonis.'

'Or the Capomontis?'

'*Or* the Capomontis!'

'You didn't like them?'

446

'We didn't *know* them! They kept to themselves. Other Jews came and they lived among their own. It's that simple.'

'It's *not*.' Adrian knew the answer was within reach. Hidden, perhaps, from Goldoni himself. 'Something happened in July of 1920! What was it?'

Goldoni sighed. 'I can't remember.'

'July the fourteenth, 1920! What *happened*?'

Goldoni's breath was shorter, his large jaws taut. The massive stumps that once were legs twitched in the wheelchair. 'It doesn't mean anything,' he whispered.

'Let me by the judge of that,' said Adrian.

'Times have changed. So much has changed in a lifetime,' said the Alpiner, his voice faltering. 'The shame was felt by everyone.'

'July the fourteenth, 1920!' Adrian zeroed in on his witness.

'I tell you! It is meaningless!'

'*Goddamn you!*' Adrian leaped from the chair. Striking the helpless old man was not out of the question. Then the words came.

'A Jew was beaten. A young Jew who entered the church school ... was beaten. He died three days later.'

The Alpiner said it. But only part of it. Fontine backed away from the wheelchair. 'Leinkraus's son?' he asked.

'Yes.'

'The church school?'

'He couldn't enter the state school. It was a place to learn. The priests accepted him.'

Fontine sat down slowly, keeping his eyes on Goldoni. 'There's more, isn't there? Who gave the beating?'

'Four boys from the village. They didn't know what they were doing. Everyone said so.'

'I'm sure everyone did. It's easier that way. Ignorant children who had to be protected. And what was the life of one Jew?'

Tears came to the eyes of Alfredo Goldoni. 'Yes.'

'You were one of those boys, weren't you?'

Goldoni nodded his head in silence.

'I think I can tell you what happened,' continued Adrian. 'Leinkraus was threatened. His wife, his other children. Nothing was said, nothing reported. A young Jew had died, that was all.'

'So many years ago,' Goldoni whispered as the tears fell down his face. 'No one thinks like that any more. And we have lived with what we did. At the end of my life, it grows even more difficult. The grave is close at hand now.'

Adrian stopped breathing, stunned by Goldoni's words. The *grave* is close ... The *grave*. My God! Was that *it*? He wanted to jump out of the chair and roar his questions until the legless Alpiner remembered! *Exactly*. But he could not do that. He kept his voice low, incisive.

'What happened then? What did Leinkraus do?'

'Do?' Goldoni shrugged slowly, sadness in the gesture. 'What could he do? He kept silent.'

'Was there a funeral? A burial?'

'If there was, we knew nothing of it.'

'Leinkraus's son had to be buried. No Christian cemetery would accept a Jew. Was there a burial place for Jews?'

'No, not then. There is now.'

'*Then!* What about then? Where was he *buried*? Where was the *murdered son* of Leinkraus *buried*?'

Goldoni reacted as though struck in the face. 'It was said the father and the brothers – the men of the family – took the dead son into the mountains. Where the boy's body would not be further abused.'

Adrian got out of the chair. There was his answer.

The grave of the Jew. The vault from Salonika.

Savarone Fontini-Cristi had found an eternal truth in

a village tragedy. He had used it. In the end, not letting the holy men forget.

Paul Leinkraus was in his late forties, the grandson of the merchant and a merchant himself, but of a different time. There was little he could relate of a grandfather he barely knew, or of an era of obsequiousness and fear he had never known. But he was a man of acumen, bespeaking the expansion for which he was responsible. As such, he had recognized the urgency and legitimacy of Adrian's sudden call.

Leinkraus had taken Fontine into the library, away from his wife and child, and removed the family Torah from the shelf. The diagram filled the entire back panel of the binding. It was a precisely drawn map that showed the way to the grave of Reuven Leinkraus's first son, buried in the mountains on 17 July 1920.

Adrian had traced every line, then matched his drawing with the original. It was precise; he had his last passport. To where, he was certain. To what, he could not know.

He made a final request of Leinkraus. An overseas telephone call to London for which, of course, he would pay.

'Your grandfather made all the payments this house can accept. Make your call.'

'Please stay. I want you to hear.'

He had placed a call to the Savoy in London. His request was uncomplicated. When the American embassy opened, would the Savoy please leave a message for Colonel Tarkington of the inspector general's office. If he was not in London, the embassy would know where to reach him.

Colonel Tarkington was to be directed to a man named Paul Leinkraus in the town of Champoluc in the

Italian Alps. The message was to be signed Adrian Fontine.

He was going into the mountains on the hunt, but he had no illusions. He was not ultimately a match for the soldier. His gesture might be only that: a gesture ending in futility. And very possibly his own death; he understood that, too.

The world could survive very well without his presence. He wasn't particularly remarkable, although he liked to think he had certain talents. But he wasn't at all sure how the world would fare if Andrew walked out of the Champoluc with the contents of an iron crate that had been carried on a train from Salonika over thirty years ago.

If only one brother came out of the mountains and that man was the killer of Eye Corps, he had to be taken.

The call finished, Adrian had looked up at Paul Leinkraus. 'When Colonel Tarkington makes contact with you, tell him exactly what happened here this morning.'

Fontine nodded to Leinkraus in the doorway. He opened the door of the Fiat and climbed in, noticing that he had been so agitated upon his arrival that he'd left the keys in the car. It was the kind of carelessness no soldier would be guilty of.

The realization caused him to reach over and pull down the panel of the glove compartment. He put his hand inside and took out a heavy, black, magazine-clip pistol; the loading mechanism had been explained to him by Alfredo Goldoni.

He started the ignition and rolled down the window, suddenly needing the air. His breath came rapidly; his heartbeat vibrated in his throat. And he remembered.

He had fired a pistol only once in his life. Years ago at a boys' camp in New Hampshire when the counsellors had taken them to a local police range. His brother had been beside him, and they had laughed together, excited children.

Where had the laughter gone?

Where had his brother gone?

Adrian drove down the tree-lined street and turned left into the road that would take him north to the mountains. Above, the early morning sun was hidden behind a blanket of gathering clouds.

The sky was angry.

CHAPTER THIRTY-TWO

The girl shrieked and slipped on the rock; her brother whipped around and grabbed her hand, preventing the fall. The plunge was no more than twenty feet, and the soldier wondered whether it might be better to break the grip between them and let her fall. If the girl snapped an ankle or a leg, she wouldn't go anywhere: she certainly could not make it down through the trails to the flat ground and the road below. It was twelve miles behind them now. They had covered the initial terrain during the night.

He could bypass the initial trails of the journey into the mountains fifty years ago. If others began the search, they wouldn't know that; he did. He could read maps the way most men read simple books. From symbols, colours, and numbers, he could visualize terrain with the accuracy of a camera. There was no one better in the army. He was a master of everything *real*, from men to machines to maps.

The detailed map used by climbers in the Champoluc district showed the railroad from Zermatt angling west around the curve of the mountains. It straightened out for approximately five miles before the station at Champoluc. The areas directly east of the final flat stretches of track were heavily traversed throughout the year. These were the first trails described in Goldoni's journal. No one concealing anything of value would consider them.

Yet farther north, at the start of the railroad's western

curve, were the old clearings that led to the numerous trails specifically listed in the pages he had ripped out of the Goldoni ledger for 14 and 15 July of 1920. Any of these might be the one. Once he saw them in daylight, and studied the possibilities, he could determine which of the trails he would trace.

Those selections would be based on fact. Fact one: the size and weight of the vault mandated vehicle or animal transportation. Fact two: the train from Salonika made its journey in the month of December – a time of year when the weather was bitter cold and the mountain passes clogged with snow. Fact three: the spring and summer thaws, with their rushing waters and erosion of earth, would call for a recess in the high ground to hide the vault, enveloped by rock for protection. Fact four: the recess would be away from frequently travelled areas, high above an established route, but with an offshoot trail that could be negotiated by an animal or a vehicle. Fact five: that trail had to emanate from a section of the track where a train could pull to a stop, the ground level on both sides flat and straight. Fact six: the specific clearing, in current use or abandoned, would lead to the crisscrossing trails recorded in the Goldoni ledger. By retracing each one to the tracks and picturing the feasibility of travelling over it – in the cold and snow, by animal or vehicle – the number of trails would be further reduced until there was one that led to the hiding place.

He had time. Days, if he needed them. He had supplies for a week strapped to his back. Goldoni, the woman, Capomonti, and Lefrac and his family, were too frightened to make a move. He had covered himself brilliantly. The unseen was always more effective than the observable in combat. He had told the terrified Swiss that he had associates in Champoluc. They would be watching; they would get word to him in the mountains should a Goldoni or a Capomonti or a Lefrac reach the police. Communications were no problem for soldiers. And the result of their reaching him would be the execution of his hostages.

He had fantasized the presence of Eye Corps. Eye Corps the way it had been – efficient, strong, quick to manoeuvre.

He would build a new Corps one day, stronger and more efficient, without weakness. He would find the vault from Salonika, carry the document out of the mountains, summon the holy men, and watch their faces as he described the imminent, global collapse of their institutions.

... The contents of that vault are as staggering to the civilized world as any in history ...

That was comforting. It could not be in better hands.

They were on a flat stretch now, the first elevation to the west no more than a mile away. The girl fell to her knees, sobbing. Her brother looked at him, his eyes conveying hatred, fear, supplication. Andrew would kill them both, but not for a while. One disposed of hostages when they no longer served a purpose.

Only fools kill indiscriminately. Death was an instrument, a means to be used in reaching an objective or completing an assignment, and that was all it was.

Adrian drove the Fiat off the road into the fields. The rocks ripped the undercarriage. He could drive no farther; he had reached the first of several steep hills that led to the first plateau described on the Leinkraus diagram. He was eight and a half miles north of Champoluc. The grave was precisely five miles beyond the first of the plateaux that were the landmarks of the journey to the burial ground.

He got out of the car and walked across the field of tall grass. He looked up. The hill in front of him sprang suddenly out of the ground, an impromptu bulge of nature, more rock than greenery with no discernible path on which to scale it. He knelt down and retied the laces on his rubber-soled shoes as tightly as he could. The weight of the pistol was heavy in his raincoat pocket.

For a moment he closed his eyes. *He could not think. O God! Keep me from thinking!*

He was a mover now. He got to his feet and started to climb.

The first two railway clearings proved negative. There was no way animal or vehicle could traverse the routes from the Zermatt railway to the eastern slopes. Two more clearings remained. The names on the old Champoluc map were Hunter's Folly and Rook; no mention of hawk. Still, it had to be one of them!

Andrew looked at his hostages. Brother and sister sat together on the ground, talking in quiet, frightened whispers, their eyes darting up at him. The hatred was gone now, only fear and supplication remained. There was something ugly about them, thought the soldier. And then he realized what it was. Across the world in the jungles of South-east Asia, people their age fought battles, weapons strapped to their backs over uniforms that looked like pyjamas. They were his enemy over there, but he respected that enemy.

He had no respect for these children. There was no strength in their faces. Only fear, and fear was repulsive to the major from Eye Corps.

'Get up!' He could not help himself; he shouted angrily at the sight of these pampered, weak brats with no dignity in their faces.

Christ, he despised the spineless!

They would not be missed.

Adrian looked back across the ridge to the plateau in the distance, thankful that old Goldoni had given him gloves.

Even without the cold, his bare hands and fingers would have been a bleeding mass of flesh. It wasn't that the climb was difficult; a man used to minimum exercise in the mountains would find it simple. But he had never been in the mountains except on skis, where tows and trams did the uphill work. He was using muscles rarely employed and had little confidence in his sense of balance.

The last several hundred yards had been the most difficult. The trail in the Leinkraus diagram was land-marked: a cluster of grey rock at the base of a crystalline schistose embankment that all climbers knew should be avoided, for it cracked easily. The crystalline rock evolved into a cliff that rose about a hundred feet from the schist, its edge sharply defined. To the left of the crystalline sheet were abrupt, dense Alpine woods that grew vertically out of the slope, a sudden, thick forest surrounded by rock. The Leinkraus trail was marked off at ten paces from the embankment. It led to the top of the wooded slope whose ridge was the second plateau; the end of the second leg of the journey.

The trail was nowhere to be found. It had disappeared; years of disuse and overgrowth had concealed it. Yet the ridge could be seen clearly above the trees. That he could see it was an indication of the angle of ascent.

He had walked into the dense, Alpine underbrush and made his way, yard by yard, up the steep incline, through nettled bush and the skin-piercing needles of the pines.

He sat on the ridge, breathing heavily, his shoulders aching from the constant tension. He estimated the distance from the first plateau to be at least three miles. It had taken nearly three hours. A mile an hour, over rocks and down miniature valleys, and across cold streams, and up endless hills. Just three miles. If that were so, he had two miles to go, perhaps less. He looked up. The overcast had lasted the entire morning; it would continue on throughout the day. The sky above was like the North Shore sky before a heavy squall.

They used to sail in squalls together. Laughing as they bested the weather, sure of their abilities in the water, pitting themselves against the rain and the wind of the Sound.

No, he would not think of that. He got to his feet and looked at his tracing of the Leinkraus diagram, copied from the inside binding of a family Torah.

The diagram was clear but the rising terrain beyond him wasn't. He saw the objective – due north-east, the third plateau, isolated above a sea of Alpine spruce. But the ridge he was on swept to the right, due *east*, leading into the base of yet another mountain of boulders, away from any direct line to the plateau in the distance. He walked around the ledge past the border of the dark, sloping woods he had climbed through. The drop below was sheer and the rocks beneath rose like a bubbling river of stone. The trail as marked in the diagram went from forest to ledge to forest; there was no mention of intersecting rock.

Geological changes had taken place in the intervening years since any member of the Leinkraus family had journeyed to the burial ground. A sudden shift of nature – a quake or an avalanche – had eliminated the trail.

Still, he could see the plateau. What separated him from it seemed impenetrable, but once through it – and over it – he could make out a winding trail on the higher ground that led to the plateau. It was doubtful that that had been altered. He slid down the embankment on to the river of stone, and awkwardly, trying to keep his feet from slipping into a hundred miniature crevices, climbed towards the forest of spruce.

The third clearing was it! *Sciocchezza di Cacciatori!* Hunter's Folly! Long abandoned but once perfect for removing the vault. The trail from the mountains to the Zermatt railway was passable, and the area around the tracks was flat and accessible. At first Andrew had not been sure; in spite of the level ground on either side of the tracks, the stretch was short, blocked by a curve. Then he remembered: his father had said that the train from Salonika had been a short freight. Four wagons and an engine.

Five railway units could easily pull beyond the curve and come to a stop in a straight line. Whatever car the vault had been in could have been unloaded without difficulty.

But what now convinced him he was near his goal was an unexpected discovery. West of the tracks were the unmistakable signs of an abandoned road. The cut through the woods was defined, the trees in the cut shorter than those surrounding them, the brush closer to the ground. It was no longer a road – not even a path – but its former existence was undeniable.

'Lefrac!' he yelled at the eighteen-year-old. 'What's down there?' He pointed north-west, where the cut in the forest sloped.

'A village. About five, six miles away.'

'It's not on the railway line.'

'No, *signore*. It's in farm country, below the mountains.'

'What roads lead to it?'

'The main road from Zürich and—'

'All right.' He stopped the boy for two reasons. He had heard what he wanted to hear, and twenty feet away the girl had got to her feet and was edging towards the woods on the eastern side of the tracks.

Fontine took out his pistol and fired two shots. The explosions thundered throughout the woods; the bullets detonated on the ground on either side of the child. She screamed, terrified. Her brother lunged at him in a frenzy of tears; he sidestepped and smashed the barrel of the pistol on the side of the boy's head.

Lefrac's son fell to the ground, sobs of frustration and anger filling the silence of the abandoned railroad clearing.

'You're better than I thought you were,' said the soldier coldly, raising his eyes, turning to the girl. 'Help him. He's not hurt. We're heading back.'

Give the captured hope, reflected the soldier. The younger and more inexperienced they were, the more hope they should be given. It reduced the fear which was, in itself, detrimental to rapid travel. Fear was an instrument, too. Like death. It was to be used methodically.

He retraced the trail from the Zermatt tracks for a second time. He was certain now. There was nothing that would prevent an animal or a vehicle from negotiating it. The ground was clear and mostly hard. And more important, the terrain rose directly towards the eastern slopes, into the specific trails recorded in the faded pages of the ledger. Light snow and layers of frost covered the earth. With every yard the soldier in him told him he was nearing the enemy zone. For that was what it was.

They reached the first intersecting trail described by the Goldoni guide on the morning of 14 July 1920. To the right, the trail angled downward into some kind of forest, a thick wall of dark green, laced with a roof of white. It seemed impenetrable.

It was a possible hiding place. That mountain forest would not be tempting to the casual climber, and without interest for the experienced. On the other hand, it *was* a forest – wood and earth, not rock – and because it was not rock he would not accept it. The vault would be protected by rock.

To the left, the trail continued up, veering obliquely into the side of a small mountain above them. The trail itself was wide, on solid rock, and bordered by foliage. Boulders rose sharply to the right, forming an abrupt sheet of heavy stone. An animal or a vehicle still had space to walk or roll; the direct line from the Zermatt tracks was unbroken.

'Move it!' he shouted, gesturing to the left. The Lefrac children looked at each other. To the right was the way to Champoluc – the way back. The girl grabbed her brother; Fontine stepped forward, broke the grip, and propelled the girl forward.

'*Signore!*' The boy shouted and stepped between them, his arms raised in front of him, his young palms flat – a very penetrable shield. 'Don't do that,' he stammered, his voice low, cracking with young fear, his own anger challenging himself.

'Let's go,' said the soldier. He had no time to waste on children.

'You hear me, *signore!*'

'I heard you. Now, move.'

At the western flank of the small mountain the width of the rising trail abruptly narrowed. It entered an enormous, natural archway cut out of the boulders and led to the face of a hill of sheer rock. The geologically formed archway was not only the logical extension of the trail, but the mountain of rock beyond must have been irresistible to novice climbers. It could be scaled without great effort, but was sufficiently awesome by its breadth and height to be a good start for the higher regions. Perfect for an enthusiastic seventeen-year-old, under the watchful eye of a guide and a father.

But the width under the arch *was* narrow, the rock floor too smooth, especially when heavier snows fell. An animal – a mule or a horse – might cross under but there was considerable danger that hooves would slip.

No vehicle could possibly get through.

Andrew turned and studied the approach they had just

made. There were no other trails, but about thirty yards back on the left the ground was flat and filled with Alpine brush. It extended to a short wall of rock that rose up to the ridge of the mountain. That wall, that short cliff, was no more than twenty feet high, almost hidden by shrubs and small, gnarled trees growing out of the rock. But the ground beneath the cliff, beneath that ridge, was flat. Natural obstructions were everywhere else, but not there, not in that particular spot.

'Walk over there,' he ordered the young Lefracs, both to keep them in sight and to provide perspective. 'Go into that flat area between the rocks! Spread the bushes and walk in! As far as you can!'

He stepped back off the trail and studied the ridge above. It, too, was flat or at least appeared so. And it was something else, something that might not be noticed except, perhaps, from where he stood. It was . . . defined. The edge, though jagged, formed a nearly perfect semicircle. If that circle continued, the ridge itself was like a small, out-of-the-way platform on a small, unimportant mountain, but still high above the lower Alpine hills.

He judged the height of Lefrac's son as five feet ten or eleven. 'Raise your hands!' he shouted.

Arms extended, the boy's hands were just below the midpoint of the short cliff.

Suppose the method of transport was not an animal but a vehicle. A heavy-wheeled piece of machinery, the carriage a plough, or a tractor. It was consistent; there was no part of the route from the Zermatt tracks or up the Goldoni trail that such a piece of equipment could not traverse. And ploughs and tractors had winch machinery . . .

'*Signore! Signore!*' It was the girl; her shouts conveyed a strange exultation, a cross between hope and desperation. 'If this is what you *look* for, let us *go*!'

Andrew raced back into the trail and towards the Lefracs. He sped into the tangled shrubbery to the face of the rock.

'Down there!' The girl shouted again.

On the ground in the light snow, barely seen through the underbrush, was an old ladder. The wood was rotted, the steps swollen out of their sockets in half a dozen places. But otherwise it was intact. It was not now usable, but neither had it been abused by man. It had lain in that shrubbery for years, perhaps decades, untouched except by nature and time.

Fontine knelt down and touched it, pried it off the ground, watched it crumble as he lifted it. He had found a human tool where none should be; he knew that not fifteen feet above him . . .

Above him! He whipped his head up and saw the blurred object crashing down. The impact came; his head exploded in a flashing of pain, followed by an instant numbness, a hundred hammers pounding. He fell forward, struggling to shake the effects of the blow and find light again.

He heard the shouts.

'*Fuggi! Presto! In la traccia!*' The boy.

'*Non senza voi! Tu fuggi anche!*' The girl.

Lefrac's son had found a large rock on the ground. And in his hatred he had lost his fear; holding the primitive weapon in his hand, he had crashed it down on the soldier's head.

The light was returning. Fontine started to get up and, again, he saw the unfocused hand descending, the rock slashing diagonally down.

'*You little fuck! You fuck!*'

Lefrac's son released the rock, hurling it into the soldier's body – anywhere, a final assault – and ran out of the snow-covered shrubbery on to the trail after his sister.

Andrew recognized the pitch of his own fury. He had felt it perhaps a dozen times in his life, and it had always been in the molten heat of combat when an enemy held an advantage he could not control.

He crawled out of the bush to the edge of the trail and looked below. Beneath him on the winding path were brother and sister, running as best they could over the slippery trail.

He reached under his jacket to the holster strapped to his chest. The Beretta was in his pocket. But the Beretta would be inadequate; it was not that accurate. He pulled out the .357-calibre Magnum he had bought at the Leinkraus store in Champoluc. His hostages were about forty yards away. The boy took the girl's hand; they were close together, the figures overlapping.

Andrew squeezed the trigger eight times in succession. Both bodies fell, writhing on the rocks. He could hear the screams. In seconds the screaming subsided into moans, the writhing became twists and lurches at nothing. They would die, but not for a while. They would go no farther.

The soldier crawled back through the shrubs into the flat *cul de sac* and removed the pack from his back, slipping the straps off slowly, moving his bleeding head as little as possible. He opened the pack and slipped out the canvas first-aid kit. He had to patch the broken skin and stop the bleeding as best he could. And move. For Christ's sake, *move*!

He had no hostages now. He could tell himself it made no difference, but he knew better. Hostages were a way out. If he came out of the mountains alone, they'd be watching. *Jesus* they'd be watching for him – he was a dead man. They'd take the vault and kill him.

There was another way! The Lefrac boy had said it!

The abandoned road west of the abandoned clearing

called Hunter's Folly! Past the tracks, down to a village whose main road led to Zürich.

But he was not going to that village, to that road that led to Zürich, until the contents of the vault were his. And every instinct he possessed told him he'd found it.

Fifteen feet above.

He unwound the ropes clamped to the outside of the pack and spread the grappling hook from its axis; the prongs locked into position. He stood up. His temple throbbed and the wounds stung where he'd applied the antiseptic, but the bleeding had stopped. He was focusing clearly again.

He stepped back and lobbed the grappling hook up to the ledge. It caught. He yanked on the rope.

The rock splintered; fragments plummeted down, followed by larger sections of limestone. He sprang to the side to avoid the falling hook; it embedded itself through the thin layers of snow into the ground.

He swore and once more heaved the hook skyward, arcing it over the ledge, far into the flat surface above. He tugged in swift, short movements; the hook caught. He pulled harder; it held.

The line was ready; he could climb. He reached down, grabbed the straps of his pack and slipped his arms through, not bothering to secure the front clamps. He yanked on the rope a last time; he was satisfied. He jumped as high as he could, thrusting his legs out against the stone, allowing himself to swing back into the rock as he manipulated his hands – one over the other – in rapid ascent. He swung his left leg over the jagged ledge, and pushed his right hand against the stone beneath, forcing his body into a lateral roll that propelled him on to the surface. He started to get up, his eyes travelling to the source of the grappling hook's anchor.

But he remained kneeling in shock as he stared at the strange sight ten feet away, in the centre of the plateau.

Embedded in the stone was an old, rusted metal star: a Star of David.

The grappling hook enveloped it. The prongs moored around the iron.

He was looking at a grave.

He heard the echoes throughout the mountains like repeated, sharp cracks of thunder, one right after another. As if bolts of lightning had sliced through the roof of the forest, splitting the wood of a hundred trees around him. But they signified neither lightning nor thunder; they were gunshots.

In spite of the cold, perspiration streamed down Adrian's face, and despite the darkness of the forest, his eyes were filled with unwanted images. His brother had killed again. The major from Eye Corps was efficiently going about his business of death. The screams that followed the shots were faint, muted by the forest barrier, but unmistakable.

Why? For God's sake, *why?*

He could not think. Not about things like that. Not now. He had to think only on one level; the level of motion. He had made half a dozen attempts to climb out of the dark labyrinth, each time allowing himself ten minutes to see the light of the forest's edge. Twice he had allowed himself extra time because his eyes played tricks, and in each case there was only further darkness, no end in sight.

He was rapidly going out of his mind. He was caught in a maze; thick shafts of bark and unending, prickling branches and cracked limbs creased his face and legs. How many times had he gone in circles? He could not tell. Everything began to look like everything else. He'd *seen* that tree! That particular cluster of branches had been his wall five minutes ago! His flashlight was no help. Its illuminations imitated themselves; he could not tell one from another. He was lost in the middle of an impenetrable slope of Alpine woods. Nature had altered the trail in the decades since the Leinkraus mourners made their final pilgrimage. The seepage of melting summer snows had spread, inundating the once-negotiable forest, providing a bed of moist earth receptive to unlimited growth.

But knowing this was as useless as his flashlight's distortions. The initial reports of gunfire exploded from over *there*. In *that* direction. He had very little to lose except his breath and what remained of his sanity. He began to run, his head filled with the echoes of the gunfire he had heard seconds ago.

The faster he ran the straighter seemed his course. He slashed a path with his arms, bending, breaking, cracking everything that got in his way.

And he saw the light. He fell to his knees, out of breath, no more than thirty feet from the forest's edge. Grey stone, covered with patches of snow, rose beyond the dense trees and surged out of sight above the highest limbs. He had reached the base of the third plateau.

And so had his brother. The killer from Eye Corps had done what Goldoni believed he could not do: he had taken long-forgotten descriptions written down a half century ago and refined them, made them applicable to the present search. There was a time when brother would have taken pride in brother; that time had passed. There remained only the necessity of stopping him.

Adrian had tried not to think about it, wondering if he'd be capable of accepting it when the moment came. The moment of anguish unlike anything in his imagination. He was accepting it now. Calmly, strangely unmoved, though filled with a cold sadness. For it was the only eminently logical, undeniable response to the horror and the chaos.

He would kill his brother. Or his brother would kill him.

He got to his feet, walked slowly out of the forest and found the path of rock diagrammed on the Leinkraus map. It wound up the mountain, a series of wide curves to lessen the angle of ascent, veering always clockwise until it reached the top. Or almost the top, for at the base of the plateau was a sheet of rock that Paul Leinkraus recalled was quite high. He had made the journey only twice – in the first and second years of the war – and was very young. The sheet of rock might not be as high as he remembered it to be, for the memory was in the context of a boy's perspective. But they had used a ladder, he recalled that clearly.

A solemn service for the dead and a young's boy's sense of life were incompatible, Leinkraus had admitted. There was another way to the plateau, hardly practical for old men, but explored by a youngster lacking the proper respect for religious observance. It was at the very end of the seemingly vanished path, well past an enormous natural arch that was the continuation of the mountain trail. It consisted of a series of jagged rocks that followed the line of the narrowing summit, and necessitated sure feet and a willingness to take chances. His father and older brother had scolded him severely for using it. The drop was dangerous; probably not fatal, but sufficiently deep to break an arm or a leg.

If an arm or a leg were broken now, thought Adrian, the danger *was* fatal. An immobilized man was an easy target.

He started up the winding path, between the intermittent rocks, crouching to conceal his body below their height. The plateau was three hundred to four hundred feet above the path, the distance of a football field. A light snow began to fall, settling itself delicately on the thin layer of white that already covered much of the rock.

467

His feet slipped continuously; he balanced himself by grabbing shrubs and projections of jagged rock.

He reached the midpoint of the climb and pressed his back into a concave flute of stone to catch his breath unseen. He could hear sounds above him, metal against metal, or rock against rock. He lunged out of the recess and ran as fast as he could, up and around the next four bends of the trail, falling once to let untrapped, unswallowed air fill his lungs, to give his aching legs a chance to rest.

He pulled the Leinkraus diagram from his pocket and checked off the curves on the map; he had covered eight, he thought. Whatever, it wasn't any farther than a hundred feet to the arch symbolized by an inverted U on the diagram. He raised his head, his face bitter cold from the temporary pillow of frost and snow. There was a straight stretch of trail, bordered on both sides by grey, gnarled shrubbery. According to the map, there were two more hairpin curves above the stretch and then the arch of rock. He jammed the diagram into his pocket, feeling the steel of his gun as he did so. He pulled his legs up under him to a crouch and raced on.

He saw the girl first. She was lying off the trail in the shrubs, her eyes wide, staring at the overcast sky, her legs stretched rigidly in front of her. There were two bullet holes above each knee, the blood matted about the cloth. A third puncture could be seen above her right breast, below her collar bone; blood had formed a solid stream down her white Alpine jacket.

She was alive, but in such a degree of shock that she did not blink her eyes against the particles of falling snow. Her lips were moving, trembling, melted snow forming rivulets of water at the edges. Adrian bent over her.

At the sight of his face, her eyes blinked into focus. She raised her head in convulsion, coughing the start of a scream. Gently he pressed his gloved hand over the mouth, supporting her neck over his other hand.

'I'm not him,' he whispered.

The brush above them moved. Adrian whipped up, releasing the girl as carefully as he could, and sprang back. A hand edged its way over the snow – what was left of a hand. It was bloodstained flesh, the glove blown off, the fingers shattered. Fontine crept over the girl and up into the tangled, gnarled shrubbery, ripping the intertwined, branches apart. The boy lay on his stomach in a bed of wild mountain grass. A straight line of four bullet wounds angled diagonally along his back across his spine.

Adrian rolled the youth carefully over on his side, cradling his head. Once again he gently pressed a hand over a mouth in shock. The boy's eyes locked with his and within seconds Adrian's meaning was clear: he was not the killer. That the boy could speak at all was extraordinary. His whisper was nearly covered by the growing wind, but Fontine heard him.

'*Mia sorella.*'

'I don't understand.'

'Sister?'

'She's hurt. So are you. I'll do everything I can.'

'*Pacco.* The pack. He wears a pack. *Medicina.*'

'Don't talk. Save your strength. A pack?'

'*Si!*'

. . . *An Alpine pack is not a mere collection of straps and leather casing. It is a work of master craftsmanship . . .* His father had said that.

The boy would not stop. He knew he was dying. 'A way out. The Zermatt railroad. A village. Not far, *signore.* North, not far. We were going to run.'

'Shh. Don't say any more. I'm going to put you next to your sister. Keep as warm as you can.'

He half carried, half dragged the boy over the grass to the girl. They were children; his brother murdered

469

children. He removed his raincoat and jacket, tearing the lining of the jacket in order to tie the strips around the girl's wounds. There wasn't much he could do about the boy's, so he avoided his eyes. He covered them both; they held each other.

He put the heavy pistol in his belt beneath the heavy black sweater and crawled out of the sanctuary of the bushes. He raced up the path to the arch, his eyes stinging but his breath steady, the pain in his legs gone.

It was one against one now. The way it had to be.

CHAPTER THIRTY-THREE

The sound of cracking came louder, hammer-like and furious. It was directly above him, above the sheer sheet of rock that sprang up, facing the small, defined plateau on the north side. The ground at his feet was disturbed; snow and earth were intermingled, footprints and broken shrubbery formed a semi-circle beneath the overhang. Fragments of rock signified the method of ascent; a rope had been thrown above, with a hook attached, and the first throw or throws had not been successful.

A rotten ladder lay in the snow-laced, grey bushes, a number of its steps torn from the frame. It was the ladder Paul Leinkraus remembered. It was at least twenty feet long, on end, slightly higher than the sheet of rock in front of which Adrian crouched.

The burial ground is really a surface of shale. It cracks easily under the force of a pick to the earth beneath. The child's coffin was placed in the ground and a thin layer of concrete spread over it. The words of Paul Leinkraus.

Above him his brother had broken through the layer of concrete described by Leinkraus. The hammering stopped; a metal instrument was thrown aside on the hard surface. Large particles of cement plummeted down, kicked by impatient feet, joining the fragments of rock on the ground and the bushes. Adrian got to his feet quickly and pressed himself into the miniature cliff. If he was seen, he was dead.

The spray of cement stopped. Adrian shivered; he

knew he had to move. The cold was penetrating the black sweater, his breath formed billows of vapour in front of his face. The brief, light snowfall was letting up; a shaft of sunlight broke through the clouds, but brought no warmth.

He edged his way around the sheet of rock until he could go no farther, blocked by a projecting boulder bulging out of the mountain-top. He stepped forward on to the shrub-covered, snow-layered ground.

Suddenly, the earth gave way. Adrian leaped back and stood motionless, petrified, at the side of the boulder. The sounds of falling rock carried on the wind. He heard the footsteps above – heavy, abrupt – and held his breath so no steam would emerge from his mouth or nostrils. The sound of footsteps stopped – except for the wind, only silence remained. Then the footsteps started again – less heavy, slower. The soldier's alarm had subsided.

Adrian looked down in front of him. He had come to the end of Paul Leinkraus's path; there was only mountain now. Below, beyond the edge of broken earth and wild grass, was a drop, a wide, sweeping crevasse whose empty space separated the ground of the summit from the shallow ledge of earth across from it that led to higher regions. The crevasse was far deeper than Leinkraus remembered; it was well over thirty feet to a floor of jagged rock. The boy had been reprimanded by his elders, but not so truthfully as to frighten him, or instil a fear of mountains.

Adrian swung his body around and, clinging to the uneven surface, inch by inch, testing each, he moved out, pressing his chest and legs into the boulder, holding whatever sharp point he could grasp. On the other side was a narrow mass of indiscriminately formed rock that angled sharply up to the flat surface of the peak.

He was not sure he could reach it. A small boy could walk on the ledge away from the immediate base of the projecting boulder; it would not give way under his weight. A grown man was something else. It had not taken Adrian's weight; it would not take it.

The distance from the central point of the boulder – where he was – to the first promontory of rock was about five feet. He was over six. If he could angle his fall, with his arms outstretched, there was a good chance his hands would reach. More of a chance if he could narrow the distance.

The muscles of his feet were in agony. He could feel cramps forming in both insteps; the strain on his calves swelled his skin, the tendons beneath aching nearly beyond endurance. He forced all thoughts of pain and risk out of his mind and concentrated only on the inches he could cover around the massive boulder.

He had gone no more than a foot when he felt the ground sinking beneath him – slowly, in minute, hypnotizing stages. Then he could hear – actually *hear* . . . the cracking of stone and frozen earth. He thrust out his arms in the last half second. The ledge fell away and for a moment he was in the void, suspended. His hands clutched out crazily; the wind whipped against his face in mid-air.

His right arm crashed over the jagged rock somewhere above him. His shoulder and head slammed into the rough, shagged surface. He clamped his hand around the sharp stone, arching his back instinctively to absorb the shock of the impact.

He swung like a puppet on the string of his own appendage, his feet dangling. He had to drag himself up. *Now!* There were no seconds to waste! No time to adjust to his own disbelief!

Move!

He clawed the uneven cliff with his free left hand; his feet pumped insanely until his right shoe caught a tiny ridge that supported his weight. It was enough. Like a panicked spider he scaled the wall of jagged rock, throwing his legs one after another over the diagonal incline, slamming his body into the base of the inner surface.

He was out of sight from above, not out of hearing. The sounds of the falling ledge brought Andrew to the edge of the plateau. The sun was behind him on his right, casting his shadow across the crevasse, over the rock and snow. Again, Adrian held his breath. He had a window on his own lantern show, played out in the now-blinding Alpine sun. The soldier's movements were not only clear, they were magnified. Andrew held an object in his left hand: a climber's folding shovel.

The soldier's right arm was angled at the elbow; the shadow of his forearm joined the shadow of his upper body. It took little imagination to visualize what the right hand held: a gun. Adrian moved his own right hand to his belt. The pistol was still there; he was grateful for its touch.

The shadow moved about the ledge above, three steps to the left, four to the right. It bent down and then stood up again, another object now in its right hand. The object was thrown off; a large fragment of cement plummeted down no more than two feet from Adrian's face and crashed on the floor of jagged rock below. The soldier stood motionless during the object's fall, as if counting off seconds, timing the descent. The last rolling spatters finished, the soldier walked away. His shadow disappeared, replaced by the harsh reflections of the sun.

Adrian lay in his recess, unaware of his discomfort, his face drenched with sweat. The curve of uneven rocks above his head swept sharply up, like a primitive spiral staircase in an ancient lighthouse. The sweep was about twenty-five feet in length; it was difficult to estimate for there was nothing beyond but sky and blazing sun. He could not move until he heard sounds from above.

Sounds that meant the soldier was occupied, digging again.

They came. A loud crashing of stone, the scraping of metal against metal.

Andrew had found the vault!

Adrian crawled out of his shelter and, hand over hand, silent foot after silent foot, made his way up the jagged rock staircase. The ledge of the plateau was directly above; below was no longer the crevasse but a sheer drop of several hundred feet to the winding mountain pass. There were, perhaps, eight inches between him and the open space. The wind was steady. Its sound was a low whistle.

He reached for the pistol in his belt, removed it and – as Goldoni had instructed – checked the safety. It was in upright position, locked.

He snapped it level with the trigger and raised his head over the ledge.

The flat surface of the plateau was an oval, extending thirty-five feet or more in length, twenty or so in width. The soldier crouched in the centre, next to a mound of earth covered with fragments of cracked cement. Beyond the dirt, partially concealed by the soldier's broad back, was a plain wooden casket with metal borders; it was remarkably preserved.

There was no vault. There was nothing but earth, the fragments of cement, and the coffin. But no vault!

Oh, my god, thought Adrian. We were *wrong*! *Both wrong!*

It wasn't possible. It was not possible. For if there were no vault, the killer from Eye Corps would be in a rage. He knew Andrew well enough to know that. But his brother was not angry. He was crouched in thought, his head angled down; he was staring at the grave. And Adrian understood: the vault was below, still in the earth.

It had been buried beneath the coffin, that casket its final protection.

The soldier got to his feet and crossed to the Alpine pack which lay upright against the coffin. He bent over, unsnapped a strap, and pulled out a short, pointed iron bar. He returned to the grave, abruptly knelt by the edge, and reached down with the bar. Seconds later he yanked the bar up, letting it fall to the ground, and removed a gun from his jacket. Swiftly, but carefully, he angled the weapon down into the grave.

Three explosions followed. Adrian ducked his head below the edge of the plateau. He could smell the acrid odour of the gunfire, see the billows of smoke carried above him on the wind.

And then the words came and his whole body was locked in a fear he never believed he could experience. It was the shock of the knowledge of his own immediate execution.

'Put your head up, Lefrac,' was the soft-spoken command, delivered in a monotone of ice. 'It'll be quicker that way. You won't feel a thing. You won't even hear any noise.'

Adrian rose from his narrow perch, his mind blank, beyond fear now. He was going to die; it was as simple as that.

But he was not what the soldier above him expected. Not *whom* the soldier expected. The killer from Eye Corps was suddenly, completely gripped in a shock of his own. It was so total that his eyes widened in disbelief, his hand trembled and the weapon in its grasp wavered. He took an involuntary step backwards, his mouth gaping, the skin on his face bloodless.

'*You!*'

Wildly, blindly, without thought or feeling, Adrian whipped up the heavy Italian pistol from the ledge of rock and fired at the stunned figure. He squeezed the trigger twice, three times. The gun jammed. The spits and smoke from the barrel-housing singed his flesh, stung his eyes. But he had hit the soldier! The killer from Eye Corps reeled backwards, holding his stomach, his left leg buckling beneath him.

But Andrew still had the pistol in his hand. The explosion came; a crack of air detonated above Adrian's head. He lunged at the fallen man, crashing the jammed pistol down in the area of the face. His right hand shot out, grabbing the hot steel of Andrew's gun, slamming it against the hard surface of the plateau. His own pistol found its mark; the bridge between the soldier's eyes erupted; blood flowed into the corners of his sockets, blurring his vision. Andrew's pistol flew out of his hand. Adrian sprang back.

He aimed his gun and squeezed the trigger with all his strength. It would not operate, it would not *fire*. The soldier got to his knees, rubbing his eyes, his mouth emitting grunts of fury. Adrian lashed out his foot, catching the killer from Eye Corps at the temple; the soldier's neck arched back, but his legs shot forward, twisting, kicking, slamming into Adrian's kneecaps, causing him to lurch to the side, his knees suddenly in agony.

Adrian could not stay on his feet. He rolled to his right as the major leaped up, still wiping his eyes. Andrew sprang off the ground, hands now outstretched like rigid hooks, directly at the intruder's neck. Adrian recoiled farther, crashing into the casket at the side of the grave. The soldier's lunge was uncontrolled; the screaming pitch of his anger caused him to lose his balance, and he fell, one arm plunged into the mound of earth and fragments of concrete. The earth flew; an eruption of dirt and snow and rock.

Adrian dived over the open space of the grave; on the opposite side was the iron bar. The soldier followed; he lunged up, screaming at Adrian, his hands locked above his head into a hammer – a monstrous bird screeching in for the kill. Adrian's fingers were on the bar, and he lashed it up at the plummeting figure.

The point plunged into the solder's cheek, stunning him. Blood burst again from Andrew's flesh.

Adrian lurched away as fast as his exhausted, aching legs could propel him, dropping the bar. He saw the soldier's pistol lying across the flat stone surface; he lunged for it. His fingers wound around the handle; he raised it.

The iron bar came slicing though the air, creasing the skin of his left shoulder, tearing the sleeve half off his sweater. The shock sent him reeling back to the edge of the sheet of rock. He had brought the hand with the gun across his chest in panic; he knew the instant he did so it was the fraction of a second the soldier desperately needed. A wall of earth and stone came at him, the space between himself and the killer from Eye Corps was filled with debris. It smashed into him; sharp pieces of rock pummelled his face, his eyes. He could not see.

He fired. His hand recoiled violently from the explosion of the weapon; his fingers arched from the vibration.

He tried to get to his feet; a boot hammered into his neck. He caught the leg as he fell back, his shoulders over the edge of the sheet of rock. He rolled to his left, holding the leg until he felt the barrel of the gun against the flesh.

He pulled the trigger.

Flesh and bone and blood filled his universe. The soldier was blown off the ground, his right leg a mass of red-soaked cloth. Adrian started to crawl but he could not; there was no strength left, no air in his lungs. He raised himself on one hand and looked over at Andrew.

The major writhed back and forth, moans coming from his throat, his mouth filled with blood and saliva.

He pushed himself off the ground, halfway to his knees, his eyes staring insanely at what was left of his leg. He looked over to his executioner. And then he screamed.

'*Help me!* You can't let me *die*! You *don't have the right*! Get me the *pack*! He coughed, holding his shattered leg with one hand, his other trembling, gesturing at the Alpine pack against the coffin. The blood flowed everywhere, saturating his clothes. The poisons were spreading rapidly; he was dying.

'I don't have the right to let you live,' said Adrian weakly, gasping for air. 'Do you know what you've done? The people you killed?'

'Killing's an *instrument*!' screamed the soldier. 'That's all it is!'

'Who decides when the instrument's used? *You?*'

'*Yes!* And men *like* me! We know who we are, what we can do. People like you, you're *not* – For Christ's sake, *help me*!'

'You make the rules. Everybody else follows.'

'Yes! Because we're willing to! People everywhere, they're not willing. They want the rules made for them! You can't deny that!'

'I do deny it,' said Adrian quietly.

'Then you're lying. Or stupid! Oh, *Christ* . . .' The soldier's voice broke, interrupted by a spasm of coughing. He clutched his stomach and stared at his leg again, and then at the mound of dirt. He pulled his eyes away and looked at Adrian. 'Here. Over *here*.'

The major crawled towards the grave. Adrian rose slowly to his feet and watched, mesmerized by the horrible sight. What was left of his compassion told him to fire the weapon in his hand, end the life that was nearly finished. He could see the vault from Salonika in the ground; slats of rotted wood had been pulled away, revealing the iron beneath. Strips of metal had been shattered by gunfire, a coil of rope lay on top. There were torn pieces of heavy cardboard with faint markings that looked like circles of thorns around crucifixes.

They had found it.

'Don't you understand?' The soldier could barely be heard. 'It's there. The answer. The *answer*!'

'What answer?'

'*Everything* . . .' For several seconds his brother's eyes lost muscular control; they rolled in their sockets, and for an instant the pupils disappeared. Andrew's speech had the inflections of an angry child; his right hand extended into the grave. 'I have it now. You can't interfere! Any more! You can help me now. I'll let you help me. I used to let you help me, remember? You remember how I *always used to let you help me*?' The soldier screamed the question.

'It was always your decision, Andy. To let me help you, I mean,' said Adrian softly, trying to understand the childlike rambling, hypnotized by the words.

'Of course my decision. It had to be *my decision*. Victor's and mine.'

Adrian suddenly recalled their mother's words . . . *he saw the results of strength; he never understood its complications, its compassion* . . . The lawyer in Adrian had to know. 'What should we do with the vault? Now that we've got it, what should we do with—'

'*Use it!*' The soldier screamed again, pounding the loose rock at the edge of the grave. '*Use* it, use it! Make things *right*! We'll tell them we can ruin *everything*!'

'Suppose we can't? Suppose it doesn't matter? Maybe there's nothing there.'

'We tell them *there is*! You don't know how to do it. We tell them anything we *want* to tell them! They'll *crawl*, they'll *whine* . . .'

'You want them to do that? To crawl and whine?'

'Yes! They're weak!'

'But you're not.'

'No! I've *proved* it! Over and over and *over again*!' The soldier's neck arched and then snapped forward convulsively. 'You think you see things *I* don't see. You're *wrong*! I see them but they don't make *any difference*, they don't *count*! What you think's so goddamned *important* ... *doesn't* ... *matter*!' Andrew spaced out the words: it was a child's cry of defiance.

'What's that, Andy? What is it I think is so important?'

'*People!* What they *think*! It doesn't *count*, doesn't *matter*. Victor knows that.'

'You're wrong; you're *so* wrong,' interrupted Adrian quietly. 'He's dead, Andy. He died a couple of days ago.'

The soldier's eyes regained part of their focus. There was elation in them. 'Now everthing's *mine!* I'll do it!' The coughing returned; the eyes wandered again. 'Make them understand. They're not important. Never were ...'

'Only you.'

'Yes! I don't hesitate. *You do!* You can't make up your mind!'

'You're decisive, Andy.'

'Yes, *decisive*. That's important.'

'And people don't count, so naturally they can't be trusted.'

'What the hell are you trying to say?' The soldier's chest expanded in pain; his neck arched back, then shot forward, mucus and blood coughed through his lips.

'That you're *afraid*!' shouted Adrian. 'You've always been afraid! You live scared to death that someone'll find that out! There's a big crack in your armour ... you *freak*!'

A terrible, muted cry came from the soldier's throat; it was at once guttural and clear, a cross between a roar of final anger and a wail. 'That's a *lie*! You and your goddamned words ...'

Suddenly there were no more words. The unbeliev-able was happening in the blinding Alpine sunlight, and Adrian knew only that he would move or die. The soldier's hand was in the grave. He whipped it out. In his grip was a rope; he lurched off the ground, swinging the rope violently. Tied to the end was a grappling hook, its three prongs slashing through the air.

Adrian sprang to his left, firing the enormous weapon at the crazed killer from Eye Corps.

The soldier's chest exploded. The rope, held in a grip of steel, swung in a circle – the grappling hook spinning like an insanely off-course gyroscope – around the soldier's head. The body shot forward, over the sheet of rock, and plummeted down, its scream echoing, filling the mountains with its pitch of horror.

With a sudden, sickening vibration the rope sprang taut, quivering in a thin layer of disturbed snow.

There was the sound of cracking metal from the grave. Adrian whipped his eyes over to its source. The rope had been lashed to a steel band around the vault. The band had snapped. The vault could be opened.

But Adrian did not go to it. He limped to the edge of the plateau and looked over the sheet of rock.

Suspended below was the soldier's body, the grappling hook imbedded in his neck. A prong had plunged up through Andrew's throat, its point protruding from his gaping mouth.

He filled the large Alpine pack with the three steel, airtight containers from the vault. He could not read the ancient writing etched in the metal. He did not have to; he knew what each container held. None was large. One was flat, thicker than the other two; within it were the documents compiled by the scholars of Constantine 1,500 years ago, studies that traced what they believed was the theological inconsistency – raising a holy man to one substance with God. Questions for new scholars to ponder. The second container was short, tubular; it held the Aramaic scroll that had so frightened powerful men thirty years ago that strategies of global war were secondary to its possession. But it was the third container, thin, no more than eight inches wide, ten high, that held the most extraordinary document of all: a confession written on a parchment, taken out of a Roman prison nearly 2,000 years ago. It was this receptacle – black, pitted, a relic of antiquity – that was the essence of the vault from Salonika.

All were the denials; only the confession on the Roman parchment could produce an agony beyond men's minds. But that was not for him to judge. Or was it?

He put the plastic bottles of medicine into his pockets, threw the pack down on the ground, lowered himself over the edge of the sheet of rock – next to the soldier's body – and dropped to the earth beneath. He strapped the heavy pack on his back and started down the trail.

The boy was dead. The girl would live. Together they would somehow walk out of the mountains, of that Adrian was convinced.

They travelled slowly – a few steps at a time – down the trail towards the Zermatt tracks. He held the girl so that as little weight as possible was forced on her wounded legs.

He looked back up the mountain trail. In the distance the soldier's body hung suspended against the white sheet of rock. It could not be seen clearly – only if you knew where to look – but it was there.

Was Andrew's the final death demanded by the train from Salonika? Were the documents in that vault worth so much life? So much violence for so many years? He had no answers.

He only knew insanity was given unearned stature in the name of holy things. Holy wars were primeval; they always would be. And he had killed a brother for their part in an unholy war.

He felt the terrible weight on his back. He was tempted to remove the steel containers and heave them into the deepest gorge in the mountains. Broken, left to wither into nothing with the first touch of air. Swept away by the Alpine winds into oblivion.

But he would not do that. The price had been too steep.

'Let's go,' he said to the girl, gently placing her left arm around his neck. He smiled at the child's frightened face. 'We're going to make it.'

PART FOUR

CHAPTER THIRTY-FOUR

Adrian stood by the window overlooking the dark expanse of Central Park. He was in the small staff lounge at the Metropolitan Museum. He held the telephone to his ear and listened to Colonel Tarkington in Washington. Across the room sat a priest from the Archdiocese of New York, the monsignor named Land. It was shortly past midnight; the army officer in Washington had been given the private number of the museum. He was told that Mr Fontine expected his call, regardless of the hour.

Official documentation of events surrounding Eye Corps would be issued by the Pentagon in due time, the officer told Adrian. The administration wanted to avoid the scandal that would result from charges of corruption and insurrection within the armed forces. Especially as a prominent name was involved. It did not serve the interests of national security.

'Stage one,' said Adrian. 'Cover-up.'

'Perhaps.'

'You're going to settle for that?' asked Fontine quietly.

'It's your family,' replied the colonel. 'Your brother.'

'And yours. I can live with it. Can't you? Can't Washington?'

There was silence on the other end of the line. Finally the officer spoke. 'I got what I wanted. And maybe Washington can't. Not now.'

'It's never "now".'

'Don't preach to me. Nobody's stopping you from holding a press conference.'

It was now Adrian who was momentarily silent. 'If I do, can I demand official documentation? Or would a dossier suddenly appear, describing—'

'Describing in psychiatric detail,' interrupted the colonel, 'a very disturbed young man who ran around the country living in hippie communes; who aided and abetted three convicted army deserters in San Francisco. Don't kid yourself, Fontine. It's on my desk.'

'I thought it might be. I'm learning. You're thorough, aren't you? Which brother's the lunatic?'

'It goes much further. Family influence used to avoid military service; past membership in radical organizations – they're using dynamite these days. Your odd behaviour recently in Washington, including a relationship with a black attorney who was killed under strange circumstances, said black lawyer suspected of criminal activities. Lots more. And that's only you.'

'What?'

'Old truths – documented truths – are dragged up. A father who made a fortune operating all over the world with governments many believe are inimicable to our interests. A man who worked closely with the Communists, whose first wife was killed years ago under very odd circumstances in Monte Carlo. That's a disturbing pattern. Questions are raised. Can the Fontines live with *that*?'

'You make me sick.'

'I make myself sick.'

'Then why?'

'Because a decision had to be made that goes beyond you and me and our personal revulsions!' The colonel raised his voice in anger, then controlled himself. 'I don't like a lot of the bullshit players upstairs. I only know – or think I know – that maybe it isn't the time to talk about Eye Corps.'

'So it goes on and on. You don't sound like the man I talked to in a hotel room.'

'Maybe I'm not. I only hope for the sake of your righteous indignation you're never put in a position like this.'

Adrian looked at the priest across the room. Land was staring at the dimly lit white wall, at nothing. Yet it was in his eyes, *it's always in the eyes*. A desperation that consumed him. The monsignor was a very strong man, but he was frightened now. 'I hope I never am,' Adrian said to the colonel.

'Fontine?'

'Yes?'

'Let's have a drink some time.'

'Sure. We'll do that.' Adrian hung up.

Was it up to him now? wondered Adrian. Everything? Was the time ever right to tell the truth?

There'd be one answer soon. He'd got the documents from the vault out of Italy with the colonel's help; the colonel's payment was a body suspended in front of a sheet of rock in the mountains of Champoluc. Brother for brother. Debt paid.

Barbara Pierson had known what to do with the documents. She contacted a friend who was a curator of relics and artefacts at the Metropolitan. A scholar who had devoted his life to the study of the past. He had seen too much of antiquity to make judgements.

Barbara had flown down from Boston; she was in the laboratory with the scholar now. They'd been there since five-thirty. Seven hours. With the documents from Constantine.

But there was only one document that mattered now. It was the parchment taken out of a Roman prison 2,000 years ago. The parchment was everything. *Everything*. The scholar understood that.

Adrian left the window and walked across the room to the priest. Two weeks ago, when his father was close to death, Victor drew up his list of men to whom the vault of Constantine was to be delivered. Land's name was on that list. When Adrian contacted him, Land began saying things to him he had never said to Victor Fontine.

'Tell me about Annaxas,' said Adrian, sitting down opposite the priest.

The monsignor looked away from the wall, startled. Not by the name, thought Fontine, but by the intrusion. His large, penetrating grey eyes under the dark brows were momentarily unfocused. He blinked, as if remembering where he was.

'Theodore Dakakos? What can I tell you? We first met in Istanbul. I was tracing what I knew was false evidence. The so-called destruction by fire of the Filioque documents. He found out I was there from the Vatican archives. We talked; we were both curious. I, why such a prominent man of commerce was so interested in obscure theological artefacts. He, why a Roman scholar was pursuing – *allowed* to pursue, perhaps – a thesis hardly in the Vatican's interests. He was very knowledgeable. Each of us manoeuvred throughout the night, both of us finally exhausted. I think it was the exhaustion that caused it. And the fact that we thought we knew one another, perhaps even liked one another.'

'Caused what?'

'The train from Salonika to be mentioned. Strange, I don't remember which of us said it first.'

'He *knew* about it?'

'As much, or more, than I. The engine driver was his father; the single passenger, the priest of Xenope, his father's brother. Neither man ever returned. In his search he found part of the answer. The police records in

Milan contained an old entry from December 1939. Two dead men on a Greek train in the freight yards. Murder and suicide. No identification. Annaxas had to know why.'

'What led him to Milan?'

'Over twenty years of asking questions. He had reason enough. He watched his mother go insane. She went mad because the church would give her no answers.'

'Her church?'

'An arm of the church, if you will. The Order of Xenope.'

'Then she knew about the train.'

'She was never supposed to have known. It was believed she didn't. But men tell things to their wives they tell no one else. Before the elder Annaxas left early that morning in December 1939, he said to his wife that he was not going to Corinth, as everyone believed. Instead, God would look favourably on them for he was joining his brother Petride. They were going on a journey far away. They were doing God's work.'

The priest fingered the gold cross hanging from a cord on the cloth beneath his collar. His touch was not gentle; there was anger in it.

'From which he never came back,' said Adrian quietly. 'And there was no brother in the church to reach because he was dead.'

'Yes. I think we can both imagine how the woman – a good woman, simple, loving, left with six children – would react.'

'She'd go out of her mind.'

Land let the cross drop, his eyes straying back to the wall. 'As an act of charity, the priests of Xenope took the mad woman in. Another decision was made. She died within a month.'

Fontine slowly sat forward. 'They killed her.' It was not a question.

Land's gaze returned. There was a degree of supplication in his eyes now. 'They weighed the consequences of her life. Not against the Filioque, but in relation to a parchment none of us in Rome ever knew existed. I'd never heard of it until this evening. It makes so many things so much clearer.'

Adrian got out of the chair and walked back to the window. He was not ready to discuss the parchment. The holy men no longer had the right to direct inquiries. The attorney in Adrian disapproved of the priests. Laws were for all.

Down in Central Park, along a dimly lit path, a man was walking two huge Labrador retrievers, the animals straining at their leashes. He was straining on a leash of his own, but he could not let Land know it. He turned from the window. 'Dakakos put it all together, didn't he?'

'Yes,' replied Land, accepting Adrian's refusal to be led. 'It was his legacy. He vowed to learn everything. We agreed to exchange information, but I was more forthright than he. The name Fontini-Cristi surfaced, but the parchment was never mentioned. The rest, I assume you know.'

Adrian was startled by the priest's words. 'Don't assume anything. Tell me.'

Land flinched. The rebuke was unexpected. 'I'm sorry. I thought you knew. Dakakos took over the responsibility of Campo di Fiori. For years he paid the taxes – which were considerable – fended off buyers, real-estate developers, provided security, and upkeep—'

'What about Xenope?'

'The Order of Xenope is all but extinct. A small monastery north of Salonika. A few old priests on diminished farmland, with no money. For Dakakos, only one link remained; a dying monk at Campo di Fiori. He couldn't let it go. He extracted everything the old man knew. Ultimately, he was right. Gaetamo was released from prison; the banished priest, Aldobrini, came back from Africa dying of assorted fevers and finally, your father returned to Campo di Fiori. The scene of his family's execution. The terrible search began all over again.'

Adrian thought. 'Dakakos stopped my brother. He went to extraordinary lengths to trap him, expose Eye Corps.'

'To keep him from the vault at all costs. The old monk must have told Dakakos that Victor Fontine knew about the parchment. He understood that your father would act outside the authorities, use his sons to find the vault. He had to. Weighing the consequences, there was no other course. Dakakos studied both of you. Actually he had you watched for several years. What he found in one son shocked him. Your brother could not be permitted to go further. He had to be destroyed. You, on the other hand, were someone he felt he could work with, if it came to that.'

The priest had stopped. He inhaled deeply, his fingers once again around the gold cross on his chest. Thought had returned to him and it was obviously painful. Adrian understood; he had experienced the same feeling in the mountains of Champoluc.

'What would Dakakos have done if he'd found the vault?'

Land's penetrating gaze settled on Adrian. 'I don't know. He was a compassionate man. He knew the anguish of seeking painful answers to very painful questions; his sympathy might have guided his judgement. Still, he was a man of truth. I think he would have weighed the consequences. Beyond this I can't help you.'

'You use that phrase a lot, don't you? "Weighing the consequences".'

'I apologize if it offends you.'

'It does.'

'Then forgive me, but I must offend you further. I asked your permission to come here, but I've changed my mind. I'm going to leave.' The priest got out of the chair. 'I can't stay. I'll try to put it simply—'

'Simply *put*,' interrupted Adrian harshly, 'I'm not interested.'

'You have the advantage,' replied Land quickly. 'You see, I'm interested in *you*, in what you perceive.' The priest would not be stopped; he took a step forward. 'Do you think doubts are erased because vows are taken? You think seven thousand years of human communication is somehow voided for us? Any of us, whatever the vestments we wear? How many gods and prophets and holy men have been conjured over the centuries? Does the number lessen the devotion? I think not. For each accepts what he can accept, raising his own beliefs above all others. My doubts tell me that thousands of years from now scholars may study the remnants of what we were and conclude that our beliefs – our devotions – were singularly odd, consigning to myth what we think most holy. As we have consigned to myth the remnants of others. My intellect, you see, can conceive this. But now, here, in my time – for me – the commitment is made. It's better to have it than not to have it. I do believe. I am convinced.'

Adrian remembered the words. '"Divine revelation cannot be contravened by mortal man"?'

'That's good enough. I'll accept that,' said Land simply. 'Ultimately, the lessons of Aquinas prevail. They're not the exclusive property of anyone, I might add. When reason is exhausted, at its last barrier, faith becomes the reason. I have that faith. But being mortal I'm weak. I haven't the endurance to test myself further. I must retreat to the comfort of my commitment, knowing I'm better with it than without it.' The priest held out his hand. 'Good-bye, Adrian.'

Fontine looked at the outstretched hand and accepted it. 'You understand that it's the arrogance of your "commitment", your beliefs, that disturbs me. I don't know any other way to put it.'

'I understand; your objection is noted. That arrogance is the first of the sins that lead to spiritual death. And the one most often overlooked: pride. It may kill us all one day. Then, my young friend, there'll be nothing.'

Land turned and walked to the door of the small lounge. He opened it with his right hand, his left still holding the gold cross, enveloping it. The gesture was unmistakable. It was an act of protection. He looked once more at Adrian, then walked out of the room, closing the door behind him.

Fontine lighted a cigarette, then crushed it out. His mouth was sour from too many cigarettes and too little sleep. Instead, he went to a coffee maker and poured himself a cup.

An hour ago Land, testing the metal rim of the hot plate, had burned his fingers. It occurred to Adrian that the monsignor was the sort of man who tested most things in life. And yet he could not accept the final test. He merely walked away; there was a kind of honesty in that.

Far more than he had shown his mother, reflected Adrian. He had not lied to Jane; it would have been useless, the lie known for what it was. But neither had he told her the truth. He had done a far more cruel thing: he had avoided her. He was not yet ready for confrontation.

He heard footsteps in the corridor outside the lounge. He put his coffee down and walked to the centre of the room. The door opened and Barbara entered, the door held for her by the scholar, still in his laboratory smock, his horn-rimmed glasses somehow magnifying his face. Barbara's brown eyes, usually so filled with warmth and laughter, were sharp with professional involvement.

'Doctor Shire's finished,' she said. 'May we have coffee?'

'Sure.' Adrian went back to the table and poured two cups. The scholar sat down in the chair from which Land had risen just minutes ago.

'Black, if you please,' said Shire, placing a single page of paper in his lap. 'Your friend has left?'

'Yes, he left.'

'Did he know?' asked the old man, accepting the coffee.

'He knew because I told him. He made his decision. He left.'

'I can understand,' said Shire, blinking his old eyes beyond the glasses in the steam of his coffee. 'Sit down, both of you.'

Barbara took the coffee but did not sit. She and the scholar exchanged looks; she walked to the window as Adrian sat across from Shire.

'Is it authentic?' asked Fontine. 'I imagine that's the first question.'

'Authentic? As to time and materials and script and language ... yes, I would say it will survive those examinations. I'm going under the assumption that it will. Chemical and prismatic analyses take a long time, but I've seen hundreds of documents from the period; it's authentic on these points. As to the authenticity of the contents, it was written by a half-crazed man facing death. A very cruel and painful form of death. That judgement will have to made by others, if it's to be made at all.' Shire glanced at Adrian as he placed the coffee cup on the table beside the chair and picked up the paper on his lap. Fontine remained silent. The scholar continued.

'According to the words on that parchment, the

prisoner who was to lose his life in the arena on the following afternoon renounced the name of Peter, given him by the revolutionary named Jesus. He said he was not worthy of it. He wanted his death to be recorded as that of one Simon of Bethsaida, his name at birth. He was consumed with guilt, claiming he had betrayed his saviour ... For the man who was crucified on Calvary was *not* Jesus of Nazareth.'

The old scholar stopped, his words floating, suspended, as if broken off in mid-sentence.

'Oh, my God!' Adrian got out of the chair. He looked at Barbara by the window. She returned his gaze without comment. He turned back to Shire. 'It's that specific?'

'Yes. The man was in torment. He writes that three of Christ's disciples acted on their own, *against* the carpenter's wishes. With the help of Pilate's guards, whom they bribed, they took an unconscious Jesus out of the dungeons and substituted a condemned criminal of the same size and general appearance, dressing him in the carpenter's clothes. In the hysterical crowds the next day, the shroud and the blood from the thorns were sufficient to obscure the features of the man under and on the cross. It was *not* the will of the man they called a messiah—'

' "Nothing is changed",' interrupted Adrian softly, remembering the words. ' "Yet all is changed".'

'He was involuntarily removed. It was his intention to die, not to live. The parchment is clear on that.'

'But he didn't die. He *did* live.'

'Yes.'

'He was *not* crucified.'

'No. If one accepts the word of the man who wrote the document – under the conditions he wrote it. Barely on the brink of sanity, I should think. I wouldn't accept it merely because of its antiquity.'

'Now you're making a judgement.'

'An observation of probability,' corrected Shire. 'The

writer of the parchment lapsed into wild prayers and lamentations. His thoughts were lucid one moment, unclear the next. Madman or self-flagellating ascetic? Pretender or penitent? Which one? Unfortunately, the physical fact that it's a document from two thousand years ago lends a credibility that would certainly be withheld under less striking circumstances. Remember, it was the time of Nero's persecutions, a period of social, political, and theological madness. People survived more often than not on sheer ingenuity. Who was it, *really*?'

'The document spells it out. Simon of Bethsaida.'

'We have only the writer's word for it. There is no record of Simon Peter's having gone to his death with the early Christian martyrs. Certainly it would be part of the legend, yet there's no mention of it in biblical studies. If it were so, and overlooked, it's an awesome omission, isn't it?'

The scholar removed his glasses and wiped the thick lens with a corner of his smock. 'What are you trying to say?' Adrian asked.

The old man put the glasses back on his face, magnifying his thoughtful, sad eyes. 'Suppose a citizen of Rome, scheduled for a most horrible form of execution, invents a story that impugns the hated mark of an upstart, dangerous religion, and does so in a believable manner. Such a man might find favour with the praetors, the consuls, with a ceasar himself. A great many tried it, you know. In one form or another. There are remnants of scores of such "confessions". Is there any reason to accept it more than the others? Merely because it *is* complete? Ingenuity and survival are commonplace in history.'

Adrian watched the scholar closely as he spoke. There was a strange anxiety in the words. 'What do *you* think, doctor?'

'It's not important what I think,' said Shire, momentarily avoiding Adrian's eyes.

There was silence; it was profoundly moving. 'You believe it, don't you?'

Shire paused. 'It's an extraordinary document.'

'Does it say what happened to the carpenter?'

'Yes,' replied Shire, staring at Adrian. 'He took his own life three days later.'

'Took his *own life*? That's contrary to everything—'

'Yes, it is,' interrupted the scholar softly. 'The consistency is found in the time factor: three days. Consistency and inconsistency, where's the balance? The confession goes on to say that the carpenter reviled those who interfered, yet still at the end called upon his God to forgive them.'

'That's consistent.'

'Would you expect otherwise? Ingenuity and survival, Mr Fontine.'

Nothing has changed, yet all is changed.

'What's the condition of the parchment?'

'It's remarkably well preserved. A solution of animal oils, I think, pressed into a vacuum, covered by heavy rock glass.'

'And the other documents?'

'I haven't examined them, other than to distinguish them from the parchment. The papers that I presume trace the Filioque agreements as seen by its opponents are barely intact. The Aramaic scroll is, of course, metallic and will take a great deal of time and care to unravel.'

Adrian sat down. 'Is that the literal translation of the confession?' he asked, pointing to the page of writing in the scholar's hand.

'Sufficiently so. It's unrefined. I wouldn't present it academically.'

'May I have it?'

'You may have everything.' Shire leaned forward. Adrian reached out and took the paper. 'The parchment, the documents; they're yours.'

'They don't belong to me.'

'I know that.'

'Then why? I'd think you'd be pleading with me to let you keep them. Examine them. Startle the world with them.'

The scholar removed his thick glasses, his tired eyes creased with exhaustion, his voice quiet. 'You've brought me a very strange discovery. And quite frightening. I'm too old to cope with it.'

'I don't understand.'

'Then I ask you to consider. A death was denied, not a *life*. But in that death was the symbol. If you raise that symbol into question, you risk casting doubt on everything that symbol has come to mean. I'm not sure that's justified.'

Adrian was silent for a moment. 'The price of truth is too steep. Is that what you're saying?'

'If it's true. But again, there's the terrible absolute of antiquity. Things are accepted because they exist. Homer creates fiction, and centuries later men trace sea routes in search of caves inhabited by one-eyed giants. Froissart chronicles the history that never was and is hailed a true historian. I ask you to weigh the consequences.'

Adrian got out of the chair and walked aimlessly to the wall. The same area of the wall that Land kept looking at: dimly lit white paint. Nothing. 'Can you keep everything here for a while?'

'It can be stored in a laboratory vault. I can send you a receipt of acknowledgement.'

Fontine turned. 'A vault?'

'Yes. A vault.'

'It could have stayed in another.'

'Perhaps it should have. For how long, Mr Fontine?'

'How long?'

'How long will it remain here?'

'A week, a month, a century, I don't know.'

He stood by the hotel window overlooking the Manhattan skyline. New York pretended to sleep, but the myriad lights below on the streets denied the pretence.

They had talked for several hours, how many he didn't really know. *He* had talked; Barbara had listened, gently forcing him to say it all.

There was so much to do, to go through, before he found his head again.

Suddenly – the sound somehow terrifying – the telephone rang. He wheeled around, too aware of the panic he felt, knowing it was in his eyes.

Barbara got out of her chair and walked calmly over to him. She reached up and held his face with her hands. The panic subsided.

'I don't want to talk to anyone. Not now.'

'Then don't. Tell whoever it is to call in the morning.'

It was so simple. The truth.

The telephone rang again. He crossed to the bedside table and picked it up, sure of his intention, confident of his strength.

'Adrian? For God's *sake*! We've been tracing you all over New York! A colonel at IG named Tarkington gave us the hotel.'

The caller was one of the Justice lawyers recruited by Nevins.

'What is it?'

'It's happened! Everything we've worked for is falling into place. This town is blown apart. The White House is in panic. We're in touch with the Senate judiciary; we're after a special prosecutor. There's no other way it can be handled.'

'You've got concrete evidence?'

'More than that. Witnesses, confessions. The thieves are running for cover. We're back in business, Fontine. Are you with us? We can *move* now!'

Adrian thought only briefly before he answered. 'Yes, I'm with you.'

It was important to keep moving. Certain struggles continued. Others had to be brought to a close. The wisdom was in deciding which.

All Orion/Phoenix titles are available at your local bookshop or from the following address:

Mail Order Department
Littlehampton Book Services
FREEPOST BR535
Worthing, West Sussex, BN13 3BR
telephone 01903 828503, *facsimile* 01903 828802
e-mail MailOrders@lbsltd.co.uk
(Please ensure that you include full postal address details)

Payment can be made either by credit/debit card (Visa, Mastercard, Access and Switch accepted) or by sending a £ Sterling cheque or postal order made payable to *Littlehampton Book Services*.
DO NOT SEND CASH OR CURRENCY

Please add the following to cover postage and packing

UK and BFPO:
£1.50 for the first book, and 50p for each additional book to a maximum of £3.50

Overseas and Eire:
£2.50 for the first book plus £1.00 for the second book and 50p for each additional book ordered

---

BLOCK CAPITALS PLEASE

name of cardholder .... *delivery address*
                       .... *(if different from cardholder)*
address of cardholder ....
....
....
....
        postcode ....   *postcode* ....

☐ I enclose my remittance for £ ....

☐ please debit my Mastercard/Visa/Access/Switch (delete as appropriate)

card number ☐☐☐☐☐☐☐☐☐☐☐☐☐☐☐☐

expiry date ☐☐☐☐   Switch issue no. ☐☐

signature ....

prices and availability are subject to change without notice